Outstanding praise for the novels of Timothy James Beck!

HE'S THE ONE
A Booksense 76 Pick!

"Second novels are usually not as good as first novels, especially when first novels are as excellent as Timothy James Beck's first work, *It Had to Be You*. So it was with surprise and delight that I found Beck's second work, *He's the One,* to be not just as good—but better! Funny and touching with wonderful characters."
—*The Texas Triangle*

"Another romantic comedy from the author of the equally engaging *It Had to Be You.*"
—*Booklist*

"This second madcap Manhattan romance from Beck has sexy boys, mild comedy, and even a little amateur sleuthing. Beck seems to have found his calling serving up featherweight fun."
—*Publishers Weekly*

"A delightful sophomore novel . . . smart and breezy."
—*OutSmart* (Houston, Texas)

"*He's the One* stands out for good writing and a fairly inventive plot. This book is a good, quick read, just what everyone needs in the summer. You can enjoy it during an afternoon by the pool or an evening when you don't want to go out or watch TV. Pick it up and see if you don't agree."
—*The Bottom Line* (Palm Springs)

IT HAD TO BE YOU

"A charming, humorously appealing tale . . . Readers will find the overall mood light and the action absorbing enough to keep the pages turning."
—*Publishers Weekly*

"*It Had to Be You* is a rousing story of finding yourself after you've spent years thinking you already had. While much of this book is laugh out loud funny, there are plenty of serious moments as well . . . Dry, witty, touching and loads of fun, *It Had to Be You* is a novel that manages to easily and expertly straddle the fence between serious and hilarious."
—*The Texas Triangle*

Books by Timothy James Beck

IT HAD TO BE YOU

HE'S THE ONE

I'M YOUR MAN

SOMEONE LIKE YOU

Published by Kensington Publishing Corporation

Someone Like You

TIMOTHY JAMES BECK

KENSINGTON BOOKS
http://www.kensingtonbooks.com

KENSINGTON BOOKS are published by
Kensington Publishing Corp.
850 Third Avenue
New York, NY 10022

All Kensington titles, imprints and distributed lines are available at special quantity discounts for bulk purchases for sales promotion, premiums, fund-raising, educational or institutional use.

Special book excerpts or customized printings can also be created to fit specific needs. For details, write or phone the office of the Kensington Special Sales Manager: Kensington Publishing Corp., 850 Third Avenue, New York, NY 10022. Attn. Special Sales Department. Phone: 1-800-221-2647.

ISBN 0-7582-1035-3

First Kensington Trade Paperback Printing: April 2006
10 9 8 7 6 5 4 3 2 1

Printed in the United States of America

For John Scognamiglio

Acknowledgments

Belgian waffles from Congreve room service to: Tom Wocken, Dorothy Cochrane, Paul Enea, Bill Thomas, and Alison Picard.

Drink for Your Health smoothies to: Rebecca and Brian Baker, Shanon Best, Sean Brennan, Tim Brookover, famous author Rob Byrnes, Jason Cabot and Jeff Heilers, Susan Caretti, the Carter family, Carol E. Charny, Jean-Marc Chazy, Clea, Darryl Coble, the Cochrane family, Steve Code, Andre Coffa, Dalton DeHart, Caroline De La Rosa, Lynne Demarest, Jonathan DeMichael, Jone Devlin, the Ellner family, the Enea family, Laura Enea, Jim, Alex, and Alana Fitzgerald, Kitty Fontaine, the Forry family, the Garber family, Amy and Richard Ghiselin, Cullen Graff, Lowry Greeley, Kimberly Greene and River Heights Productions, Terri Griffin, Kate and Chris Guerrette, Victoria Harzer, Larry Henderson, Greg Herren, Alan Josoff, Judge Joe B., Christine and John Kovach, the Lambert family, Lee Linden, Amy Littlefield, Pierre Lombardini, Ellie Marshall, James McCain Jr., Marla McDaniel, Robin McElfresh, the Miller family, Debbie Milton, Helen Morris, Riley Morris, Eric Newland, Steve Nordwick and Doug French, David Outlaw, Pete and Sonja, Rachel Polintan, Pootz 'n Mootz, Ron Pratt, Todd Rainer, the Rambo family, Lori Redfearn and Bob Corrigan, Tandy Ringoringo, the Rose family, Carmella Roth, Rhonda Rubin and Lindsey Smolensky, Michael Ryan, Terry and Allen Shull, Leah Siegel, Laurie and Marty Smith, Sylvia and Angelo, Amy Terrell, Denece Thibodeaux, Matthew Thornton, Steve Vargas, Michael Vicencia, Ellen Ward and Pat Crosby, Don Whittaker, Sarena P. Williams, the Wocken family, Yojo, OUTeverywhere, AOL and Yahoo message boards and chat room friends and supporters, and everyone at Kensington who pulls it all together.

Treats to: Arthur, Brandi, Guinness, Hailey, Lazlo, Margot, and River.

Events and people in this novel are entirely fictitious. Especially the managers. The Mall of the Universe does not exist, but thank you to some Indiana resources, including Anne, Linda, Myra, Rob, Craig M. Bell, and Traci Lenzi, for helping provide a context within which it could be imagined. Thank you, Tracy Wilson, for providing a little bit of Dollywood.

1

Fruit of the Loom

Derek Anderson had been sixteen years old before he had room service for the first time. His parents' idea of a family vacation was visiting historic battlefields, homes, and monuments. They could never stay at a hotel. Their chosen vacation locations were invariably in close proximity to a campsite, where the nearest thing to room service was Derek's mother poking her head inside the tent to tell him something charred over a campfire was done cooking.

Deprived of entertainment, Derek was forced to devise his own. His growing up was measured by the nature of his fantasies. To the young Derek, a muscular man at an adjoining campsite was a superhero in disguise. Derek would envision Muscular Man saving the world—or at least one very bored eight-year-old. A few years later, Muscular Man was all human, more Indiana Jones than Superman. Derek would imagine going on adventures with him as they searched for magical artifacts buried in a Civil War battlefield or hidden within a dead hero's tomb.

Then Derek hit adolescence and his mental scenarios didn't require props, costumes, locations, or complicated plots. Nor could he focus on only one man when there were so many men everywhere. Shirts off and sweating as they set up tents. Stripped to cutoffs, trunks, or Speedos as they dove into lakes. Tanned muscles on display as they stood in tourist lines wearing shorts and tank tops. Wherever he looked, Derek saw a tantalizing feast that he wasn't allowed to taste. He was trapped in a world of scorched eggs and incinerated hot dogs.

Reuben, his best friend, took him away from all that. Reuben's parents won a trip for four to New York City, and since Reuben was an only child, they asked Derek to go along. After much begging and pleading, the Andersons relented, and Derek got to stay in a real hotel. Reuben and Derek shared their own room. On their first morning, Reuben dialed room service and ordered Belgian waffles topped with strawberries and whipped cream. After Derek took his first bite, while sitting in bed and watching television, he swore he'd never spend another summer roughing it in the wilderness like a male version of pioneer girl Caddie Woodlawn.

After that, Belgian waffles became Derek's comfort food. On his first day of employee orientation for Drayden's department store, he sat at a table in the back of a conference room and promised himself a heaping plate of waffles if he didn't run out the door before it was all over. A tall woman dressed in an eggplant-colored suit and brown high heels stood at the front of the room, droning on about the history of Drayden's.

"Bjorn Henry Lvandsson founded Drayden's in 1951. When Mr. Lvandsson's farm was wiped out by a tornado, his wife, Greta, pawned her loom so the young couple could try their hand at retail. The original Drayden's, which was named after Mr. Lvandsson's first-born son, was a tiny shop in St. Paul, Minnesota, and sold denim clothing and boots to area farmers. Offering sturdy, no-frills work clothes at low prices paid off. Mr. Lvandsson was able to get his wife's treasured loom out of hock and expand the business to include a line of hunting wear in 1954."

It was the hokiest story Derek had ever heard. His eyes glazed over as boredom became exhaustion. He stared at the Human Resources associate, studying her tight-lipped, hatchet face and wondering if she ever smiled. To keep himself from giving in to monotony, he made up a second job for her. In his daydream, she led a secret life as a stripper by night. Her routine as Lydia the Librarian was a favorite among the blue-collar patrons, earning her hundreds of dollars, which she earnestly socked away so she could get out of Indiana in style.

Derek smiled, but his glee vanished when he opened his eyes and the bright lights, dollar bills, and stripper poles faded from his imagination. He was back in the windowless conference room with a dozen other new hires. Derek sighed resolutely and tried to concentrate as the HR associate continued.

"People from all over Minnesota flocked to Drayden's in the late fifties, when the Lvandssons introduced a line of livestock blankets. Woven by Greta Lvandsson on the loom that started it all, they christened the livestock line Fruit of the Loom. Unfortunately, the underwear empire caught wind of the copyright-infringing horse blankets and threatened to sue Drayden's. 'We never hear of underwear from a loom,' Mr. Lvandsson insisted. 'We only wear Hanes,' his wife declared. The publicity from the case brought more customers into the 'Little Store That Could,' and people everywhere snatched up the newly christened Cattle Cozy line to keep their livestock warm on those harsh winter nights."

Derek didn't know which was worse, the story or the bad Scandinavian accent the HR associate used while speaking as the idiotic Lvandssons. He thought about excusing himself to go to the bathroom and not returning, or faking a seizure. Instead, he reminded himself that he needed the job, the money it would provide, and the sense of independence it could give him.

A black woman with big, curly hair chose that moment to stride into the conference room and say, "Sorry I'm late. Is this orientation?"

"Yes, it is. We were going over the history of Drayden's. If you'll find a seat, we can continue."

As the HR storyteller continued describing Bjorn Henry's foray into hunting and camping gear, Derek watched as the hair that ate Terre Haute sat next to him at his table.

"My curling iron made me late. It wouldn't heat up," his seatmate whispered.

"Sounds like my boyfriend," Derek said. When her eyes lit up, he added, "Sometimes it helps to plug it in."

"Oh, I like you," she said. "We'll get along fine. I'm Vienna."

"Derek," he whispered, pointing at himself.

They stopped talking and listened to their Drayden's history lesson, which became more palatable now that Derek had Vienna to alleviate his boredom. As Drayden's expanded into new markets, Mr. Lvandsson tried to engage his children in the business. His eldest son, Drayden, ran off to Hollywood. Sven, the next in line, headed for New York City and went to work on Wall Street after he received his MBA. Lastly, Henrietta, the only daughter, not to mention the family's bad seed, grabbed her automotive engineering certificate and raced off to join a pit crew at the Indianapolis 500. Other than Greta, who would greet Drayden's visitors from her loom, which was positioned in front of the main doors of the original store, the only family member to actively join in the business was Gertrude, the family cow. When Greta accidentally mixed up her Christmas card list with the customer database, Drayden's catalog business was born. The store was inundated with calls from people who had to have the festive sweater a perky Gertrude sported on the front of the Lvandsson family Christmas cards.

"Is this shit for real?" Vienna whispered.

Derek could empathize with the Lvandsson children. A career in the retail industry was not his ultimate goal in life, and he understood why they wanted to get as far away as possible from their parents' dreams. Derek's dream had been to be pampered and privileged. To eat Belgian waffles in bed. Maybe be famous for being famous. However, that sort of lifestyle was usually reserved for people with money. Or at the very least, for their children. Derek's parents were not rich. They were comfortable and happy. But they assumed their son would want the life they lived and never bothered to show him that his life had possibilities. Instead of preparing him for a future, they immersed him in a past of on-this-spot battlefields and crumbling buildings.

Derek explained that to Vienna when they were allowed to leave for lunch.

"I hear you, Derek," she said as they left Drayden's and wandered into Mall of the Universe. "My parents were very old-fashioned. Even though I did well in school, they never dreamed that I'd want to go to college. They thought I'd turn out just like my mama, living and breathing for my man. I worked hard to go to college, and I got my education. On my own, thank you."

"What's your degree?"

Vienna mumbled something that Derek couldn't understand. There were a lot of people in the mall, voices and footsteps echoing off the tile and glass interior of the corridors, so he asked her to repeat herself.

"Psychology. I got my B.S. at Indiana University," she said.

"I get mine from my boyfriend," Derek quipped. "I don't get it. Why are you here with me, working at a mall, when you could rake in the dough from an office somewhere in the real world?"

"My license to practice was suspended," she said. "Hey, let's go visit my friend Davii."

They pushed their way through throngs of people and crossed the main floor of the mall. When Derek was a boy, he'd seen a drawing of a space colony that might house thousands of people sometime in the future. It looked like a gigantic, high-tech wagon wheel floating through the galaxy. Mall of the Universe was similarly shaped, but firmly planted on the ground with a planetarium at its hub. The mall contained not only hundreds of stores, but also a nightclub, a roller rink, and a bowling alley, as well as a hotel and an apartment building on opposite sides of the mall, and a mid-rise condominium standing sentinel over all four mall levels, which were named Earth, Moon, Sun, and Stars.

Derek had assumed they would meet Davii in the food court, since there was one on the Earth level, but they walked past it, then Vienna pulled him into a hair salon. He was overcome by loud music and the acrid smell of perm solution, which almost made him yearn to return to Drayden's and the insufferable Lvandsson legend. Vienna dragged him to the end of a row of chairs, where a handsome man dressed in black was cutting a client's hair.

"Davii!" Vienna shrieked.

"Vienna!" Davii roared. He flung his arms around Vienna, and for a moment Derek was afraid Davii had plunged his scissors into her back. He couldn't bear the thought of returning to Drayden's without her.

"I missed you," Vienna said. "This has been the longest day ever."

"I know," Davii commiserated. He resumed snipping his client's hair as he said, "I've been slaving away here for hours. Ages!"

"It's only noon," Derek said, checking his watch to be sure. Davii looked at him with an unreadable expression. Derek immediately worried that Davii hated his hair.

"Davii, this is Derek," Vienna said, putting her arm around Derek's waist. "He's been my saving grace today. We're in training together, and he's been so witty and clever, providing a much-needed stimulus in a dull setting. Very entertaining. He reminds me of you."

"Really?" Davii said, looking skeptical. Derek felt dubious about her remark as well. Visually, he and Davii were polar opposites. Davii was tall and lithe; his face angular and striking, with deep blue eyes framed by long eyelashes. His black hair was cut in a trendy, spiky style. If Derek's look was as American as apple pie, then Davii was a crème brulée or an Italian pastry. Something European and decadent; Derek couldn't be sure exactly. Davii arched an eyebrow and said, "Oh, well, any friend of Vienna's—"

"Should be isolated and studied in a controlled environment!" Vienna interjected, and the two of them burst out laughing. The client in Davii's chair looked mildly annoyed, until he stopped laughing and turned her head sharply to the left so he could cut the back of her hair.

"I've got stories," Davii stated.

"Who?" Vienna asked.

Though her chin was pushed down into her chest, Derek saw the client's eyebrows perk up at the mention of gossip.

"Glenda, our manager, was fired," Davii stage-whispered, though it was unnecessary because of the loud music.

"No. Really?" Vienna said. "What happened?"

"She was taking long lunch breaks," he answered.

"That doesn't seem like a reason to fire someone," Derek said.

"It does when you spend your lunch breaks in the broom closet," Davii said.

"Why would she eat her lunch in a broom closet?" Vienna asked. "Did she have an eating disorder? Sometimes bulimics binge in private."

"Glenda was bingeing, but not on food," Davii said. "And she wasn't eating alone, either. Did I mention that Betty, the shampoo girl, was fired, too?"

Vienna's perfectly lined eyes grew wide, and she covered her mouth with her hands. "Oh, that's—"

"Stupid, right? I mean, when I want a nooner, I'll go to the top floor of the parking garage like a normal person!" Davii exclaimed.

"Are you going to try to get her position?" Vienna asked.

"I could," Davii mused, "but I'm not that nimble. It's an awfully small closet."

Derek laughed, and Vienna admonished, "Don't encourage him, Derek."

"No. I don't think so," Davii answered. "I'm not nearly responsible enough to be a manager. Nor would I want to be. Too much time would be taken up organizing and running this place. I'd rather do hair and collect tips."

"I suppose you're right," Vienna said.

"I'm always right," Davii said emphatically. He surveyed his client's hair and said, "Listen, you two had better run along. I don't want you to be late getting back to work, and I'm fucking up Brenda's hair."

Davii's client lifted her head in alarm and stared at herself in the mirror, looking for carnage.

"Okay. I'll see you later," Vienna said and kissed Davii's cheek.

"It was nice to meet you, Davii," Derek said.

"You, too. I'm sure I'll see you soon. We'll all go for drinks sometime. Ciao, *bello*! Ciao, *bella*!"

"He's a trip," Derek remarked once they'd left the salon.

"Davii? Yeah. You could say that," Vienna said. "But outside the salon he's not so—"

"Theatrical?" Derek suggested.

"I was going to say flaming, but that will do," Vienna said. "It's all a performance. He's giving his clients what they expect of him. Playing up the stereotype. Oddly enough, they tip him more if he does."

"That's ridiculous."

"No, it's true. At home, Davii is really quiet and reserved. We share an apartment in the Galaxy Building." She pointed toward the apartment tower at the end of the mall. "It's a two-bedroom. Davii's not my boyfriend or anything."

"I figured as much," Derek said. "But that's not what I meant."

"I know what you meant," Vienna said. "Listen to me, Derek. I'm giving you some free advice. You're a gay man who's about to begin a career in sales. You don't think people will look at you and draw their own conclusions without knowing you? Get real. If you play it straight, they won't listen to a word you say and you won't sell anything. If you gay it up a notch, they'll think you're a genius. Think about the gay stereotype. Supposedly all gay men have amazing style and can make anything or anyone fabulous. Davii could give a woman a Mohawk and make her think she's transformed for the better. Like my daddy always said, it takes a lot of manure to make a garden."

"That sounds like Drayden's propaganda to me," Derek said.

Vienna grabbed his arm and pulled him toward the food court, saying, "Speaking of which, if we don't get moving, we'll be late."

After a hurried lunch, they returned to the store for more

History of Drayden's 101. The Lvandsson family saga continued into the eighties, when Drayden Lvandsson finally returned from Hollywood to help his father run the company. Drayden had connections in the fashion industry and convinced many of them to sell their clothes and accessories in his stores. Business boomed, and Drayden's opened stores all over the Midwest.

After the market crash of 1987, Sven Lvandsson returned to handle Drayden's economic concerns. Henrietta retired from the racing circuit a few years later and secured a job as Director of Operations. Though she ran routine inspections of every store and made sure they functioned like a well-oiled race car, she spent the majority of her time managing the shipping and receiving warehouse.

Surprisingly, Derek enjoyed the rest of their orientation. Drayden's was a respected department store chain, often recognized for enriching and giving back to the communities where its stores were located. The stores carried the finest quality merchandise and had beautifully inventive window displays. The atmosphere inside buzzed with creativity and excitement. The salespeople were all polite and well dressed. He wanted to be part of it.

But he still had training to get through. Not to mention scads of paperwork to fill out. While a different HR associate stood at the front of the conference room and discussed the employee handbook page by page, Vienna and Derek sat together and made up games to pass the time.

"If you had to have sex with one person in this room, who would it be?" she asked.

Derek scanned the room for someone attractive but couldn't spot anyone who was his type. "Nobody," he answered.

"Not even me?" Vienna asked, feigning hurt.

He bit his lip, pretending to mull it over as he looked her up and down. She had on black high heel pumps, a short skirt, a white shirt, and a fitted jacket. Her body was all curves, but very toned, and her makeup was minimal. She was attractive, and if Derek hadn't had a boyfriend, he thought he might be persuaded to give heterosexuality another try. "Sorry. No," he said.

"It's okay. You're not my type either."

"Why? Because I'm white?"

"No, fool. Number one, you're too young. I like my men a little older."

"Really? How—"

"Don't you even ask that," Vienna whispered threateningly. "Number two, I like to make more money than the men I date."

"That's absurd. I'm going to be selling shoes. You'll be selling cosmetics. We'll be on equal financial footing."

"That's not what I meant," Vienna explained. "I'm talking about independence. I don't like to rely on other people for anything. You, on the other hand, have no problem in that respect, do you?"

"How can you say that? You don't even know me."

Vienna looked smug as she said, "I know all about you."

"But we just met."

"Trust me. I know everything that goes on in this mall."

Derek eyed Vienna suspiciously while she secured her wild hair behind her head and began filling out an insurance form. Her self-confidence and insight made him nervous. He hardly knew her, so how could she know anything about him?

Vienna glanced over and saw him staring at her. "We're supposed to be filling out these forms. You'd better get to work."

"Are you playing mind games with me? What do you think you know about me?" he asked.

Vienna smiled and said, "I know you live in the hotel." Then she added, "And I know you're a kept boy."

Suddenly Derek wanted Belgian waffles more than ever.

2

Oops . . . I Stabbed You Again!

Vienna Talbot never hesitated to pamper herself. In her thirty-five years on earth, she'd learned that everyone was looking out for himself, so she'd better follow suit. If she had a long day, nothing soothed her nerves like a pedicure. If she saw an outfit in a window, she told herself that it wouldn't look better on anyone else; she'd then prove her assumption correct by trying it on and buying it. She liked to be surrounded by beautiful objects. For breakfast, she preferred freshly sliced fruit with yogurt in a Baccarat bowl.

Davii often called her a diva. Vienna hated the word. It had connotations she didn't relate to: a pushy, demanding bitch who always had to be the center of attention and get her way. Vienna knew she was the complete opposite of that description. Sure, she enjoyed getting her way every now and then, but she was more than willing to learn from her mistakes. She felt more comfortable on the edge of a crowd, observing, taking in a scene, rather than making one.

From the time she was a little girl, she'd known she was pretty. A fact confirmed by the members of her father's parish, who were quick to point out her beauty when they saw her at church or when they came to the Talbot home for dinner. She appreciated a compliment and was quick to offer thanks for an accolade, but it wasn't the be-all and end-all of her existence. Her self-confidence was strong and she didn't demand compliments, or anything else, from anyone.

Vienna stood in front of a full-length mirror in a dressing room at Drayden's, comparing the little girl from her memory to the woman she'd become. She ran her hands over her stomach and scrutinized her reflection. She was tall, but not exactly slender. Her body could be described as womanly, curvy, but nothing kept moving after she stood still. She ate right, and her only vice was alcohol, but not in excess. Vienna turned and looked over her shoulder to examine her butt in her black lace panties.

"Ain't no junk in my trunk," she said to herself.

"Did you call me?" a perky voice called to her through the dressing room's curtain.

"No," Vienna said quickly and firmly. She'd finished her last day of training, four hours of register procedures and three hours of diversity class, and decided to reward herself with lingerie. She hated it when salespeople didn't respect a closed curtain. "I'm fine. But could you find me this set in red, too? And can I try the merry widow that's on the mannequin?"

"Of course."

Vienna readjusted a bra strap and tried to look at herself as if she were a stranger. Or how a man might view her. She smiled, liking the way her light brown skin looked in spite of the fluorescent lighting. Her high cheekbones and almond-shaped eyes were free of makeup, save a light foundation and eyeliner. Her lips, however, were painted a dark red, drawing attention to her mouth, which she thought was her best feature. Although with the way the new bra lifted her breasts, she began to reconsider.

"I'd do me," she decided aloud.

"Here you are," her sales associate said, passing the requested items through the curtain.

"Thank you," Vienna said.

"My name is Jeanine. Call me if you need me."

"I will," Vienna said, even though she knew she wouldn't. There was no way Vienna would ever wear red lingerie. She'd only asked for it to give Jeanine something to do, to keep her out of the dressing room. However, Vienna had always wanted to try on a merry widow. It was something she never would've considered buying before she moved to Terre Haute. It wasn't becoming for a preacher's daughter or a respected psychologist.

But the Vienna in the mirror, in her lacy black bra and panties, looked like a completely different person from the girl from Gary, Indiana. Just thinking about Gary made Vienna cringe. She couldn't wait to leave her hometown when she was young. She wanted to get away from the industrial fumes, the suburban boredom, and her overbearing, hypercritical mother. Vienna knew the key to escape was her mind. She studied hard and accepted the first scholarship that came her way, taking her to Bloomington. Even at Indiana University, Vienna kept her nose to the grindstone, never deviating from her plans for success. However, a defensive lineman named Kevin did sidetrack her.

Kevin Martazak was a star on the field and off. A physiology major, he was on the dean's list, and he danced with IU's African American Dance Company, though he swore he did it only to help his agility on the field. Kevin and Vienna met in statistics class when they both knocked their textbooks off their desks at the same time. They introduced themselves after class, and Vienna stated that the odds of them having the same accident at the same time were one in fifty. Kevin asked what the odds were for going out on a date, to which Vienna replied, "From where I'm standing, they're looking good. Better by the second."

They lived together for three years before they got married. After graduation, they got an apartment off campus and pursued their master's degrees while holding down part-time jobs. Then Kevin, working as a therapist in a downtown hospital, supported her while she got her doctorate. Eventually they bought a house in the suburbs, with matching Volvos and hectic lives. Vienna found an office with a group of psychologists in a professional building near their new home.

Their life seemed perfect. Vienna enjoyed being married. She liked coming home from work and cooking dinner for her husband. She liked taking care of him. She liked picking up their dry cleaning. She liked grocery shopping. She liked massaging Kevin's shoulders until he fell asleep on the couch while watching a movie in their home.

She enjoyed her career. Vienna liked helping people; guiding them to make better decisions about their lives and to see things about themselves that they'd never realized. Maintaining her home and career was difficult, but she managed quite well. Vienna used her maiden name at work, and sometimes she felt like two different people. By day she was Dr. Talbot, saving people from their inner demons. At five o'clock each evening, she'd resume her true identity as Mrs. Martazak, devoted wife of Kevin.

All her years of dreaming and planning had paid off. Vienna felt like she'd broken free from the shackles of Gary to become her own person. She loved that her patients felt safe enough to confide in her. And if she ever doubted that her life was perfect, she need only listen to the awful truths her patients revealed to make her count her blessings.

Until one afternoon a patient unwittingly offered Vienna a dose of reality she couldn't bear to swallow. Her patient, Laura, was having an affair with a married man. Vienna listened to Laura for weeks with an open mind, despite the fact that deep inside, she hated her. In Vienna's opinion, what was worse than the affair was that Laura got sloppy as the weeks went by, as if she wanted her husband to find out what she was doing. Laura didn't work, but she'd come home late, telling her husband that she'd been grocery shopping. Yet she arrived home empty-handed. Another time, Laura came home from a liaison with her lover, fixed dinner for her family, did the dishes, watched television with her husband, and went to bed as if nothing had ever happened. Which was what she normally did, but this time, her lover's dried semen was still on her legs, since she hadn't taken a shower after they met that afternoon.

Vienna was appalled. But all she could do was ask Laura what she would have done if her husband wanted to make love and wondered what was on her leg. After a long pause, Laura said, "I think I wanted him to find out. And I think I would've told him. Kevin's an amazing lover and a good man. I'd rather be married to him than to my husband. Maybe I should ask for a divorce. What do you think, Dr. Talbot?"

"This is a breakthrough, Laura. But it changes your original goal. You came here hoping to end your affair and keep your husband. Now it sounds as if you're changing your mind. To answer your question, it doesn't matter what I think. What do *you* think?" Vienna asked. Then, before Laura could answer, Vienna heard herself add, "I'm sorry. Did you say Kevin?"

"Yeah," Laura answered. "I mean, you have to admit that Mrs. Martazak sounds better than Mrs. Bartlebaum."

"You're right. That does sound better. But then, I'm rather partial to the name," Vienna said. "Talbot is my maiden name. My husband's name is Martazak. Which makes me Mrs. Martazak. Mrs. Kevin Martazak."

The last thing Vienna remembered was Laura's startled face as she put two and two together. Vienna had never been a firm believer in temporary insanity, but she changed her point of view when she stabbed Laura in the leg with a letter opener.

Vienna stared at herself in the mirror at Drayden's. Even though she was no longer Vienna the preacher's daughter from Gary, or Mrs. Martazak from Bloomington, the merry widow still wasn't for her. She was neither merry nor a widow. She was a bitter divorcée.

After she dressed, Vienna tossed the merry widow aside, handed the lingerie to Jeanine, and said, "I'll just take these, please."

The magic of purchasing with a discount faded faster than the image on a falling Etch A Sketch when the sales associate said, "The name on your license is Vienna Martazak, but the Visa card says Vienna Talbot."

"I'm divorced. It's easier to get a new Visa than it is to spend a whole day at the DMV. Talbot's my maiden name."

"Oh. I'm so sorry."

"Do you have unpleasant associations with the name Talbot?" Vienna asked.

"What? No," Jeanine said. "I meant that I'm sorry your marriage didn't work out."

"Oh. Thanks," Vienna said. She felt pitied and didn't like it at all. "Can I sign so I can get home?"

"Sure. Sign here, then add your employee number and extension." While Vienna signed, Jeanine asked, "Was it a bad divorce?"

"No, it was fabulous! We sang Gershwin tunes throughout the whole hearing. My divorce was sold out for weeks." Seeing the sales associate's discomfort, she quickly apologized and added, "I don't think divorces are ever good."

"I shouldn't have pried," Jeanine said.

"It wasn't all bad," Vienna said offhandedly. "I got to keep my car and the money from selling the house."

"What did he get?" Jeanine asked.

"He got to live," Vienna said. When Jeanine laughed, she added, "I didn't think that was fair, but who am I to question a judge?"

Walking through the mall on her way home, Vienna watched the people around her and wondered if their lives had turned out as planned. She tried to ignore all the couples walking hand in hand, but there were too many of them. People came from all over the world to visit Mall of the Universe, and they seemed to do it in pairs. She tried to avert her eyes, but everywhere she looked she saw them. Then she ran into a woman and said, "Excuse me. I'm sorry."

"That's okay," the woman said. "Do you regularly get manicures? Would you like to try our new hand cream? It's great for problem cuticles."

Vienna looked around in horror, finally realizing what had happened. She wasn't paying attention and had run into one of the Cart People.

"No. I just got a manicure. I don't need anything," Vienna said quickly and tried to get away. Before she could, the other Cart People saw her, grabbed samples from their carts, and began moving toward her.

"Isn't this hat great?"

"Do you need sunglasses? We have the latest styles!"

"These earrings would look fabulous against your neck! They're stainless steel."

Vienna felt like the town tramp with a broken heel in a slasher flick as hordes of zombies moved in for the kill. She swung her Drayden's shopping bag to ward off the Cart People, screamed, and ran for her life.

By the time she got home, Vienna was extremely annoyed. The scads of people in love ticked her off, but her own feelings of inferiority bothered her even more. Not to mention the Cart People. She slammed the door to her apartment, threw her shopping bag into her room, and headed for the refrigerator.

"You're in a mood," Davii observed as he turned to look at her from their sofa. Though their apartment was fairly large, the kitchen, dining area, and living room had no walls, so Davii and Vienna could carry on a conversation even though they were in separate rooms. "Rough day in the kohl mines, dear?"

Vienna shut the refrigerator door and said, "Why don't we have any decent food? Do we have any cupcakes? I want cupcakes."

Davii turned off the television and said, "You threw out all the junk food last week when you went on fad diet number five this year."

"That was stupid. Why didn't you stop me?"

"Ever try to stop a moving train?" Davii asked. "This can't be about cupcakes. What's wrong?"

"Why can't it be about cupcakes?"

"Because that would be insane," Davii said.

"Technically, it would be obsessive. Actually, it's more compulsive behavior," Vienna said.

Davii patted the cushion next to him and said, "Come on, Vienna. Tell me all about it."

Vienna made a big show of exasperation as she crossed the room to sit down, but inside she was grateful. She wanted to talk to someone. Someone other than a sales associate at Drayden's. "I hate people," Vienna said after she sat down.

"No, you don't," Davii said.

"Okay. Just people in love."

"No, you don't," Davii repeated. "You hate that you're not in love."

"No, I don't," Vienna retorted. "What I hate is people who watch talk shows and think they know everything there is to know about psychology. I'm upset because my husband left me."

"Your husband didn't leave you. He had an affair."

"Same thing," Vienna said. "He left me sexually."

"The sex is always better on the other side of the fence," Davii stated. "So this bad mood is all your ex-husband's fault?"

"Isn't everything?" Vienna asked.

"I meant—"

"I know what you meant," Vienna said. "I was just using humor as a shield. I'm in a bad mood because a sales associate at Drayden's brought up my divorce while I was shopping."

"How did that come up?" Davii asked. "Did she ask, 'Would you like to try on that dress? What size are you? An eight, or a divorcée?' "

"I'm a six," Vienna lied emphatically. She told Davii what happened in the store, then said, "It's not so much the divorce that's bothering me. It's the fact that it's been two years since it happened and I'm still in the same place I was then."

Davii looked puzzled as he said, "I thought that all happened in Bloomington."

"Not literally," Vienna said with an exasperated sigh. "I mean figuratively. Emotionally. Davii, I haven't been with another man since Kevin."

"I live in the same apartment. You don't have to convince me."

"Hey! I could be like you and have quickies all over this mall. You don't know what I do outside our apartment."

Davii rolled his eyes and smirked, his silence saying more about

Vienna's character than words ever could. They'd lived together for almost two years, and Davii was the only person that Vienna trusted with her secrets. If she had an illicit fling, Davii would be told. He knew that she had problems trusting people, especially men. She knew that he felt sorry for her, though he'd never say that out loud. Davii understood that Vienna was a romantic woman who grew up with notions of princes on horses who would rescue her from her bedroom window in Gary. Now that she lived with Davii on the eighth floor of the Galaxy Building, she wasn't sure the princes would be able to reach her.

Davii said, "Don't underestimate the power of a good quickie. It could be just what you need."

"Do you see me disagreeing?" Vienna asked. "Davii, I bought lingerie today after work. Do you know how depressing it is to try on lingerie, look at yourself in the mirror, then realize you have nobody to wear it for?"

"You could wear it for me," Davii said.

"Honey, that's even more depressing," Vienna said with a good-natured laugh. "I'm better off wearing it for myself."

"At least then you're more likely to have an orgasm. I can't guarantee the same results as your right hand."

"I'm left-handed."

"Whatever."

"I just want a man who respects me," Vienna said. "A man who won't give up on me would be nice, too."

"So you haven't given up on love?" Davii asked.

"No. But don't let that get around. Unless you happen to run into Lenny Kravitz."

"I'll see what I can do," Davii promised. He fingered one of Vienna's curls and said, "I'll bet Lenny would love a woman with braids."

"With red extensions woven into them?" Vienna asked hopefully.

"I'll see what I can do," Davii repeated. "By the way, how is that friend of yours from work? Darren?"

"Derek?"

"The guy you brought by the salon?"

"That would be Derek," Vienna confirmed. "He's all right. I guess. I haven't had much time to talk to him. He's been in seminars learning how shoes are made."

"Sounds fascinating," Davii said dryly.

"No more fascinating than learning about lipstick and mascara. Anyway, once we're settled into our new jobs—"

"You'll quit and get a new one," Davii interrupted. "You've had thirty different jobs in two years. All in this mall, too."

"I don't think it's quite that many. Besides, if I hadn't quit that job at the Fabric Mart, I wouldn't have gotten a job as a receptionist in your salon, and I wouldn't have met you. My job-hopping paid off, so lay off." Vienna suddenly thought to ask, "Why are you asking about Derek?"

Davii examined his cuticles and said, "I don't know. You've never brought a co-worker to meet me before, so I was curious."

"Not to mention he's cute," Vienna added.

"Yes. There's that. Is he single?" Davii asked.

"No. It's not like I was presenting you with a gift."

"Should I let that stand in my way?"

Vienna paused in thought. Finally she said, "I don't know enough about his relationship to answer you, but I don't think he's looking for a rendezvous in the parking garage."

"Who says that's what *I'm* looking for?" Davii asked.

Vienna eyed him a minute, then said, "All this interest on the basis of one brief meeting?"

"I'm good at reading people," Davii said. "It goes with my job."

"Speaking of your job—"

"You only keep me here for your hair," Davii said. "Let's get started."

3

Kept Boy

When Derek's parents had sat him down the summer before his senior year of high school and asked what he planned to do after graduation, he certainly hadn't blithely responded, "I want to be a kept boy!" Nor had that been his ambition while he was growing up. He hadn't been sure what he wanted to do, but he knew he had a college fund. He assured his parents that lots of people started college without a set plan, found out what they were good at, then made their decision.

In due course, he went north to Terre Haute and Indiana State University. It was only a hundred miles from home, but that was far enough to be an inviting new world for him. He loved his parents, but they could be a little smothering. They'd married in their late twenties and tried unsuccessfully for fifteen years to have a child. His mother initially thought he was a symptom of early menopause.

He didn't mind having parents who were the age of some of his classmates' grandparents. His father's tool and dye business provided a comfortable living. If he didn't get everything he wanted, like a car, at least his parents hadn't lived beyond their means or inflicted him with the messy divorces and child custody fights he saw all around him.

But George and Terri Anderson were also nobody's fools. When they saw his lackluster grades at the end of his first college semester, Derek was warned to show improvement or continue his education while living at home. They knew what he was capable of, because he'd made good grades in high school. They were sure, and correctly so, that the only subject Derek had focused on was Party 101.

What they didn't know was how enthusiastically he'd embraced the chance to be openly gay in a place where he found like-minded and able-bodied men. He wouldn't have called himself a slut; he didn't have to, since his friends said it for him.

Derek heeded his parents' warning and finished his freshman year with a much-improved grade point average. Thus he was allowed to return to Cromwell Hall—his parents were still reluctant to approve off-campus housing—as a sophomore. A year wiser, he kept his grades up for two more semesters, but he'd despaired of ever figuring out what he wanted to be when he grew up. He'd fulfilled all his general requirements, and it was time to narrow his field of study.

He'd been pondering that on his last day as a part-time employee at Drink for Your Health Juice and Smoothie Bar. Business was slow, since finals were over and students were beginning their mass exodus to hometowns, beaches, or summer jobs. Most of his friends were already gone. Derek had only a few things left to pack and a few precious days of freedom before his father came to get him for a boring summer of helping with inventory and shipments at Anderson Tool and Dye.

After his last customers left, he was desultorily wiping down their table, trying to ignore that year's song-that-must-be-played-until-everyone-hates-it. He glanced through the plate glass window and his heart skipped a beat when he spied one of Indiana's scenic wonders: a man bending to lock his bicycle. He was wearing Lycra cycling shorts, and while they showcased his ass to good advantage—and for that matter, his package, when he turned around—they also appealed to Derek's weakness for great legs.

The cyclist's legs were long, muscular, tanned, and covered with hair sun-bleached to nearly white. Derek was practically drooling about his powerful thighs when the man opened the door to the shop and stopped short on the threshold.

"I'll give you twenty dollars if you'll change the radio station," he said, brushing his sweat-soaked hair back with one hand.

"I'll do whatever you want for nothing," Derek said brazenly, then darted behind the counter and changed the station. He met the cyclist's intense blue eyes and said, "What else?"

"Strawberry lemon smoothie. Large."

"Are you sure that's what you want?" Derek asked.

One corner of the man's mouth twitched, and he said, "Is there something else you'd recommend?"

As if channeling some turn-of-the-century floozy from an ice cream parlor, Derek said, "Most of my customers appreciate my finesse with a banana." He grabbed one from the counter and, keeping his eyes locked on the cyclist's, began to unpeel it.

"I usually like something more tart," the man said, playing along.

Derek shrugged and said, "Then I may as well eat this."

He proceeded to slide the banana between his lips, provoking a reluctant laugh from his customer, who asked, "When do you get off?"

Derek slowly drew the uneaten banana from his mouth and said, "*That* depends on you. The shop closes at six."

"I'll be back at six," the cyclist said, turning to leave.

"Aren't you going to satisfy your craving for something tart?" Derek asked.

"That depends on *you,*" the man said, mimicking Derek, and kept walking.

Derek sighed with longing as he watched the cyclist cross the street and unlock his bike. Derek didn't really believe he'd be back, but at least he'd be a good fantasy on boring summer nights in Evansville.

Derek's boss, Tyrone, a hippie throwback who'd dropped out of Indiana State in the seventies, came in before six to write out his final paycheck and lock up. Just as Derek stepped out of Drink for Your Health, his Mystery Date wheeled up to the curb in a silver Jaguar convertible. Derek didn't even hesitate before stepping into the car. It was only after they pulled away that it occurred to him that he knew nothing about his companion, not even his name, beyond how appealing he looked in biker shorts.

Derek scrutinized him while he drove. His hair, fine and straight, looked blonder now that it was dry. In spite of his deep tan, there were no faint lines around his eyes, which made Derek guess he wasn't that much older, definitely under thirty. He was clean-shaven and wore no jewelry except a watch with a silver band. His black jeans, black leather lace-up boots, and crisp white linen shirt made Derek feel frumpy in his khaki shorts, faded T-shirt, and sneakers. He was grateful that Tyrone hadn't expected him to wear something like the bright orange uniform shirt he'd worn in his previous job as a fry cook.

Without turning his head, the man said, "Now can you tell me my sun sign, my favorite color, and what brand of toothpaste I prefer?"

"You could tell me your name," Derek suggested.

"Is it customary for an abductor to provide details like that?"

"I'm Derek Anderson," Derek volunteered.

"Hunter," the man said, which drew only silence as Derek contemplated whether that was his first or last name.

Derek also wondered why they were driving toward Indianapolis. "I hope my parents can find a good photo for my milk carton shot."

Hunter laughed but offered no more information, so Derek faced forward and considered the consequences of his heedless flirting. When they took the exit for Mall of the Universe, his worry evaporated. Maybe Hunter just wanted to take him to the retail mecca of the Midwest and buy him some decent clothes.

They drove to the outside entrance of the Hotel Congreve. If Derek was in for a one-nighter, he'd be doing it in style. They got out of the car, and Derek watched as Hunter tossed his keys to the uniformed doorman with a nod. Since the Hotel Congreve was way beyond Derek's means, he had no idea whether it was customary for a doorman to also act as a valet. However, both men seemed to know what they were doing, so Derek just shrugged and followed Hunter into the opulent lobby, noticing how heads turned to watch as they strode toward the elevator. Hunter seemed oblivious to the stir he caused. Once the elevator doors cut the two of them off with a soft whoosh, Derek watched as Hunter punched some numbers onto a keypad.

Then Hunter turned to him and said, "Let's see what that mouth does with something other than smart-assed comments and bananas, shall we?"

Derek felt Hunter's kiss all the way down to his toes. It left him swooning like the heroine in a romance novel. The next few hours were a blur, because Hunter was a sensational lover, without inhibitions. They didn't do anything Derek hadn't tried before, but he'd never done it all with one man. Especially a man with Hunter's skill.

Later, Hunter watched with an amused expression as Derek polished off a massive room service order. He'd given Derek a silk robe to wear. Since Hunter was a larger man than Derek, he had to roll up the sleeves to keep them out of his waffles, which made him feel like a kid. Hunter didn't help matters when he said, "How old are you?"

"Twenty."

"That explains your appetite."

"Why, how old are you?"

"Twenty-seven." Hunter patted the bed. "Come back here."

Derek dropped the robe and joined him under the sheets, game for another session if Hunter was. But Hunter's amorous mood had faded. He lay quietly against a stack of pillows, smoking and absently rubbing Derek's skin, which looked milky white compared to Hunter's.

"This is a huge suite," Derek said, looking around. "The bathroom is twice the size of my dorm room." The silence was making Derek edgy, and he always talked too much when he got nervous. "It's kind of weird that your stuff is all over. The bathroom, I mean. And your drawers and closets are full of clothes. You must be planning to stay in Indiana quite a while?"

"This isn't a hotel suite," Hunter said. "It's my home."

Derek mulled that over for a few minutes, then, deciding he had nothing to lose, said, "I guess you're loaded. Living at a hotel must be—"

"I work here," Hunter said abruptly. "The apartment is part of the package. Tell me about you. You're a student?"

True to form, Derek began rattling off the details of his life, up to and including his imminent summer exile to Evansville. In an attempt to keep his narrative from boring Hunter, he tossed in stories about other people. His parents' crazy neighbor, who let her German shepherds eat at the table. His father's delivery driver, who claimed to be distantly related to John Wayne and hid his male-pattern baldness under a cowboy hat. A friend on his floor in Cromwell Hall who could belch "March On You Fighting Sycamores," Indiana State's fight song. He didn't know if Hunter was listening, but he sure smoked a lot.

"Doesn't all that smoking interfere with your cycling?" Derek asked.

Hunter gave him a look he couldn't read, stubbed out his cigarette, and said, "I gather you have no interest in the tool and dye business?"

"Not much," Derek admitted. "That's okay with my dad. He's already handpicked someone he's going to sell the business to when he retires."

"Your father sounds like a reasonable man." Hunter was silent a while, then said, "What if I could offer you a job at the hotel? Our athletic club has a smoothie bar. You've shown your skill at satisfying your customers."

The slight irony in his tone made Derek wince, and he said, "It's not like I make a habit of this. It was my last day. I was feeling bold."

"That's not an answer," Hunter said.

"I don't have a place to live. And I don't think my parents will go for it. They sure won't pay for me to stay here to work in a smoothie bar."

"Call your father and tell him you've found another way to get home," Hunter said. "I'll take you to Evansville in a few days."

Derek sat up and looked at him, saying, "You're used to getting your way, aren't you? Do you do the hiring for the hotel, or what?"

This elicited a faint smile before Hunter said, "Congreve."

"Right. The Hotel Congreve."

"You asked for my name. It's Hunter Congreve."

So began Derek's association with one of the descendants of a family who not only routinely made Forbes' list of wealthiest Americans, but as far as Derek knew, had erected their first hotel within view of Plymouth Rock just after disembarking from the Mayflower.

When Hunter had left him in Evansville a few days later, Derek tried to convince himself that his sinking mood would pass; that before the end of summer, Hunter would be nothing more than a sexy memory. Hunter hadn't asked for the Andersons' number, nor did Derek call Hunter at the hotel. His parents seemed to notice his uncharacteristic silence, as well as his lack of enthusiasm about getting in touch with old friends, but they asked no questions.

He'd been in Evansville less than two weeks when he rode home from work with his father one night to see the silver Jaguar parked in front of their house. When they went inside, it had taken all his self-control not to run into Hunter's arms. Hunter had calmly repeated his offer of a job, but one look at Derek's face told his parents the whole story.

They'd disguised their shock at the realization that he was gay with protests that a job at the hotel—or anything at the hotel—might derail Derek's education. Hunter made it clear that as far as he was concerned, finishing college was Derek's top priority. He displayed an attitude that Derek would come to know well; when Hunter wanted something, he persisted until he got it. The Andersons finally gave in, perhaps believing that a relationship between two people of such disparate backgrounds would quickly fizzle out. They'd been wrong. Although the health club job had never materialized, the Hotel Congreve became Derek's home.

In the beginning, Derek tried to maintain the pretense that he was a hotel employee who just happened to use the extra bedroom in Hunter's luxurious apartment. Each morning after Hunter left to go biking, Derek would mess up the extra bed before Juanita, the only member of the housekeeping staff who took care of Hunter's residence, arrived. She always smiled and nodded with a cheery "*Buenos dias,*" and Derek assumed she spoke little English. Until one day, as he was leaving to wander the mall while she was there, she gripped Derek's arm and pulled her wallet from her apron pocket, flipping it open to a photo of a lovely young woman with coal black hair and a gorgeous smile.

"Consuela," she said. "My other half. Stop forcing me to change two beds, please."

"I'm sorry," Derek stammered, blushing.

"Don't be sorry. I'm just letting you know I don't care where you sleep. You make Mr. Hunter happy. When he's happy, it's better for everyone."

"You're a big fraud, too, you know, pretending you couldn't speak English," Derek complained.

"You assumed," she said. "Let's be friends, you and me. We both take care of Mr. Hunter. He was very unhappy before you came."

Over time, it was Juanita, not Hunter, who gave Derek some of the details of Hunter's life. He was the youngest of five children and apparently had an overbearing father. He'd been uninterested in the hotel business. His passion was competitive racing, until an accident irreparably damaged tendons and ligaments in one of his knees. His cycling career finished, he succumbed to his father's wishes and agreed to manage the mall hotel. He rarely talked about his work, but as Derek came to understand him better, he recognized that Hunter's genius was in knowing whom to hire and how to delegate.

Hunter asked very little of Derek, not even monogamy, although Derek was faithful. Hunter occasionally traveled for work, and Derek thought there might be other men, but they didn't talk about it. There was a lot they didn't talk about, and sometimes it maddened Derek. Hunter could be aloof, noncommunicative, and moody, but he also had a wonderful sense of the ridiculous and knew how to make Derek laugh.

Derek made himself useful to Hunter in any way he could, and Hunter made regular deposits to Derek's bank account. It was like *Pretty Woman,* only Richard Gere owned the hotel and Derek didn't have Julia Roberts's dedication to flossing. Whenever Derek got uneasy about the money, Hunter reminded him that his focus should be on finishing college. He'd have the rest of his life to work; in the meantime, Hunter was simply investing in Derek's future. It was Hunter who suggested that Derek's innate love of storytelling made English the perfect major for him. Derek wasn't sure what he'd do with a degree in English, but Hunter had been right. Once Derek began taking more literature classes, he became a better student.

Hunter also insisted that Derek travel to Evansville regularly to see his parents and spend holidays with them. Hunter never went with him, nor did he ever invite Derek to go to the Congreve family home. *Any* of the Congreve family homes. Only once had Derek suggested spending Christmas in Massachusetts with Hunter, who'd given him a sardonic look and said, "We don't exactly roast chestnuts, Derek. I get my performance appraisal and my bonus check from the old man. Then we all go our separate ways to drink heavily and pretend he doesn't own us."

Derek had breaks from school other than Christmas. During these, he traveled with Hunter to places like Fire Island, Palm Springs, Key West, and Provincetown, where he felt a little overwhelmed among Hunter's A-list acquaintances. He was never sure why they went. He liked exploring new places with Hunter, but he was less enthralled by the bounty of drugs and bodies they were offered. All those beautiful, pumped-up men intent on pleasure made Derek feel that he was being presented with an excess of rich desserts when what he really wanted was meat and potatoes.

Or more honestly, all he really wanted was Hunter. Even though Hunter remained something of an enigma to him, Derek was completely in love. Since Hunter was not the kind of man who expressed his emotions, Derek didn't feel free to vocalize his own feelings, but he told himself it didn't matter. He learned to read Hunter's moods and knew his lover wasn't unhappy, which seemed almost as good as knowing he was happy.

Sexually, Hunter preferred quality over quantity, and Derek adjusted his expectations accordingly. He loved going to bed with Hunter even when they didn't make love. He liked lying in his arms and telling him stories in the dark. He liked waking up to the sound of Hunter getting ready for work. In the winter months, Derek would get up and make breakfast for the two of them. During good weather, when Hunter got up earlier to ride, Derek would order from room service and linger over his morning coffee until Hunter's return, giving them a few minutes together before they went their separate ways.

Derek grew comfortable with their routines. Because he saw his friends when he went to class, it wasn't until he graduated that he realized school was the only place he saw them. As the months passed, he found himself with too many hours on his hands and nothing to do. He began leaving the hotel during the day to wander through the mall, and for the first time in more than two years, he began to really notice other men. He reverted to his childhood hobby of observing and making up stories about men who appealed to him.

At Venus Video, he could check out Hey Boy, who wore faded jeans and had biceps that threatened to rip the seams of his plaid shirts. Derek liked to rent obscure movies from the top shelf just to make Hey Boy strain for them, causing his shirt to rise up and reveal his treasure trail.

Jade Eye Knight, slender and shy, worked the counter at Sirius Dogs and never got any of Derek's lame innuendos about footlongs, relish, or special sauce. Glute Guy bowled with a league on Wednesdays and had no idea that Derek sometimes followed him across the Earth level just to look at his amazing ass.

On his mall excursions, Derek often saw MCI Man, so named because he constantly talked on his cell phone through a headset while he went in and out of stores. MCI Man dressed as tastefully as Hunter and had steely gray eyes and flawless skin. Derek noticed that he wasn't MCI Man's only fan; he left a trail of lovelorn females wherever he went. On the single occasion that Derek got within five feet of MCI Man, he caught an appealing scent that he'd never been able to find in any men's fragrance department.

The only one of them that Derek knew was gay was Lube Job, an employee with a blond ponytail at Satellite Drugs who'd gotten his nickname when he'd recommended a better brand of lubricant to Derek while admonishing him to always be safe. Lube Job was too serious and hardworking to flirt, but he didn't seem to mind Derek's loitering among the magazines and greeting cards as a way of watching him.

On nights when Hunter had to entertain hotel guests, Derek went online and talked to men all over the country. He entertained his online friends with stories about his Mall Men. If they occasionally flirted with him, he reassured himself that anonymity and distance made it harmless. He never talked about his personal life, but one night in a chat room, a man happened to mention that he worked the night shift at a hotel. Derek stared at his monitor with dismay when it appeared that almost every man there had a story of tricking with a hotel employee. The transient nature of hotels provided the perfect setting.

Derek had signed off and gone to the one place he was always assured of privacy when he needed to think: the roof of the Congreve. He stared at the stars and faced some hard facts about his relationship. Hunter had a career and an entire life that didn't include Derek. Derek had only Hunter. Hunter paid the bills, made the decisions, and never offered any promises about fidelity or a future. Derek had allowed himself to become dependent on Hunter and made his lover his entire life. Not only was that bad for him, but sooner or later, Hunter would surely tire of being with a man who had so little to offer him.

Derek decided it was time for a change, and the first thing he needed was a job. He sent out résumés online and filled out applications at several places in the mall. Unwilling to take any more help from Hunter, he didn't tell him he was even looking for a job until he received the offer from Drayden's.

He'd been so excited that he made a rare visit to Hunter's office on the executive floor of the hotel. Hunter sat back in his leather chair and heard Derek out, occasionally tapping a finger on his lower lip, a familiar signal that he wasn't happy. Derek was confused, having expected Hunter to be proud of him for showing initiative.

"If you need more money—"

"No, you're always generous," Derek said. "I understood that you wanted to help me when I was in school. But now I need to start taking care of myself." He waited for some declaration of Hunter's feelings. Even anger would have been more welcome than his silent perusal.

"I'll cancel your flight to Miami. You obviously won't be able to go if you're starting a new job."

Your flight, Derek heard loud and clear. Not *our* flight. So Hunter intended to go even if Derek couldn't go with him. Hurt, Derek said, "How long will you be gone?"

"A week. That was the plan." Hunter's expression indicated that if there was nothing else, Derek was dismissed.

"Have a great time," was all Derek managed to say before he turned and left the office.

He didn't understand why Hunter had reacted so coldly, and he felt unjustly accused of something, although he wasn't sure of what. He decided not to go to their apartment. A few hours away from him might give Hunter time to adjust to the news about the Drayden's job, or at least to compose his thoughts so that he could tell Derek why he didn't like the idea.

Derek went to Patti's Pages, where he spent over three hundred dollars on biographies ranging from Ann-Margret to Zelda Fitzgerald. Then he ate a solitary dinner in the Jupiter Lounge and had a couple of cosmopolitans at the bar afterward.

When he went home, Hunter wasn't there. Derek watched the clock; as the hours passed, he began to get angry. He knew Hunter was staying away on purpose, something Derek saw as an unnecessary power play, a reminder that Hunter would always have the upper hand in any contest between them. He decided to fight back by not waiting up. He was asleep when Hunter got into bed and woke him with soft kisses on the nape of his neck.

"Derek, wake up. I need you," Hunter whispered.

Derek turned into Hunter's arms, too sleepy to hold on to his anger. After they made love, Derek drifted off again. When he awoke, it was morning and Hunter wasn't in bed. Derek walked through their apartment, but it was empty. With a groan of frustration, he called Riley, Hunter's assistant.

"Is Hunter in the hotel?"

"He was driven to O'Hare airport about an hour ago," Riley said.

"Did he leave a message for me?"

"Not with me," Riley said.

"I'll call him later in Miami," Derek said, trying to sound nonchalant. The last thing he needed was the hotel staff gossiping about whether he was being dumped.

It was Hunter who called first. Derek could hear crowd noise through the phone, and he asked, "Where are you?"

"The airport," Hunter said.

"In Miami?"

"In Los Angeles. Change of plans. The manager of the Sydney Congreve was fired. The old man's sending me to Australia."

"Australia! How long will you be gone?"

"I'm not sure, Derek. I would suspect anywhere from six to twelve weeks. It's a shame you couldn't come with me. Australia would be quite an adventure for you."

The silence on the line stretched between them. Hunter wasn't going to unbend enough to ask Derek to decline the position at Drayden's. Derek wasn't going to halt his baby steps toward a sense of independence. They'd reached an impasse.

"Come home soon," Derek said.

"I'll be in touch."

The days that followed were the loneliest of Derek's life. Hunter's absence forced him to acknowledge that he no longer had friends who could support him through a bad time. It was a grim reminder of how things would be if Hunter was finished with him, which seemed likely. When he expressed those fears to Juanita, she shook her head and said, "Mr. Hunter is not tired of you. You're tired of yourself. It's time for you to make a life of your own. Not without him. But something that is yours, apart from him."

All of that was weighing on Derek when he began his new job at Drayden's, but he was determined to make the best of things. Not only would he be earning his own money, but he hoped to make friends. Vienna had seemed to fulfill that hope. She was funny and nice, and she'd immediately introduced him to Davii. Derek was a little intimidated by Davii's bold attitude and good looks, but he yearned to have another gay friend like the ones he'd known in college. He also envied the affection that Vienna and Davii shared; he wanted to be part of it.

Vienna's comment that he was a kept boy had jarred him, reinforcing his fear that Hunter saw him that way, too. But what was he being kept for? Some rainy, romantic Sunday when Hunter might finally realize and verbalize feelings of love? As much as Derek wanted that, he was no longer naïve enough to expect it. Instead, he'd pared down his expectations to a single objective. For his own self-respect, he needed to prove that he wasn't the kind of man who was just looking for a bank account, a circuit party, or a room service life.

4

Bland Ambition

After Riley Blake called in changes to the Congreve room service menu, he settled into Hunter's leather chair and indulged himself with a Gitane from the gold cigarette box on the desk. One of the perks of working for a smoker was that Riley could light up in the office. Of course, Hunter didn't smoke the pungent Gitanes himself; they were kept for visiting dignitaries. Hunter preferred Marlboro Lights in a box, and Riley kept a desk drawer supplied with cartons for his boss.

With Hunter on another continent, Riley could smoke the Gitanes without fear of detection. Not that Hunter would give a damn. If he knew that Riley enjoyed the French cigarettes, he'd have urged him to take all he wanted. But Riley liked the feeling he got from stealing the Gitanes, as if he was pulling a fast one on Hunter.

It was the same feeling he got when he powered up his laptop and accessed the private accounts of Hunter and his loathsome boy toy, Derek. That had been so simple to arrange. Hunter had wanted a computer system in his office and apartment that was independent of the Congreve network. Riley figured Hunter knew that his father, Randolph Congreve, wouldn't hesitate to order his lackeys to monitor Hunter's private e-mail and computer use. Old Randolph's spies were everywhere. It hadn't taken long for Riley to suspect that the chanteuse in the hotel's piano bar, Sheree Sheridan, kept an eye on both of them and reported back to the elder Congreve.

Riley had discreetly hired someone to set up a separate computer system. What he didn't explain to Hunter was that he'd had the consultant link the computers with another line on Riley's desk, giving Riley the control of a network administrator via his laptop. Riley could read the files and e-mail on Hunter's and Derek's PCs. He could track what Web sites they visited, know what games Derek played and for how long, and access Hunter's financial records. Riley understood that knowledge was power, particularly when he was the only one with the knowledge. He hoarded all the information he got, sure that it would prove useful to him one day.

He checked Hunter's READ mail and found a recent message from Hunter's best friend, Garry Prophet.

Con,
Australia, huh? When you say distance, you aren't kidding. No, I don't think you're an asshole for asking the old bastard to send you there. Derek will survive. The separation may do him some good, too. Not that I'm in any position to give you relationship advice. But I know better than anyone all the ways you drive the boy crazy—bad and good.

Screw e-mail. As soon as you're there and I figure out the time difference, I'll call you. If you're not already stateside by then. Or maybe Derek will have decided to join you in Sydney.
Pro

Riley scowled and closed the e-mail. *Pro and Con.* So precious it made him want to retch. It had probably started when they were roommates at Andover and continued through their tenure at Yale. He wondered how many other people had figured out the true nature of their relationship. Probably both families. That was why the Prophets were trying to force Garry into a sham marriage with pimento heiress Buffy Barlow. Hunter wasn't as malleable as his friend-slash-lover. He'd apparently never made a secret of his sexual orientation, whereas Garry continued to maintain the charade that he was straight.

None of that mattered to Riley. Although he was himself gay, his interest in Hunter was not romantic. A cruel twist of fate had tied his destiny to his boss's. When Hunter prospered, so did Riley. If Hunter failed, Riley would be banished from the Congreve dynasty.

It was a bitter pill to swallow after fourteen years of fighting his way up the Congreve ladder. He'd left San Antonio a seventeen-year-old runaway, ending up in Boston because that's where his money ran out. The first job he'd been able to get was shining shoes at the Boston Congreve. From there, he'd been a doorman, bellhop, and desk clerk. After years of ass kissing, blackmailing, and otherwise manipulating himself into better positions, he'd been accepted into the hotel's management training program.

He stubbed out the Gitane and lit another, brooding over the injustice of it all. A few years earlier, just when Riley was sure he was poised to take over any of the more elite hotels in the chain, Hunter had abruptly entered the family business. Since Hunter was too pampered to start at the bottom, Riley had been transferred to this godforsaken hotel in the middle of nowhere to make sure the youngest Congreve heir didn't screw things up too badly. Instead of being master of his own domain, Riley was nothing more than a glorified secretary.

In all fairness, he had to admit that Hunter didn't treat him that way. He gave his assistant the authority to act on his behalf, and Riley made the most of it. Around Hunter, he adopted a self-effacing facade. But Riley ruled the rest of the hotel staff with steely resolve. He couldn't afford for anything to go wrong and bring down Randolph Congreve's wrath on his son and, consequently, Riley.

Riley went to great pains to know his new boss, although it wasn't easy. Hunter was not a man who invited confidences, nor did he talk about himself. It seemed that Hunter was no happier than Riley to be in Indiana; Riley took satisfaction in this. If he was discontented and bored, Hunter would move on sooner, either taking Riley with him or getting out of his way. It pleased him to see that Hunter made no real friends, nor did he seem eager to find male companionship.

Until Derek Anderson. In the beginning, Riley had regarded Derek as a harmless distraction, someone who could keep Hunter occupied while Riley ran the hotel. He'd expected that when the relationship died a natural death—which it was sure to do, since Hunter and Derek came from different worlds—Hunter would ask for a transfer. Then Riley could take over the mall hotel and prove his value to the Congreve empire.

It hadn't been the most attractive solution, since it left him exiled in the wasteland between Terre Haute and Indianapolis. But

Riley figured it was an easy proving ground. The more upscale Congreve hotels hosted world-famous figures from the entertainment industry, royal families, and governments. The best bookings Riley could get were those connected with beauty pageants, colleges, agriculture, small-town governments, and families succumbing to the allure of a super mall.

He shuddered inwardly at this last group. It was the final irony that he had to promote the hotel as a family-friendly environment, because children were the bane of his existence. While parents conducted business or shopped, their children ran the halls early in the morning and late at night, tied up the elevators, turned the swimming pool into a piss pit, and threw up junk food in the well-appointed rooms. No matter how many guided visits Riley arranged for them to such mall attractions as the planetarium, the arcade, the roller rink, and the bowling alley, it seemed their major source of entertainment came from wreaking havoc in his hotel.

But he smiled, kept his mouth shut, and buffered Hunter from the more hideous realities of their clientele. He inflicted his vengeance on the housekeeping staff, who were expected to immediately eliminate all evidence of the destruction caused by the Lollipop Guild.

That had nearly proved to be his undoing when Randolph Congreve dispatched someone to find out why housekeeping had such a high turnover rate. Hunter had sought answers from the only hotel employee other than Sheree Sheridan who was bulletproof, his personal housekeeper, Juanita.

Juanita Luna was the unofficial leader of what Riley privately called the Disunited Nations, the melting pot of college students, blacks, Hispanics, Middle Easterners, and Asians who composed the housekeeping staff. Riley knew Juanita didn't like him, and he'd fully expected her to use her inside track to Hunter to bring him down. He'd even armed himself with a counterattack. Juanita might consider herself as cunning as General Santa Anna, but Riley didn't intend to let her turn the hotel into his Alamo.

Juanita, however, had outmaneuvered him, presenting her opinion that the high turnover rate was caused by employee anxieties and misunderstandings based mainly on language barriers. With Hunter's oversight and the old man's grudging consent, hotel conference rooms were turned over to the staff once a week. The college students taught English. Groups representing different cultures explained their customs, religions, and social structures. They had fashion shows. The hotel chefs prepared ethnic foods. Families were invited.

The turnover rate dropped, and Riley knew a crisis had been averted. He became more circumspect in how he handled the housekeeping staff, and he gave Juanita a wide berth. Not only did she have Hunter's ear and the staff's respect, but he knew from reading Derek's e-mails to his cyber pals that she doted on Hunter's insipid little boyfriend.

Riley finally allowed himself a satisfied smile. This time, he'd outfoxed Juanita. When he'd found out Derek was looking for employment, he called in a favor from one of Drayden's Human Resources managers, and Derek's new job was a done deal. If Riley was reading Garry Prophet's e-mail correctly, Hunter was apparently unhappy enough with his boy-toy-turned-shoe-salesman to have requested the temporary assignment to the Sydney Congreve.

Riley intended to take advantage of Hunter's absence. He would not only run the hotel flawlessly, but he'd also find a way to get rid of Derek Anderson. He was sure both accomplishments would score points with Randolph Congreve. Before long, he'd resume his climb up the ladder, finally making it to the pinnacle—management of the Manhattan Congreve, where he could rub shoulders with real power.

He lit another Gitane and electronically tiptoed his way through Derek's computer. None of Derek's e-mails provided any useful information about his relationship with Hunter, and Riley rolled his eyes at the history trail of porn sites Derek had looked at. These did nothing for Riley, but hopefully they'd whip Derek into such a frenzy of lust that he'd start cheating on Hunter. That might prove to be his final undoing. With Hunter in another country and Derek on his way out the door, Riley's cigarette took on the taste of victory.

5

That Witch!

Natasha Deere dropped the remainder of her microwaved waffle down the garbage disposal and listened to the grinding noise with a fleeting wish that bland people could be as easily discarded. She took her coffee with her to the bathroom, where she pulled back her long, dark hair and wound it into a tight bun. She put on her makeup, then dressed in a black suit with a red silk blouse. After downing the rest of her coffee, she swished some mouthwash and spit it into the sink with deliberate aim.

Today was going to be a good day. For her.

Mondays were always her favorite day. They were symbolic of new beginnings. Sundays were for sissies, total throwaway days. It also didn't hurt that most people hated Mondays. That made Natasha love them all the more. The productive week began on Monday, and for as long as Natasha could remember, she'd been driven to conquer one Sunday after another.

As a little girl growing up in Los Angeles, she'd attended the finest private schools. Her parents, who could barely stand her—the feeling was mutual—surrendered to their true feelings about their daughter and sent her to boarding school when she was a teenager. Although never popular, she was invited to all the other girls' parties for the simple reason that her parents always sent great presents, and word had gotten around. Most birthday girls' only problem with accepting the present was having to put up with Natasha for a few hours at the party.

Natasha couldn't have cared less. It wasn't like she actually chose the present. She just told her mother during their weekly phone call that she'd been invited to a birthday party, and the present would arrive, already wrapped, with a card for her to sign and attach, in plenty of time for the festivities. It was always something expensive and tasteful, classic and timeless. The Perfect Gift. The birthday girl would coo, and her bimbo friends would make comments of admiration. Natasha could see the pupils of their eyes turn into dollar signs, as in a cartoon.

Natasha wasn't bothered by the fact that they liked her gifts more than they liked her. She had a plan, and it didn't allow for emotional attachments. People were a necessary evil, something to put up with while she worked toward her goal. Occasionally, one might serve as a vehicle to get what she wanted. More than anything, she wanted to be rich and free of her parents.

By the time Natasha started working, her ambition and drive were the most noticeable parts of her personality. The less noticeable part, by comparison, was her striking beauty. If she chose to leave it down, her bouncy, dark hair was full of body, and her watery blue eyes could have been mistaken for pools. She had high cheekbones and a strong but not too defined jaw. Her figure was mannequin-perfect; it always had been. Her legs were long, and she looked great in anything she wore.

Natasha had grown up in a world where beauty was bankable. Her mother belonged to a group of women whose lives were a futile quest to find the right cream, the right plastic surgeon, or the right drug to preserve beauty. Natasha refused to foolishly turn herself into a simpering female who traded on her looks. Beauty was brief. Financial freedom was forever.

She worked the whole time she was in college, not because she had to, but because it was part of the plan. She maneuvered her way through a number of departments in the Neiman's on Wilshire Boulevard in Beverly Hills while she got her business degree at USC, then her MBA at UCLA. She could be found anywhere, from Cosmetics to Fine Jewelry, from Handbags to Furs.

After completing her MBA, Natasha told her parents, during a conversation at some holiday function that she had long since blocked out, that she didn't need them or their money. The latter of the two declarations she would come to regret. It had seemed like a good idea at the time.

Natasha knew that she'd formed her only significant relationship with the retail world. It was the best vehicle to show off what she was capable of. She hadn't wanted to stay in California, and she found herself going from place to place. She'd work her way up the ladder at one location, then move on to a more upscale store somewhere else.

As she climbed the ladder, and occasionally slept under it, she came to realize that it mattered even less than she'd thought whether people liked her. Business was not about making friends. What a useless endeavor that would be. *Friends.* Natasha scoffed at the thought.

But she also learned that it paid to make a few of the others think she was their friend. It didn't have to be true, but if she pretended to bond with a couple of the people on her staff, it made life easier. The ones who hated her—and there were always plenty—would inevitably say something to one of the others who didn't, and someone would at least try to make it seem like Natasha wasn't entirely evil. Not that she cared if they thought she was evil. The payoff was in finding out *who* thought she was evil, and whether they could in any way threaten her, and if so, how to eliminate them.

She strode with purpose through the employee entrance of Drayden's, and the graveyard shift security guard greeted her. "Good morning, Ms. Deere."

"Good morning," she replied with a nod and kept her pace steady as she continued down the hall.

"Had a good day yesterday, did we?" the guard persisted.

"We always do," Natasha said.

She turned the corner and set her handbag on her desk, then went to the sales floor. Her first task was always making sure that those who'd closed the night before had left things ready for the start of a new day.

She stopped short when her vantage point allowed her to see that a shoe on the wall display had not been properly replaced. "Idiots," she said aloud. She marched over and replaced the shoe on its shelf.

She then moved from table to table with an imaginary white glove, making mental notes of who'd worked the night before. Finally, she went back to her computer and checked the previous evening's sales figures for each person who'd been scheduled, comparing those figures to what that person was expected to sell per hour. As she looked at the sales figure for Jonquil, she frowned.

How could someone be here for a full seven working hours and sell only $152, when everyone else sold over $1,000 during their shifts? she wondered. *What the hell was she doing the whole time she was here? Giving blow jobs in the men's room?*

The door pushed open from the back hallway, and two of her sales associates walked in. They were laughing and joking—until they saw who was waiting for them.

"Which one of you closed last night?" Natasha demanded.

"Um, I did," Erik volunteered, and Missy looked sheepish.

"Who was the senior person in charge of closing last night?"

"I was," Erik answered.

"Can you give me a good reason why the displays look so awful this morning?" Natasha asked, folding her arms across her chest.

"Well," Erik began, "each person was in charge of their own area. That's the way we always do it."

"So in other words, you're not supposed to have any responsibility for this, even though you were in charge of making sure it was done properly. Even though you're the senior person on the schedule, I'm not supposed to hold you or anyone else accountable, because you all stick up for each other, right?"

"The company does promote teamwork," Missy volunteered.

"Missy? Did anyone ever tell you that perfume you're wearing smells like bug repellant?" Natasha paused, and Missy blushed. "Would you like to wash it off, or have me call the Orkin Man to see if he wants a date?"

Missy fled, and Erik said, "You know, you don't have to—"

"What?" Natasha interrupted. "Let her know that she smells like she should be wearing a fumigation tent instead of that horrible Kmart blouse?"

"Oh, you recognize it?" Erik got one dig in.

"Not as well as I recognize someone who pictures himself as an assistant manager but clearly isn't qualified," Natasha snarled.

Erik turned crimson at the mention of his submitting his name for the cross-department promotion as the assistant manager of Men's Shoes. He obviously hadn't realized that she knew about it. She'd never stand in the way of a valuable employee succeeding, but if the employee simply wasn't up to the task of managing a department in a large, successful business, it was her duty to thwart him. *Valuable* was certainly in the eye of the beholder.

The door to the stockroom opened again. Natasha heard footsteps, which seemed to hesitate, turn around, then stop completely. "Hello?" a voice called.

"Can I help you?" Natasha answered.

"I'm looking for Natasha?" The voice spoke again with a note of uncertainty.

Natasha rose from her desk and stood tall, as though an invisible hand pulled her up by the crown of her head. "I'm Natasha," she said.

She scrutinized the young man in front of her, first noting his expensive suit. Either he had money, or he'd been taking advantage of deep discounts as a retail employee. Other than his clothes, he was nothing special. He was shorter than she was, with mousy brown hair cut short, clear skin, brown eyes that watched her with apprehension, and a hesitant smile. Her split-second judgment categorized him as the warm and fuzzy type.

"I'm Derek Anderson. I was told to report here for work this morning," he said tentatively as the silence stretched between them.

Great, Natasha thought bitterly, noticing the way Erik hovered protectively near Derek, as if eager to absorb him into the little group of friends who plagued her department. Why couldn't she ever get an employee who had her drive, her vision, her devotion to hard work?

"I don't remember asking for additional help," she finally said. "I guess calling HR is just one more thing I have to do now. Erik, take him to the floor and show him around."

After they left, she tapped her fingernails on her desk while she thought it over. Drayden's procedure was to screen prospects, then let the department manager interview them and make the hiring decision. Since the usual channels had been subverted, Derek must have been placed with her by someone with clout. She'd have to find out who before she decided on her next move.

Natasha smiled. The only thing better than a normal Monday was a Monday that held the promise of a new power struggle for her to win. She brushed Derek aside as nothing more than a little bug who had whetted her appetite for larger prey.

6

Trying to Keep the Customer Satisfied

Vienna's sandwich seemed to lose its flavor, so she dropped it and brushed crumbs from her hands, saying, "That's not the worst of it. The little bitch's mother came up and dragged her away, saying, 'Come on. You don't want *her* waiting on you.' "

"Ew!" Davii exclaimed. "How hateful."

"Nasty," Derek agreed.

"You never get used to prejudice," Vienna said, shaking her head. She absently tore the crust from her discarded sandwich. "I'm sure I'm preaching to the choir."

Derek and Davii looked at each other and grinned, singing, "Hallelujah!"

"I thought so," Vienna said, finally smiling.

"Back home," Derek began, after thinking it over, "boys in cars used to yell things at me. But nothing like that's happened in a long time."

"I hate it when guys do that," Vienna said. "Why do they think people can understand them when they're buzzing by at fifty miles an hour?"

"Because they're stupid?" Davii guessed. "I used to get threatened all the time in high school. This one guy picked on me every day. I even had a girlfriend at the time, and he'd still call me a fag and throw things at me."

"What did you do?" Derek asked.

"I slept with his girlfriend," Davii said matter-of-factly.

"Rock on," Derek said in awe.

"Solved all kinds of problems," Davii said. "My girlfriend broke up with me. His girlfriend broke up with him. And even though it didn't endear me to him, at least he stopped calling me names. Who wants to be known as the guy whose girlfriend dumped him for a fag? There's always a way to fight back."

"Reminds me of Darlene Patterson," Vienna said. "I hated that snotty little bitch. She'd follow me around, making up new lyrics to 'Four Women' with my name in it. 'My hair is nappy. My clothes are borrowed. What do they call me? They call me Vienna.' One time she put gum in my hair. She thought I couldn't do anything, because I was the preacher's daughter. I had to love the sinner and hate the sin. All that crap."

"What did you do?" Derek asked.

Vienna shrugged and said, "I hated the sinner and scratched her eyes out after school. I got a licking when my mother found out, but it was worth it to see that skinny-assed bitch run crying. I don't approve of violence, but—"

"Oh, no. Not you," Davii interrupted.

She glared at him, then continued. "Sometimes you have to stand up for yourself. If you're being forced down, you have to claw your way up again."

"When I'm forced down, I find that it helps to relax the muscles in my throat," Davii said, and ducked when Vienna threw her bread crust at him. He pointed at her and shouted, "Oppressor!"

"Oh, please," Vienna drawled. "You don't know oppression. Oppression is putting lipstick on women with chapped lips. Oppression is doing someone's eyeliner, then realizing she has pink eye. Oppression is putting polish on someone's toes."

"That can be sexy," Davii countered.

"Maybe on a guy," Vienna conceded.

"I've only been selling for a couple of weeks, and I'm already grossed out by people's feet," Derek stated. "I never thought feet were particularly sexy. Before this job, I might've been convinced otherwise. But now? No way. Some of the feet I've seen are just nasty."

"Please stop," Davii begged, waving his sandwich. "I'm eating."

"We do what we have to do to get by," Vienna said.

"Amen, sister!" Davii exclaimed.

"How does a woman with such religious parents end up living with a gay man?" Derek wondered aloud.

Vienna smiled, thinking about her father. He was always her rock. Not to mention the buffer between her and her mother when they'd get into arguments. He was the kindest and noblest man Vienna had ever known, the ruler against which all the men in her life would forever be measured.

"Daddy always said that love is love," Vienna said. "Love doesn't follow creed, race, or whatever mental roadblock you want to put in front of it. Love is from the heart and soul. It has nothing to do with our bodies."

"Speak for yourself," Davii muttered.

"I think that's wonderful," Derek said.

"Daddy knows the Bible cover to cover," Vienna stated, "and he knows a lot of people twist its meaning to fit their own agenda. He never preached hate, only acceptance. As long as two people love each other, what's the harm in that?"

Derek looked at his watch and groaned. "I have to get back to work. I wish Natasha had gone to your daddy's church."

"Praise be to God," Vienna said, rolling her eyes. "I still have a half hour. I'll see you later."

As Derek left, Davii said, "I love to watch him walk away."

"It might help your agenda if you flirted with him once in a while," Vienna said. "Especially when he's actually at the table."

"I can't help it if I'm subtle," Davii said demurely.

"Please. You're about as subtle as a fox in a chicken coop with a red rubber glove on his head."

Davii pondered her words and asked, "What's that supposed to mean?"

"Daddy would've said it better," Vienna admitted. "Why do you need me to feel out the Derek situation? Why don't you just ask him out?"

"How do I say this?" Davii asked aloud. He thought for a moment, idly making trails in a blob of ketchup with a french fry. "Derek's not like the guys I usually date."

"Fuck," Vienna clarified. "I'm sorry, but you don't date."

"Fine," Davii admitted, dropping the french fry and throwing up his hands in defeat. "He's not like the guys I usually pursue. He's sweet, has integrity, and he's smart."

"He has a boyfriend," Vienna reminded him. "I'm the result of a broken marriage. I'm not too fond of the idea of interfering in theirs."

"They're not married," Davii said.

"Unfortunately, that's not an option for them. But that's a lunch-time topic for another day. I get the idea that Derek needs friends, not a new boyfriend. I know I said I'd help you, but—"

"He makes me want to be a better person, okay?" Davii blurted. "There. Happy? I see Derek and want to be more like him. I'd like to end up with a guy like him. And from what you tell me, if this current boyfriend of his doesn't appreciate him, why can't I?"

"Fine," Vienna relented. When Davii grinned like a boy who'd worn down a parent to get a puppy, she added, "But I mean it—I'm not wild about interfering. Give me a little more time to feel out the situation."

"If you need any help feeling him out, let me know."

"I'm about to be late," Vienna announced and began collecting her things.

"Do you need another shot of Drayden's Kool-Aid?" Davii asked.

"Our customers are our neighbors, and we must always treat them as if we're in their backyard," Vienna intoned, speaking in a zombielike trance. She brightened and said, "Nope. I'm good to go. See you tonight at the Galaxy."

7

Other People's Money

Christian Mercer rode the Galaxy Building's elevator to the ground floor, where he accessed Mall of the Universe via the Light Year Passage. Space-age music played in the corridor, which was lit to resemble the winter sky over the Northern Hemisphere.

Hello, Orion, Christian thought as he walked beneath the constellation.

His phone vibrated on his hip, and he hit the SEND button and kept walking while a distraught client's voice pierced his hands-free headset. "She quit! I've got a presentation tomorrow at ten, my slide show isn't ready, and she just walked off the job!" Shauna wailed.

Christian ducked into Comet Cleaners. Kate was in the back, and she nodded to let him know she'd be right with him before she darted into what he assumed was the employee bathroom.

"Shauna, calm down," Christian said soothingly. "Who quit?"

"My secretary! I don't even know how to open Power Point! Crap, hold on. My other line's ringing."

Christian hummed along to the hold music until Kate joined him at the counter, having obviously brushed her hair and applied a fresh coat of lipstick.

"Hi, Christian," she said brightly, taking the pile of shirts from him. She looked them over and asked, "Do you ever actually wear your clothes? They look like you take them off the hanger and bring them here."

"I do," he agreed. "It's all an excuse to see you."

She laughed and said, "Right. Seriously, do you ever sweat?"

"Like a Chinese fortune cookie," he answered with sparkling eyes. When she looked bewildered, he added the popular fortune cookie ending. "In bed."

"I don't have a spare secretary in my bed," Shauna said acidly through his headset.

"Just a second, Shauna," Christian said, then asked Kate, "Day after tomorrow?"

"Unless you need them back sooner. I can rush it."

"No need. You'll be here when I come back, right?"

"Whoever she is, don't rely on her if she's a secretary," Shauna warned.

"I'll be here," Kate promised.

He stepped out of the dry cleaners and said, "Shauna, take a deep breath. You need someone proficient in Power Point. Anything else?"

"Willing to work overtime," Shauna said. "But there's no way—"

"Have you forgotten who you're talking to? I'll have a temp there before noon. Take care of what you can, don't panic, and I'll see to it that your presentation is in capable hands."

"What would I do without you?" Shauna said. "You're saving my life."

"Keep it up and I'm adding ten percent to your bill," Christian said. He disconnected the call and hit speed dial for Terre Temps.

"Christian!" Debby said when she heard his voice. "It's been too long!"

He told her what he needed, and Debby assured him that she'd have the right match for Shauna well within his time frame. After they hung up, he took out his PalmPilot and made a notation on Shauna's account. It was going to cost her, but she wouldn't complain. No matter how daunting his clients' needs, he always delivered, and they knew it.

Fifteen minutes later, freshly shampooed, he sat back in a chair and relaxed, knowing he was in the capable hands of Davii. Davii was just about the only person who could tame Christian's unruly auburn curls, not to mention that he knew how to properly tweeze a man's eyebrows. The one time Christian had gone to Star Power Salon and Spa, he'd emerged looking like a four-year-old had scrawled brick crayon across his brow. He cared about his image too much to entrust it to an amateur. CosmicTology also carried more skin and hair products for men than any other salon in Mall of the Universe.

"Who's the lucky man?" Davii teased, meeting his eyes in the mirror.

Before Christian could answer, his phone vibrated again, and he reached for his headset while Davii frowned. "Christian Mercer."

"Mr. Mercer, this is Emily-Anne Barrister."

Christian's eyes widened, and he went into full work mode, saying, "What can I do for you, Ms. Barrister?"

"Emily-Anne," she said. "I'm planning an event, and everyone tells me that you're the go-to person."

Yes! Christian thought. Emily-Anne was the wife of Cortlandt Barrister, whose family had founded and bought newspapers throughout Indiana, Illinois, and western Ohio, as well as other publications, including an oddly successful magazine titled *Hoe & Sew*, which was geared toward the wives of farmers. Getting the Barristers as clients opened up a new world of possibilities for Christian. He reached under the black smock and extracted his PalmPilot, saying, "I'm sure I can help you. If you give me some of the details—"

"Oh, I'm not going to tie up your time on the phone," Emily-Anne said. "I'll make an appointment."

Christian checked his calendar, they settled on a day and time, and he disconnected the call after a cordial good-bye. He was startled when Davii not only removed his headset but took the phone and turned it off. "Hey!" he protested.

"I realize you're melded to that thing, but unless you want a nipped ear—or even worse, a bad haircut—while you're here, you're mine." When Christian gave him a meek look, Davii smiled and repeated his earlier question. "Who's the lucky man?"

"You're the only man in my life, and you know it," Christian replied.

"Oh, what a great liar you are. I've heard that one before."

"I never lie."

"Are you sure?" Davii asked.

"Why would I lie?"

"That's not what I mean," Davii said, staring pointedly at Christian's reflection.

"I guess there's a shortage of available men here, but I'm afraid I won't be any help."

"A boy can dream." Davii sighed as a tight curl fell to Christian's vinyl smock with a whisper, then said, "The prospects have improved. My roommate recently introduced me to one of her new co-workers."

"Cute?"

"Edible," Davii assured him, then chatted about other things while he cut and forced Christian's hair into submission. He did a stellar job, as usual.

Unfortunately, Christian could never re-create Davii's stylishly disheveled handiwork. He eyed himself in the mirror, thinking that Davii had managed to make him look like a soap actor or someone in a fashion magazine. "Your talents are wasted here. Ever consider moving on to greater possibilities?"

"Are you trying to persuade me to come to one of your seminars?"

"No, not at all. I'm completely serious."

"Who knows what the future holds?" Davii asked with a shrug.

Christian went to the cashier and paid. He discreetly slipped a substantial tip into a tip envelope, wrote Davii's name on the outside, and walked into the mall, checking his watch. He wouldn't have time to eat anything before his next appointment, but hopefully he could squeeze in a half hour for himself before his evening seminar. If not, he'd gone without meals before. He'd survive.

While he headed toward Drayden's, he called the Hotel Congreve and confirmed that his conference room would be ready that night. The popularity of the seminar mandated that he hold one every two months. Luckily, it was one of his favorites, titled, "The Importance of 'Me' Time: Fitting Your Dreams Between Soccer Practice and Work." It was most rewarding when a busy career mom wrote him an e-mail to gush about how much his seminar had helped her. One woman in particular came to mind. A harried mother with four kids, Angela had decided to wake up two hours earlier than normal every day to experiment with baking pastries. After only four months, she had regular wholesale customers and would soon be able to quit her full-time job and work for herself. It was that kind of story that made Christian's job worth it.

He found Leslie Harper on Drayden's second floor in Women's Haberdashery and gently eased a red suit from her hands, saying, "Red *is* a power color, Leslie, but this will make your complexion look cerise."

"Is that bad?" Leslie asked with a stricken look. "I've got a promotion riding on this."

He deftly grabbed a charcoal gray suit from a rack and said, "This one. Trust me. Try it on over your T-shirt."

Later, after they paid for the suit and found a blouse and undergarments—when Leslie resisted, Christian reminded her that it was important to feel well-dressed from the skin out—he guided her downstairs to Cosmetics. The associate who helped them quickly allied herself with Christian while he gave Leslie makeup advice.

As Leslie signed her credit card slip, she said, "I sure hope all this is worth it."

"It'll pay for itself when you get your promotion," Christian promised. "Shoes."

"I can't afford to buy shoes at Drayden's!" Leslie yelped, and the Clinique associate cast a sad look her way.

"You can't afford not to," the associate said. "You should trust Mr. Mercer's judgment."

Christian was surprised that she knew his name and said, "I don't believe we've met."

"I'm Kiki," the woman said. The name seemed familiar, and Christian tried to place her. She laughed and said, "You don't know me. You helped my boyfriend's ex-wife when they were going through their divorce."

"Oops," Christian said. "Do you hate me?"

"Are you joking? Her demands were killing us. Then she went to your 'Don't Look Back' seminar. Now she makes twice as much as he does. I think I got the wrong half of the couple."

Leslie looked at Christian and said, "Shoes," in the submissive tone of a Stepford wife.

As they neared Women's Shoes, Christian regretted his decision. Two associates were with other customers, which left him at the mercy of the department manager, Natasha Deere, who was circling a display table like a marauding shark, followed by a young man in a dark suit. Christian did a double take, sure that the suit was Hugo Boss. Pricey for someone who appeared to be not only very young but a trainee.

He was relieved when an employee summoned Natasha to the cash wrap area, leaving the young associate free to approach Christian and Leslie.

"How can I help you today?" he asked Leslie, who turned toward Christian.

But Christian, having had a few unpleasant shopping encounters with Natasha in the past, was still keeping a wary eye on her and said, "I'll bet if you cut her open, that Kintner boy would fall out."

Leslie giggled, and the associate looked confused and said, "Who, Natasha? What?"

Christian laughed and said, "Maybe you've never seen *Jaws*. That woman's always reminded me of something that should be approached only from the protection of a cage. I'm sorry. I shouldn't make fun of your manager. I'm Christian Mercer, and this is Leslie Harper." He paused to unzip the garment bag he was holding and said, "Ms. Harper is looking for a pair of shoes to go with this suit."

"There's got to be something around here that will match that color," the associate said blandly.

Christian resisted the urge to ameliorate his selling skills, merely asking, "Is there anything in particular you might suggest?"

The boy looked at the suit, then at Leslie, and asked, "Is there a style that appeals to you?"

Christian wished he'd gotten something to eat after all as his temples began to throb. At that moment, Natasha advanced on them and said, "I'm sorry, Mr. Mercer, Derek is still in training. How can we assist your client today?"

Within seconds after seeing the gray suit, Natasha rattled off a list of brands and styles at Derek before sending him to the stockroom. Christian dreaded seeing what he'd bring back, but to his surprise, the stack of boxes included exactly what Natasha had requested plus a few of Derek's own selections. Just as he was ready to revise his assessment of Derek, he saw Leslie wince when Derek amateurishly slid a shoe onto her foot.

"Snug?" Derek asked sympathetically. "If you've been shopping a while, your feet may be a little swollen. Let's try this one."

Natasha watched with a sour expression as Derek exchanged the Marc Jacobs for a Cole Haan. Christian was startled, wondering if Derek understood the concept of commission. When Natasha was pulled away again, Derek looked up at Leslie and softly said, "These are on sale for half the price of those others, and they're twice as comfortable. They'll look great with your gray suit, and no one should work with aching feet."

"Thanks," Leslie said, smiling down at Derek. She looked so grateful that for a minute, Christian thought she was going to kiss him.

Christian conceded that Derek was nice, but if he wanted to continue to buy expensive suits, he'd have to learn how to be nice *and* sell.

Natasha surfaced again, baring her teeth in what could have been mistaken for a smile if her jaw muscles weren't twitching. "Did you find what you were looking for?" she asked, then frowned as she saw which shoes Derek was boxing up for Leslie.

"I sure did," Leslie said, smiling again at Derek.

Once the transaction was complete, Christian carried Leslie's bags to her car and sent her on her way with a few more reassuring words. When he walked back through Drayden's, Derek was straightening a display and Natasha was nowhere in sight. Christian paused and said, "That was nice. Bringing Leslie the less expensive shoes. Even though you're a trainee, aren't you working on commission?"

Derek shrugged and said, "Did you see her eyes when she saw the price of those Marc Jacobs pumps? She seemed like someone who needed a break. I pictured her as a single mom, struggling to dress herself on a budget. I couldn't see forcing her kids to eat mac and cheese out of a box just so I could make a few more bucks."

"Leslie is a top seller in a commercial real estate firm. She's trying to be promoted to their Indianapolis office. She is single, but I don't think her goldfish eats mac and cheese." He felt contrite when Derek blushed, adding, "It's the thought that counts."

Derek's face fell as he looked past Christian, who turned around and spied Natasha at a perfume counter. "We're gonna need a bigger boat," Derek said glumly.

Christian laughed and said, "So you have seen *Jaws!* You're funny, Derek. I have to run; I've got another appointment. What time do you get off?"

Derek blushed again and stammered, "Uh . . . well . . . I close tonight."

"Would you like to meet for a drink or something?"

"Well . . . um . . ."

"If you feel like a drink after work, I'll be at the Aurora piano bar in the Congreve at about nine. If I don't see you, no big deal." He smiled at Derek again and escaped just as Natasha glided up.

When he left the store, he had to maneuver his way through the usual crowd of children who surrounded Gert, a fiberglass cow that had once been part of the Chicago Cows on Parade exhibit. Gert was dressed in an original Drayden's Cattle Cozy and was a silent testament that someone in the Drayden's organization had a sense of humor. She seemed to be staring balefully toward the moon that hung outside the planetarium at the center of the mall. The only things missing were the Dish and the Spoon. His observation reminded Christian that he was hungry. He grabbed a veggie wrap at Sirius Dogs and ate it while he walked to the Congreve, listening to his messages on the way.

It wasn't until midway into his seminar that it struck him why Derek had been flustered by his suggestion that they meet for a drink. Maybe he'd thought Christian was asking him out. Which meant that Derek was probably straight and now thought Christian was gay. It was a misunderstanding that would clear itself up if the need arose. Christian had actually intended to disguise a mini lesson in salesmanship as a social meeting. Derek could use the help.

A couple of hours later, Christian let a dirty martini work its magic, bringing him down a notch from the high energy level of his seminar. With the smoky tones of the piano bar's chanteuse in the background, he read over his notes for a self-help book he intended to write as a supplement to his classes. When he spotted Derek entering the bar from the hotel lobby, he quickly gathered up the papers and placed them in his bag, then stood as Derek gave a meek, self-conscious wave before he walked toward him.

"I'm glad you made it! Can I get you something from the bar?" Christian asked cheerfully.

"I'll get it," Derek said.

Christian noticed that the bartender slid a drink across the bar before Derek had a chance to order. Nor did Derek pay for it. He was apparently a regular at the Aurora and ran a tab. That interested Christian as much as Derek's casual attire. The blue-and-green-striped shirt was definitely Paul Smith, and Christian was sure he saw the signature red stripe of Prada at the back of Derek's black shoe. There had to be a story that explained Derek's clothes. Maybe he was selling shoes because he'd been disowned by a wealthy family. Or he was a Lvandsson grandson working his way up the ladder.

When Derek plopped down in a chair across from his and slung one arm over its back, Christian decided that Derek would benefit not only from a lesson in salesmanship but in posture. Since it was obvious that he'd endured a harrying day, Christian merely asked, "Tough day in the trenches?"

"It wasn't so bad. I was actually able to help a few customers without Natasha the Hun spearing me."

"I think Attila would have been afraid of Natasha Deere. I do admire her selling skills and good taste, though." Christian grimaced as he heard "Morning Train" blare in ring tones from his bag. He thought he'd turned off the phone before the seminar.

"Do you want to get that?" Derek asked.

Christian pulled the phone from his bag, squinting apologetically at Derek as he flipped the cover open.

"Chrissie! It's your mother."

Christian flinched, sure that Derek had heard his mother call him by his childhood nickname. "Mother, you know I've told you—"

"Yes, they're both two syllables. I remember, *Christian.*"

He closed his eyes for a moment, trying to shut out the memory of "Happy Birthday, Chrissie!" on his ninth birthday cake. Assuming the cake was for a girl, the baker had frosted it with tiny yellow roses and daisies embellished with pink swirls. Of course, his friends had howled, and until they moved, he was stuck with "Chrissie."

He came back to the present when he heard his mother saying, "So I need you to call a few galleries. The Rania, Lee Young, um . . . Who else is showing my work?"

"Wait, you need what? Where's your manager?" Christian asked.

"Simon? He ran off to Acapulco for the week with his latest bimbo."

"Mother, you can't afford to have unreliable people in charge of your career."

"But I have you, dear! Anyway, Simon's not unreliable. He just cracked the West Coast market for me. Beverly Hills, no less. So I want to move some paintings around—"

"Okay, I'll make the calls." Christian looked remorseful and made talking motions with his hand, though Derek didn't seem the least bit fazed. In fact, Derek was barely able to tear his eyes from the stage, where the singer was crooning a melancholy ballad.

Christian began to feel a bit melancholy himself as his mother rattled off the names of people she wanted him to call while he made notes in his PalmPilot.

"I love you, Chrissie," she finally said to signal that she was finished with business.

"Love you, too, Mother," Christian whispered into the phone before he snapped it shut. "I'm so sorry about that. You know how mothers can be."

"What does your mother do? She sounds like a busy woman. Does she live around here?"

"She's a self-absorbed artist. Patricia Mercer. You may have heard of her?" When Derek shook his head, Christian said, "It doesn't matter. We lived all over the place when I was growing up, ending up in Terre Haute. When she moved back to Manhattan, I stayed. What about your family? Are they nearby?" Derek shook his head, then shifted his eyes, gazing at a couple a few tables away. After a few seconds, Christian asked, "Is that someone you know? Do you want to invite them over?"

Derek jerked his head around as if he'd been caught putting a sale tag on a full-price pair of Bruno Magli pumps, and said, "No. I mean, I don't want to invite them over." He must have noticed Christian's curious expression because he said, "That's Hannah. She comes from a wealthy family who sent her to the best schools and had high expectations of her. Then she met *him*."

Christian glanced again at the man with Hannah, seeing nothing about him that warranted Derek's ominous tone. "Who is he?"

"Damien? He's a drug dealer."

"He doesn't look like a drug dealer," Christian said after a more circumspect peek at Damien.

"That's why he's so good at it. No one suspects him. It's really sad, because you just know he'll ruin Hannah's life. But she loves him. Love is such an irrational emotion."

Christian frowned and said, "They look like a couple of tourists. Are you sure—"

"I told you, appearances can be deceiving," Derek said, interrupting him. "See that guy at the end of the bar?"

Christian looked where directed and saw an older man staring at the bottom of his empty glass. "Yeah?" he asked.

"What do you think he does?"

Christian looked again and hesitantly said, "Sells farm equipment?"

"That's really good," Derek praised. "He does sell farm equipment. Including backhoes. Which is exactly why his next-door neighbor has been calling the police about him for the past five years."

"His neighbor doesn't approve of backhoes?" Christian asked, bewildered.

"The neighbor insists that Ralph—that's his name—dug up his backyard and installed a fish pond about the same time his wife ran off with another man. The neighbor is sure that Mrs. Ralph is actually buried under the fishpond."

"Oh, my God, are you serious?" Christian asked, gaping at Ralph.

"No."

Christian swung his eyes back to Derek, who was grinning like a little kid. "You made that up? About Ralph?"

"His name's not Ralph. It's Buzz."

"Buzz?"

"Yes. They call him that because he's a beekeeper. It's kind of funny, because his wife's name is Honey. It's her real name, not a nickname."

Christian narrowed his eyes and said, "You're making that up, too, aren't you?" When Derek didn't answer, Christian said, "Hannah? And the drug dealer?"

"Probably here on their honeymoon from Billings, Montana."

Christian started laughing and said, "You're insane, Derek."

"Maybe," Derek agreed. "But I never buried anyone under a fishpond."

"There's always Natasha Deere," Christian said, laughing again as Derek's eyes brightened.

8

Down in the Valley of the Dolls

Natasha flew across the sales floor, having just come from a meeting of the department managers, the expression on her face leaving no doubt that it hadn't been positive. She made a beeline to the sales desk, looked at the schedule, then demanded, "Where's John?"

"He's at lunch," Missy answered.

"Lunch? He's only been here an hour!"

"He had something he had to do, and we're slow, so Erik said he could—"

"Erik." Natasha spat the name in disgust. "Hasn't he done enough damage around here?"

Missy wisely kept her mouth closed, and Natasha scanned the schedule, comparing it to Erik's list of the staff's responsibilities for the day. The "Chore List," as the sales crew referred to it. She made a mental inventory of all the tasks that were supposed to have been done by now and weren't, then retreated to her office.

She sank to her desk, exhausted. It had been quite a day, not at all like the one she'd envisioned when she got up that morning. First she'd had to intervene when that imbecile Derek screwed up a phone order. After nearly a month, he remained one of her most inept employees. Then she'd been stuck in that endless meeting, where Oscar, manager of Men's Shoes, had complained about Natasha encroaching on his floor space and his sales. For months, her requests to get Men's Shoes moved away from her department had been ignored. But all Oscar had to do was whine about her, and suddenly the idea of separating the departments was treated like a brilliant concept that Oscar had come up with. She mentally filed her grievance against him, knowing that sooner or later, she'd get her revenge.

As if she hadn't endured enough, she was informed that her only competent assistant manager was being promoted and relocated to one of the Wisconsin stores. The regional manager had suggested that she replace the assistant with Erik. Natasha had pleasantly replied that she'd be considering *all* qualified candidates for the job, but inside she was seething, recognizing his suggestion for the decree it was. Especially after Hershel, the store manager, mentioned that he'd gone to business school with Erik's father. There was no doubt about it; she was surrounded by fools of the Old Bores Network.

She sat motionless for a few moments, wondering if she shouldn't just pack up her things and head home. This was, after all, her day off. Not that she ever really took one. She grabbed her phone when it rang and snarled, "Natasha Deere."

"I got it," a gravelly voice on the line said with no other greeting.

Natasha gasped and looked over her shoulder to make sure there was no one in the stockroom with her. Her voice was almost a whisper when she said, "I told you not to call me here."

"Do you want it or not?" the voice responded.

"Of course I want it."

"Meet me at the usual place. One hour." The line went dead.

Natasha felt her heart race with adrenaline as she fumbled to hang up the phone. This was so wrong, and she knew she shouldn't be doing it. If anyone ever found out, her reputation would be ruined. But although she could barely admit it to herself, and certainly to no one else, it was her compulsion. Her only other compulsion besides work, and the one thing that made her daily suffering of fools bearable.

She quickly gathered up her things, threw her bag over her shoulder, and strode toward the sales floor. She could hear the associates scurry like rats at the sound of her approach. By the time she set foot on the floor, they were scattered throughout the department, attempting to look busy. It was a dance that had had many rehearsals. Erik was the only person behind the counter when she approached.

"That will be four-hundred forty-six dollars and sixty-seven cents," Erik enunciated loudly. "Would you like to put that on your Drayden's card today?" He glanced over his shoulder as if to make sure Natasha had heard the size of the sale he'd just made.

Natasha stepped in closer, saying softly, "I have to leave. You're in charge."

Before he could answer, she was gone. She half jogged through the Final Frontier Passage to the Rings of Uranus, the building of condominiums where she lived. It stood fifteen circular stories tall, providing sweeping views for most of its tenants. Natasha often wondered why that was supposed to be a selling point in the middle of Nowhere, Indiana, and generally kept her vertical blinds closed.

She impatiently tapped her foot as the elevator climbed to the thirteenth floor. The only other occupant of the car was a good-looking man in his twenties who was obviously returning from a visit to the workout room. The doors of the elevator slid apart, and the man opened his mouth as if to say something. Natasha shot him a look that said, *Don't bother, loser,* when she got out of the car. The man's mouth snapped shut as if he'd heard her.

She walked into her apartment, slamming the door behind her, then threw the deadbolt and dropped her keys on the table in the small entryway. Moving as quickly as she could, time being of the essence, she undressed as she went to her bedroom. She tossed the discarded clothing on her bed and stopped at the bedside table. She slowly opened the drawer and lifted up a false bottom, removing a tiny key. She looked over her shoulder, as she always did when taking out the key, in spite of knowing how silly it was to be furtive in her own home. She maintained her stealth as she went down the hall to a closed door. She inserted the tiny key into a padlock, slid the lock off, and slipped inside the room, relocking the door behind her. Only then did she feel safe enough to release the breath she'd been holding.

Without taking the time to look around, she quickly applied more makeup and got dressed, finally pinning up her hair and putting on a hat. Only then did she look at herself as objectively as possible in the full-length mirror on the back of the door. One corner of her mouth turned slightly upward.

Good God, she thought, *I hardly recognize me. I'm getting better at this all the time.*

She left the room and relocked the padlock from the outside. She went back to her bedroom, replaced the key, and found a large pair of sunglasses, which she slid on carefully so they wouldn't get tangled in the blond extensions that were attached to her hat.

She picked up a paper bag from the counter and tucked it into her dress pocket before walking to the door and looking out the peephole. Slowly, carefully, Natasha opened the door just an inch. She listened for footsteps or voices and heard neither. She darted out the door and ducked into the stairwell, walking down to the ninth floor before slipping into the corridor and taking the elevator.

She continued in the same clandestine fashion to the section of the mall anchored by Kohl's department store. It wasn't an area she normally ventured to, given that most of the businesses were discount stores. That was what made it the perfect rendezvous place. She sauntered into a bar located near the entrance to Kohl's and surveyed the room without removing her sunglasses. She spotted the owner of the gravelly voice sitting at a table not too near the bar in a dark corner.

He was wearing bib overalls and a T-shirt, which had some sort of condiment stain on it. His oily hair was thinning, but was long on the sides and in the back. His long beard undoubtedly doubled as a flytrap when he rode his motorcycle on the highways.

Natasha sat opposite him and brushed back the hair hanging from her hat like any actress working with a prop. "You have it?"

"I said I did when I called, didn't I?"

"Let me have it," Natasha demanded.

"First things first. You know that," the man chastised her. It was annoying to be admonished by one of Hell's Angels, but she reached into her pocket without argument.

"Here," she said with disdain, taking the bag from her pocket and pushing it across the table, casually glancing around to make sure no one saw. A ferret-faced man at the bar was looking in their direction, but Natasha dismissed him with contempt. In spite of his cashmere sweater, he looked like a big loser who wouldn't know his ass from his elbow.

"And here's to you," her companion said, pushing a similar bag across the table toward Natasha. When she anxiously started to open the bag, he said, "Are you sure you want to do that here?"

"Huh?" Natasha asked, her hand already inside the bag. She was delirious with anticipation.

"We have enough history that I don't feel out of line saying that you don't want to do that here," he commented.

Natasha caught herself, finally understanding his warning. Without another word, she got up from their table and hurried back to her apartment, her fingers tingling where they clutched the bag in her pocket. Once inside, she retraced her earlier steps, getting the key and letting herself into the locked room. Then she gently placed the hat with attached extensions on the one empty Styrofoam head among many neatly lined up in a row, each wearing wigs of various styles, lengths, and shades of blonde.

Natasha sat in a chair and reached into the bag, touching something wrapped in tissue paper. She pulled it out and gently placed it on her lap. After carefully folding the brown paper bag and putting it on the table in front of her, she gazed expectantly at the clump of tissue, inhaling sharply at the bright colors bleeding through the thin paper.

She barely breathed as she carefully unwrapped the tissue to reveal a tiny patchwork coat in perfect proportion, about four inches long and half as wide, quilted with the love and care of an eighty-seven-year-old Amish woman. It was brilliant in design and color, the stitching perfect, and hemmed just so.

Natasha held it carefully in the palm of one hand, like a little girl who'd found a baby bird on the sidewalk. With the index finger of her free hand, she gently traced the stitching, squirming at the sudden dampness between her legs. She shifted in her chair just a bit, and as her fingernail bumped over the precise stitching, she let out a soft, "Ohhhhhh."

She fondled and inspected the tiny coat for almost an hour, turning it every which way, hypnotized by the colors and the flawless detail. Finally, she gently put the coat on the tissue paper and set it all on the table so she could reach up to a shelf. She took down a doll that resembled how Barbie might look after she'd stuck her finger in a light socket. The blond hair on the doll was enormous.

Natasha took a tiny blue sequined jacket off the doll and delicately set it on the table, then picked up the patchwork coat. With all the finesse and precision of a surgeon, she slipped the coat onto the doll and admired how perfectly it fit.

"It's beautiful," she whispered. With the tracing fingernail, she brushed a bit of hair from the doll's face, drawling, "You're beeeeautifuuuuul . . ."

She reached over to push a button on a nearby remote, and Dolly Parton's voice filled the room. Natasha stood to look at the other dolls on the shelf. Dolly in one of her less overwhelming hairstyles, wearing a white satin dress slit all the way up her thigh, with tiny pearl beads on the bodice. Dolly in red, white, and blue sequins, wearing a jaunty cap over her blond shag. Dolly with spiral curls cascading over her black turtleneck sweater, jeans tucked into her black boots. Dolly in a red sequined calico dress, her hair in a beautiful updo. Dolly in shimmering white lace, curls flowing to her waist from a tan cowboy hat. Dolly in a black bustier, garter, and stockings. Dolly in tight, dark denim, wrists weighted with red bracelets, and red earrings peeking out from her blond tresses.

There were more than a hundred in all, and Natasha sighed with contentment as she inventoried her little World of Dollys. She swayed back and forth, crooning to the Dolly in her new coat of many colors, conveying in song that she wished her joy and happiness, but above all that: She would always, always love her.

9

Why the Long Face?

Although Derek's paychecks were relatively meager in the World of Hunter, he'd earned more in a month than he had during any of his college semesters. He bypassed the mall office of First National Bank, where Hunter had set up an account for him, and went to the mall branch of Indiana State's credit union. Half an hour later, he emerged with his temporary checks and a new sense of independence. A man on a mission, he resisted the siren calls of Aveda, Guess, and Mars Music as he walked through the mall.

He'd decided what his first major purchase would be after his evening with Christian. It had been so bizarre to actually meet MCI Man for drinks, especially when their conversation was interrupted several times by Christian's phone. He still wasn't exactly sure what Christian did for a living, but the phone made him seem industrious and in charge in a way that Derek envied.

Later, when he left Energy Electronics, he was a little disappointed because the battery on his new cell phone had to charge overnight before he could use it. Nonetheless, it was gratifying to know that friends could call him without going through the hotel receptionist. Although the friends were still mostly illusory. He rarely got calls from anyone but his parents. Still, it was his phone, paid for with his money, from his job. And it felt good.

He bought a latte at Brew Moon Café, sitting at one of their bistro tables to people watch. Most of his fellow employees swore they shunned public places on their days off, citing retail-induced agoraphobia. But Derek was tired of spending his nights at the Congreve chatting online to people thousands of miles away. Or endlessly changing television channels. Or waiting for Hunter's e-mails, which were usually short and only minimally affectionate.

Then again, the apartment seemed really tempting when he saw Natasha Deere emerge from Ann Taylor. Fortunately she didn't spot him, although he doubted that she'd have acknowledged him. Natasha didn't really see people unless she had a reason to castigate them.

His boss baffled him. He'd quickly placed her in his mental A-B-C file drawer, for abhorrent, brutal, and cold, among less savory words that began with the same letters. Then out of nowhere, she'd pulled him off the floor a few days before to have "a little chat." He'd expected to be fired for something he didn't know he'd done wrong.

Instead, Natasha had said, "Congratulations on your sale to Mr. Mercer's client."

"Thanks," Derek said, waiting for the other shoe to drop.

"Do you know who Christian Mercer is?"

The first man who might tempt me into cheating on my boyfriend, Derek thought of saying, but merely asked, "Someone important?"

"He's a glorified errand boy for influential people in Terre Haute. Or at least those who like to think they're influential. Maybe he'll bring more of them your way. Try not to foul it up."

Since then, his manager hadn't seemed quite as frigid, but Derek knew not to get comfortable. He saw the way she treated Erik, who had their department's highest sales. If Natasha's lifeless, Prada-clad feet were ever spotted sticking out from under a stack of shipping crates, Erik would be the first suspect. And Derek would have to stand in a long line of people willing to provide him an alibi.

Derek didn't really care if Christian brought him more customers. He'd rather see Christian, whose attention had reminded Derek that he was still a young man with a healthy libido. A lonely young man, in fact. Which seemed exciting and dangerous, a deadly combination.

He finished his latte and walked to the Congreve, edging his way through the crowd of people who were there for a Midwestern mayors' conference. Normally he'd scan them for possible stories to entertain his Internet buddies, but his thoughts were consumed by Christian.

Derek had been hesitant to meet MCI Man at the Aurora, right under the noses of Hunter's employees. He'd chastised himself for succumbing to the alluring contrast of Christian's dark auburn hair and gray eyes, the way his clothes fit his body as if they'd been custom-tailored, and for some bizarre reason, his fingers, which had struck Derek as artistic and sensual. After Christian removed his suit jacket and rolled up his sleeves, Derek had watched the play of the muscles in his forearms and hands when he made notes in his PalmPilot or drummed his fingers on the table.

But it wasn't Christian's obvious physical appeal that Derek couldn't forget. There was something intense about the way Christian sized him up, taking in every detail of his appearance. Maybe Christian was just a label queen, but he'd seemed to want to probe beneath Derek's clothes and find out who he was. Derek's fantasies about MCI Man had left him self-conscious about being with the real person. He'd also wanted to avoid any discussion of Hunter, so he'd nervously tried to direct Christian's attention to other people in the bar.

It had worked, and Christian seemed to be charmed by Derek's gift for improvising stories about people. But in the cold light of day, Derek wondered why it had been so important to charm Christian. Was he really ready for a fling? A different relationship? Had he given up on a future with Hunter? Would he have followed through if Christian had suggested moving their meeting into the closest available bedroom?

When he let himself into the apartment and plugged in his cell phone to charge it, it occurred to him that the closest available bedroom would have been Hunter's. Which was too far outside the realm of decent behavior for Derek to even contemplate. It was time to make some changes.

He moved his things from Hunter's room into the suite's other bedroom, then checked his e-mail. There was nothing from Hunter, so he threw himself on the sofa to watch television. Two hours, one dinner, one fantasy about Hunter, and two fantasies about Christian later, he was climbing the walls. He dug through the slips of paper and cards he'd piled on his dresser until he found Vienna's number. She and Davii were probably inundated with things to do on a Friday night, but he figured he'd give it a shot.

When no one answered at the apartment, he tried Davii's cell phone. After getting voice mail, he left a message suggesting that they meet him at the Aurora if they got home early enough. Since the chance of seeing them was slim, he might as well drink close to home.

Sheree Sheridan was in the middle of a set when Derek settled himself at the bar with a martini. Hearing her mourn the man that got away in her husky voice hit a little too close to his heart, so he focused on the way she looked, something he never tired of.

Having seen the telltale lines around her eyes and mouth, Derek knew Sheree had to be fiftyish, but to him, she was timeless. Her hair, blonde courtesy of a hairdresser, was teased and pulled into a loose knot, with wisps falling artfully down the back of her neck and around her face, softening her features. She was in stage makeup—heavy on the foundation, false eyelashes, lots of contouring and shading—and he thought she looked fabulous. The blue sequins of her dress caught the light and shot beams into the room, casting glamour on the crowd that always filled the bar on Friday nights, a mixture of locals and hotel guests.

Everything about her—whiskey voice, glittering costumes, fading beauty—bespoke a world-weary attitude. And then her eyes registered. No woman of her years and experience should have eyes that still looked dreamy and hopeful. From the first time he saw her and listened to her sing, Derek had adored her.

He still remembered that night. He and Hunter had gone into Terre Haute for dinner, a rarity in itself. When they'd returned to the hotel, some sad song was drifting through the lobby like smoke, and Hunter had suggested they stop in and listen to Sheree. Later, in bed, Hunter had been unusually expansive. Derek didn't know if it was Sheree's singing or the numerous cocktails that loosened Hunter's tongue, but he listened, spellbound, to the story in their dark bedroom.

"That woman," Hunter said, "is the closest thing to a conscience Randolph Congreve ever had."

Apparently, it was one of the family's open secrets that Sheree was Hunter's father's mistress. The girls weren't supposed to know about her, but the boys had occasionally seen her in their father's company at symphony performances, the opera, and the ballet. Any time his sons were bold enough to speak to their father and Sheree, she always knew them by name without being introduced, and could even converse knowledgeably about their hobbies and interests. Sheree was the only proof that their father knew what his sons did with their time. Somebody had to have told her.

"Sheree is all heart," Hunter said. "Way too good for the old man."

"So what's she doing here?" Derek finally thought to ask.

"Maybe he got tired of her. Maybe she's getting too old, so he found a younger version. Although she's one of a kind. Or maybe he's just too old and tired himself to continue to maintain a mistress. Who knows?"

The subject never came up again, but many times when Hunter was out of town, Derek spent his nights in the piano bar watching Sheree cast her spell on the crowd. He rarely saw her during the day, although she, too, had an apartment at the Congreve. Sometimes he'd spot one of the bellhops walking her Italian greyhound, or catch a glimpse of her getting into a hotel courtesy car. He didn't really want to see her outside the bar, preferring that she remain a mysterious, sultry creature of the night.

He automatically joined in the applause when she finished her set. After being stopped by a few of the patrons, she came to the bar, where the bartender handed over her usual glass of sparkling water with a twist of lemon.

"Hi, Buddy," she said to Derek, giving him one of her languorous smiles. She always made it sound like his name, although he knew that she was fully aware of who he was.

"Hi, Sheree," Derek said, smiling back as she slid onto the stool next to his. "You sound great, as always."

"Honey, it's the songs. I haven't sounded great since God was a boy, but thank you for saying so. You look a little gloomy. Is that the songs, too? You came in during the sad set."

He shook his head and said, "The sad set is my favorite."

"Mine, too," she said. "I wonder why a broken heart is always more interesting than a light one?" He'd been staring toward the stage, but that made him turn a startled look her way. "Feeling lonely and abandoned?" she asked.

"A little," he admitted. "Sort of like I've overstayed my welcome. I don't know what I'm supposed to do if he's tired of me."

"Depends," she said with another slow smile. "Can you sing?"

He caught her meaning and returned an equally wistful smile, saying, "If only I could."

She placed one beautifully manicured hand on his arm and said, "There's more than one way to make music, Buddy. You just need to find your voice."

Wondering if she'd noticed him the night he'd met Christian in the bar, Derek decided it might be prudent to change the subject and said, "Let's play the guessing game."

Sometimes, if she was in the mood, she'd join him in picking out people from the crowd and making up stories about them. Although his own tales were improbably outrageous, he was willing to bet hers were almost always accurate. Not much got past Sheree.

"Okay. But you pick," she said.

He looked at the crowd, spotted a face he'd seen in the newspaper, and said, "The woman with the curls."

"That wouldn't be fair," she said. "I know who she is."

He shrugged and said, "Tell me anyway."

"Emily-Anne Barrister. The people she's with are from out of town. Maybe business associates of her husband. Or from one of the conglomerates that keep trying to buy him out. It'll never happen. Cort's got ink in his veins; he'll die owning those newspapers."

"Which one is he?" Derek asked.

"The stocky one with the unlit cigar. His doctor told him no more smoking, but he can't give them up, so he just doesn't light up. Cort thinks Emily-Anne hung the moon, but she's a troubled soul. They never had the children they'd hoped for. And these days, many of their friends are on their second or third trophy wives. Emily-Anne's solution is surgery. She's got so much plastic in her, they should stamp 'Mattel' on her ass." Derek let out a bark of laughter, and Sheree shook her head. "It's sad, really. When a man falls in love with who you are, why keep trying to be someone else?"

He met her eyes again, wondering if she was trying to convey advice.

"Your public awaits," the bartender said.

Sheree patted Derek's arm again and said, "Goodnight, Buddy."

"Goodnight, Sheree."

After Sheree took her spot next to the piano and began singing "Smoke Gets in Your Eyes," Derek saw Davii enter the Aurora. He was dressed in jeans and a fitted black T-shirt with Keith Haring drawings dancing over his chest. Derek waved to him and watched as Davii's face lit up before he walked toward the bar.

"I'll have what I'm having," Davii said to the bartender as he commandeered the stool next to Derek's. "A cosmopolitan," he clarified.

"Where's Vienna?" Derek asked. "I assumed you two were out together."

"I checked my vulva at the door," Davii quipped. Derek winced, which made Davii laugh. "She and I were at Asteroid Arcade when you called. I was in the middle of defending my high score on Ms. Pac-Man; otherwise I would've answered. Vienna was complaining about a headache or something, so she went home. Ah, sweet nectar of the gods. Thank you."

When Davii reached for his wallet, Derek said, "It's on me. Thanks for coming out tonight. I needed company."

"Tonight? I came out long before tonight." Davii sipped at his drink before picking it up. "I was a young lad of twelve in Muncie when reality hit me."

"Reality or puberty?" Derek asked.

"A little of both, actually. I was getting a haircut when I realized my barber was a hot stud. I had fantasies about locking the door and letting him have his way with me. But of course, fantasies rarely become reality. He was a married father of three and also went to our church." Davii gulped at his drink, then continued. "Cut to the mall, six years later, when I finally acted on my feelings and picked up some guy at Pluto. It wasn't great, but it was good to finally feel like I was . . . myself, I suppose. Does that make any sense?"

"Completely," Derek replied, thinking about how he'd felt the same way when he was in college. "Have you ever had a boyfriend?"

"I guess it would depend on—hey! How do you keep doing this to me? I came here fully intending to get to know more about you. Whenever we get together, you somehow get me talking about myself. You hardly ever talk about yourself," Davii complained good-naturedly. He playfully tapped Derek's knee and prodded, "Go ahead. Talk about you."

"You want me to open up?" Derek asked.

Davii looked over the rim of his glass and arched an eyebrow. "Oh, yeah. Open up for me, baby."

"I don't open up for just anyone," Derek said, matching Davii's suggestive tone.

"We'll see about that," Davii said. Neither one of them went any further, so Davii added, "I'll just sit here and sip quietly until you're more forthcoming. I can hold out all night if I have to."

"Check!" Derek exclaimed.

10

Don't You Step on My Blue Swarovski Shoes

Vienna checked out her reflection in the mirrored wall of the elevator. She was on the verge of being late for work. She had an errand to complete and ten minutes before her shift. She left the elevator, ran down the Light Year Passage, and turned her heel when rounding the corner into the mall, losing her balance.

"Jesus!" she exclaimed as she felt gravity being thwarted by a man's arms.

"Are you okay?" the man asked, still holding on to her waist. Vienna looked into concerned eyes as she gripped his shoulder and flexed her ankle.

"I think so," she said. She examined her ankle, which felt fine, then worried for her Gucci heels. They were intact, without a scratch, and she breathed a sigh of relief. Realizing that she was still in the man's arms, she extricated herself from his grasp and took a step back. He seemed concerned, attractive, and oddly familiar, but she was a woman with places to go. "I'm fine, thank you. I'm sorry, but I'm about to be extremely late for work."

Before he could answer, Vienna headed toward Drayden's, walking with the speed of Jackie Joyner-Kersee on a fashion runway. About halfway between the Galaxy Building and Drayden's, she stepped nimbly onto an escalator and went up to the Moon level. Directly opposite the top of the escalator was a Krispy Kreme storefront, where Vienna ordered two large boxes of assorted donuts. "I don't care what kind you put in there," she said. "Just make sure none of them have powdered sugar on top. Powdered sugar plus couture equals disaster. Hurry, please!"

Moments later, Vienna dashed into Drayden's, carefully carrying her booty before her like an offering to the gods.

"Hi, girls!" she called to the other Cosmetics associates as she wended her way to the Lillith Allure counter. Hungry eyes watched when she stashed the boxes under her counter, a Friday morning tradition that Vienna had started when she began working at Drayden's. Food on the sales floor was prohibited, but the Cosmetics manager overlooked the rule, since she was addicted to maple-glazed Krispy Kremes. For the next three to four hours, the Cosmetics associates would create reasons to pass by Vienna's counter and nip behind it for a sugar rush. Vienna loved being able to provide her co-workers with a guilty pleasure on an otherwise ordinary day. Nor could she deny the popularity and attention the donuts garnered her. Plus, as people stopped by to eat, they talked, and Vienna was more than happy to listen.

"Sorry I'm late," Vienna said to her counter mate, Bianca, a willowy redhead with an inferiority complex and a pale complexion. "Are you okay to watch the counter while I run to the time clock? If I pretend that I forgot to punch in one more time, HR is sure to bust me for it."

"It's okay," Bianca said, eyeing the donuts. "But if you leave me here with those fat pills, I can't be held accountable if I eat them all."

"There's no way you could eat thirty donuts on your own," Vienna said, stashing her purse in a drawer.

"Don't be so sure. I'm no stranger to bingeing. That's why I'm so fat," Bianca moaned.

Vienna looked at Bianca's near-perfect figure and was ready to protest when she remembered the time. Instead, she said, "Honey, I've told you a hundred times that you're gorgeous. You're on your own. Be right back."

She raced across the store and into the shoe stockroom, where she keyed her employee number into the time clock. She was only five minutes late, an infraction that she knew her lenient department manager would overlook, but she mentally reprimanded herself anyway.

Though retail wasn't her career trajectory, Vienna liked her new job. It wasn't so much the job itself, but the environment. She liked being in a larger store instead of a cramped boutique because it allowed her to observe people in larger numbers. Her immediate supervisors and co-workers all took their jobs with an easygoing attitude. They knew they weren't moving mountains, and as long as everyone completed their tasks pleasantly and efficiently, there was no reason for stress and strife. Unfortunately, not everyone in Drayden's shared that mentality. Vienna looked around for Natasha Deere and, not seeing her anywhere, quickly got a cup of water from the cooler next to the time clock, downed it, and hurried away.

She checked the schedule at the Women's Shoes cash wrap to see when Derek was working. He was closing and wouldn't be there for another four hours. Vienna sighed and headed back to her counter. Although she didn't mind her job, it was more tolerable when Derek was working, too. He would often crank call her when Natasha wasn't around, pretending to be a customer.

"Do you have any frosted blue eye shadow?" he'd ask in a hideously high-pitched voice. "I can't get enough of the stuff. Tubs! I want tubs of blue eye shadow! Can you help me?"

"No. All the shrinks in the world couldn't help you," Vienna would reply. "But let me ask you something. Do you have any pumps in a size fourteen narrow?"

They'd also begun a routine of sometimes meeting for breakfast before work if they were both scheduled for the opening shift, kvetching about their jobs over Belgian waffles and coffee. If their shifts weren't the same, they'd try to meet for lunch, often joining up with Davii. Vienna would watch her two favorite men talk, trying to make each other laugh and competing for her approval. She'd watch Derek carefully and covertly during lunch, observing his body language and looking for clues as to his interest in Davii.

Even though she'd practically promised Davii that she would set him up with Derek, she wanted to be sure that Derek was attracted to Davii. Derek already had a boyfriend, and she didn't want to disrespect their relationship, although she knew enough about Hunter Congreve to have already formed an unfavorable opinion. Vienna had encountered him many times in various stores in Mall of the Universe. She'd sold him a suit in Mercury Man, served him drinks in the Jupiter Lounge, offered advice about a stereo in Energy Electronics, and noticed Derek wearing several of the shirts she'd selected for Hunter during her stint at Gucci. Each time, Hunter had regarded her as if he'd never seen her before and barely spoke to her. Vienna had quickly diagnosed him as a pompous snob with a daddy complex and possible racial prejudices, and regarded him with equal indifference.

Now she was looking for cracks in the veneer of Derek's relationship with Hunter—the fact that Hunter had left Derek behind to go to Australia being a titanic hint that their ship might be sinking. But whenever she asked Derek about his lover, he'd become guarded and assure her that everything between them was fine. He'd told Vienna how he met Hunter and other facts, but when it came to emotions and how he felt about Hunter, Derek would shut down and change the subject.

Vienna never pushed Derek when he got to that point, not wanting to offend him and risk their growing friendship. Which was another reason she was reticent to fix up her two friends. What if Derek and Davii didn't click as a couple and things grew awkward between them? Vienna didn't relish the thought of her only friends being at odds with each other, or of trying to protect the frail, histrionic egos of two gay men.

Natasha moved from behind a column and blocked her path when Vienna was just steps away from the divide between Women's Shoes and Cosmetics. She reminded Vienna of a villain in a Grimm's fairy tale—a wolf blocking a forest path, hoping to gobble up innocent girls like Vienna for breakfast.

"Can I help you with something?" Natasha growled.

"I don't think so," Vienna said dismissively and walked around her to the safety of the Cosmetics floor.

Vienna never liked to waste her time and energy on people who were beyond redemption. She tried to avoid Natasha as much as possible. Whenever Vienna's department manager was tied up in a meeting upstairs or was off the floor for an extended period of time, Natasha would never hesitate to use her authority and make the lives of the Cosmetics employees a living hell. Vienna hurried back to the Lillith Allure counter, feeling like a child playing freeze tag who'd just reached the safety of home base.

"I hate that woman," Vienna said to Bianca, who was guiltily and hastily swallowing a donut.

"Me, too," Bianca replied, which surprised Vienna, who'd never known Bianca to hate anyone or anything. Hate required a spine.

Just then, a drab and nerdy teenaged girl approached the counter, inquiring about Lillith Allure's Zodiac products, and

Vienna switched into work mode. She recommended Zodiac's Sagittarius line, which was more subdued and might work with the girl's Plain Jane appearance.

"Let me apply some samples, if you've got time, so I can show you how they'll work with your look," Vienna said.

"I'm going to a party and hoped to look like her," the girl said, pointing to a picture of Sheila Meyers, Zodiac's spokeswoman, who was decked out in red leather and festooned in glam and glitz in an ad for Zodiac's Cancer line.

Bianca stood behind Vienna and murmured, "Sure, Vienna. I'll start the cauldron boiling. You get the eye of newt."

Vienna suppressed her laughter and walked around the counter to work some magic. Time flew by as she transformed the girl into Sheila Meyers's mousy-haired Mini-Me. Several customers stopped by to observe her work, while Bianca reeled them in with her standard "I could never pull this off, but it would look fabulous on you" shtick. After a few hours, Vienna had unloaded sixty dollars worth of Zodiac on Mini-Me and made over five other women, as well.

While she was contouring another customer's cheekbones with pale pink Lillith Allure rouge, Vienna noticed Derek enter Drayden's. He was wearing a charcoal suit, and his hair, which Davii had recently trimmed, was styled in a deliberately messy way that made him look like he'd stepped out of a magazine ad. Vienna was impressed and smiled. Derek saw her and waved. As she returned the gesture, she noticed the man walking behind him, who'd followed Derek's gaze and was now staring at her. Recognizing him as the man who'd caught her earlier when she tripped, Vienna felt her face grow hot with embarrassment. He smiled and nodded briefly, but turned his attention to the woman next to him, much to Vienna's relief.

"I don't think I like this color," Vienna's customer said. "Do you have anything else?"

"You're right," Vienna said. "Let's try something a little more natural."

Vienna's curiosity took hold, and she stole glances at Derek and the couple with him while she worked, wondering how Derek knew them. They were obviously buying shoes for the woman. Even at fifty feet, Vienna could tell she was a "second draft," her term for a woman who'd had plastic surgery. The man obviously had control issues, since he was the one picking out shoes for her and putting them on her feet. Derek was little more than a gofer, running back and forth to the stockroom for different sizes and styles. Natasha prowled nearby, which made Vienna wonder if the couple was of importance. It was difficult to tell, since Natasha often lurked, hovered, and circled like a vulture.

When their counter was clear of customers, Vienna gestured to Women's Shoes and asked Bianca, "Who's that couple that Derek's assisting?"

Bianca squinted, then said, "Emily-Anne Barrister. God, I wish I had her breasts."

"You should ask her where she got them," Vienna advised. "Maybe if she referred you, you could get a discount."

"You don't think they're real?" Bianca asked incredulously.

"Oh, girl, please," scoffed Vienna. "Who's the guy? I know I've seen him before."

"Christian Mercer. Don't you think he's cute? He organizes people's personal lives, or shops for them, or something."

With a little effort, Vienna began to remember other times she'd seen Christian and mused aloud, "I thought he was schizophrenic."

"What?" Bianca said with a shocked look.

"He seemed to spend a lot of time talking to himself or hearing voices," Vienna explained. "Then I realized he wears a headset connected to his cell phone. Those things have altered our entire way of diagnosing human behavior."

"Uh-huh." Bianca seemed a little puzzled. "So then you do know him."

"When I worked at Mercury Man, I helped him and some of his clients. And I sold him a digital camera at the electronics store. I don't really *know* him. We've made small talk, but that's about it." She paused and regarded Christian. He was an arresting man. But it was his smile and poise, the way he put himself together, that made him attractive. Vienna recalled the strong arms that had caught her earlier and studied him as if he were a painting on display. "I guess he's cute. Whose bus do you think he's riding?"

"What?" Bianca asked.

"On which side is his bread buttered?" she inquired. When Bianca still looked confused, she said bluntly, "Is he gay?"

"Probably," Bianca said. She flushed crimson and quickly busied herself by restocking a display with eyebrow pencils.

Vienna was intrigued and said, "You know something you're not telling me."

"No, I don't," Bianca said quickly. Too quickly. When Vienna stared hard at her, Bianca put down the box of eyebrow pencils with a defeated sigh. "My friend Kate? Who works at Comet Cleaners? She's been trying to get a date with him forever. She got this brilliant idea. Kate's really bold. I could never—"

"What was the idea?" Vienna asked, losing her patience.

"She slipped a pair of her sexiest panties into the arm of one of his dry-cleaned shirts. Just to make sure he got the message, she wrote her phone number on the crotch."

"Were the panties clean?" Vienna asked, scandalized in spite of herself.

"Of course!" Bianca said. "But he never called."

"Maybe she should have—"

"Don't," Bianca said with a grimace. Then she stared wistfully at Christian and said, "So anyway, he's probably gay. It would be just my luck. Not that it matters. He'd never go for me. I'm too—"

"Oh, shut up," Vienna interrupted. "You're beautiful, and every straight man in this store wants your body. I know it. You know it. Free yourself. Have a donut. If you don't mind, I'm taking fifteen."

"Donuts?" Bianca gasped.

"Minutes."

Bianca didn't mind, so Vienna crossed over into Women's Shoes and pretended to look at a display of new merchandise while surreptitiously watching Derek, Christian, and Emily-Anne. It bothered her that Bianca knew more about Christian than she did, so Vienna was determined to learn everything she could about him. She idly thought about Christian as a potential back-up romance for Davii, who could use a little organization in his life.

She watched as Christian strapped a pair of white sandals on Emily-Anne's feet, while Derek stood by with an empty shoebox in his hands. Once the silver buckles were all fastened, Emily-Anne crossed her legs, admiring the sandals.

"Christian, they're beautiful," she purred. "I was right to get in touch with you."

"I didn't design them," Christian joked. Vienna rolled her eyes at his lame attempt at humor and noticed that, across the floor, Natasha was mirroring her. Vienna carefully moved behind a nearby column to stay out of Natasha's line of sight. She heard Christian say, "The heels are pretty high. Try walking in them."

Vienna couldn't see what was going on, but after a pause, she heard a clattering noise, followed by Emily-Anne squealing, "Oops! Sorry!"

Vienna peeked around the column to see Derek and Natasha rushing to a table that Emily-Anne had apparently bumped into. Shoes were tottering and falling off stands, raining down and hitting the floor like fashionable hailstones.

"Don't worry about it. It happens all day," Derek said while picking up shoes.

Natasha was also grabbing at shoes. Then she wrenched a pair of yellow mules from Derek's hands and snarled, "I'll take care of these! Help your clients."

Christian, who'd observed the scene from the sofa as if he was at home watching a sitcom, laughed silently with his hands over his mouth. He turned and spotted Vienna, who quickly picked up a shoe and began examining it. She realized it was a hideously ugly orthopedic-looking loafer and dropped it back on the shelf as if it had bitten her.

"These would look fabulous by the pool. I have to have them," Emily-Anne said, returning to the sofa. She kissed Christian on the cheek and exclaimed, "I love them!"

Vienna was shocked at the familiarity implied by the kiss and didn't know how to interpret it. Was Christian buying the shoes for her? Were they having an affair? Or was Emily-Anne a gal pal bussing her gay friend? Vienna was more intrigued than ever.

"I'll add them to the pile," Derek said.

"Actually, these would look even better poolside," Christian said, producing a pair of blue-and-pink-flower-patterned mules with a huge Lucite wedge.

"What goes on at her pool?" Vienna whispered to herself.

"Should I ask how much?" Emily-Anne asked Derek, then giggled.

Derek said, "They're only a hundred and fifty dollars."

Christian looked pleased with Derek's response, as he added, "That's nothing."

"Yeah, but in addition to all those," Emily-Anne said, pointing to the pile of shoeboxes, "I must have over a thousand dollars in shoes so far."

Vienna was aghast; Emily-Anne's new shoe collection cost more than Vienna's rent. Surely, Christian couldn't afford to buy her that many pairs of shoes. Maybe she was a client. A man that into shoes had to be gay.

"And they're worth every penny," Christian stated. "You're worth every penny. Try on the wedges."

Emily-Anne shrugged and put the shoes on her feet. She stared at them silently.

"What do you think?" Derek prodded. "Will they work with what you need them for?"

Emily-Anne smirked and said, "I don't know. Let me see."

She flopped onto her back on the sofa and lifted her feet in the air. Vienna's mouth fell open, as did Derek's. Christian laughed out loud and said, "Oh, come on! That can't be true."

"You're right," Emily-Anne agreed. "That's what my Louis Vuitton shoes are for!"

Laughing at her own joke, Emily-Anne, whose feet were still in the air, suddenly kicked, launching a shoe from her foot. Vienna, Derek, and Christian followed the blue-and-pink-flowered wedge's trajectory, watching it sail across the store like a football over a playing field. It was easily a thirty-yard pass, and Vienna was impressed. The wedge finally succumbed to gravity and arced down toward the replica of Mrs. Lvandsson's loom, which was positioned in the middle of the store, by the escalators.

"Girl," Vienna quietly drawled.

"Uh-oh," Christian said.

"What?" Emily-Anne asked, rising to a seated position and looking around. "Where did it—"

She was cut off as the wedge crashed loudly into the loom, reducing it to kindling. Several customers leaped away in terror, one of them knocking over a pair of nearby mannequins, another upsetting a counter display.

Emily-Anne bit her bottom lip in embarrassment, then said, "I think my Drayden's account just increased."

"Don't worry. It happens all the time," Derek said.

"I don't think anyone was hurt. Pay it no mind," Christian said sweetly. "Forget the mules and look at what I found. I was thinking this pair would go with the blue gown you just bought."

Vienna peered around the column again, and her eyes widened as she watched Christian slip another pair of stilettos onto Emily-

Anne's feet. The sandals had intricately woven straps crossing over the instep that were beaded with blue and clear crystals, a toe loop with one large blue crystal on top, and long satin straps that wound around and tied at the ankle in a bow. Vienna stared, coveting them, and wondered how much they cost.

"They're five hundred and twenty dollars," Derek suddenly said, as if reading Vienna's mind.

"Those are Swarovski crystals. That's actually a good price," Christian hastily added. "There must be a purse that goes with them."

Derek, catching the hint, said, "I'll find out," and hastened toward Accessories on the other side of the store. He didn't get too far, because he spotted Vienna loitering behind the column and hissed, "What are you doing?"

"Looking at shoes," she calmly replied. "I'm on a break."

"You look like you're spying on me," Derek said suspiciously.

"Don't be ridiculous," Vienna indignantly responded. "You'd better hurry up and find that purse."

Derek frowned at her but hurried away. While he was gone, Vienna turned back to watch the Christian and Emily-Anne Show, but instead found herself on display, as they were now staring at her.

"I said, what do *you* think?" Emily-Anne asked.

"Me? Uh, what size are you?" Vienna stammered before she knew what she was saying.

Emily-Anne looked horrified and said, "Size nine. But I don't see what that has to do with anything."

"Dammit, so am I," Vienna muttered, wishing she'd seen the shoes first. Even with her discount, however, she could never afford them, so she quickly composed herself and said, "They look fantastic on you. Of course, I don't know what your dress looks like, but they'd make anyone and any outfit look like a million bucks."

"Thank you," Emily-Anne replied. Christian winked at Vienna, who tried to look blasé, since she mistrusted winkers. "I think they'll be perfect, Christian. What would I do without you?"

Save money, stay at home, and stop risking other people's lives, Vienna thought.

Emily-Anne walked to a mirror on the other side of the sales floor. Vienna used the opportunity to say, "You really know your shoes."

"I just fake it really well," Christian said. "Clothes are basically an extension of our personalities. It's all a matter of finding clothes that match a client's personality."

"So she's a client?" Vienna asked, gesturing subtly toward Emily-Anne, who was surveying the shoes from every angle in the mirror and asking other people for their opinions.

"Emily-Anne's a new client, yes," Christian answered. "This is our first meeting, if you can believe it. She's not what I imagined at all. But I like her. She's fun." Vienna nodded, happy to have one question answered, but still wondering about Christian's sexuality. "What happened to your job at Mercury Man?" Christian continued. "That's the last place I remember seeing you."

"Oh, good," Vienna said. "I was worried you'd only remember me as the klutz who crashed into you this morning. Sorry about that."

"Don't worry about it," Christian said gallantly, then he imitated Derek, saying, "It happens all the time." When she snickered, he added, "It was my pleasure."

Vienna was about to ask a leading question loaded with innuendo when Derek jogged up to them, slightly out of breath, holding a small handbag encrusted with blue and clear crystals. Emily-Anne rejoined them and exclaimed, "What a cute purse! I love it. These will match the gown perfectly." She sat down to remove the shoes.

"Perfect. Well done, Derek," Christian praised, taking the bag from him and adding it to the pile of shoes. "Maybe we could get you a little help carrying all this stuff to the register. Excuse me, Natasha?"

Natasha turned around with an expression that bore a striking resemblance to an African funeral mask that had hung in the office of one of Vienna's former colleagues. Vienna turned back to the shelves of shoes circling the column, hoping to go unnoticed.

"Yes?" Natasha hissed.

"Would you be a lamb and help Derek with these boxes? Thank you so much," Christian said, not waiting for a favorable response. Emily-Anne looked at her loot with affection, oblivious to Natasha's withering gaze, as Derek began carrying an armful of shoeboxes to the cash wrap. When Natasha begrudgingly began to help, Christian linked arms with Emily-Anne and led her toward the registers, but not before adding, "Mind the purse, Natasha. We don't want any crystals popping off."

Before she could catch herself, Vienna sniggered audibly. In a second, Natasha was standing up and staring at her. She said dryly, "Miss Talbot, shouldn't you be behind a counter hawking lipstick?"

"I'm on a break," Vienna said, hoping Natasha wouldn't realize that she'd been there for nearly a half hour.

"How nice for you that we have such lenient labor laws in this state and that you have a department manager with a lackadaisical attitude toward the rules. I'm sure if I looked behind your counter, I wouldn't find any food at all. Correct?"

"It's past noon. By now, it's surely all been eaten or disposed of," Vienna said. Natasha's eyes narrowed, and her face slowly burned scarlet. Vienna thought about asking her to get a pair of shoes to try on but decided not to push her luck. Instead she said, "I'll let you get back to work. That's quite a sale Derek made, isn't it? See ya!"

Vienna hurried back to her counter, relieving Bianca, who dashed to the women's restroom. Fifteen minutes later, she watched as Christian and Emily-Anne left Women's Shoes. Vienna picked up her phone and dialed Derek's extension.

"Thank you for calling Drayden's shoe salon. This—"

"Hi, it's me," Vienna interrupted.

"Hello," Derek said a little too enthusiastically.

Vienna looked across the store and saw Natasha standing next to him, drumming her fingers on the counter and fuming. "Oh, crap. I think I pissed off the dragon lady. I'm sorry. Please forgive me."

"No. We don't accept that coupon here," Derek said.

"I'll make it up to you with lunch," Vienna offered.

"That could be arranged," Derek said. "But it might take some time."

"She's going to saddle you with some heinous task, isn't she?" Vienna guessed.

"That's correct. Let me check to see if we have that shoe in stock, and I'll call you back later," Derek said. "Let me take down your number."

"That number is one eight hundred your manager is a bitch," Vienna replied. "Call me when you can get away."

Later, in Bert's Bar & Grille, Vienna treated Derek to lunch.

Derek was aggressively cutting into his steak and complaining about Natasha. "Then she had me relocate all the high heels from downstairs to upstairs," Derek griped. "It would've taken me over an hour if our stock guy hadn't risked his job to help me."

"I had no idea there are two levels to your stockroom," Vienna said dreamily. "All those shoes. So little time."

"I can't stand that evil woman," Derek said, tearing into his steak again.

"Slow down and enjoy your food. You're tearing into that thing as if it were Natasha's heart," Vienna said.

"Don't be silly," Derek said before taking a bite. "She doesn't have one."

"Oh, yeah, what was I thinking?" Vienna said. "If you hate her so badly, why don't you transfer to another department? Or just quit?"

Derek swallowed and answered, "I tried that. There are no openings in any other departments. And I can't quit. I need this job."

Vienna looked skeptical as she said, "I don't want to risk offending you, but come on, Derek. You live in the Congreve with your boyfriend, who just happens to *be* a Congreve."

"Yeah, and you have alimony," Derek snapped. There was an uncomfortable moment of silence as Derek cut into his steak again and Vienna toyed with her Cobb salad. Finally Derek said, "I'm sorry. That was rude of me."

"Not to mention incorrect," Vienna stated. "I don't receive alimony. Can I have your steak knife?"

"Why?"

"There's a certain hairdresser that I need to murder," she coolly answered. When Derek stared at her, aghast, she said, "No matter. Using his own scissors would be more poetic."

"He told me when I was getting my hair cut," Derek explained. "I shouldn't have said anything. Davii told me in confidence."

"I told him in confidence!" Vienna shrieked, causing several of their fellow diners to look her way. "I'm sorry. I'm losing control of my base emotions. I need water." She took a long drink of water, swept her red and black braids back, and said, "I'm fine. No harm's been done. And I'm sorry for my assumptions about your situation."

"No harm, no foul," Derek agreed. "Besides, I'd say we're even now for you getting me in trouble with Natasha."

"Her emotional and irrational behavior is beyond my—" Vienna stopped when she saw Derek's sour expression and hastily said, "Fine. We're even. Tell me about this Christian guy. He obviously can't stand Natasha either. I like that in a man. When did you meet him?"

Vienna listened as Derek related his story. She took notice of how Derek's eyes lit up when he talked about Christian, how he leaned forward as he spoke, and how he stopped eating altogether as he waited for her reaction.

"He sounds like a nice person," Vienna said.

"He seems to be," Derek agreed, still not eating. "It was definitely nice of him to bring Emily-Anne Barrister to me and help my sales."

"Eat your steak. We're running out of time," Vienna urged, watching as Derek seemed to come back to earth, realizing there was food in front of him and why it was there. "Christian's an attractive man, isn't he? Do you think he's gay?"

"I have no idea," Derek said.

"I mean, he knows about fashion. He doesn't mix stripes with plaid. He's attractive," Vienna stated. "He's got to be gay."

"You think?" Derek asked.

"Do you want him to be gay?" Vienna asked.

"I don't know!" Derek exclaimed. "Why are you asking me all these questions?"

Vienna knew he was shutting down, so she said, "I don't know. I just think he's really attractive."

Derek nodded slowly and said, "Oh, I get it. You're hoping he's not gay."

"That's not it at all," Vienna calmly argued. "It seemed to me that you were open to the idea of Christian possibly being gay. That's all." Derek stared at her. Vienna reached over to take his hand and said, "I know your pride is bigger than my hair, and you'd never admit to me that your current relationship has problems. But if you ever want to discuss it, I'll listen. I'm only prying right now because I know someone who's interested in you."

Derek looked surprised and somewhat pleased as he asked, "Who? Not that guy who sells perfume at Drayden's, I hope. He's nice, but he's not my type."

"No. I know that," Vienna said. She wondered fleetingly if she should keep quiet and not complicate the lives of her two friends. Then she remembered how Davii had spilled her secret. "It's Davii. He wants you bad."

"Davii?" Derek said. He looked stunned and repeated, "Davii? You're kidding, right?"

"Why would I? He's a guy. You're a guy. Makes sense to me," Vienna said.

"He flirts a lot when we get together, but I never thought of him that way," Derek said.

"Oh, trust me, he's a guy."

"But he's so . . ."

"What?" Vienna prompted. "Bitchy? Arrogant? Tall? Italian?"

Derek laughed at her impatience and said, "No, none of that. Sometimes I think of myself as a boy from a small town who's still ignorant about the ways of the world. Davii is completely opposite. It surprises me that someone like him is interested in someone like me."

"Someone like him? Someone like you?" Vienna parroted. "Please, the boy is from Muncie, Indiana. That ain't so glamorous, baby. Besides, you're both human beings. That's all that matters. Everyone's different, and nobody is better than anybody else."

"I know all that," Derek said.

"Davii likes you. It's that simple. Don't make it any more complicated than it has to be," Vienna advised.

"Easy for you to say," Derek said. "What about Hunter?"

"What about Hunter?" Vienna asked.

"Forget it," Derek said, waving away the thought. "Too complicated."

"Fine," Vienna said as she signed the charge receipt. "We've got to get back to work. What should I say to Davii? If you want, I could pretend like I never told you."

Derek stood in thought for a moment and finally said, "No. Tell him I'm interested, too."

11

Heels Over Head

Christian hadn't really been interested in giving a mini lesson in yoga, but Trudy Wyler had sounded so stressed when she called that he'd relented. He slowly raised his left leg behind him, focusing all his energy on holding his leg straight while he lowered his upper body until it was parallel to the floor. His right leg trembled a little as it strained to support the weight of his body. He stayed focused and stared straight ahead at Trudy as she mirrored his movements.

"That's it, Trudy," Christian encouraged softly. "You're doing it. Reach forward with your arms as you come down. It will help maintain your balance."

"I feel like Supergirl," Trudy said. "Do I look like I'm flying?"

"Yes," Christian said, trying to be patient with his client. She wasn't focusing and kept cracking jokes, which he found annoying. Why was he bothering with this session if she wasn't going to take anything seriously? "Now we'll move into the Warrior Pose. Slowly bring yourself back to a standing position. Yes. Now take a step forward with your left foot. Good. Lean into it with your arms outstretched. Great. Inhale and feel your chest expand. Air is very important in yoga. Oxygen is important to the body and spirit. Fallen leaves don't move on their own. The wind moves them."

"Christian, you are the wind beneath my wings," Trudy quipped.

"That's wonderful," Christian said dryly.

With Trudy still mirroring his movements, Christian sat on a mat with his limbs twisted and extended in directions that would have made him a hit at the circus. Or maybe at an orgy. He fixed his eyes on a point on the wall directly in front of him and tried to clear his mind of big tops and sex parties.

Trudy giggled loudly as she attempted to fold her legs over each other. Her foot kept slipping off her thigh no matter how hard she struggled to keep it there. She finally threw up her hands in a gesture of defeat and said, "I know this is supposed to help me relax, but it's stressing me out so much that I can't do it."

"You don't seem stressed out to me," Christian said. "When you got here, you were ready to quit your job at the factory. Now you're giggling like a ten-year-old at recess. Which do you prefer?"

Trudy lay back on her mat and stared at the ceiling as she said, "You're right, as usual. I'm just tired of the same thing over and over. Go to work. Manage my team. Take the heat from my bosses when we don't make our quotas. Go home. Manage my home. Take the heat from my husband when dinner's late and the kids haven't done their homework."

"You need to delegate at home as much as you do at work," Christian said carefully.

Trudy quickly sat up and said, "Oh, no. Fred helps out all the time. He's great. Sometimes I just think about the choices I made and wonder if I did the right thing. Does that make any sense? Do you do that?"

Of course not! Christian wanted to say, but it would have been a lie. Whenever he allowed himself to slow down, he questioned his decision to remain in Indiana. He'd been so tired of moving with his mother to whatever place appealed to her artistic sensibilities. She'd been enamored with the sparse and flat expanses of the Midwestern landscape, which was how they'd ended up in Terre Haute. But after drawing her inspiration from that environment for a few years, she'd begun to miss the buzz and crackle of big city living as she'd experienced it in New York, Boston, and London. About the same time that she'd succumbed to her desire to return to urban life, Christian had decided to stop living at the mercy of his mother's whims.

He still remembered the hollow feeling in the pit of his stomach on the day he waved goodbye when her cab pulled away from the old farmhouse they'd shared for three years. Only a few hours later, the moving van had followed in her wake. By the end of that week, a new family was in the farmhouse, and Christian was settling into his apartment in the Galaxy Building.

He'd been determined to make a life and a name for himself. Nothing had turned out the way he'd envisioned it on that day, but as he always told his clients, "You can't control everything, but you can adapt and benefit from what the world has to offer."

Trudy jerked him back to the present when she hopped up and said, "Look at the time. I've got to pick up my youngest from practice in fifteen minutes. How much am I paying you?"

Christian told her the amount and followed her into the dining room, where she'd left her purse. He dropped two beginning yoga tapes into her bag and urged her to find some quiet time alone to practice the poses. "I promise you it'll help you relax. Better yet, make it a family activity some weekend. This is something you could all do together for fun."

"That's a nice theory. You obviously don't have teenagers," Trudy said wryly as she handed Christian a check. "Besides, I'm in the middle of redecorating the family room. Nobody's going to relax until I'm done with that project." She glanced around. "I wish I'd asked you to help me. I love the colors in here. And this table is great."

It was a beautiful room, decorated to perfection with deep-wine-colored walls, a small crystal chandelier, and tasteful prints. But he'd never used it for entertaining. The mahogany dining table had become the place where he spread out calendars, plans, workshop syllabi, and even fabric swatches and catalogs for his clients.

Trudy continued to gush about how much she loved his sense of style and color as they walked back through the apartment. He looked around and tried to see it objectively. His living room was spacious, with high ceilings and large windows that provided a view of the distant airfield. It had been the view that made him choose the apartment. He loved watching planes land and take off, sometimes wishing he was on one headed somewhere.

Trudy babbled on, asking where he'd gotten the Eames chair and the large, intricately woven wire sculpture. He explained that it was from an artist who was a family friend. Trudy stopped at a large painting on one of the walls. She stared at it for a moment before saying, "This is incredible. Did you do this?"

"No," Christian answered. Although it was his personal favorite of his mother's work, it was also a constant reminder that he was in her artistic shadow. A red barn and white farmhouse were set in an expansive wheat field. In the center of the field, a skyscraper towered over an adjoining parking lot. The sky was the color of peach flesh.

It was a painting that he'd been part of from beginning to end. He'd played apprentice to his mother, fetching paint and linseed oil, cleaning her brushes, and offering suggestions. She'd taken the time to explain her technique, how she replicated the light at sunset on the side of the skyscraper or thinned paints to let the base coats show through. He'd witnessed the whole process, and when she put the paintbrush down after the final stroke, he was in complete awe. His mother had watched him as he regarded the piece, finally saying, "This one is for you." She was quick to add, "After the exhibit is over."

Once Trudy had left, Christian wished that it was as easy to peel off his memories as his yoga attire, or that disappointments could swirl down the drain with the lather he rinsed from his hair. He laughed ruefully at the realization that he needed to attend one of his own "Don't Look Back" seminars. Funny how much easier it was to dole out advice to other people.

While he shaved, he checked out his abs as the towel slowly inched its way down from his waist. Even when yoga failed to discipline his mind, at least it kept his body toned. He tried to remember the last time he'd been on a date, or at least the last time he'd had sex, and frowned. It wasn't possible that his schedule was that busy, but he drew a blank. Had it been two months? Four? It was pathetic that nothing came to mind. Yoga notwithstanding, maybe it was time to get *out* of focus. Or at least out of his apartment for a reason other than work.

He finished styling his hair, wishing he could make it look like Davii did, then went into his bedroom to dress. He chose a green turtleneck sweater, noting the striking way it contrasted with his auburn hair. After he finished dressing, he did a final mirror check, happy with the brown boots he'd recently bought at Drayden's and with his weathered jeans. He looked good enough for a night out in the mall.

Just before he left, he surveyed his bedroom. Unlike the rest of the apartment, it was a horror show of disorganization and clutter. The far wall was stacked halfway to the ceiling with shoeboxes. Shirts and pants were strewn across the floor as if they should have chalk outlines around them, and socks were flung over the arms of the overstuffed chair in the corner. The only positive thing about the room was that the bed was made.

"If I were my own client," he said aloud, "I'd point out how this bedroom clearly indicates that I don't plan to bring home a date any time in the near future."

A few minutes later, he slid onto a stool at the Jupiter Lounge and smiled at the bartender, whom he didn't recognize. She flicked her long brown hair behind her shoulder, affording him a bold view of her plunging neckline, then leaned across the bar and said, "What can I get for you tonight?"

"Something sweet?" he suggested.

"Daiquiri? Bellini?"

"Sex on the Beach?" he asked.

"Too bad we're landlocked," she said, rolling her eyes to let him know that she'd heard his line many times before.

Suitably admonished, he said, "Dirty martini, please." He reclined on his bar stool as he surveyed the room. Anyone he found even mildly attractive was engaged in conversation with someone equally attractive. They all looked like matched sets, and they all seemed years younger than he was. Even though he was barely twenty-five, his most serious relationship, which had lasted only a year, had been over for a long time.

The bartender actually reminded him of Aline, a French woman who'd worked as a paralegal for one of Christian's first clients. He still had canvases he'd painted of Aline tucked away in the closet of his extra bedroom: Aline sitting naked on the bed in his apartment; draped with a silk sheet in the garden of the vacation house they'd rented by Lake Michigan; smoking her Gauloise cigarettes. When he wasn't painting his lover, Christian had worked on a series of paintings that mixed abstraction with realism. He'd been proud of them but was disappointed by the reaction they elicited from Aline.

"Christian," she'd said, drawing out the *n* with her accent, "I can see so much of your mother in these." Christian realized later that it was meant to be a compliment, but at the time it had bruised his ego. It was the beginning of the end of their relationship.

"He's dressed as if he's on the prowl, but he can't get his job off his mind. He thought maybe a drink would help, but he's barely touched it."

Christian spun around, glad that his thoughts had been interrupted, and said, "Derek! Good to see you."

"You, too," Derek said with a big smile. "Which desperate client are you scheming to save now?"

"I'm having a client-free night," Christian vowed. He became aware of a commotion in the mall outside the bar and said, "What's going on out there?"

"It's Miss Indiana," Derek said. "She's posing for a twenty-dollar donation."

"For a photograph?" Christian asked.

"No. For twenty dollars, you get to sketch her. The donation goes to breast cancer research. At some point, the drawings are going to be auctioned to raise more money."

"That must be the group Emily-Anne Barrister is chairing," Christian said. "I'm actually helping her organize that event, although I don't know all the details yet."

"You want to check it out?"

"Sure," Christian said, finishing his martini and following Derek outside the Jupiter Lounge. He smiled, looking around at all the people seated at easels who stared intently at the wholesomely stunning Miss Indiana while they tried to draw her. It reminded him of a trip he'd taken to New Orleans and the artists in Jackson Square. "Let's do it."

"Forget it," Derek said. "I can't draw."

"Anybody can draw," Christian argued. "Besides, who cares what it looks like? It's for a good cause."

With a shrug of resignation, Derek reached into his pocket, and within minutes they were seated at easels on opposite sides of Miss Indiana. Christian began with the intention of doing only a quick sketch, but he became absorbed by the woman's beautiful face as she smiled a little shyly at the would-be artists around her. He'd completely lost track of time when he heard Derek's voice behind him.

"Okay, my sketch must be burned immediately and never spoken of again," Derek said. Christian turned around to see Derek's eyes fixed on his drawing. "You told me that your mother is an artist. You never said you are," Derek griped.

Christian blushed and said, "I'm not. This is just—"

"Humiliating beyond all belief," Derek said, holding up his sketch for Christian's perusal.

After a minute, Christian gently said, "You are definitely a better shoe salesman than an artist."

"That's the lamest attempt at a compliment I've ever heard," Derek complained. When he saw Christian's abashed expression, he burst out laughing and said, "There's no way I'm signing this."

"Oh, you have to," Christian insisted. "Remember, it's for—"

"A good cause, I know," Derek said, rolling his eyes. He grabbed Christian's sketch pencil and signed the sketch "Derek 'Picasso' Anderson" with a huge flourish. Christian cracked up when Derek added, beneath his name in block letters, "AGE THREE."

After Christian signed and turned in his own sketch, he said, "It's not that late. Do you feel like going back to my place? I can throw a pizza in the oven or something."

"Sure," Derek said. He maintained a running commentary on the people around them as they walked toward the Galaxy Building, stopping only once to stare at a suit in the window of Mercury Man. "Help me before I charge again," he moaned.

Christian grabbed his arm and dragged him away from the store, saying, "You don't need another suit. Although I must admit, your taste in clothes is impeccable."

"Thanks. I had some guidance picking out my suits, though. Had I known you before, I might have hired you to help me."

"I'm glad you didn't, because I usually don't consider my clients for any relationship beyond business," Christian said. They were quiet in the elevator. Then, as Christian ushered Derek into his apartment, he asked, "Would you like the grand tour?"

"Absolutely," Derek said. "This is the biggest apartment I've seen in this building."

"The ones on the lower floors were too small for me. Rumor has it that the penthouse is spectacular. I have no idea who lives there, though."

Christian led Derek through the apartment. Derek seemed to like the view as much as he did, and his eyes grew wide when he turned to face the paintings on the opposite wall.

"Wow, that's a huge print," Derek said, pointing to the painting of the skyscraper in the field. "I think I saw the original at the Whitney Museum in New York."

"Probably. I loaned it to them for their Patricia Mercer exhibit," Christian said.

After a pause, Derek said, "It's official. I have absolutely no cultural credibility at all. I can't draw, and I can't tell a painting from a print. Nor did I connect that painting to your mother. Does that window open? Can I hurl myself through it?"

"No," Christian said. "I mean, it opens, but I can't eat a whole pizza by myself, so you'll have to stay alive long enough to help me."

"What about that one?" Derek asked, pointing at a small abstract portrait of a naked man. "Is that your mother's, too?"

"No," Christian said and turned Derek toward the back of the apartment.

"It's yours, isn't it?" Derek demanded, looking over his shoulder. "It's excellent."

"Actually, I do have a work in progress," Christian said, pushing him down the hall to the room that doubled as his office and his studio. Derek waited while he moved some training materials out of the way and uncovered a pastel he'd been working on.

"That white dog is kind of scary," Derek said with a semi-horrified look on his face.

"Who, Perky? That's Emily-Anne's dog. The eyes do look slightly alien. The other dog is Jitters. I've only met them once, but she dotes on them like they're children. I thought giving her a drawing of them would be a nice way to cement our new relationship." Christian paused, then said, "I guess that leaves the kitchen."

"What about the bedroom?" Derek asked, then he blushed, biting his lip. "I mean, you haven't shown me your bedroom."

"If you think that dog is scary, you'll be terrified by my bedroom."

"I doubt it," Derek said.

With a resigned sigh, Christian led Derek to the bedroom and opened the door. Derek stumbled over a stray shoe but caught himself on the edge of the bed and sat down to survey the room. He looked up at Christian, who remained standing by the door.

"I told you, it's a mess."

"My room gets much worse than this. Do you think you have enough shoes?"

"I can never have enough shoes. Just call me Imelda Mercer." Christian mentally kicked himself for such a feeble joke, even though Derek laughed.

Derek drummed his fingers on top of the comforter. He finally pointed to the corner of the room where Christian kept his yoga mat and accessories, and asked, "What's all that for?"

"Yoga. I've been going for about two years now. You should come to class with me sometime as a guest. The yoga studio is on the Stars level."

"So you must be pretty flexible?" Derek asked.

"After the first year, I was able to do splits and put my legs behind my head."

"I'd love to see that!" Derek yelped.

"I'm going next Tuesday, if you'd like to join me."

Christian saw a bewildered look flicker over Derek's face. He wondered if Derek thought he was trying to recruit him into some strange yoga cult. Embarrassed, he turned and headed for the kitchen. After a few moments, Derek joined him, sitting on a stool and talking about his co-workers while Christian baked the pizza and prepared salads for them.

While they were eating, Christian described some of his clients until Derek abruptly asked, "Are you happy with what you're doing?" Derek blushed. "That sounded rude. I asked because I feel like I'm in the wrong job, but I don't know what I want to do."

"Sort of like an interim job," Christian said with understanding. "I feel that way, too, sometimes. When I was younger, I wanted to be an artist, but that's my mother's job. What about your parents? Do you get along with them?"

"They're great," Derek said. "They pushed me hard when I was in college, but they take a philosophical approach to my job at Drayden's. My father says that I can turn any experience to my advantage in the future. I love living and working at the mall because it gives me a chance to study a large cross section of people."

"What do you plan to do with that information?" Christian asked. His work with his clients had taught him that it was better to let people discover what they wanted for themselves, although it didn't hurt to give them an occasional nudge. Since he was more interested in having Derek as a friend than a client, he tried to determine an approach that would give Derek insight without crossing boundaries.

Instead of answering, Derek asked, "Do you mind if I use your bathroom?" Christian directed him down the hall and stood up to start loading the dishwasher when he heard Derek exclaim, "Jesus!"

Christian flinched, hoping he hadn't forgotten to flush or something, then he hurried down the hall to see Derek staring around him with his mouth open. Christian didn't see anything amiss and said, "What?"

"This," Derek said, waving his arms.

Christian frowned and said, "The wallpaper? The towels? What?"

"You have three different eye creams. Four different shaving gels." Derek paused, still gaping. "I feel like I just stumbled into homo heaven."

"I guess it is excessive," Christian said, a little surprised by Derek's choice of words.

Derek shook his head and said, "It's not how much you've got. It's the total absence of brand loyalty. Kiehl's. Aveda. Phyto. Redken. Biotherm. Clarins. Clinique. Paul Mitchell. Is that more shampoo back there? Who knew you had such product promiscuity? Have you no shame?"

"I like variety," Christian said defensively.

"Oh, yeah?" Derek asked, grinning as he turned his head and met Christian's eyes. Christian suddenly realized that their faces were uncomfortably close, and he stepped back. Derek frowned and said, "Do you have a boyfriend or something?"

"No," Christian said. "I mean . . . I guess it might be easier to get one if I were gay."

"Oh, God, I'm sorry," Derek said, looking mortified.

"It's okay. I'm learning to deal with it," Christian said and laughed.

"I meant that I'm sorry I assumed."

"The funny thing is, until you started your tirade about my grooming products, I thought you were straight." After a moment, he realized he sounded rude and added, "Not that it makes a difference."

"I guess that explains why you didn't respond to my less-than-subtle advances. I was beginning to think I had bad breath or something."

"I've got something for that," Christian said reassuringly.

"About ten somethings, no doubt," Derek said. "However, I really only need to pee." When Christian didn't move, he added, "Alone would be better."

"Suddenly I'm the most inept host on the planet," Christian moaned, backing out of the bathroom.

"In the Universe, actually," Derek quipped just before Christian closed the door.

Christian went back to the kitchen, rolling his eyes at how tactlessly he'd handled their exchange and how clueless he'd been about picking up Derek's signals.

Derek came back to the kitchen, saying, "Let's get this straight. So to speak. You didn't know I was gay—"

"And you didn't know I was straight," Christian said. "I'm sorry if I misled you."

"No, I'm sorry. I've fallen prey to stereotypical thinking. I mean, you've got great hair, a thousand pairs of shoes, original art, and enough personal products to stock your own shop. Not to mention that you seem to have a complicated relationship with your mother, and you don't have a girlfriend. Plus, and I don't mean this in a bad way, you're kind of a flirt."

Embarrassed and hoping to shift the focus back to Derek, Christian asked, "Do you have a boyfriend?"

"I do," Derek said. He seemed uncomfortable. "He's a great person, but . . ."

When Derek didn't finish his sentence, Christian said, "What does he do?"

"He works at the Congreve."

"I wonder if I know him. I use their conference rooms for my seminars."

"It's nearly midnight?" Derek asked abruptly. "I have to open tomorrow. Thanks for dinner. And for the company. I had a good time."

It wasn't a subtle evasion, but it was effective, and Christian suppressed his smile as he walked Derek to the door, saying, "You're welcome. I'm serious about yoga. Once you empty your mind, you can get a fresh perspective on things."

"My sketch of Miss Indiana is ample proof that perspective is not one of my strengths," Derek said. "But I think I've mastered the empty head."

12

I Got a Brand New Pair of Roller Skates

Happiness radiated through Derek when Hunter wrapped his strong arms around him and said, "How could you doubt the way I feel? I love you. I honestly love you." Derek's eyes closed as Hunter kissed him; when he opened them, he looked with confusion at the empty pillow next to his.

Awareness arrived with a thud that seemed to land somewhere in the vicinity of his stomach. He'd been dreaming, and Olivia Newton-John was warbling at him from his clock radio. A violent toss of the extra pillow sent her sailing from his dresser to the floor, cutting her off mid-anguished note.

"Are you okay in there?" he heard Juanita call from outside his door.

"Couldn't be better," he yelled back, then turned over and buried his face in his pillow, wishing he could go anywhere but Drayden's.

After a minute, he remembered that it was his day off. He hadn't set the alarm because of work. He was supposed to see Davii to get his hair trimmed again. The appointment had made him happy when he'd scheduled it, but his residual embarrassment over misreading Christian had left him leery. He no longer trusted his ability to judge Davii's signals correctly.

He'd been out of the dating pool too long. Even in the days before Hunter, his dates had been casual, almost accidental. The whole idea of asking someone out, figuring out what to wear, deciding where to go, and actually going through with it seemed daunting. He was ready to give up the idea before he even got to step one.

Besides, dating was for the single. He was still part of a bihemispheric couple. He rolled his eyes, knowing that he was using Hunter as an excuse. He certainly hadn't agonized over his decision to go to Christian's apartment after their chance meeting in the Jupiter Lounge. But Christian had been so hot. He'd also been so straight.

He thought about Christian for a while to the comforting sound of the vacuum cleaner. Derek's interest had been bolstered on the day that Christian brought Emily-Anne Barrister to Drayden's. He and Christian had worked well together as they indulged Emily-Anne's tendency to overspend, and Derek had appreciated the way Christian cut Natasha down to size. But his assumptions about Christian's motives had proved to be inaccurate. They were clearly destined to be friends, not lovers. That was fine; he needed friends.

Which brought his thoughts back to Davii. Because he'd spent a lot of time with Vienna and Davii, he thought of Davii as a friend who he didn't want to lose to a failed romance. But if Davii was interested, it wouldn't hurt to attempt a date. At least he knew Davii wouldn't humiliate him with a sudden declaration of heterosexuality.

But what would they do on a date? He supposed they could go to dinner. The mall had several nice restaurants. He imagined sitting with Davii at a linen-covered table, bathed in the warm glow of candlelight. Davii wouldn't be like Hunter, removing the menu from Derek's hands and saying he'd order for both of them so Derek wouldn't end up with a cheeseburger. Which was so unfair. Derek had never been reluctant to try any of Hunter's suggestions or embark on culinary adventures of his own.

He remembered his first taste of steamed crabs at a restaurant on the Inner Harbor in Baltimore. Hunter had taught him how to pick and hammer the crabs, both men laughing at the mess they made of the table and themselves. It had been so much work that Derek had felt justified in ordering two desserts, and Hunter had sat back with his after-dinner drink and cigarette, shaking his head at how much Derek could eat. Later, they'd taken a walk along the harbor, finally going back to their hotel room . . .

But he wasn't thinking about Hunter and the past. He was thinking about Davii. Unfortunately, there wasn't a good restaurant in the mall that he hadn't been to with Hunter. There would be a ghost at their table. Dinner was out.

They could always go to a movie, something he and Hunter rarely did. Movies were nice first dates, because you didn't have to make conversation until afterward, and then you could talk about the movie when there was a lull. If he and Davii were so inclined, they could hold hands in the darkened theater. It had been a long time since he'd held hands with anyone, and he remembered it as being sweet and sexy.

He wondered what kind of movies Davii liked. Derek always picked the movies that he and Hunter watched, and if he selected anything romantic, Hunter would usually end up dozing on the sofa, with his feet in Derek's lap. It took suspense or humor to keep Hunter awake . . .

"Argh!" Derek shouted, sitting up in bed. Why did everything always end up being about Hunter?

He hurried to the bathroom to get ready for his appointment, grimacing at the sight of his bed head in the mirror. At least if they woke up together some morning, Davii was already familiar with his difficult hair.

By the time he was ready to leave, Juanita was sitting near the door, doing something with a screwdriver and the vacuum cleaner cord. She watched him grab his cell phone and key, then said, "You're not starting your day with breakfast?"

"No time," Derek said. "I have an appointment to get my hair cut."

"Again?" Juanita asked, staring at his head with a small frown. Derek wondered if he'd overlooked the big red *A* tattooed on his forehead.

"I have to do it more often with this new style," Derek said. "Or else I'm all cowlicks."

"It seems strange that you spent all that time with hairspray and the hair dryer when you're about to get it cut," Juanita commented.

"I don't use hairspray," Derek said and quickly added, "What's that you're doing to the vacuum cleaner?"

"It needed a new plug," Juanita said.

"Couldn't maintenance—"

"I can do it faster," she said.

"I wish I was as self-sufficient as you are," he said, hoping flattery would erase her scowl.

"That can be highly overrated," she answered.

"Gotta run," he said. "If I don't see you later, have a great weekend!"

What is it with women, he wondered while he waited for the elevator. Vienna seemed to know everything about his personal life. Sheree could tell when his heart was aching. Natasha apparently anticipated every mistake he was going to make at work, since she was always there, ready to point them out. And Juanita treated a simple visit to a salon as an assignation.

He inhaled when he stepped inside CosmicTology. The scent wasn't overpowering; apparently no one was getting a perm. The music was still too loud and muffled everyone's conversations. As a kid, he'd spent many Saturday afternoons at the beauty shop with his mother. He would color quietly or pretend to read magazines, and the women would forget he was there. He heard a lot of good dirt that way. Not to mention it had left him nearly qualified to be an OB/GYN. That had served his gal pals well in high school, since he could tell them things their mothers were too embarrassed to discuss.

As Derek stepped up to the counter, Davii looked over from several stations back, where he was combing someone out, and called, "I'll be with you in a minute, Derek."

"Thanks," Derek said.

One of the shampoo girls started toward him, and Davii said, "That's okay, Marcy. I'll take care of this one."

He figured Davii was trying to spare him the expense of tipping her, but when they went to the shampoo area, Davii whispered, "Marcy is the worst. She's all about the shampoo, and there's so much more to it than that."

As Davii went to work on him, Derek understood what he meant. Davii took his time, massaging deeply into Derek's neck muscles. It felt wonderful, and Derek melted under his hands. Then Davii lightly rubbed his ears and scalp instead of just slapping on conditioner and sending him on his way.

"I could fall asleep," Derek said. "Why didn't you do this last time?"

"The other shampoo girls don't appreciate me taking their business," Davii said. "Marcy's lazy, so she doesn't care."

When they went to Davii's chair, Derek felt soothed and relaxed, in spite of the nagging voice in his head that kept saying, *What are you waiting for? Just ask him.*

Davii stood behind Derek and began playing with his hair. He stared into the mirror and said to Derek's reflection, "This is where I'm supposed to ask you about your love life. If you're seeing anyone special. But I guess I already know the answer to that. Is Hunter still in Australia?"

"Shouldn't this be the moment you ask what sort of haircut I'd like?"

"Don't be ridiculous," Davii said. He began combing Derek's wet hair and snipping haphazardly. "So the cat's still away, huh? Are you being a good little mouse?"

Derek squinted at the mirror, eyeing Davii suspiciously as he said, "Why do you ask?"

"You sound guilty."

"Me? I've done nothing. Hey, what song is this? I like it."

"So that's how it is," Davii said. He dropped his scissors on top of his supply cart and withdrew an electric razor. Flipping the switch, he put Derek in a headlock and said, "We have ways of making you talk."

"Okay!" Derek yelped. Davii laughed and let go. As he put away the razor, Derek could still smell the scent of Davii's skin. It made him feel light-headed. He reasoned that could be caused by skipping breakfast. "Maybe you should shave my head after all. I'm a bit wary of coming off like an idiot in this story."

"What you perceive as idiotic I might find absolutely charming," Davii said.

"It's too embarrassing," Derek said. Davii's expression made it clear that until he got details, he wasn't proceeding with the haircut. Derek sighed and told him about the unplanned meeting at the Jupiter Lounge that had led to an invitation to Christian's apartment.

"What's it like?" Davii asked.

"Big," Derek said.

"I meant the apartment," Davii said with a grin.

"Trust me, the apartment's the only thing I can describe," Derek said. "It was interesting. Christian's a man who tells people how to organize their lives, yet his bedroom is in complete disorder."

"Really?" Davii asked. "I had him figured as one of those men who color-coordinates his closet and puts cedar inserts in his sock drawers. You know the type."

Derek frowned and said, "How do you know him, anyway?"

"I cut his hair. Keep talking."

"The living spaces and kitchen are fine. But his bedroom and the room he uses for his office are total chaos. That's another thing. For someone who provides advice on career planning and advancement, he's obviously not doing what he's meant to." Davii's expression was thoughtful as Derek told him about Christian's Miss Indiana sketch, the painting of the male nude, and his drawing of Emily-Anne's dogs. "He's very gifted. I guess Vienna would say his refusal to paint has something to do with his mother." Derek stopped talking and made a little whimpering noise.

"Now what?" Davii asked.

"I mistook a famous painting—by his mother—for a print."

"You couldn't tell the difference between a painting and a print? Do you need glasses?"

"The lighting was subdued," Derek said, defending himself. "As you'd expect for a seduction scene."

"Yeah, let's get to the hot stuff," Davii demanded.

"There was a lot of playful flirtation, a few jokes about the limbering effects of yoga—"

"How flexible is he?" Davii asked in a lascivious tone.

"I never found out. He's straight."

Davii tried not to laugh, but he obviously couldn't help himself. "Poor Derek. Those metrosexuals make the dating world so tricky."

"I told you I come off like an idiot in this story," Derek lamented.

"I think it's charming," Davii said. "Don't ask me why."

After a pause, Derek asked, "Why?"

"I told you not to ask me that," Davii admonished, giving Derek's head a playful shove. When Derek rolled his eyes, Davii said, "It's kind of sweet that you put yourself out there like that. At the mercy of the object of your affection. It's so tragic in a *Pretty in Pink* kind of way. Or am I thinking of *Sixteen Candles*? Anyway, it sounds like a real Molly Ringwald moment."

Derek and Davii locked eyes in the mirror and said simultaneously, "Jake Ryan."

"See? I knew I could make you forget about what's-his-name," Davii said. "I just wish I'd known you were carrying a torch for him so I could've set you straight. So to speak."

"You knew Christian was straight?" Derek exclaimed. "Why didn't Vienna tell me?"

"We don't tell each other everything! She probably doesn't even know he's my client," Davii explained. "Now you know that she's not the only one who's got the goods on the people in this mall. Next time you have a rampant crush on someone, come to me."

"I'll try to remember that," Derek said.

"Or just come to me," Davii said. "My last appointment's at six."

Derek wondered what he meant. Was it the prelude to asking for a date? He took a deep breath and said, "Are you asking me out?"

Davii said, "Yeah. I know I'm not straight—"

"Stop!" Derek pleaded, completely embarrassed. "I'm serious."

"So am I," Davii said. "I think there's a dog show at the Hulman Center. That might be fun."

"Neither of us has a car," Derek reminded him. "I mean, I could have a Congreve car—"

"No, you're right," Davii said, cutting him off. Maybe he, like Derek, thought it was in bad taste to use the Congreve to help Derek cheat on its owner. "Something closer to home. Do you bowl?"

"I'm actually pretty good," Derek said. "In high school—"

"I'm lousy, so that's out. What about skating?"

"I'm not very good," Derek said.

"The roller rink it is," Davii said with a malicious grin. "See, *I'm* good at that."

When Davii leaned against him to reach for his electric clippers, Derek was sure Davii knew that his goods were parked firmly against Derek's biceps, as if giving a preview of coming attractions. Derek could already tell it was going to be much better than any movie he would have picked out.

"Tonight at eight at the Launch Pad," Derek said agreeably, then added, "I can't wait to check out your payload."

One of Davii's eyebrows shot up, and he said, "Don't forget to bring your rocket."

"Liftoff!" Derek said.

"I gotta get out of this mall," Davii said. "The double entendres are killing me."

Derek left Davii's tip with the woman at the counter when he paid. He couldn't figure out the etiquette of tipping someone with whom he'd be on a date in a few hours. Then he went to Diesel, where he was checking out his butt in a pair of jeans when his cell phone rang. He looked at the display, rolled his eyes, and answered, "Already?"

"I'm sure I don't know what you're talking about," Vienna said. "But you work fast, honey."

"You work faster. Did he call you?"

"Actually, I called him, and he told me. I thought I'd warn you. The boy can skate."

"So I've heard. We all have our talents."

"I didn't tell him, so I'm telling you; I'll be out very late tonight," Vienna said. "Just in case."

"It's only a first date."

"Right. I'd better call first before I come home. Have fun." She hung up.

Derek's euphoria at having an actual date carried him through the rest of the day. He avoided his computer. The last thing he needed was another e-mail from Hunter that would make him feel like crap.

But his timing was off, and he found himself dressed way too early in his new jeans and a black crewneck sweater that made him look more buff than he was. He fidgeted. Times like these made him wish he smoked. He checked his reflection for the hundredth time, then he couldn't avoid the darkly beckoning gaze of his monitor any longer. He powered on the computer.

> *Derek,*
> *Sorry I've been out of touch. I went on a three-day dive trip. Oh, God, Derek, it was amazing. I can't do it justice with words. I kept looking to my right, as if you were there next to me, wanting you to see what I was seeing. You have to take diving lessons. You have to see this for yourself one day. But if your boss has soured you on swimming with the great whites and you must stay on the beaches, there's plenty to enjoy there. Sydney has the hottest men in the world. G'day—Hunter*

Don't think about it, Derek warned himself. *He's not doing anything you aren't doing. Let it go. Don't let it spoil your night.*

It was Hunter's contradictions that left Derek reeling. He couldn't just leave it at the hint of I-wish-you-were-here. He had to add the part about the great men. Hunter gave and he took away all in one paragraph.

"Fuck him," Derek said. "I'm tired of this cycle."

His spirits lifted when he saw Davii outside the Launch Pad. He was wearing the same jeans as Derek, and they eyed each other and laughed. At least Davii's sweater was navy instead of black, but they still looked like a somewhat mismatched pair of twins. Davii was definitely hotter.

"You look so handsome," Davii said with a smile.

"Of course you'd say that. I look like I dressed out of your closet."

"Babe, trust me. Clothes don't always make the man. You'd look good in—" Davii glanced around until his eyes fell on a middle-aged man wearing a plaid shirt in neon colors and a pair of brown Sansabelt slacks, and he finished, "—that."

"Thank you. I think," Derek said, and Davii gently shoved him toward the entrance of the roller rink. He tried to pay, but Davii wouldn't let him.

"You can pay next time. Let's get our skates."

As promised, Davii was a skating fiend. He was all over the place with gravity-defying smoothness an ice-skater would have envied. Derek didn't care. He was content to roll along the perimeter with the parents, gazing with fondness at Davii just as they stared at their daring children. He flinched as he maneuvered around Sansabelt Man. At least he wasn't a threat to other skaters.

While he watched Davii, Derek had the uncomfortable realization that his date reminded him of Hunter. They both had a natural athletic grace that was a pleasure to look at. The most enjoyable part of the circuit parties Derek had gone to with Hunter had been the dancing. Derek and Hunter both loved to dance, and Derek often thought it was the one thing that let Hunter forget everything but his joy in the moment. They'd be on the floor among hundreds of beautiful, gleaming men, and Derek couldn't tear his gaze from Hunter, who flirted and teased Derek with his body and his eyes. When other men would touch either of them, Hunter would just smile, until finally he'd reach for Derek and slowly pull him closer. Their first kiss would seem to last until they were back in their bed, gorging themselves on each other's scents and tastes in moments of sweaty passion.

Derek shook off the image, reminding himself of how distant Hunter was off the dance floor. Although, he couldn't say it was a physical distance. Hunter had never given a damn what anybody thought, probably because he'd grown up feeling entitled to the world's approval. If he wanted to drape an arm over Derek's shoulders, kiss him hello, or pull out a chair for him, he just did it, no matter where they were.

As Derek watched Davii wind his way through couples, he knew he'd been spoiled. Middle America was not a place where two men could dance together, or even skate together, without fear. So his eyes widened when Davii skated toward him with an outstretched hand.

"Come on," Davii said.

"I can't," Derek said, darting a look around.

"You can," Davii said. "Just take my hand. I won't let you fall." Derek absolved himself of consequences and let Davii lead him to the center of the rink, blurring his eyes so he wouldn't be tempted to watch if dozens of straight people grabbed their children and fled the scene. "When you have the right partner," Davii said, "it all becomes so easy."

"Okay," Derek said, leaning into Davii's body when he felt Davii's arm slip around his waist.

When the song ended, Davii gave him a hug and said, "Told you. You're a natural."

"I think . . . I'm ready . . . to go," Derek said, looking at Davii's mouth.

"It's not good to just stop," Davii said, his breathing a little heavy. "We should cool down."

"We'll take the outside path to the Galaxy Building," Derek said.

Davii gave him a perplexed look and said, "Are you okay?" When Derek mutely nodded, Davii shrugged and said, "All right. Let's get our shoes." They didn't speak again until they stepped outside the mall, when Davii took a deep breath and said, "Do you ever get tired of being inside that bubble? Sometimes I feel like I'm suffocating."

Derek thought of the times he'd traveled with Hunter and how he always felt a little displaced until he was back in the Congreve. Before he could answer, he heard a voice behind them call, "Cocksuckers."

"Shit," he said and tried to walk faster, but Davii stopped short and turned around.

"Excuse me?" Davii asked.

Derek turned back and saw two teenaged boys getting closer.

They looked stupid and mean, and he softly said, "Davii, they have no necks. They look like offensive linemen. Keep walking."

"They're offensive, all right," Davii said, standing his ground. "I'm sorry. Were you speaking to us? I didn't quite catch what you said."

"Fucking fags," one of the boys said.

"You looked real pretty in the skating rink," the other one said. "We thought you might like to dance with us. Which one of you wants to be my girl?"

"Fuck you, asshole," Davii said, and Derek tensed as the boy lunged for Davii. Davii moved so fast that until the boy was bent double, gasping, Derek didn't realize what had happened. Davii was looking at the other boy and was poised to strike again. "Come on. Maybe you're tougher than your buddy."

"I can't breathe," the first boy gasped. "Get him, Billy."

"Fuck that," Billy said, backing away from Davii. "Let's get out of here."

"Good idea," Davii said. "I don't want to see either of you again unless you're getting those unibrows waxed." Davii watched alertly until Billy had helped his friend walk back inside the mall, then he relaxed and gave Derek a little smile.

"What the hell just happened?" Derek asked.

"Tae kwon do. Third-degree black belt," Davii said.

"Jesus, Davii. You're my hero."

"It was just a kick," Davii said with a shrug. "It's a simple move. Makes 'em feel like they've had the shit knocked out of them, but if done right, there's no permanent damage. Maybe a bruise. I could teach it to you in five minutes."

"I'd rather just swoon from fear," Derek said with a wary look. "You're scaring me."

"I wouldn't hurt you," Davii vowed.

"I think I love you," Derek said.

"Aw, don't be so easy. I haven't even shown you my original artwork and subdued lighting yet." He started giggling and said, "Sorry. Adrenaline. I'm kind of giddy."

"Come on, Bruce Lee. Let's get out of here before the bad guys come back with their friends."

Davii frowned and said, "Bruce Lee was jeet kun do."

"Well, I'm jeet kun don't," Derek said. "Let's go."

As they walked, Davii said, "I don't want you to get the wrong idea about martial arts. I'd never be aggressive toward anyone except in self-defense. It's about mastery of the self, not fighting. Fear is a natural reaction when threatened."

"Uh-huh, my natural reaction almost made me ruin my Diesel jeans," Derek said.

Davii laughed and said, "The fear is what you have to fight against. Not some redneck assholes who challenge you."

When they were safely inside Davii's apartment, Derek shook his head and said, "I could be in an emergency room right now."

"I think there's an emergency in my bedroom," Davii said in a helpful tone. Derek followed him there, watching while Davii lit some candles and turned on his stereo. When Davii lit a stick of incense, Derek sniffed the air with a pleased expression. "Nag champa," Davii said. "Preferred by eight out of ten action heroes." He patted the bed. "Get comfortable."

"I'm kind of dazzled by you right now," Derek said. "You might take unfair advantage of me."

"Only in self-defense, remember," Davii said, grinning at him. When Derek dropped on the bed next to him, Davii rolled onto his back and stretched out his hands, saying, "I'm wide open for attack. This is the perfect opportunity." Derek moved in close to him and lifted up his sweater a little bit. "Oh, somebody help me," Davii said. Derek laughed and leaned in to kiss Davii's stomach. Suddenly Davii yelped and drew his knees upward, knocking Derek in the head. "I'm sorry!" Davii said, sitting up to put his arms around Derek, who was holding his head and cursing. "I'm a little ticklish."

"You are? I didn't notice," Derek said sarcastically.

"Here, let me try to make it better," Davii said. He kissed Derek's temple carefully and gently. "How's that?"

"A little better," Derek said.

"What about this?" Davii asked, then kissed Derek's forehead.

"Much better," Derek murmured.

While Davii kissed Derek's other temple, Derek put his hands under Davii's sweater. Davii pulled back and raised his arms so Derek could remove the sweater. As he pulled the sweater over Davii's head, it got caught on Davii's earring. Davii said, "Hold on. Don't pull it—it's caught!"

After two minutes of untangling, Derek asked, "Are you okay?"

"I'm fine," Davii said, rubbing his ear.

Derek tossed both sweaters aside and looked longingly at Davii, who crept toward him on the bed. He rested his hands on Derek's thighs and moved in to kiss him. Unfortunately, Derek shifted his weight and they knocked their teeth hard as they kissed.

"Ow!" Derek exclaimed, putting his hand over his mouth. "Can we stop for a minute?"

They both rolled over on their backs and stared at the ceiling. Davii started laughing and said, "You don't need tae kwon do. Just try to kiss your attacker, and you'll be fine." When Derek didn't respond, he propped himself on his elbow. "Grasshopper, I sense a lack of confidence in your troubled soul. Admittedly, some of my insight has come from Vienna."

Derek frowned, uneasy with the thought of Vienna analyzing him behind his back, and said, "What was her theory?"

"Hunter Congreve," Davii said. "Vienna has worked all over this mall, and she's waited on him several times. I get the impression he's aloof, domineering, and full of himself."

"You've been misinformed," Derek said, wishing he didn't sound so prissy.

"Vienna's a pretty astute judge of character," Davii disagreed. "He sounds like the kind of person who'd tear you down."

Before he could stop himself, Derek said, "Not at all. Hunter and Vienna come from different worlds; she doesn't understand him. People take advantage of Hunter unless he keeps his distance. It's not his problem; it's theirs. As soon as they hear the Congreve name, people treat him differently. Mostly like he owes them something. It's hard for him to trust people when they're so eager to use him in some way."

"Excuse me, but I find it difficult to feel sorry for someone of the privileged class who whines about how tough he has it," Davii said.

"Hunter would never whine, and he's not the one who's saying this. He wouldn't, because he's probably never figured it out himself. It's the way *I* see him. He's *my* boyfriend; I think I know him better than Vienna does." Derek paused, then went on. "Why is this date suddenly going south? And not in a good way?"

Davii shook his head and said, "I think you just answered your own question. He's your boyfriend. So what are you doing with me?"

"I just—I don't know," Derek admitted. He desperately wanted to change the subject and looked at a pile of papers and magazines on the floor next to Davii's bed. "What's all that?"

Davii looked down and said, "Articles on salons in New York and L.A."

"Trying to get ideas?" Derek asked.

"Getting applications," Davii said. "I would love to move away from here."

"I didn't know that," Derek said.

"I'm sure you would if Vienna knew," Davii said. "I haven't talked about it to her. I mean, if nothing comes of it, why upset her?" He was quiet for a few seconds, then he said, "Vienna is really the only thing that keeps me here. I know she puts on a good act, but she's been through a lot. I told you about her divorce."

"Yes. She was pissed that I knew."

"I know. But underneath her tough exterior, Vienna can be a little fragile. She has some demons of her own to master. I don't think I could leave her hanging, even if it means I'm stuck here for a while."

"If you really feel like you're stuck here, I think Vienna would hate thinking she's holding you back," Derek said.

"I agree. That's why I don't talk about it. Besides, it's not forever. When the time is right, we'll both know it."

"I'll always be here," Derek said. "I can't protect her from the unibrows of the world, but I'd be the best friend I could to her."

Davii nodded thoughtfully, then said, "Do you listen to yourself, Derek?"

"Huh?"

"You're not going anywhere. You're in love with Hunter. Maybe you've got problems, but you're still very much in that relationship. You should forget pretty men like Christian, straight or gay, and skating hairdressers, and focus on your relationship. Even if Hunter screws it up, you won't be finished with it until you've given it your best effort."

"I guess I ruined the mood, didn't I?" Derek asked somberly.

"So we won't have hot man sex in here tonight. We'll always have that really hot kiss," Davii teased. "That doesn't mean I'm not glad you're here. Or that I want you to leave. We're friends. Maybe one day; who knows."

"But not this day." When Davii shook his head, Derek said, "That takes a certain pressure off. Let's make popcorn and watch a DVD or something."

"Thank God," Davii said. "I can put on my raggedy sweatpants. I think these jeans are a size too small. I wanted to show off my assets."

Derek nodded with understanding and said, "You wouldn't by chance have an extra pair of sweats?"

Davii laughed, hugged him, and said, "I can cover your assets, too."

13

Two Doors Down

Riley surveyed the Congreve lobby from the mezzanine and congratulated himself on what an asset he was to the hotel. They hadn't experienced any kind of crisis since Hunter's departure, confirmation that Riley knew what he was doing and that his boss's presence was unnecessary. Riley almost regretted not having to prove himself further by deftly handling an emergency, but he wasn't one to look a gift horse in the mouth. He was sure the lull would end all too soon. Besides, he'd kept himself busy with the matter of Natasha Deere.

People were amazingly simple if one took the trouble to watch them and do a little legwork. A few weeks before, while strolling through Drayden's to meet his contact, Craig, for lunch, Riley had witnessed Derek getting reamed by his manager. He faked an interest in a new fragrance so he could edge closer to the two of them, but he hadn't been able to overhear anything except Derek muttering that he was going on break. Riley noted that Natasha's jerky movements and twitches vanished as soon as Derek did. She was obviously one of those people who exhibited strong physical reactions to stress.

Riley had squelched the cologne queen who kept hitting on him and committed the Derek incident to memory, wondering if there was a way to use it to his advantage. Later, when Craig was ecstatically inhaling the dessert Riley had insisted he order, his careful interrogation began.

"Hey, I've been meaning to ask you. How's Derek Anderson working out?"

Craig rolled his eyes, swallowed, and said, "He's a good kid, but his sales are shit. He's lucky that he's gotten excellent customer service cards filled out for him, or I wouldn't be able to keep his manager from dumping him."

"He doesn't like Derek?" Riley asked cagily.

"She," Craig corrected. "As far as that goes, Natasha doesn't like anyone. But she does have the best Women's Shoes numbers of all the Midwestern stores, so she doesn't appreciate having a nonperformer thrust on her. I'm not sure how much longer I can protect him. I know you wanted me to help him out. There are more easygoing managers. I could probably get him transferred to a different department."

"What about a different store?"

"Any other store would look at his numbers and decline to hire him," Craig said, then smacked his lips over his last bit of chocolate sauce, making Riley's skin crawl.

Craig had really let himself go since he'd gotten a boyfriend, and Riley, who kept trim through rigid self-control and excessive smoking, thought Craig was being shortsighted. One day, he'd be on the market again, and he'd remember just how unforgiving buyers could be. He realized that Craig was watching him expectantly and said, "What?"

"You asked about a different store. Does Derek want to move?"

"Beats me. I don't know him that well. I was just doing a favor for my boss," Riley lied. He adopted a placating tone when he went on. "I don't want to cause you any trouble. Don't worry about it. Let the kid fail or succeed on his own. He has to learn how to deal with the Natalies of the world."

"Natasha," Craig corrected. "Trust me, there's only one Natasha Deere. The world couldn't handle another."

"Bitch, huh?"

"An epithet hasn't been written that can sum up Natasha. I don't know how she got hired by a warmhearted organization like Drayden's. Well, she knows how to butter up the brass, and she operates totally by the book. She'd never give anyone a reason to get rid of her. But she doesn't have a drop of human kindness in her veins."

"I've met a lot of people from the Northeast like that," Riley said, fishing.

"Northeast? She's from southern California. One of those spoiled Beverly Hills kids. She probably has to work for a living because her family disowned her. Although it's more likely she was raised by wolves."

Feeling smug at how well his conversation was paying off, Riley smoothly snatched the check from the waiter and said, "It's on me. The least I can do after sticking you with Derek."

"Thanks, Riley," Craig said. "Generous, as usual. Don't give the Derek thing another thought. I was happy to help you out."

Instead of returning to the hotel after their lunch, Riley had taken a walk through the mall. He needed to think, and there were too many interruptions at work. It was a fortunate choice, because as he strolled into the corridor that ended at Kohl's, he realized something was nagging for his attention. He rapidly looked around until his gaze fell on a woman walking in front of him.

Drag queen! was his instant thought. Long blond curls hanging from a hat; tiny, cinched-in waist of a dress that seemed to undulate because of its metallic, varicolored threads; flat ass; and four-inch stilettos. Most notably, the stilted walk was evidence of someone who wasn't at ease in those clothes.

Two thoughts struck him simultaneously. The few drag queens he'd known were more comfortable inside drag than in their regular clothes. And this person's crablike walk reminded him of Natasha Deere's jittery movements.

A man on a mission, he rushed past the woman, stopped, and pretended to look at the window display at Patti's Pages, then turned to let his eyes casually drift over her as she came his way. It took effort to suppress his gasp when he realized that, except for her height, and even partially concealed by sunglasses, the woman was a dead ringer for Dolly Parton.

So it was a female impersonator after all. Not a common sight in the mall, and certainly not someone who wanted to go unnoticed. Riley fell into step behind her, noting with amusement the double takes and widened eyes of the people who glanced "Dolly's" way. He wasn't sure why he kept following her, except that something didn't add up. If she didn't want to be noticed, why was she dressed so outrageously? But if she liked attention, why were her movements erratic, almost stealthy?

When she hesitated, Riley slowed down, wondering if she'd realized she was being followed. Then she slipped into Galileo's Glass and, after a few moments, Riley followed her. When he saw where she was sitting, his interest waned. A drag queen and a bit of rough trade, like a porn movie without the flesh.

Since he was already inside, he sat at the bar and ordered a drink, glancing back at the table just in time to see an exchange of paper bags. It was even less interesting than he'd thought—probably a drug transaction. He yawned, but before he could turn away, "Dolly" spun around, and Riley got a good look at her face before she put on her sunglasses. She was no drag queen. She was not only female, but he was convinced he was looking at Natasha Deere in disguise.

Riley didn't see how this information could help him in his quest to banish Derek Anderson, but it was intriguing. After Natasha left the bar, her companion called out to the bartender, asking if he could change the TV station to the game. It didn't sound like the man was planning to leave any time soon, so Riley made a quick decision.

A half hour and several credit card transactions later, Riley emerged from Kohl's wearing faded jeans and a distressed leather jacket over a white T-shirt. The clothes he'd changed out of were being delivered to the hotel, and Riley felt oddly vulnerable in his generic—and discounted—outfit. If his new getup was suitable for cruising, it would also blend in among the unsavory clientele in Galileo's Glass.

Rough Trade had moved to the bar, and Riley slid onto the stool next to him, ordering another drink and frowning when his neighbor's pistachio shell landed on his arm.

"Sorry, dude," Rough Trade said. When Riley stared pointedly at the pistachio shell, Rough Trade swiftly tapped it off his arm. "Nice jacket."

"Thanks," Riley said, then moved his gaze to the TV.

"Can you believe the score? This game sucks. I'm DeWitt."

More like DeWittless, Riley thought, but improvised, "My friends call me RB."

"So we're friends now, huh?" DeWitt asked, and Riley realized the man's arm was suddenly very close to his. Interesting.

"Weren't you in here with your girlfriend earlier?" he asked.

DeWitt looked confused for a minute, then said, “Oh, her? Hell, no.” He dropped his voice when he said, “I’m in the Brotherhood of the Machine.” When Riley gave him a blank look, he said, “Great Lakes Harley Riders?”

“Uh-huh,” Riley said. Not a group he was likely ever to book at the Congreve.

DeWitt sighed and said, “Gay. We’re gay men who own Harleys.”

“Ahhh,” Riley said. He realized that he’d been caught glancing at his companion’s long, oily hair when DeWitt whipped out a bandana and tied it around his head. Not great, but an improvement.

“It gets greasy when I ride,” DeWitt said apologetically. “So, you ever been on a Hog?”

Riley rapidly discarded a dozen sarcastic answers and replied, “No. Not my thing.”

“I wouldn’t mind checking out your thing,” DeWitt said with a grin.

Riley’s senses went into danger mode, but he forced himself to entertain a vision of Hunter and Derek in tuxedos at a commitment ceremony. With an inward shudder, he said, “Listen, I need to be honest with you.”

“I’m not stupid. And you’re not straight.”

“No,” Riley said, forcing himself to laugh. “It’s about the woman you were with. I’m a store detective here at the mall, and our shrinkage consultant thinks she may be a shoplifter.”

“Nat? She’d never do that. Unless maybe you work at the Barbie store?”

“Kohl’s,” Riley said, the first name that came to mind.

“Then I know she’s not your thief. Nat would never shop at Kohl’s. Don’t let her outfit fool you. Can you keep a secret?”

“To the grave,” Riley said.

“She’s got a little Dolly Parton obsession.”

“Like a stalker?” Riley yelped.

“No. She just loves Dolly. Truth be told, so do I.”

“Stand by your man,” Riley commented.

“That’s Tammy. It’s a long story, but Nat and I do a little business. That’s all.”

“What kind of business?” Riley asked.

DeWitt blushed and said, “She buys Barbies and dresses them as Dolly. In clothes that I sell her.” When Riley stared at him, DeWitt turned a deeper shade of red. "I sew them myself, okay? I happen to be handy with a needle. I make a lot of money off of Nat. And she's *not* a shoplifter."

Riley wasn't sure why, but DeWitt's confession made him seem bizarrely endearing. With a shave and a haircut . . . Riley looked at the bib overalls and repressed a tremor. Only in an alternate universe.

Or after several drinks, Riley remembered while he stared at the Congreve lobby. As tricks went, it hadn't been bad. In spite of the beard. DeWitt had been eager to please, and Riley hadn't minded playing Hoosier Daddy with him. It wasn't always easy to find gay men in rural America, and Riley was baffled as to why Indiana had been chosen as the location for a super mall. It *was* an alternate universe in Riley's opinion, so he supposed his dalliance with DeWitt was justifiable.

"Thinking of jumping?" Juanita Luna asked, jolting Riley back to the present as she stopped behind him.

He turned around and met the challenge in her eyes by saying, "I couldn't trust you to adequately clean up the mess."

When he got back to his office, he powered up his laptop to link to Hunter's network and check his boss's e-mail. Hunter had sent a half-dozen messages to his friend Garry, and it appeared Garry had finally answered. Riley opened his e-mail and frowned as he read it.

> *Con,*
> *I know. I know. I've left town on business. At least that's the official story. But really it's an escape. The Buffy situation is heating up, but I'm not. So I've sort of dropped out on a mini-vacation. I'm on a mission. More later. Hope things are better with you and Derek. Any idea how much longer you'll be in Australia?*
> *Pro*

Mission? Riley wondered. *What the hell does* that *mean?* He lit a cigarette, then read a new series of e-mail exchanges between Hunter and Derek.

> *H. I hate my boss. You wouldn't believe this woman. Take every foul quality you can think of, multiply it by a hundred, and that's Natasha. Juanita was asking when you'd be home. D.*

Derek,
Quit. You don't have to work. I don't understand why you took the job in the first place. Tell Juanita I don't know. I can't treat my job like a whim.—Hunter

H. You don't take me seriously. My job may not be ideal, but it is not a whim. I'm making money and good friends. There's more to life than dressing up and attending functions, you know. Juanita looks at me like I've driven you away. D.

Derek,
You haven't driven me away. I'm working. WORKING. Not all work involves punching a time clock. Stop talking to me through Juanita. It's juvenile.—Hunter

H. You know what? It sounds like I'M the whim. Fuck you, Hunter. D.

Derek,
Take the hostility down a notch and tell me about your friends. What does Juanita think of them?—Hunter

Then there was nothing, which meant that Derek must not want Hunter to know about his new friends. Riley, however, had his own means of finding out what Derek was up to. He checked his mall directory and called Drayden's, asking the operator for Women's Shoes. "Natasha Deere, please," he said sharply to the man who answered.

"Certainly. Just a moment."

While Riley waited, he cued up the CD player. As soon as he heard Natasha's voice, he hit PLAY and listened to the dulcet strains of Dolly Parton bemoaning her nine-to-five existence. When the song finished, Natasha weakly said, "Hold, please." He waited, and her voice was biting when she returned. "DeWitt, this isn't funny."

"It's extremely funny. Who's DeWitt?"

"Who is this?" Natasha demanded. "I don't know what kind of game you're playing—"

"Dolls," Riley said. "Do you like to play dolls, too?"

"Listen, you freak, I don't think you realize who you're dealing with."

"No, that's *you,*" Riley said. "But I'm willing to introduce myself. Your little hobby is really of no interest to me. Although your employees would probably get a kick out of it."

He heard a sharp intake of breath, then Natasha said, "What do you want?"

"Meet me tonight at nine in the Aurora piano bar at the Congreve. In costume or out—it doesn't matter to me. I'll recognize you."

"Just tell me what you want," Natasha snapped. "I don't have time for this nonsense."

"Tonight," Riley said and hung up.

He called the Aurora and left a message for Sheree Sheridan, then read a few of Derek's e-mails to his online friends. They were as boring as ever, mostly forwarded jokes, stupid stories he made up, or celebrity gossip. He powered off the laptop and went back to work.

That night, after dinner, he dressed as meticulously as if for a date. He wanted Natasha to realize she was not dealing with some ordinary schmuck, but an accomplished player who was holding all the cards. He knew she would arrive at the Aurora well before the designated time in hopes of figuring out who he was before he spotted her. Amateur.

He saw her as soon as he walked into the bar. Her corner table gave her a good view of the room, which her eyes swept with a chilling gaze every few seconds. She wasn't dressed in Dolly attire, however, but an exquisite black Ann Taylor sheath. Even Riley had to admit that she was a striking woman. No one would ever guess what a freak show she was.

As he'd requested, when Sheree saw him come in, she began singing "Jolene." Natasha's spine straightened, and she looked right at him, her eyes narrowing when he gave her a little nod. He stopped at the bar and ordered a whiskey sour, then casually drifted to her table. In the dim light, he could make out bright spots of color staining her high cheekbones.

"Miss Deere," he said, taking a seat. "I was hoping to see you in one of your fetching costumes tonight."

"Who the hell are you?" she snapped.

"So uncivil," Riley replied. "I always thought people from Southern California were mellow and polite."

Natasha's eyes flickered; when Sheree switched to "Coat of Many

Colors," her body seemed poised to attack him. As an adversary, Natasha was too easy. Maybe she'd turn out to be more fun as an ally.

"You have one minute—"

"I only want to make a little deal with you," Riley said soothingly. "My silence in exchange for a small favor."

"I don't do favors," Natasha said. She waited, and when Riley said nothing, she said, "Apparently we're done here."

"Not so fast," he said as she started to get up. "You only have to give me information on Derek Anderson."

"Derek?" Natasha questioned, her tone equal parts contempt and confusion. "Derek is less important to me than this cocktail napkin. I know nothing about him."

"But you're in a position to know who his friends are, what he does after hours, anything you may overhear or observe."

"I don't spy on my employees," Natasha said. "I have no intention of doing it for you."

"It would be so easy for me to undermine your authority with your staff," Riley reminded her. "And give your fellow managers a titillating piece of gossip about your proclivity to play Dress the Dolly."

Natasha stared at him with rage, then suddenly slumped. Riley might have felt sorry for her if he was a less perceptive man.

"I only know that someone with influence in the Drayden's organization helped him get his position," Natasha said. "Perhaps if I knew who that person was, I'd be able to tell you more."

"If that's a pathetic attempt to extort information, you can drop it," Riley said. He suppressed a smile when Natasha sat up, abandoning her pose of weakness with a withering look. "My request is actually quite modest and requires almost nothing on your part but vigilance. Or perhaps you might have to befriend him a little under the guise of being a good manager."

"I'm not interested in becoming embroiled in some Ruckus of the Rump Rangers, helping Derek's ex-boyfriend, or whatever you call yourself, get information," Natasha said, reaching for her purse. "If you want to spread rumors about me, go ahead. I can't imagine that anyone would think poorly of me for buying dolls and doll accessories for sick children. In fact, my employer would probably recognize my act of compassion with a commendation."

Riley gave her a look of admiration and said, "You're good. But I'm better."

"I don't think so."

"Judge Shipman," he said, and Natasha, in the act of rising, fell back to her chair with a genuine loss of composure. He went on. "Bluffing never works in my game. I know people everywhere. You have an unusual name and an unusual hobby; yours was one of those quirky cases people like to talk about. Would your employer be interested to learn the reason you were sent to that exclusive boarding school? Or that your juvenile record was expunged at great cost to your father?"

"I don't know what you're—"

"Stealing lingerie from Frederick's of Hollywood. How tacky. Then assaulting the arresting officer."

"You have no proof," Natasha said from between gritted teeth.

"And when a police detective who knew your father took you home, he made your parents unlock your bedroom closet, finding rhinestone-studded outfits, blond wigs, and pictures of Dolly Parton. Speaking of records, have you bought her latest one? Miss Sheridan seems to have finished her Dolly set, but I'm sure she'd take a request. Perhaps 'Starting Over Again'? Or 'Halos and Horns'? The game has changed. I'm dealing the cards, and I make the rules. I'll be in touch."

Riley finished his whiskey sour and watched Natasha stumble blindly from the bar. As he'd anticipated, she'd crumbled. He'd found a forty-hour-a-week source of information that might prove useful against that little twerp Derek Anderson.

14

Totally Pauley

"Do you ever feel like somebody's out to get you?" Derek asked, dropping into his chair at a table in Quasar Kitchen, where Davii, Christian, and Vienna were waiting for him.

"That's called paranoia," Davii said quickly and smirked at Vienna, who closed her mouth on whatever she'd been about to say and frowned at him.

"In my case, it's called Natasha Deere," Derek said and ordered a drink.

"Going back to work cocktailed?" Christian asked.

"I don't have to go back," Derek said.

"She didn't fire you, did she?" Vienna asked with a look of alarm.

"No," Derek said. "Once Natasha was sure that Jonquil was in tears, John was feeling castrated, and Missy was cowering in the stockroom, she left. Erik said we were overstaffed and offered one of us our freedom. Since the others were already on her shit list, they told me to make a run for it. We all figured she'd come back when she realized that her tirade had missed me. She'll probably torture Erik for helping me escape."

"You make it sound like the Underground Railroad," Christian said.

"My name is Kunta Kinte," Derek said. "I would have gone home and changed clothes, but I didn't want to keep you waiting any longer. Plus I needed this drink." He swallowed half of his cosmopolitan in one gulp.

"It's okay," Davii said. "Vienna's off; I'm done for the night, and look—Christian isn't wearing his headset."

"How'd you talk him into that?" Derek asked.

"I'm not that bad," Christian protested.

"You are, too," Davii said. He looked at Derek. "If you want to run up to our apartment, I can loan you something to wear."

"That'd be great," Derek said, then looked at the others. "If you don't mind waiting a little longer?"

"Go," Vienna said, waving her hand dismissively. "If we're going to hang out, you might as well be comfortable."

Davii chattered about the salon all the way to the apartment, but once they were inside the door, he turned and put his arms around Derek. "Is it just work?"

"I don't know," Derek said, grateful for the hug. "Thanks for not asking in front of the others."

"I've picked up that you don't want to tell Christian who your boyfriend is," Davii said.

"I figure he probably knows Hunter through work," Derek said. "It would make me uncomfortable to talk about him." He followed Davii to his bedroom and watched him paw through jeans to find some that would fit. He took off his tie and began unbuttoning his shirt. "Can I wear your gray sweater?"

"You have good taste," Davii said, tossing him the jeans and opening a drawer to get the sweater.

"Blame Hunter," Derek said.

"There's enough of that going around already," Davii said.

Derek paused in the act of zipping the jeans. "What does that mean?"

"It means I blame Hunter for your bad mood," Davii said. "Don't get defensive. Tell me what's going on."

"These jeans are going on," Derek said, turning to check the fit in the mirror. "How come you have jeans in my size?"

"I might have had a boyfriend or two who left some things behind," Davii said.

"Hmmm," Derek said. "Is it good for me to wear an ex's clothes? Does it remind you of happier or sadder yesterdays? Does it doom our friendship? Will it—"

"Give you something to ramble about so you can avoid answering me? Yes," Davii said.

"I want to know that he misses me the way I miss him," Derek confessed. "It makes me crazy to never know how he feels. Why couldn't I have fallen in love with one of those men who never shuts up? You know, like me."

Davii ran his fingers through Derek's hair after he pulled on the sweater and said, "You're fine. Your hair and your personality."

"My shoes?" Derek asked.

"I can't help you there; we're not the same size. Don't do it," Davii said, holding up his hand. "No size jokes."

"I'm so predictable. No wonder he can spend weeks—months—away. I'll be the same old me when he gets back."

Davii let out a noise of frustration, pulled Derek to him, and kissed him hard. After a moment's shock, Derek kissed him back, until Davii broke it off, saying, "I'm glad we finally managed to get that right. I'm only going to say this once; are you listening?" Derek nodded. "A rough patch in your relationship doesn't mean you're boring, ugly, stupid, or worthless. Hunter's never said anything like that to you, so stop saying it to yourself. You know I can kick your ass if you keep it up, right?"

"Uh-huh," Derek said. "Or kissing works, too."

Davii grinned and said, "I'll keep that in mind. Come on; Vienna and Christian are waiting."

Derek's mood was greatly improved when he sat at the table for the second time and ordered a fresh drink. He caught Vienna looking from Davii to him a couple of times, but there was nothing for her to see. Derek knew that even if Davii's kiss had gone beyond friendly, friendship was its motivation. He'd almost forgotten what it was like to relax with a group of people who genuinely liked him and shared a common language and an easy companionship. He mentally summed up what he admired about each of them as they talked.

Despite the way he looked, Christian was more than a pretty face. He could talk about almost anything, but he really lit up when the subject was art. He'd been excited to find out that Derek could tell him about writers who'd been influenced by some of Christian's favorite artists. Derek had loaned him novels and poetry anthologies, and Christian returned the favor by loaning Derek art books.

Or they met at Patti's Pages to find new things together. Derek felt mentally stimulated by Christian, and he also felt like he might be helping Christian renew his interest in an old passion.

If Christian was good for his mind, Vienna was good for his heart. She acted tough and irreverent on the outside, but Derek realized Davii was right—Vienna was a little fragile. He didn't know the whole story of her divorce, but she'd obviously been through an ordeal. Yet she was still able to open herself up to new friendships. He knew that if he, Davii, or Christian needed her, she'd be there for them, no questions asked. He hoped that when the right man came along, Vienna would let herself fall in love again, because in the short time he'd known her, she'd taught him a lot about love, loyalty, and acceptance. They took care of each other, especially at work.

Derek decided that the characteristic that set Davii apart from the other two was that he was fearless. Christian had let something or someone divert him from his talent as an artist, and Vienna's heartbreak made it hard for her to trust people. But Derek saw Davii as courageous. As a teenager, as well as with those two losers who'd followed them from the skating rink, Davii fought back when someone came after him. More than that, however, he hid nothing. He could play the campy hairdresser for his clients or ask a man to skate or dance in his arms without hesitation. Derek sensed that Davii would always go after what he wanted without worrying what people thought, but he wasn't ruthless, as he'd proved by respecting the boundaries of Derek's relationship with Hunter.

"He's doing it again," Christian said.

"Derek, come back," Vienna said.

Derek realized they were talking about him and looked around the table at his friends. Christian seemed to be scanning the surrounding area to see what might have diverted Derek's attention. Vienna was staring at him with an expectant expression, as if waiting for a story. Davii was giving him a pointed look and tilted his head. Derek followed Davii's eyes and saw one of the mall's maintenance men standing on a ladder in the courtyard, showing his physique to good advantage as he replaced a lightbulb.

Vienna intercepted their look, rolled her eyes, and said, "According to Kinsey, fifty-four percent of men think about sex every day or several times a day."

"Not me. I'm above average," Christian said.

"Not if you're in the forty-six percent," Vienna said.

"I meant the 'several times,' " Christian said. "I guess it depends on your definition of 'several.' "

"Math and sex don't mix," Davii said.

"I'm not so sure about that," Derek disagreed. "I had this algebra teacher in college. I never skipped one of his classes. When he wrote on the board, I couldn't take my eyes off—"

"What was your grade?" Davii interrupted.

"I passed. Barely."

"That's what I'm saying. Math and sex don't mix."

Disgruntled, Derek said, "Do you want to hear this story or not?"

"Yes!" Christian said. When Vienna turned to him and pointedly arched a penciled eyebrow, he added, "If the only sex I get is vicarious, I don't care who the players are."

Derek and Davii stared at him for a moment, then Derek said, "Anyway, Dr. Bunn—"

"You're making that name up," Davii said.

"—had the most amazing ass. He'd work out problems on the board, and I had no idea what he was talking about. Even if I tried to think of him as *x* and me as *y,* my fantasy about what came after the equal sign was usually both of us, multiple times. This wasn't conducive to learning algebra, something I couldn't explain to my parents when my grades arrived during Christmas break."

"How old were you?" Vienna asked.

"Almost nineteen," Derek said.

"And Dr. Bunn?"

"I don't know. I thought he was old at the time, but he was probably in his late twenties."

"Tell the story," Christian said.

"After I promised to apply myself, my parents sent me back second semester. It was really cold that year, so when a friend invited me to a party some graduate student was having, I almost didn't go. At the last minute, I changed my mind. It was snowing when we walked to this dumpy old house that had lousy heat, so I kept my coat on, even though everybody else was leaving theirs in a back bedroom. I did a couple of tequila shots to warm up. I was bored and would have left, but I couldn't stand to think of going back outside. And then Dr. Bunn showed up."

"Details," Davii ordered when Derek paused.

"Dr. Bunn was immediately surrounded by fawning students and wasn't paying any attention to me. I was just some geeky freshman lacking math skills. A boy has to work with what he's got, so off came the coat, and I went into hyper mode, going from group to group, cracking jokes, telling stories, always moving on as soon as I had everyone laughing loudly enough for Dr. Bunn to notice. Once I was sure I had his attention, I picked up my coat and walked to the back bedroom. Then Dr. Bunn came in and closed the door behind him. He rested against it, looking at me as if daring me to make the first move. I crossed the room, put my hands on his biceps, pushed him against the door, and kissed him hard. Our mouths stayed fused while our hands fumbled and strained at our clothes, and finally, I stepped back to look at my fantasy."

Derek paused again. They were all leaning forward, including Vienna, and Davii finally broke the silence by prompting, "And?"

"And nothing. I'm just making this shit up as I go along," Derek lied.

"I knew it," Davii said.

"Damn," Christian said, looking crestfallen.

Vienna stared at Christian. "You're sounding very bi-curious."

"I can satisfy your curiosity," Derek volunteered.

"I knew him first," Davii said.

"I'd already turned Dr. Bunn into a woman in my mind," Christian said. "I was just trying to cast her from among a group of actresses."

"Right. When somebody's talking about biceps, most people start visualizing actresses," Vienna scoffed. "Derek's story does have a moral."

"I like immoral stories better," Davii said.

"The moral is that I should have gone to college so I'd have my own stories," Christian said.

"The moral is that Derek learned to be rewarded for showing off," Vienna corrected. "A hot encounter with Dr. Bunn, our undivided attention—it's all the same."

"Um, not really," Derek said. He grabbed the check when the waiter brought it to the table and said, "I'm getting this one."

"At least let me take care of the tip," Christian said.

"No. You guys are always paying for everything."

"I hate it when people haggle over a check," Davii said.

Vienna grinned at him and said, "That must be why you never pick one up."

Derek listened to them banter as they walked into the courtyard. Vienna was wrong—he didn't need their undivided attention. It was enough that he had friends whose laughter and conversation could get him through bad moments. "I don't feel like going home. Let's do something else," he begged.

"We could catch a show at the planetarium," Christian suggested.

"Hello," Davii said. "We can walk outside and see the stars for free."

"Not the way we can see them in the planetarium," Vienna said. "Unless you have a telescope."

"I was wondering what he had in his pocket," Derek said.

"Fine," Davii said, cuffing Derek's neck. "The planetarium it is."

When they got there, Derek smoothly stepped in front of them and once again whipped out his Visa card. As he handed them their tickets, Vienna gave him her thank you with a mild scowl, and Christian gave him a look of reproach. Davii just hugged him, seeming to understand that Derek needed to treat them.

They walked inside the planetarium, which was nearly empty. A little girl sat with her father about midway around. A couple sat in the back row on the far side. A man by himself was on the first row in front of the couple.

"They're really packing them in tonight," Vienna said.

"It's the dinner hour," Davii said. "This is the best time to come here if you want to—"

"Which we don't," Vienna cut him off, plopping into a seat in the front row directly opposite the solitary man.

Christian sat on one side of her and Davii sat on the other, leaving Derek to take the seat next to Davii. He settled back to stare up at the dome. It was their constellation show, narrated by Indianapolis's favorite daughter, Jane Pauley. Still full from dinner, Derek became drowsy and leaned his head on Davii's shoulder. Davii shifted so Derek would be more comfortable, and he dozed a little, having already seen the show several times in the past.

He thought about Dr. Bunn. That incident seemed like it had happened to a different Derek. He'd forgotten how aggressive he was back then. But hadn't that brazen quality been what made him come on so strong to Hunter in their first meeting? He couldn't understand when he'd lost his cocksure attitude.

He jerked himself fully awake when Jane's voice trailed off mid-sentence.

"Something's always breaking here," Christian whispered as everyone sat quietly, waiting for the film to resume.

"I have to pee," Vienna said.

Davii and Derek stood so she could get past them. When they didn't sit back down immediately, Christian got up, too, and the three of them stood shoulder to shoulder, staring up at the stars frozen on the dome.

Derek could hear the whispers of the couple across the room, then the little girl said, "Daddy, I'm bored."

"Shhh," her father said. "They'll fix it in a minute."

Everything was quiet again, until Davii, in a surprisingly strong baritone, was apparently inspired by the stars to sing a line from "Somewhere Over the Rainbow." Christian sang the next line with him, and Derek joined in with "behind me."

"The only thing behind you, Dr. Bunn, is me," Vienna said. Davii reached back and pulled her in between him and Derek.

Derek heard the man on the other side of the planetarium say, "Fags."

As Davii tensed, Derek called out, "Looking for a date?"

The couple giggled, and the man with the little girl said, "I never miss *Will and Grace.*"

Davii started laughing, and Vienna softly said, "Some of my best friends—"

". . . don't form alone, but in clusters or clumps," Jane Pauley boomed over the speaker system.

"Come on, clumps, let's get the hell out of Oz," Christian said.

As they walked out arm in arm, Davii said, "The only thing missing is the little dog."

"I could borrow one of Emily-Anne's," Christian volunteered.

Vienna clicked her heels and said, "There's no witch."

Derek had a vision of Natasha riding by on one of Hunter's bikes and said, "I love you guys. Let's go to the Little Dipper and get some ice cream."

"My treat," Vienna insisted.

15

Shuffle Up and Deal

Natasha leaned against her kitchen counter, a cup of coffee cooling next to her bagel, and thought, *No one treats me that way and gets away with it.* She hurled the bagel into the trash, her appetite gone, and drummed her fingers as she replayed her meeting with the man at the Aurora piano bar, her lips drawn in a tight line. She picked up the cup and turned her back to the counter, resting her backside against it as she analyzed the situation.

Who the hell was this guy, and how did he know so much about her? She'd been pondering those questions every day since their meeting. She took a sip of coffee and set the cup down, protectively folding her arms in front of herself. Why would he give a shit about a nobody like Derek? It was impossible that anyone had any use for that loser who couldn't sell water in the desert.

As little as Natasha might like Derek, however, she wasn't about to accept a directive from some queer Columbo to snoop into his private life, particularly not by *befriending* him, as that ferret had suggested she do. Although she wasn't above the pretense of friendship if it served her interests, she wasn't so sure that it did in this case.

"What if I don't do it? What if I don't play your stupid little game?" she defiantly asked out loud. She pondered his threats to undermine her authority with her staff and, worse, to tell what he knew about her arrest record. "Bastard!" she spat. How the fuck had he found out all that stuff?

Natasha picked up her coffee again, mentally reviewing the measures she'd taken to ensure that no one would know about her . . . passion.

Her eyes flew open with sudden suspicion. She set down the cup with such force that it almost cracked. Racing to her bedroom, she dug out the key to the padlock and strode down the hallway to the locked door. She fumbled to fit the key in the lock, unlocked the door, and secured herself in the room, turning on the light.

He must have broken in. There had to be some evidence. She'd find it, move her "supplies" to another location, and have this asshole arrested. Let *him* find out what it was like to answer a few questions for the police. He thought he held the cards. He didn't know the first thing about who he was fucking with. She'd crapped bigger turds than he was.

Careful not to move, she leaned against the door, taking note of the location of every wig, doll, cosmetic, and CD. Everything was meticulously in place, just as she'd left it.

Fucker, she thought. *Either he's really good, or he found out some other—*

DeWitt! It had to be DeWitt. She *knew* she'd seen the Ferret before. He'd been sitting at the bar in Galileo's Glass the last time she met DeWitt. They must be in it together. They'd set her up!

Rage built inside her. She let herself out of the room, went back to the kitchen, and picked up the phone. As she dialed the number from memory and waited for DeWitt to answer, she reminded herself to be careful how she approached him or she wouldn't get any information.

DeWitt picked up the phone on the fourth ring. "Hello?"

"It's Natasha."

"I didn't expect to hear from you so soon." He sounded puzzled.

"I have another little something I'd like to commission from you," Natasha said, trying her best to sound sincere.

"Great. You want to meet, or do you want to describe what you want so I can get to work on some drawings?"

"I think it's better if we meet to discuss this one."

"The usual place? Around two?"

"Fine." She hung up without waiting for any parting pleasantries, then walked back to her Dolly room and looked around. It was important that she have the advantage during this meeting. DeWitt would recognize her in her Dolly wardrobe, but the Ferret had seen her as Dolly *and* Natasha. Maybe she could sneak in early and catch them together if neither of them saw her first.

She stared at the blond wigs with a frown, wondering, *What would Dolly do?*

Then she remembered that momentous day on eBay when she'd bid on seven Dolly dolls and a *9 to 5* wig. The dolls had been a decent investment. They now stood on their own shelf, appropriately attired, really not looking much more like Dolly than the Barbies. But the wig . . . The shock she'd gotten when she excitedly opened the box to find a Lily Tomlin wig rather than Dolly's *9 to 5* coif still rattled her. She'd hurled the wig to the back of her closet with a shudder. But it might finally be useful.

At a quarter 'til two, she strolled into Galileo's Glass in her brunette shag. She spotted DeWitt at the usual table, but he was alone, sipping on a beer. She did a quick scan of the bar but saw no trace of the Ferret, so she approached DeWitt's table. He glanced up without recognition.

"It's me," she hissed.

"Nat? Who're you supposed to be now, Keith Partridge?" She slid into her seat without comment, and he said, "What's up?"

"Funny. I was just about to ask you the same thing."

He looked at her as if evaluating her body language. "What do you mean?"

"What do you mean?" Natasha mimicked in that most annoying of child's games.

DeWitt let out a deep sigh. "Nat," he began.

"Natasha," she corrected.

"Sorry. Natasha," he amended, "do you need me to make something for you or what?"

"Yes, I need you to make something for me, all right. I need you to make something clear. Then I'm going to make something clear to you. But first I want you to tell me who you've been talking to about our deal."

"Who I've been talking to?"

"Is that question too hard for you? It's going to be difficult for me to deliver it in words less than a syllable. I'd draw it for you, but I don't have time to play *Win, Lose or Draw.*"

"If you're going to get bitchy . . ." DeWitt started to get up.

"Sit!" Natasha barked the command as if training a stubborn dog. DeWitt sat with a Pavlovian reflex, as did a few of the patrons who'd been standing at the bar. She lowered her voice in an effort to avoid drawing any more attention to them. "Someone knows about me. Someone other than you, and they're using what they know to—" Natasha broke off, considering for a moment how much information she wanted to divulge. "You're the only one who knows anything about our deal. I thought it was pretty simple. You make the clothes. I pay you. You keep your mouth shut. Until now, we seemed to have had an understanding. But suddenly, there's a third person in the equation. I know I haven't said anything to anyone. That leaves you. Who did you tell, and what did you say?"

"I haven't said any—"

She practically lunged across the table, scaring him into silence. "What do you think? That I'm as stupid as you are?" she whispered with a sneer. "Don't even think about finishing that sentence by telling me you haven't said anything to anyone. I didn't just fall out of a tree, you lump. You think I got where I am in this world by not knowing a thing or two about people? If two people have an agreement and one of them breaks it, then everyone who made the agreement in the first place knows who broke it. That's the magic of math. And don't think for one second that there aren't things I know about you. Everyone has skeletons. You think you're exempt? Do you think I didn't have you checked out before hiring you? I know all about the little homo-Harley-hooligan group you hang out with."

"We're not *hooligans,*" DeWitt protested.

"I'm sure it's the tip of the iceberg. It won't take much to dig up more on you. But you'll save me the trouble if you just tell me what you know."

DeWitt bit his lip and considered what Natasha had said. "I told a friend," he admitted, looking defeated.

"Now we're getting somewhere. Who is he? How do you know him? What, and I mean exactly what, did you tell him?"

"Just a friend. RB." DeWitt suppressed a brief smile.

"Arby? What the hell kind of name is that?"

"Not *Arby.* He's not a sandwich. *R-B.* They're initials."

"What do the initials stand for?"

"I don't know."

Natasha rolled her eyes. "You mean to tell me you had sex with this guy, and you only know his initials? I'd expect more from a sensitive man like you."

"Who said I had sex with him?"

"You're blushing like a stupid schoolgirl. And God knows, someone who looks like you can't possibly get any but a couple of times a year."

"What?"

"Look at you. You dress like a slob; your hair is so oily I'm surprised we still bother to use the Alaska pipeline; and that beard makes you look like you're attempting a hostile takeover of ZZ Top." She watched his face fall farther with each cut but relentlessly kept stabbing the downed man. "Can we please get back to what you said to this RB jack-off?"

"Fuck you. I don't need this shit from you." DeWitt started to get up.

"Maybe not, but I know you're strapped for money. And I know you can't afford to pay taxes on the cash I've given you. Cash, by the way, that you should be declaring as income and probably aren't. I guess we could let the IRS iron that out."

DeWitt sat down again, and she watched his face while he struggled with the math. "That's a lot of money," he said. "You'd really turn me in to the IRS?"

"Or the EPA—whoever wants you most," she said. "Let's stop this charade of you getting up, then sitting back down. Although heaven knows, I'm not trying to deny you the exercise, this isn't the time or place for aerobics. What did you say to your little butt buddy about me?"

DeWitt regarded Natasha with disdain. "I told him that you had a thing for Dolly Parton, and that you hired me to make doll clothes for you. That it was a hobby for you. And that's it!"

Natasha considered this for a moment and quickly reviewed her conversation with the man she now knew as RB. All the other references he'd made were things that DeWitt didn't know. "Christ. How could you be so stupid? What the hell were you thinking?"

"Wait just a minute," DeWitt objected. "He's the one who seemed to know all about you. He said they've been watching you at Kohl's for a while. They thought you were a shoplifter."

"What? Are you insane?"

"No, that's what he said. He said he worked here at the mall, and they thought you were stealing from Kohl's."

"Kohl's?" Natasha was disgusted. "You moron, I've never even been in that place. This guy is so full of shit. I can't believe you can't see that. For God's sake, all you have to do is look in the mirror to figure it out. He used you. He used you to find out something about me that he couldn't find out on his own. You're a fool if you think otherwise."

"That's not true. He said he really liked me. He said he'd call."

"Yeah, I'm sure your phone has been ringing off the hook. I'll tell you this much. If this guy actually is interested in you, I'll put a stop to it. Just you wait. I can't afford to have you blurting out my business to every psycho who's willing to give you a mercy fuck."

"The only reason I told him anything was because he was saying untrue things about you. I knew you didn't shop at Kohl's. I knew you weren't a thief. A royal bitch, but not a thief."

"At least you got that part right. I don't shop at Kohl's. I'm not a thief. And I am a royal bitch."

"You can say that again," DeWitt agreed with a scowl.

"I'll tell you what I won't say again."

"What's that?"

"That I'll meet you here. I have no need for people in my life who are deceptive or who I can't trust. I don't need you to defend me. I can take care of myself. There are lots of people around here who can sew. Your services are no longer required. I'm through with you."

With that, she got up from the table, abruptly leaving the bar. She adjusted her sunglasses and walked into Kohl's, looking for the nearest undercover store detective. After so long in the retail business, she could spot one of those bozos halfway across any store.

There's one now, she thought, spying a young, well-built man carrying a Kohl's bag that obviously concealed his walkie-talkie. He lurked behind a display, trying not to make it obvious that he was watching the shopping habits of a young girl with a pierced lip. The store detective wasn't RB.

In fact, it occurred to her that the Ferret didn't seem at all like a store detective. Could she be losing her touch? Impossible. Or was it?

"Can I help you?"

The question unexpectedly derailed her train of thought, and Natasha answered, "Huh?"

"I'm sorry, ma'am. I didn't mean to startle you. Did you need help with something?"

Natasha realized she was standing next to a display of men's underwear. "No, uh . . . No. I'm just looking." She picked up a package of boxers.

"For someone special?" the saleswoman prodded with a suggestive tone.

"No. For my father," Natasha lied. The woman looked at her curiously, and Natasha realized the package she'd picked up was a pair of white boxers with red hearts and the word "Sexy" scrolled across them. "Mind your own business," Natasha hissed, tossing the boxers back onto the display and walking across the floor to another department.

She surveyed the store to find the security idiot who was stalking Pierced Girl. She noticed that the underwear saleswoman was on the phone. With another glance around, Natasha spotted the store detective a short distance away, talking into his bag.

Real smooth, Natasha thought, surreptitiously watching him skirt the store while he monitored *her* every move. She blamed the Lily Tomlin wig.

She resumed contemplating the accuracy of her assessment of RB. When it came to taking care of herself in the competitive world of retail management, her instinct had always served her well. It was telling her that RB was not a store detective at Kohl's or anywhere else. For some reason, however, he'd decided to play Kojak, with Derek as his prey. In doing so, he'd stumbled onto information about her beyond what DeWitt could have provided.

Who had given it to him? Only someone from Drayden's could have told him who she was and where she was from; someone who had a grudge against her. Maybe that vindictive Oscar from Men's Shoes, who'd whined about his floor space as a way to mask his department's weak sales. Or Melanie from Cosmetics, who undoubtedly resented Natasha's superior management skills and was afraid she'd report the Cosmetics employees' many abuses of Drayden's rules. Or maybe a person still unknown, the one who'd helped that miserably inept Derek get his job in the first place.

If RB thought he held all the cards, he'd soon learn that they were playing with her stacked deck. As far as Derek Anderson was concerned, the stakes were small. The big payoff would be in bluffing until she found a way to flush out her enemy at Drayden's while also squelching RB and getting rid of a useless employee like

Derek. It wouldn't be a *straight* flush, but she'd still have the winning hand.

Natasha smirked with self-satisfaction as she left Kohl's and headed for the food court, suddenly experiencing a voracious desire for a roast beef sandwich.

16

A Model for Business and Technical Success

"I don't understand how you can eat waffles every day," Vienna stated.

"And I don't see how you can eat a fruit cup every morning," Derek said. "Doesn't it get boring?"

Vienna popped a slice of orange into her mouth and chewed methodically as she thought about it. Then she answered, "No. It's refreshing. It wakes me up. Besides, the ratio of the fruit is always different. Sometimes there's more banana. More strawberries. You get the idea. Waffles rarely change."

"There are different kinds of waffles," Derek said.

"It's all bread to me," Vienna said dismissively. "Way too many carbohydrates."

"What do you think fruit—"

"If I ate waffles every day, I'd be a tank," Vienna interrupted. "Growing up, I never got fresh fruit. It was always that stuff from a can. You know the type? Drenched in that awful syrup? Or else it was in a pie. Apple pie, rhubarb pie, peach pie; Mama was always baking a pie. Or else someone was always bringing one by the house. It was like a calling card of the neighborhood, or a moral code: *If you're going to knock on someone's door, you must have a pie in your hands.* Or cake. Bread. Any sort of baked goods, I suppose. But we were poor, so everything and anything was appreciated. Lord knows, I ate it all. Why am I telling you all this?"

Derek grinned at Vienna and said, "I have no idea. Keep talking."

They were seated at a table in the Congreve's restaurant, having one of their usual breakfasts before work. Vienna loved eating at the Congreve. It made her feel like she was in a movie or a television commercial. Something fabulous, unlike the monotony of her actual life. She loved that her fruit cup arrived in a crystal dish, which was placed on a china plate with a silver spoon resting beside it. She loved unfolding the crisp white napkin with the embroidered *C* and placing it on her lap.

What she didn't tell Derek was that her fruit cup represented her a little too perfectly. The fruit was cut into haphazard shapes and sizes. Just like her emotions, there was no rhyme or reason to the ratio of apple to banana, strawberry to orange. When you ordered a fruit cup, you never really knew what you were going to get. The little slices of mayhem were then placed into a bowl; chaos and disorder served up in a pretty package.

The only difference between Vienna and her fruit cup was that the fruit cup usually contained cherries. Although, Vienna felt like hers was about to return any day now. It had been a long time since she'd had sex, and she was beginning to feel it. She missed holding a man. She missed sleeping next to somebody, hugging him all night. Or even the feeling of waking up and knowing that she'd let go in the middle of the night, only to wrap her arms around him again.

Sometimes her need made her feel silly. Sometimes it made her feel angry. She'd remember her ex-husband and why she didn't want to get attached to anyone. It would be difficult for her to trust someone that much again.

Davii would often remind her that a roll in the hay didn't require a commitment. She didn't fool herself into thinking that it was different for gay men. Or any man, for that matter. She wasn't a believer in a woman's need for emotional intimacy with her sexual partners. Especially if the sexual partner was a man. In her opinion, men were detached anyway. Whether it was with a woman or a cantaloupe, as long as they got off, what was the difference?

Vienna silently picked at her fruit cup, remembering a time when even her husband had revealed himself as a typical man. He'd always been attentive, trying to impress and connect with her, at least for the first few years. But one night, she was feeling particularly amorous and seduced him in their living room. She was performing oral sex on him, and he was obviously enjoying it, encouraging her aloud, moaning, running his hands through her hair, but not holding on to her head and pushing it down on himself, which she absolutely hated. She felt so in control, so giving and completely able, totally in tune with his needs. She stopped right before he was about to have an orgasm, wanting him to climb on top of her.

It was then that she noticed he'd been watching television the entire time she was blowing him. She couldn't remember what was on that night, only that she felt like a rerun rather than a prime-time special episode. She'd stared at him, mentally counting to ten before she got up and went into their bedroom alone to finish what she'd started. He never said a word about it, and she didn't either. She filed the moment away, recalling her mother's advice that she had to watch out for herself. But surely her mother hadn't meant masturbation. Had she?

Vienna studied Derek as he polished off his plate of waffles, wondering if they looked like a couple to their fellow diners. She stared at him affectionately, grateful for his company and friendship. She tried to imagine them as a newly wedded couple having breakfast during their honeymoon, but the image was too blurry to look real in her mind. She knew a leopard would never change his spots, especially when animal prints were in vogue. Gay men often looked at her, but it was always with appreciation and admiration, as if she was a flawlessly decorated cake that they couldn't improve upon.

Derek noticed her staring and asked, "What?"

Vienna felt her face become hot and said, "Nothing. I was zoning out. Pay no attention to the woman with the dazed and listless expression. I'm tired."

"Me, too," Derek said, even though he sounded chipper and had wolfed down his waffles like a hungry beast.

"You should be tired. You and Davii were out late last night," Vienna admonished.

"We went to Pluto," Derek said, gulping down his orange juice. "We danced for hours; it was fantastic. Davii, of course, was up on a platform half the night, putting on his own little show."

"The Davii Show," Vienna mused. "Starring Davii. Produced by Davii. Directed by Davii. I know it well. Did either of you get lucky?

Did you finally finish that aborted date?" Derek made a face. "I'll take that as no. You two have been out together a lot since that date."

"It wasn't a date," Derek corrected. "We're just friends, and we're fine with that. I'm kind of relieved, actually. I feel like I didn't do anything wrong as far as Hunter and I are concerned."

"Ah," Vienna said.

"Do you think that's true?"

"Do *you* think it's true?" Vienna asked.

"I'm not playing psychologist and patient with you," Derek said and wiped his mouth with his napkin.

Vienna took a long sip of coffee, then said, "Neither am I." When Derek just stared at her, she added, "No, I don't think you did anything wrong. Come on; let's go."

Derek frowned and said, "But we still have a half hour before our shifts."

Vienna gave their waiter her credit card, saying, "True. But I've been late way too many times. I need to kiss a little butt. Besides, I have a lot to do today." As they walked through the mall, Vienna weighed her words carefully before saying, "I know you didn't go on real dates with Davii and Christian, but you were testing the waters. What do you think that means?"

When Derek didn't answer, Vienna wondered if she'd pushed things too far. She didn't understand the complexities of his relationship with Hunter, she was aware of that much, but she refused to let Derek walk around in denial. He had to accept that in his unhappiness with his situation, he might be pushing buttons he didn't really want to push.

"I think you're bringing up Christian because you're secretly thrilled that he's straight," Derek said, poking Vienna in the ribs.

Vienna slapped his arm. She loved it when Derek teased her, but she was slightly annoyed that he was diverting the topic. She decided to give him a break. "I have no secrets," she said. When Derek looked like he was about to challenge her statement, she continued, "I'll admit that my kitty's getting hungry and wants to be fed, but I don't think Christian's the man for the job. He's cute and all, but if you insist on being friends with him, that makes things too complicated."

"He's really nice," Derek insisted. "I think you and Christian might be a good fit."

"You make it sound like a seizure. Or like shopping."

"Dating *is* like shopping," Derek said. "You have to try a man on and make sure he's flattering, that he's the right size."

"The right fit is very important," Vienna agreed.

"Does this man make my ass look too big?" Derek pretended to wonder.

They parted company when they reached Drayden's, Derek shuffling his feet toward Women's Shoes and Vienna clocking in before heading to Cosmetics. She dreaded the day ahead. She suspected that Derek was feeling the same. Derek had told her that he'd never imagined himself selling shoes. When she asked what he'd rather be doing, he couldn't come up with anything. Because she'd been so driven all her life, that was a new concept for Vienna. Even though she'd had many different jobs in the mall since moving into the Galaxy Building, she still felt like she had a purpose. She wanted to work at every store in Mall of the Universe. Since there were more than four hundred of them, she figured it would take a long time to accomplish that goal.

Bianca had opened that day and was darkening a blond woman's eyebrows when Vienna approached. She greeted Vienna warmly, then her face clouded as she said, "I'll never be able to do eyebrows like you, Vienna. What do you think?"

Vienna stowed her purse behind the counter, then assessed Bianca's handiwork. The woman seated at the counter was younger than Vienna, with a creamy smooth complexion, cornflower blond hair, and blue eyes. She was a strange juxtaposition of ordinary features and striking beauty. Vienna could tell that she was all slender limbs and tall, despite the fact that she slouched on the stool in her loose, casual clothing. She wore minimal makeup, not that she needed any, which made the eyebrows that Bianca had filled in stand out too much. As Vienna studied her face, the woman smiled shyly, revealing a slight overbite.

"They're a little too dark, Bianca," Vienna finally said. "Try Allure's Desert Sands pencil. It's a few shades lighter."

Bianca softly stamped her foot and sighed audibly, reminding Vienna of a little girl in need of a nap. As she pawed through the samples, she whined, "Of course, you're right. You always are. I don't know why they don't fire me. What are you doing here so early anyway?"

"I thought I'd get a head start in the stockroom, getting ready for the big day tomorrow," Vienna explained. "Where's Meg?"

"Behind you," a voice said, causing Vienna to tense in surprise. She moved out of the way so a shorter Korean woman could get behind the counter.

"You're both early," Bianca stated. "Why? What's going on tomorrow?"

Vienna and Meg exchanged incredulous looks. Meg's eyes were rimmed with dark kohl, the lids painted a bright red that matched two streaks in her long, shiny hair. It was her signature look, and other than that, she didn't wear any makeup, which annoyed the other Cosmetics associates to no end. She always wore black clothes and platform boots or shoes. Her look screamed rock and roll. Or, "Don't fuck with me." Nobody ever did. Vienna respected Meg's sarcastic humor and blunt approach to people.

"We're doing a performance piece titled 'Symphony in Blue Vomit.' We have rehearsals all day," Meg said dryly to Bianca. She turned to Vienna and asked, "I hope you brought the grenades."

The blonde in the chair stifled a giggle behind her hand.

"Damn! I knew I forgot something when I left the apartment," Vienna said, playing along.

"It's okay. I borrowed enough for both of us from my mother," Meg said, rooting around in her purse. "But they're family heirlooms, so be careful with them."

Vienna laughed, but when she saw Bianca's hurt look, she explained, "Tomorrow is the Zodiac event, remember? They're filming an ad in the morning, then their spokesmodel, Sheila Meyers, is doing an in-store appearance."

As Bianca nodded her head to let them know that it was all coming back to her, she wiped off her previous work and began redoing the blonde's eyebrows.

"We have to unpack all the new products they sent for the event," Meg explained further. "Cleaning and organizing the stockroom—just what I wanted to do all day! I'm so thrilled. Not! I guess I should be grateful. My relatives back home do the same work for a dollar. Maybe less; I'm not sure."

"I'd rather spend a day in the stockroom than kowtow to some blond WASP model all day," Vienna stated. "And you know nobody's going to buy anything. They'll just come by to get her autograph and stare at her like some animal at a zoo."

"Do not feed the model," Meg quipped, as if reading a sign. The blonde in the chair laughed, causing Bianca to draw a line up her forehead. "It's going to be nothing but teenagers wanting advice on how to be a model and their overweight, undersexed fathers."

"Right? I hate these things," Vienna agreed.

"You two are awful," Bianca reprimanded as she rubbed a cotton ball drenched with makeup remover over the blonde's forehead. "I've heard that Sheila Meyers is the most down-to-earth and wonderful person."

"I've heard that, too," the blonde agreed.

"Besides, she works for Lillith Allure Cosmetics. You should watch what you say about her, especially in front of customers."

"She has a point there," the blonde said.

"Oh, please," Meg scoffed. "Why should I care what some model thinks of me?"

"It's not like Sheila Meyers is president of the company," Vienna said in rebuff.

The blonde looked up at Bianca and said, "They have a point."

"It's just not nice," Bianca said and pouted. She looked at the blonde's eyebrows and said, "That's a lot better. Can I add lipstick to balance it out?"

"Yeah, sure. I'll take a tube of Aquarius," the blonde said. She stood up, dug through her purse, and handed Bianca her credit card. She accepted a fresh tube of Zodiac's Aquarius lipstick and said to Vienna, "I can't believe I left home and forgot my makeup. I guess I'm the quintessential blonde."

"Get her," Meg whispered when the blond woman was busy applying her lipstick.

Vienna chuckled but stopped when she saw Bianca staring at the blonde's credit card with a horrified expression. Meg noticed, too, and walked over to see what was the matter. Bianca began whispering in her ear, waving the card frantically, until Meg grabbed her wrist to keep it still. After examining the card, she looked at Vienna, shook her head, and winced before pushing Bianca toward her customer.

"Could you sign at the bottom, Miss Meyers?" Bianca weakly murmured.

"Oh, God, no," Vienna said, suddenly massaging her temples.

"Actually, it's Mrs. Meyers-Clinton now," Sheila said, flashing her left hand at Bianca. She extended her hand to each of them, saying, "Hi, I'm Sheila."

"I'm so sorry," Vienna apologized.

"Usually it's me who's tactless," Bianca said.

"I'd commit hara-kiri on myself right now, but I'm not Japanese," Meg said.

"Stop! It's okay. Really, you didn't know," Sheila said brightly. "I probably should've spoken up sooner, but I was having fun listening to you. Besides, I'm not looking forward to tomorrow either. You're right about the girls and their fathers. But the fathers never do anything but stare, and the girls aren't so bad. We'll try to have fun. I swear, it will be over before you know it." Vienna could do nothing but smile awkwardly, as did Meg. Bianca nodded solemnly, as if listening to the Dalai Lama. "You guys have it easy," Sheila insisted. "I'm the one who has to get up at four in the morning for the shoot, have my hair and makeup done while I'm barely awake, put on seven different outfits until someone finally decides which one looks best, then try to look like I'm enjoying myself under hot lights while people poke and prod me into the perfect pose."

Vienna studied Sheila's earnest expression and finally said, "Oh, please. You love it, and you know it."

Sheila suddenly grinned and said, "I do! I really do! Do you guys want to watch the shoot? There'll be donuts."

The next morning, Vienna wondered if she should've begged off going to the photo shoot like Meg and Bianca, donuts or no donuts. She shuffled wearily to the Moon level, where the shoot was taking place, in the hall outside of Drayden's entrance. There were people scurrying around, shouting into headsets, setting up lights, and angling cameras. Vienna stared around her, feeling in the way and wondering if she should go back to bed.

A man with a clipboard rushed by her, stopped, and returned to ask, "Who are you? What's your name?"

"Vienna. Sheila Meyers invited me to—"

"Right," he said, cutting her off to consult his clipboard. "Follow me."

He led her to the craft services table and asked her to wait for Sheila, begging her to stay out of the way so she wouldn't get hurt. After he left, Vienna nibbled at a donut. Someone offered her a cup of coffee, which she accepted gratefully. As she sipped, she imagined that she was waiting for the set to be ready for her photo shoot and wondered what it would be like if the commotion was all about her.

"You're developing a plot to steal my job, aren't you?" Sheila asked, suddenly appearing at Vienna's side. She was wearing a diaphanous silver dress, her hair piled high on her head and a pair of silver shoes in her hands.

"No. I mean, yes," Vienna stammered. She laughed, then added, "I'm so not awake right now. I was just trying to imagine what this must be like for you."

"You haven't seen anything yet," Sheila assured her. "The bull's not even here."

"What? Did you say bull?"

"Yeah. Lillith wants new Taurus ads. In the old ads, I was a bullfighter. This year, apparently I'll be riding one. Sometimes I really hate Blaine," Sheila muttered.

"Who's Blaine? Is this safe?" Vienna asked while looking around for a charging bull.

"Blaine does all of Lillith Allure's advertising. Really, it's going to be fine. Well, you'll be fine. I'm the one on the bull. We got the same bull as last year—he was a pussycat—not to mention the same handlers and trainers. Besides, Lillith had the bull's chart done, and she assures me that today he'll be at his most tranquil," Sheila explained. "Oh, here comes Chuck now. He's the bull trainer. I have to go say hi. I'll be back."

Vienna stared after her, wondering if Sheila was on medication. Then she saw Derek, Christian, and Emily-Anne Barrister, and waved them over. "I can't believe you guys actually got up so early to come to this thing."

"Of course!" Emily-Anne exclaimed. "I hope you don't mind me showing up uninvited. Christian mentioned Sheila Meyers, and I just had to tag along. I want to see if Sheila will do an interview for my husband's paper. This is so exciting. Imagine, a real New York model in our mall."

"She walks and talks, too," Vienna said. "Sometimes at the same time!"

"Hey, where'd you get that coffee?" Derek suddenly asked a little too loudly. "Anyone want coffee?"

After waiting a while longer, things finally picked up when the director and the photographer showed up. Stand-ins for the bull and Sheila walked through the route the bull would take through the hall and into Drayden's. Lights were readjusted, cameras were positioned, and Sheila was finally called onto the set. The bull was led there by a team of handlers and trainers. Vienna's nerves were soothed when the bull seemed as bored and sedate as Sheila.

"Listen up, everyone," the director said to the crowd of staff and onlookers. "I can't shout or yell anything, or it might upset Belle."

"The bull's name is Belle," Christian whispered incredulously, which caused Emily-Anne and Vienna to snicker.

"You know that gives him gender issues," Vienna said.

"If everyone will be very quiet and keep still, this should all go off smoothly," the director continued. "Let's get into positions."

Vienna watched as a small ladder was placed next to the bull. Sheila put on her high heels and was about to step onto the ladder when her hairdresser raced up and climbed onto it instead in order to fix her hair one last time. At that moment, Emily-Anne's cell phone emitted a piercing rendition of "Flight of the Bumblebee." Vienna noticed Belle the bull's surprised expression and briefly wondered if she herself had the same look when she found out her husband had cheated on her.

A second later, Belle snorted and kicked the ladder, causing the hairdresser to fall over the saddle strapped to the bull's back. Sheila screamed, losing one shoe as she ran away from the bull. Belle charged off down the mall in the opposite direction, the helpless hairdresser clinging to the saddle for dear life.

"Cut!" the director shouted. Vienna rolled her eyes; he obviously had trouble differentiating between fantasy and reality.

The bull handlers ran after Belle. Someone overturned the craft services table, and everyone tried to cram behind it. Vienna and Derek clung to each other and peered over the edge, fearing the worst. Christian held Emily-Anne, who was shouting into her cell phone. "This really isn't a good time right now. I think I'm sitting on a donut. Can I call you back?"

Vienna watched as the handlers ran back toward them, Belle hot on their heels. The hairdresser was still hanging on and screaming as the bull charged. Two of the handlers jumped onto a large planter, and another dove into a trash can as the bull rumbled past them.

"It's coming right at us!" someone yelled in Vienna's ear.

"I hate Blaine! I hate him! I really do!" Sheila screamed as the director grabbed her and pushed her into a nearby bathroom, where several other crew members were hiding.

Belle suddenly veered right and circled around the planter again.

"I don't believe it," Derek said. "She's going the other way."

"He," Vienna reminded him.

"You don't name a bull Belle," Derek insisted.

"You name a cow Belle," Emily-Anne said, then dissolved in nervous giggles.

"He's headed right for Mikasa!" Christian exclaimed.

"At least the gate's closed," Vienna observed.

Belle charged right through the store's plate glass window. Everyone ducked and screamed again at the sound of breaking glass. Now that the bull was somewhat cornered, the handlers raced toward him again, this time armed with tranquilizer guns. Vienna heard someone announce that everything was safe.

"Safe? You call this safe?" Vienna asked, still not moving from her refuge behind the table.

"Oh, poor Rex! Is he okay?" Sheila exclaimed as she ran from the bathroom and into Mikasa. "Someone call 9-1-1!"

Emily-Anne whipped open her cell phone and began punching in the numbers.

"Now I can cross Pamplona off my list of places to visit," Christian said warily.

The handlers led a weaving and staggering Belle out of Mikasa, where he collapsed into a heap in front of Drayden's entrance.

"I swear, I'm calling in sick today," Vienna said.

Fortunately, Rex the hairdresser was alive, although he'd sustained minor cuts and bruises, along with two fractured wrists. Vienna stared with admiration when he urged Sheila and the director to finish the shoot as he was being taken away on a stretcher.

"What a trooper," Christian said.

"We can't finish!" the director shouted at a mildly hysterical Sheila. "Our bull is asleep, your hair is a mess, you have no hairdresser, and half my crew has quit! We're going to have to reschedule. Someone get me Blaine Dunhill on the phone!"

"Emily-Anne, give me your phone," Vienna said.

Fifteen minutes later, a disheveled Davii ran up to them with a tackle box full of hair products, brushes, and combs, brandishing a hair dryer as if it was a gun. Vienna rushed him toward Sheila, saying, "This is my friend Davii. He's a brilliant hairdresser. I'll help with your makeup, if you want. Let us help you salvage this shoot."

A half hour later, Sheila emerged looking none the worse for wear, her makeup flawless. Davii had sculpted her blond tresses into a modified Mohawk, pinned and lacquered into place and decorated with crystals.

"You look fantastic, Sheila," the director said. "Are you sure you still want to do this?"

"Oh, sure. A moment ago, he was yelling at her," Davii whispered to Vienna.

"I'm fine," Sheila said. "How's Belle? Poor thing."

Belle slept for another two hours, giving Sheila time to languish on the bull's back as she applied Zodiac's Taurus lipstick while gazing into a compact. The director circled around them with a handheld camera. Afterward, a photographer took stills of Sheila pretending to nap with Belle and more of her with one foot on Belle's back, her fist raised in victory, as if she'd just wrestled the bull to the ground.

Later, Sheila met Vienna, Davii, Derek, and Christian at the Jupiter Lounge. She showed Davii and Vienna Polaroids from the shoot and thanked them for coming to her rescue.

"It was nothing," Davii said modestly.

"Speak for yourself," Vienna said.

Sheila hugged her, then said, "I'm so sorry for putting you all in danger. I had no idea any of that would happen."

"It's not your fault," Vienna assured her.

"Emily-Anne feels terrible about her phone going off like that," Christian said. "She thought it was turned off."

"I know; she told me. Even though insurance will cover it, she's offered to pay for Rex's hospital bills, Mikasa's window, and any damaged equipment. I think she owns a bull now, too," Sheila said.

"How did the in-store event go?" Vienna asked her.

"I can't believe you called in sick," Sheila said. "Actually, it was great. We sold a lot of Zodiac, especially after the morning news coverage about Belle's rampage. People came in droves hoping to see a wild bull. Instead, they got me."

"I'm sure they weren't disappointed," Christian said.

"Everyone loved my hair," Sheila assured Davii. "I told them about you. You could be booked up for a while, giving lots of Terre Hautian teens mock Mohawks."

"I don't know whether to thank you or throw my drink in your face," Davii said.

"Thank me," Sheila insisted. "Because you're coming with me."

Everybody stared at her in silence until Davii asked, "What are you talking about, Sheila?"

"I've got appearances in eight major cities and a cosmetics convention in Los Angeles. I'm presenting at an awards show, and there's another ad campaign to shoot in a couple of weeks. Rex can't come with me, because he's going home to recuperate, so I need a hairdresser. You're it, mister."

Vienna held her breath, waiting for Davii's response. She couldn't imagine Davii leaving her, his job, everything, to join Sheila and her traveling circus. She tried to look excited when Davii finally exclaimed, "Yes! I'll do it! I'll be a model's stylist!"

"I feel like he's getting married or something," Derek said to Vienna, while Davii screamed and hugged Sheila. "Our little boy is growing up."

"Yeah, it's great," Vienna said placidly.

Two days later, Davii was packed and ready to leave to meet up with Sheila in Chicago. The night before he left, Vienna sat with him in the living room. They were sharing a bottle of wine while Davii waxed rhapsodic about the day they first met.

"You kept hanging up on everyone who called the salon," Davii recalled. "Then you somehow scheduled three different people for one appointment. I managed to do a perm, a full head of highlights, and a cut and color all at the same time."

"Too bad it wasn't all on the same person," Vienna said.

"If it was, I imagine I would've had to shave her head," Davii mused.

"I was a bad receptionist," Vienna admitted. "At least I got a good friend out of it."

Davii smiled and raised his glass, saying, "I'll drink to that."

"You'll drink to anything," Vienna said. "Speaking of drinking, watch out for that Sheila. She can really knock 'em back."

"Yes, Mother," Davii said.

Vienna rolled her eyes and sipped her wine. There was a lull in their conversation while she anticipated the next day, after Davii left. She tried to imagine what the apartment would be like without him in it and made a mental list of changes she'd have to face. It would be a lot quieter without his incessant club music. She wouldn't have to endure bad sitcoms anymore. Davii's ice cream addiction would no longer tempt her away from her diet. She could get more sleep, since Davii wouldn't keep her awake with salon stories. And maybe she wouldn't be late for work because of his long showers.

Vienna started to cry. Within seconds, she felt Davii's arms around her, and she rested her head on his shoulder, sobbing into his shirt. He stroked her back, whispering to her that everything would be okay. "Want me to get the tissues?" he asked. She nodded. When Davii returned with a full box of tissues, he removed one and held it to her nose. "Blow."

She batted it away from her face, saying, "I'm crying, not regressing. I'll do it myself." She dried her eyes and blew her nose. She dropped the used tissue onto the coffee table, then retrieved it and got up to throw it away in the kitchen.

"Even when you're a mess, you're obsessively clean," Davii teased.

"Yeah, and I won't have to go around cleaning up after you anymore," Vienna said.

"Yes, you will," Davii said. "I'll be back before you know it."

Vienna glared at him over the kitchen counter. She felt angry. More than anything, she hated it when people lied to her.

"You're not coming back," she stated firmly. "This is your big break, Davii. Use it. Ride the wave. Whatever cliché you need to make you see that this is your ticket out of here. They're going to love you. Sheila's going to take you back to New York with her, and you're never going to leave."

"Her husband might not like that," Davii said.

"You're going to meet some male model, or the sensible lawyer that you need to balance out your chaos and disorder. The bowl to your fruit cup."

"My what? You're not making any sense," Davii said.

"The two of you are going to be very happy, and you'll never give Indiana another thought," Vienna said.

"Get over here," Davii said, patting the sofa. Vienna grudgingly sat down next to him. "You're crazy if you think I want to leave you."

"I know you don't," she said, taking his hand in hers. "This isn't about me. It's about you wanting something bigger and better." Davii nodded and smiled. "I've known for longer than you think. I just hate to lose you."

"It's going to take a little more than a few miles for you to lose me," Davii said.

Vienna threw her arms around him again and said, "Thank you for being my friend."

"You, too, lady," he said. When they let go, Davii said, "Come on. This is my last chance to do your hair."

Vienna laughed and followed him into the bathroom, saying, "Okay. But give me something natural this time. Something that will last. It's going to take me a while to find someone I trust with my hair."

When Vienna woke up the next morning, it took her a moment to remember that it was her last day with Davii. She went into the bathroom and splashed cold water over her face. Then she ran her hands over her head, liking the feel of the newly shorn hair on her scalp.

"I asked for easy hair," she said to her reflection, "and the boy delivered."

She put on a pair of black leather pants, a black shirt and suit jacket, and boots with high heels. She wandered into the living room and found Davii waiting with his bags. She bowed slightly and said, "I'm in mourning, but I look fabulous."

"How could you not?" Davii responded. He kissed her head, then picked up his bags.

They took the elevator to the lobby, where a car waited outside to take him away from her. Vienna stopped in the middle of the floor. When Davii realized she wasn't next to him, he dropped his bags and walked back.

"This is where I get off," Vienna said.

"Right here? In the middle of the lobby? You dirty girl!"

She grinned, then said, "I think you have us confused. Look, I said good-bye to you last night. Now I'm just saying 'See you later.' "

"Okay. See ya, sweetie," Davii said after he hugged her again. Vienna watched as he walked away, picking up his bags and heading for the door. Before he went out, he turned one last time, and she waved.

Vienna turned away quickly and went into the mall. She walked aimlessly, grateful that she had the day off. She sat on a bench and watched people as they moved past her. She considered shopping but couldn't think of one thing she needed. She could have a drink somewhere, but it was too early. She pondered a quiet visit to Patti's Pages, where she could spend time reading books she never intended to buy. Then she felt guilty for not supporting the authors, even though she'd only imagined not buying them.

"I think I'm going crazy," Vienna said to herself. She knew that she couldn't self-diagnose, and that thinking she might be crazy meant she more than likely wasn't. But she definitely didn't feel like herself. She felt alone, an emotion she hadn't known for a while. She started walking again, resolving to go home and face her empty apartment. But she got turned around and didn't realize which way she was going until it was too late.

"Hi! We got some new hats in today. Would you like to try one on?"

"Can I ask you a question? Do you regularly get manicures? Would you like to try our new hand cream?"

"Your eyes are red. Would you like a pair of sunglasses?"

"No!" Vienna screamed at the Cart People. "I don't want your stinking hats! I don't want your cheap sunglasses! Leave me alone! Get away from me!"

She turned to run, but a pair of hands landed on her shoulders and guided her to a bench by a nearby fountain. She sat down, oblivious to the person next to her as she put her hands over her face and cried.

The man next to her soothed, "It's okay. You'll be fine."

"I can't seem to stop crying lately," Vienna said, calming down. She accepted the tissue the man offered and wiped at her eyes. "Thanks."

"You're welcome. My mother cries all the time, so I'm used to these sorts of things," he said. She quickly looked him over. He had kind brown eyes, sandy brown hair, perfect teeth, and a possible Oedipal complex. "Although she didn't cry because of me. Her birds kept dying." Vienna looked askance at the man. She couldn't believe he was going on about his mother's manic depression, which had nothing to do with her. "Of course, what she didn't realize was that she kept accidentally mixing gardening fertilizer in with their food. Not actual manure, but that chemical stuff. She was poisoning the damn birds and didn't even know it."

"Did she ever figure it out?" Vienna asked.

"No. My father did, but he didn't have the heart to tell her. He knew she'd be devastated if she found out she was the one killing them. He suggested moving the birds into another room, away from her gardening supplies. But she insisted that the birds loved being on the back porch. It was walled, with lots of windows. Apparently the birds needed a room with a view."

"So she just went on killing birds?" Vienna asked.

"Yes," the man said brightly.

"You're kidding."

"Yes," he repeated. Vienna stared at him, her face a mask of stone, until she shook her head and realized they were both laughing. "There. Don't you feel better?"

"I can't believe you lied to me like that," Vienna said, trying to be mad but finding it difficult.

"I had to. It was a mercy lie," he said.

"Thank you, but I try not to associate with liars," Vienna said.

"What if I told you the truth?"

"That would be a refreshing start," Vienna replied.

"Okay. Here goes. Even though your face is still a little tear-stained, I think you're the most beautiful woman in this mall," he said.

Vienna stared at him for a moment, then said, "Unlike your mother, I know fertilizer." When she stood up, so did he, which was when Vienna realized he was wearing a smock emblazoned with one of the cart logos. "You're a Cart Person?"

"I can't decide if that's politically correct or incredibly offensive," he said. "Since you're stunningly beautiful, I'll overlook the remark."

"Okay, Cart Man. Whatever you say," Vienna said offhandedly. Cart Man suddenly grabbed his heart, as if an invisible arrow had been shot into it. Vienna said, "Thanks for the tissue."

"If you could have it cleaned and pressed before you return it to me, I'd be most obliged," Cart Man said.

17

Tall, Mark, and Handsome

Derek tossed his crumpled Kleenexes into the wastebasket; the Marc Jacobs cologne had been his undoing. He'd staggered home from work mentally drained and physically exhausted. Natasha had dogged him all day, making it impossible for him to enjoy his favorite part of the job, the customers, with her incessant demands on him to inventory and move stock or change displays.

Then she'd mystified him by asking him to come to her desk in the stockroom at the end of his shift. He'd feared that she was about to fire him, but she'd done something more frightening. When he walked up, she bared her teeth in an expression approximating a smile.

"Sit down, Derek. At some point during every employee's first three months, I like to have a little chat. Are you happy in your position at Drayden's?" While Derek babbled what he knew was a feeble answer, he'd have sworn she wasn't listening. He was sure of it when she said, "Excellent. Often, a new employee benefits from mentoring by a more experienced employee. Do you have someone like that here at Drayden's?"

"No," he said, determined to quit on the spot if she offered to mentor him.

"You don't have a friend in management? Or Human Resources? Perhaps the person who referred you for your job?"

"No one referred me," Derek said. "I just filled out an application, got called for an interview with some people in HR, and received my job offer."

Natasha's smile grew more fixed, and her voice sounded almost sinister when she said, "Did you use someone at Drayden's as a reference?"

"No," Derek said. "I didn't know anyone who worked here."

"That will be all," she said abruptly, all semblance of a smile gone. "You may clock out."

All he'd wanted was the sanctity of his apartment and an endless hot shower. He paused long enough to ascertain that the phone's message light wasn't blinking, which meant that Hunter hadn't called. Rather than further torture himself by checking his e-mail, he started shedding clothes while he walked to the bathroom. After twenty minutes of being pummeled by near-scalding water, he felt almost human again. Then, as he was getting out of the shower, his elbow jostled a bottle, which shattered on the tile floor. He squatted to pick up shards of glass, and the next thing he knew he was sitting on the thick white bathmat and crying, immersed in memories of Hunter and the smell of Marc Jacobs, Hunter's signature scent.

He missed his boyfriend. He missed telling his daily stories to Hunter and hearing Hunter's version of things that went on at the Congreve. Although Hunter didn't talk much about his own job, he kept up with the drama in some of his employees' lives, plus there was never a shortage of unusual hotel guests to discuss.

Derek missed other things, too. The times he'd order lavish room service breakfasts after Hunter left to go riding, except Hunter would unexpectedly return, taking Derek back to bed, sharing breakfast with him after they made love. Unexpectedly catching sight of Hunter in the hotel lobby, his attitude as crisp and businesslike as his suit as he dealt with some aspect of hotel business. Derek would watch him and think, *He's mine. Later, I'll be there when he takes that suit off, and I can do anything I want with the body underneath it.*

He missed making love. Or having any sex at all, for that matter. And it hadn't helped that he'd been so attracted to Christian and Davii only to have it come to nothing physically. After months of self-gratification, Derek wanted another body in the bed next to him. He was used to being teased and touched, nuzzled and held.

He even missed Hunter's cigarette smoke. That smell, along with the Marc Jacobs cologne, kept him aware of Hunter's daily presence as the man in his life. It was the first thing he smelled in the morning and the last thing he smelled at night. It clung to his pillow and sometimes to his own clothes, and made him feel that Hunter was always near. Now all he felt was absence. Which would have been slightly more bearable if he knew Hunter felt the same way, and was missing Derek's scent, or the sound of his voice, or just his breathing presence in the room.

He threw the broken bottle on top of the soggy Kleenexes, made a halfhearted attempt to tame his cowlicks, and got dressed. Then he turned on the computer, slumping in his chair when there was nothing from Hunter. He answered some other e-mails without enthusiasm, then decided he had enough energy to indulge himself in an evening of people watching. It always made him feel better, and he'd undoubtedly see something that he could turn into a story with which to entertain his online friends rather than boring them with banal e-mails.

The Congreve was hosting some kind of software convention, which had evidently broken up not long before Derek went downstairs. The restaurant was busy and noisy, and Marlon, the maître d', tucked him into the kind of table that he knew Derek liked. It was a little out of the way and provided a good view of the room. The book in front of Derek was mostly a prop, because he was really reading the faces and actions of the people around him. They seemed energetic and happy. He didn't know if they were discussing software or more personal things, but the room was full of excited conversation punctuated by laughter. His spirits lifted at the sight of people enjoying themselves and one another.

When he was little, his mother's favorite TV show had been *The Love Boat.* Derek envisioned the diners around him on a cruise together. The woman fiddling with her hair was having an unexpected reunion with a man a few years older; Derek titled their story "Polly and Mr. Fincher." Mr. Fincher had been the high school history teacher that Polly had a crush on. Now both were divorced, and Polly hoped he no longer saw her as the gawky kid with braces who watched him from the fourth row.

His eyes moved on to two men in earnest conversation, setting up their story as "Betrayal." Barclay looked so serious because his business partner, William, was telling him that he'd lost all their company savings at the racetrack. The odd thing was, Barclay had dreaded this cruise because he'd intended to tell William about his affair with Mrs. William. Now he wasn't sure whether to confess and put them on equal footing or express his outrage over the money.

An older couple, smiling as they tapped their glasses together, became part of "'Til Death Do Us Part." When Larry had been diagnosed with a terminal illness, his wife, Rachel, booked them on the cruise for a last hurrah. The day before they left home, Larry got a call from his doctor explaining that he'd been given the wrong test results. Even though Larry was fine, he didn't want to tell Rachel, because this was the nicest she'd been to him in more than thirty years of marriage.

Derek played out their stories until he finished dinner, then he got another cup of coffee, content to stay where he was. He was discreetly checking out other diners' desserts, trying to decide whether or not to order one, when he realized that a man a few tables away was watching him with an amused look. He didn't break his gaze even when he saw Derek checking him out. He was a few years older than Derek, with a closely shaved head and a five o'clock shadow that matched his rumpled suit. He was wearing a red tie, but it had been loosened as if to indicate that this was the end of a long day instead of a break between meetings.

Derek dropped his eyes to his book for a few seconds, fantasizing about why the man was at the hotel. He didn't seem to be part of the software group; maybe he'd just flown in and had some kind of business meeting the next day. Maybe he was bored and lonely, hoping for the diversion of a little flirtation.

He looked over to see if Red Tie was still watching him, but found he was busy taking care of his check. Red Tie didn't glance at Derek again before leaving the restaurant. Derek sighed, thinking it was probably for the best. After Christian, he'd promised to stop assuming that handsome men who seemed to be flirting with him were gay. Apparently, he'd once again misjudged his man. Red Tie was undoubtedly the married father of two. He probably resented having business out of town. He'd been hoping to see his kids' soccer game, play poker with the guys, or do any of those other things straight guys did and Derek knew nothing about.

Derek decided against dessert, signed the check so it could be written off to Hunter, and left his usual generous tip for the waiter.

Good service was among the Congreve's claims to fame, but he was sure it didn't hurt to be Hunter's boyfriend. He supposed if Hunter dumped him, he'd find out how the staff really felt about him. Then again, if he and Hunter broke up, there was nothing at the Congreve he'd be able to afford.

He picked up a copy of the *Terre Haute Times,* one of the Barrister papers, and settled in, in the lobby. As he was turning a page, he noticed that Red Tie was also sitting in the lobby, concentrating on what looked like business papers. When Red Tie glanced around, Derek retreated behind his paper. He got interested in a story about local politics, and when he looked again, Red Tie was gone.

He watched a few other people come and go until he realized that the employees behind the desk were watching him. He didn't want to give them any reason to gossip, so he finally wandered into the Aurora, wishing Davii was still around. A little harmless flirting would be great, and Davii always made him feel better.

It wasn't one of Sheree's nights to perform, so he didn't even have the assurance of good conversation to look forward to. The bartender, Steve, was busy mixing drinks at the far end of the bar, and Derek took the only empty stool without a drink in front of it and waited patiently for Steve to get to him. He noticed Hunter's assistant, Riley, leaving the bar with a couple who were probably important hotel guests. A few minutes later, his neighbor returned from the restroom and proved to be Red Tie.

He grinned at Derek, shook his head as he sat down, and said, "Are you following me?"

"Not intentionally," Derek said.

"Damn," Red Tie said. "I'm Mark. Can I buy you a drink?"

"Derek. But I don't pay for my drinks here."

"In that case, I'll let you buy me one," Mark said. He had a beautiful smile.

Derek glanced at Steve, who nodded and, after giving Derek his usual cosmopolitan, put a fresh beer in front of Mark.

"Cheap date," Derek said, looking at the bottle.

"Especially when you don't have to pay," Mark chided. "Too bad I'm low maintenance."

"Low maintenance is good," Derek said.

"I can be more demanding elsewhere," Mark said. He waited

until Steve was out of earshot and said, "Like in room 1223. I'm guessing we should leave separately."

"I like a smart man," Derek said. He slid off his stool and shook Mark's hand as if they were brief acquaintances saying good-bye. By the time he got to the elevator, he was wondering if he'd lost his mind. The man was a guest in Hunter's hotel. Even if leaving separately fooled Steve or anyone else who noticed, there were security cameras on every floor. But as he pressed the button for twelve, he realized he didn't care. At least he wouldn't be spending another night alone.

Mark didn't make him wait long, smiling again as he slid his card key in and pushed the door open. "Welcome to my home for the night. Take anything you want from the minibar."

Derek shook his head and reached over to finish unknotting Mark's tie. By the time they made it to the bed, they were both undressed. When Mark dug into a bag next to the bed and brought out condoms and lube, Derek said, "Nothing like a Boy Scout."

"I'm gay; I can't be a Boy Scout. I'm just a very, very lucky man tonight."

Derek decided he was the lucky one. Not only was Mark sexy, he was sensual, exploring every inch of Derek to find out what pleased him. Derek returned the favor, thrilled to experience new skin, new scent, and new taste. It was like stumbling into a banquet after famine. Derek wanted some of everything.

Even better was that when the two of them were finally sated, Mark didn't drop any hints about Derek leaving. They lay on the bed together, occasionally exploring each other with their hands, and Derek said, "You have incredible skin. It feels so good." When Mark laughed, he asked, "What?"

"Have you ever noticed that when you're lying in bed with a man, thinking something nice about him, he says the same thing about you? Because I was just thinking how good your skin feels against mine. How good it feels having you next to me in general. Can you stay?"

Since he was off the next day, Derek nodded. Mark wrapped his arms around him, settling them into a spooning position, with Derek facing out. It was so comforting to be held . . .

The next thing he knew, Mark was nudging him awake. Lost somewhere between his memories of the night before and his fantasy about Mark's life, Derek asked, "Don't you have a meeting to get to?"

"That was yesterday," Mark said. "I fly out at two. But I don't have to check out—"

"Until noon," Derek said, knowing that all too well.

When he stretched, trying to feel more awake, Mark pushed the sheets down to their hips. First he kissed him, then he moved his mouth down Derek's body. Derek's back arched with pleasure, but Mark didn't let things get too far before he came back for another kiss.

"Will I make you late for class?" he asked.

"I'm not a student," Derek said. "I work here. At the mall, I mean."

"I don't know why I thought you were in college," Mark said. "I was having a little fantasy of you in a frat house."

"I live at the mall, too," Derek said, shivering as Mark traced his ear with his tongue.

Mark pulled away and said, "Really? I'm meeting a real live Mall Mole?"

Derek laughed and said, "I read that article, too. I guess I am, although I do leave the mall and see sunlight occasionally."

"You must have a million stories, considering all the people who pass through here," Mark said.

"Something like that," Derek said. Hoping to cut off the conversation, he dove for Mark under the covers.

"Come on," Mark finally said, dragging him from the bed. "We have to fuck in my fantastic bathroom. It's part of the Congreve experience."

It was hot to stare at their reflection in the mirror, and the carnelian-colored granite counters, along with the soft lighting and copper fixtures, made their skin glow. If Derek wasn't already familiar with this "Congreve experience," he might have enjoyed it even more. He felt better when they got into the glass-walled shower and lathered each other up, as if some of his guilt was washing down the drain.

Reality had hit, and again he wondered if he'd lost his mind. If the mall was like its own little city, the hotel was a neighborhood in which everyone gossiped. Juanita was going to know neither bed in his apartment had been slept in. Steve had seen them make their connection in the Aurora. There was no way of knowing what the desk clerks had noticed or what hotel security might have seen. At least Riley had left the Aurora before Derek did.

Later, when they were dressed, Mark said, "I travel to Indiana a few times a year. Can I call you?" He noticed Derek's hesitation and said, "Never mind. I've never been very good at this trick stuff."

"You have a boyfriend," Derek surmised.

"And I gathered last night that you do, as well."

"Sort of. Does yours know?"

"Yeah. It's a rare thing, but he knows. Yours?"

"I don't know. I mean, I've never—"

"Damn," Mark said, looking contrite. "I hope I didn't just fuck up a relationship."

"I had a great night. A great morning. No problem."

Later, in his own room, grateful that Juanita had already come and gone, Derek wondered if they should have traded numbers. Mark had been nice. But what would they talk about? He knew nothing about him. They'd exchanged less details with each other than body fluids. In fact, their personal histories were as safe as the sex.

And if Hunter asked questions . . .

He rolled his eyes. Hunter would never exert any effort to find out what Derek did while he was away. Nor would anyone tell him. That had been some kind of paranoid delusion.

At least I didn't tell Mark stories in bed, Derek thought.

But he'd still cheated on Hunter. The sad thing was, it didn't matter whether it was the first time or the last time. Derek was the only one who would ever regret it; Hunter wouldn't care.

18

Smells Like Teen Spirit

Christian wasn't aware of the time until a persistent whispering sound made him look up from the notes he was writing at his table in the Brew Moon Café. He located the source of the noise—four teenaged girls in school uniforms sitting a few tables away. He had a fleeting concern about whether it was advisable for teenagers to be addicted to caffeine, then nearly spit out his own coffee upon finding it stone cold. He glanced at his watch and realized he'd been taking up space at the café for nearly two hours.

He'd met with Emily-Anne Barrister and Hershel Wicks, Drayden's store manager, at the department store before it opened that morning. The event that Christian was helping Emily-Anne plan, the Big Bang Benefit for Breast Cancer, would be hosted by the planetarium. Costs had to be offset, so he and Emily-Anne had intended to pitch ideas to Hershel in hopes of getting corporate sponsorship from Drayden's.

The meeting had not begun on a high note. The Barrister dogs were in tow, and Jitters had nervously popped out what Emily-Anne euphemistically called a Tootsie Roll. Christian had grabbed a napkin, scooped it up, and tied it in a plastic bag while talking nonstop to keep Hershel's attention focused on his words rather than on what he was doing. Somehow in the confusion, Christian had ended up promising to arrange not only the catering for the event, but also the entertainment.

Although they'd ultimately gotten a substantial financial commitment from Drayden's, Christian was beginning to wonder if his association with Emily-Anne was such a good thing after all. He liked her. She was down-to-earth, friendly, and full of surprises. But he had to admit that she was a disaster on high heels. Since his public image was one of style, order, and decorum, Emily-Anne was like the anti-Christian.

The schoolgirls began to giggle and whisper again, and he realized they were staring at him. He did a discreet self-check: his zipper was fine and nothing else seemed amiss. Then he heard one of them murmur, "So cute!" and he dropped his eyes, trying not to smile. Since he was in his midtwenties, it wasn't often that girls their age noticed him. It was gratifying but a little sad, too, to think that his fan club consisted mostly of gay men, career-obsessed businesswomen, underage girls, and a dog with a tendency to soil the carpet when excited. He really needed a date.

When they'd left yoga the night before, Derek told him the same thing after pointing out that the two of them had been bitching for five minutes about the trauma of finding a new hairdresser since Davii's departure. "There are lots of hot women in our yoga class," Derek suggested.

Christian looked at him and said, "I think your version of hot women and mine may be different."

"All right, then, what about Vienna?" Derek asked.

"Never, *never* match-make your friends," Christian warned. "Somebody always gets screwed in that deal. And not in a good way. Don't you have enough relationship issues of your own? Why are you giving me advice?"

"Ha," Derek said with a gleam in his eye. "You give relationship advice to lots of your clients, and you—"

"All right," Christian said, cutting him off. "I'll get a date. On my own terms."

He packed up his papers and threw away the cold coffee, conscious that the girls were watching his every move. It really was flattering, and he gave them a warm smile before he left the café. While he pretended to window-shop, he was actually checking out mall patrons for potential romance, disheartened to see primarily tourists, young mothers pushing strollers, elderly mall walkers, and more high school kids. Although he wasn't sure about the school part unless they were all truants, since it was just after noon on a weekday.

He wandered into Drayden's, where he found Derek rearranging a display while whispering to Vienna.

"I see you don't have enough to do if you have time to stand around and chat with friends," Christian said in his best imitation of Natasha Deere.

"Your need to comment on our actions fascinates me. I have to wonder if you're projecting. Perhaps you're using us as a measure of your own self-assessment. Are you wanting more idle time?" Vienna responded.

Christian covertly studied her, thinking of Derek's suggestion that he ask her out. She was a stunning woman. Her makeup was soft and natural, unlike the wild, curly brown wig she was wearing. Apparently, the novelty of her hairstyle had worn off. She'd foregone her usual black for a pair of tan leather pants and a creamy beige angora top, which threatened to fall off one shoulder. Her Lillith Allure smock might have ruined the look, but on Vienna it seemed like the accessory of the season, as if Kate Spade had glanced up from her sketchbook and intoned, "Smocks!"

Derek left to help a customer, and Vienna hissed, "Forget your issues. That, my friend, is what we in the business call a real freak." Christian looked where she indicated and saw a petite brunette holding a red high-heeled Jimmy Choo shoe close to her mouth, as if she was about to kiss it. "Girl, get a room," Vienna said.

"Do you always get weirdos in here?" Christian asked.

"Weirdos, inferiority complexes, megalomaniacs, and fetishists of all kinds, yes."

"Drayden's Hospital for the Mentally Infirm," Christian suggested.

"Never have so many needed me so much," Vienna said. "Why do you think I take so many breaks?"

"At least you're using your talent to build self-esteem through cosmetics."

"True. That's better than some of the other jobs I've had in this mall. Which reminds me. I had a thought about the cancer benefit. Emily-Anne should ask some of the mall restaurants to donate food."

"Emily-Anne has managed to delegate that task to me," Christian said. "Thanks for the idea. You're a genius."

"That may be, though my Mensa scores haven't come in yet. I

just know that several restaurants have done that for past charity events."

"Which mall restaurant did you work at?" Christian asked.

"Which one haven't I worked at would be a better question."

"Which one haven't—"

"Galileo's Glass," Vienna interrupted, making a face.

"Good. Lukewarm buffalo wings and freezer-burned fries were not what I had in mind for the event."

"Oh, too bad. For a second there, it was feeling like home. Throw in an ambrosia salad, and we would've been on one of my mother's church picnic socials."

A voice behind them said, "I need food! Those Clinique chicks snatched up your donuts like starving Ethiopians."

They turned around to see a small Korean woman in a Cosmetics smock identical to Vienna's, and Vienna said, "Christian, this is Meg. Meg, Christian."

"I'm famished," Meg said in lieu of a greeting.

"I might have a Tic Tac," Christian offered, reaching into his pocket.

"That might work for Bianca, but I need meat," Meg insisted. "My stomach sounds like a helicopter flying low over Red Beach."

"How about a side of beef?" Vienna suggested, nodding toward a man who was hovering near Women's Shoes.

Meg rolled her eyes and said, "That's Benny from Security. I know people who've eaten from his restaurant and, from what I understand, they don't supersize, if you know what I mean."

Vienna nodded and said, "Overly pumped-up men are often trying to compensate for other shortcomings."

Christian suppressed a shudder, wondering if a date with Vienna would result in an equally cold-blooded assessment of him.

"Oh, look, there's my entrée now," Meg said perkily. Vienna and Christian followed her gaze, and Christian saw Emily-Anne leading her two dogs toward the exit. "And my dessert is sporting a diamond collar! Now that's class."

"Let's clock out and go to lunch early," Vienna said just as Derek returned. "See you later, boys."

"This is the longest I've seen you go without taking a call on your cell phone," Derek commented.

"It's turned off," Christian said. He told Derek about his morning meeting and the new responsibilities Emily-Anne had dumped on him. "So I've spent the last couple of hours strategizing, and I didn't want a lot of interruptions."

"I know someone who could fill the entertainment slot," Derek said.

"Who?"

"Sheree, from the Congreve piano bar."

"She'd be perfect. I might enlist you for a few more duties, too."

"I'll help you in any way I can," Derek promised. "Are you going to yoga tonight?"

Christian gave him a guilty look and confessed, "I need a yoga break." Derek seemed a little crestfallen, so he added, "I wouldn't mind doing something. Just something not healthy, balanced, productive, or—"

"Boring?" Derek asked.

"I am boring," Christian agreed. "I don't know why anyone ever thinks I'm gay."

"There are boring gay people, too," Derek said with a laugh. "Whenever I find myself in the mood you're in, I just ask myself—"

"What would Davii do?" Christian finished his sentence.

"He'd go for a nooner on the top floor of the parking garage," Derek said. "I'm on break in an hour."

Christian gave him a fraternal punch on the arm and said, "Sure. I'll meet you there. We can talk about babes. Anything else Davii might do?"

Derek appeared to concentrate and said, "Go dancing at Pluto, then sneak outside to the loading dock for a quickie."

"I see the Davii approach is getting us nowhere," Christian said.

Derek looked thoughtful until he finally exclaimed, "I've got it! Meet me here when I get off work at six."

Christian returned to Drayden's at the appointed hour and waited for Derek on a bench outside the store's entrance. He felt a twinge of anxiety, since he wasn't used to someone else taking the reins and planning an evening for him. He heard an incessant tapping noise and realized it was his own foot. *Get a grip,* he thought as he sat back and rested his ankle on his knee. He reminded himself that he was giving Derek a chance to do something different, too, which might help snap him out of the somewhat somber mood he'd been in lately.

"Ready for fun?" Derek asked, appearing suddenly. "Sorry if I kept you waiting. We couldn't leave until every display shoe on the floor was in its proper place. Which makes no sense because the morning staff moves everything to dust the shelves and tables, but what do I know, right?"

"What's on the agenda?" Christian asked.

"We're going to a concert," Derek said. "Come on."

While they walked through the mall, Derek seemed more like himself as he regaled Christian with stories about the crazy customers he'd assisted that day. His anecdotes ranged from an irate customer who couldn't understand why Drayden's wouldn't let her return a pair of five-year-old shoes that "hadn't worn well," to a man whose affair was revealed to his wife when their sales associate asked if she should messenger the purchase to his usual suite at the Congreve.

"She started beating him over the head with one of the shoes right there on the sales floor," Derek said.

"That's terrible," Christian said. "I shouldn't be laughing."

"We all wanted to," Derek assured him, "but couldn't, of course. Natasha was livid. But the absolute worst moment of my day was with a group of four women who made me bring out about fifty pairs of shoes for them to try on."

"Doesn't that usually happen?" Christian asked.

"Yes. But they only did it so I could take a picture of them at Drayden's trying on shoes. They had no intention of buying anything, and no regard for the fact that I brought out all those shoeboxes and had to put them back."

Christian made a face. "Bitches."

"Luckily, that's when poor Jonquil made the faux pas with the married couple and all hell broke loose," Derek said. "Natasha started screaming about how inept her staff is, that the sales floor was a mess, we have no respect for the lunch schedule, we're not ready for the Planter's Day Sale—if there was something to bitch about, she was right there bitching about it. She forced me to take lunch and made poor Jonquil put away all those shoeboxes as punishment. I felt so bad for her."

Christian was about to agree when he noticed that they were entering the Congreve lobby. "Are we watching Sheree perform? As far as I'm concerned, she's got the benefit. She doesn't have to audition. She's a shoo-in."

"Please," Derek begged. "Don't say 'shoe.' No, we're attending a different concert. But first we're having an appetizer."

Christian didn't question him further, although he wanted to when they passed the restaurant and lounges on the main floor and took the elevator to the top floor of the hotel. Derek led him to a stairwell, which they followed up to a steel door and finally onto the roof.

"Should we be up here?" Christian asked.

Derek shrugged and said, "I come up here occasionally when I need alone time. They've been talking about renovating it for the guests. Putting in a rooftop pool and a sundeck, or some such nonsense. I guess it's an adventurous and expensive project, because it hasn't happened yet. Nobody ever comes up here."

"They've been talking?" Christian repeated. "Who's 'they'?"

"Nobody," Derek said. "You know. You hang around. You hear things. Check out the view."

"It's phenomenal," Christian said, leaning on the four-foot-high wall that surrounded the edge of the hotel's roof. It was too dark to see the horizon, but Christian supposed that on a clear day, from their vantage point, he'd be able to see for miles across the flat landscape of Indiana. The only thing he could hear was the wind rushing past his ears and the occasional honk of a car horn. "You said something about appetizers?"

"Oh, yeah," Derek said. He walked behind a large air duct and returned with a paper bag. He reached inside and brought out a bottle of Jägermeister and two shot glasses. "Hope you're hungry."

One hour and several shots later, Christian and Derek were barely able to stand up. Christian looked at Derek and asked, "What were we laughing at?"

"I don't remember," Derek said.

"Man," Christian said. He tried to playfully punch Derek's shoulder but missed by several inches. "You're drunk."

Derek laughed again and looked at his watch, squinting in the dim light. "We'd better get going if we're going to make that concert on time."

"What concert? Where?" Christian asked.

"You'll see."

They retraced their route, practically falling out of the elevator and into the Congreve lobby. When Derek tripped on his own shoe, Christian caught him, saying, "Whoa, Nelly!"

"Who are you calling Nelly?" Derek asked, pointing his finger accusingly at Christian.

"Don't point at me," Christian said, trying to grab Derek's finger, but Derek pulled it away too quickly. Christian lunged at him and ended up knocking over a small potted palm. "Whoops!" They held each other for support while they laughed uncontrollably, until Christian put his arm around Derek's shoulder and said, "Lead on, McGruff."

"That's the crime dog," Derek corrected. "I think you mean Macduff."

"Whatever," Christian said.

They staggered through the mall until they reached a large crowd in the courtyard at the mall's center. A small stage had been erected behind the planetarium; hordes of teenagers and their parents were milling about.

"Who are we—" Christian was interrupted by the opening beats of a cheesy dance track and a burst of feedback from the speakers stacked next to the stage. He turned to see a trio of girls in vivid clothing and big hair skip onto the stage, waving at the crowd, until they met at center stage and began dancing in synchronized movements.

"Am I in hell?" Christian asked.

"This is Mall of the Universe," Derek reminded him. "You were expecting Aerosmith? Why do you think I got us liquored up first?"

Having acquired microphones, the girls began singing about all the men who'd done them wrong, which worried Christian, since they looked about fifteen years old. The kids in the audience seemed to know all the words to the song; they were dancing and singing along with the girls. The parents appeared bored and embarrassed, nervously looking around and exchanging withering glances. Except for the woman next to them. She looked at Christian and smiled, pushing a strand of long dark hair behind her ear as she blushed and turned her attention back to the stage.

"I think I'm being flirted with," Christian said to Derek.

"What?" Derek said absentmindedly. He was mirroring the girls' dance moves, stepping in place and doing complicated arm gestures, until he spun around and fell down. "Whoops!"

Christian grabbed his arm and hauled him up. "Stop that. That woman's flirting with me, and you're going to louse it up."

"Louse what up? What kind of woman hangs out at a Triple Threat mall show?"

"A what?"

Derek pointed to the stage and said, "Them. Triple Threat. That's their name. She's probably a mother of preteen brats just like them."

Christian glanced at the woman again. She saw him looking and smiled coyly. "There. Did you see her? She's hot," Christian said. In his mind, he was already taking her back to his place, where he'd break out a bottle of wine, they'd get to know each other, and then they'd—

"Do it all night long," the girls howled, hitting every note in their vocal register and sounding like a cat being put through a wringer.

"I haven't heard anything like that since my college roommate got plowed for the first time," Derek bellowed. "At least he was on key."

Christian laughed and said, "I hope you weren't in the room."

"No. I was staying with friends three dorms over," Derek said.

"Maybe I should book Triple Threat for Emily-Anne's benefit," Christian said. "People will pay to have them put on some clothes and shut up!" He and Derek were in the midst of another laughing fit when a purse connected with Christian's head. "Hey!" he exclaimed in surprise.

"That's my daughter you're talking about!" Christian looked up to see the woman he'd been flirting with glaring at him with what could only be described as a look of unadulterated hatred. "How dare you two?"

She swung her purse again, but Christian ducked and felt the supple leather of the handbag barely graze his cheek. He shoved Derek and yelled, "Run!"

As they dashed for the Galaxy Building, Derek said, "So. Yoga tomorrow?"

19

They Shoot Dragons, Don't They?

It was the purse that caught Vienna's eye. It was, perhaps, the largest one she'd ever seen, and she wondered what anyone had to carry that would require a purse that big. She looked at the woman holding it, and at the man with her, then trailed behind them while they wandered through Drayden's third floor. They were young, perhaps in their late twenties, both blond, both white, both dressed casually and holding hands. They never let go, which meant they had to be newlyweds. Vienna wondered if the woman's ring was digging into her husband's hand.

When they stopped in Linens to marvel at Drayden's signature burlap shower curtains, Vienna lunged at a display of towels and pretended to look through them.

"Aren't these a hoot?" the young woman asked her husband.

"They're butt ugly, if you ask me," he answered. "Who wants burlap shower curtains?"

"But look at the lettering. It's like they're old feed sacks or something," she said, ignoring her husband's sarcastic tone. Vienna had to admire her fortitude. "I think these would be so cute in our guest bathroom."

"Come on, Mary Beth, let's get out of here," he urged. "This place is dorky."

"I love this store!" Mary Beth exclaimed. "How can you say it's dorky, Richard? Where else can you find Ralph Lauren displayed next to burlap shower curtains? This place is unique, and I'm not leaving until I've seen everything in it."

Little Ricky, as Vienna immediately dubbed him, crossed his arms and pouted. He regressed so quickly that Vienna was surprised he didn't stamp his foot and suck his thumb. Mary Beth continued to look at shower curtains, ignoring her petulant husband. Vienna didn't blame Mary Beth at all. She disliked any husband who couldn't make time for his wife's interests. Shopping might not be intellectually stimulating or as exciting as a football game, but did it really require that much energy for a husband to get involved?

However, Vienna had to admit that Mary Beth wasn't being all that receptive to Little Ricky's feelings. She'd grabbed a wicker basket and was filling it with towels, not even bothering to ask Little Ricky if he liked them, completely ignoring him as he stood behind her with his arms folded. Was it really that difficult for Mary Beth to include Little Ricky in her activities? It was no wonder Little Ricky was acting like a child when Mary Beth was obviously so keen to play mommy.

When Vienna realized that Little Ricky's eyes were glued on her breasts, she decided to intervene. Turning to Mary Beth, she said, "Hi! Having fun?"

"Yes, thank you. Do you work here?" Mary Beth asked.

Before Vienna could answer, Little Ricky said, "Of course, she does, Mary Beth. Strangers don't just walk up and say hi. She's probably going to try to sell you those stupid burlap curtains."

"You'd be surprised," Vienna said. "We do our best to make Drayden's feel like a second home, so people get comfortable here and interact a lot. It's a fun place. I do work in the store, but in Cosmetics. I'm more likely to push nail polish on you than those curtains."

"Sorry," Little Ricky said, obviously chagrined.

"It's okay, honey," Vienna said. "Where are you two from?"

"We're here from Texas," Mary Beth answered.

"Texas!" Vienna exclaimed, thinking that might explain the oversized purse. "Do you like barbecue?"

"Of course!" Little Ricky said, his voice suddenly booming.

"We've got a fabulous outdoor section right over there," Vienna said, pointing across the floor. "You can even get branding irons made with your initials. You should check it out." Vienna turned to

Mary Beth and added, "They've got burlap picnic table covers, too. Go over there with him and take a look."

Vienna watched them walk away, once again holding hands. Stephanie Flaegler, the manager of Linens, walked over and said, "Vienna, I keep telling you to use your powers for evil instead of good, but you just won't listen!"

"I'm perfect, and I must be stopped," Vienna stated emphatically. "I couldn't help myself. They were so nauseatingly sweet together. I had to butt in."

"I hate to turn into a manager on you, but are you on the clock?" Stephanie asked.

Vienna smiled and said, "I'm on a fifteen-minute break."

"Exactly how many of those do you take in a given day?"

Vienna held a burlap place mat above her head and shouted, "Union!"

When she returned to the Lillith Allure counter, Meg said, "Don't get too cozy. Melanie wants to see you in her office."

"Damn," Vienna muttered, wondering if her manager was finally going to penalize her for taking unauthorized breaks.

Bianca, who was lining the lips of an elderly woman, looked up from her work and said, "I don't think it's anything bad. Melanie seemed like she was in a good mood. Besides, she likes you. I'm sure if I was called in to see her, I'd get fired."

"I'd cover you when you go in, but my mother's got my AK-47," Meg said. "Just remember my grandmother's wise words: 'Stay low and keep your knife in your right hand.' "

"How funny! My grandmother said the exact same thing to me on my wedding day!" Vienna exclaimed.

When she joined Melanie in the Cosmetics office, she was prepared for the worst and ready to resign at the slightest inkling that things were going south. She was slightly shocked when Melanie asked, "Vienna, have you ever thought about entering Drayden's management program?"

"No. But does Drayden's have a twelve-step program? I might join that."

"Meg and Bianca recently had their annual reviews," Melanie explained. "They had nothing but good things to say about you, and how much fun they have working with you. It's not just them; there are other associates at other counters who feel the same. You've only been here a few months and you have the top sales at your counter; you rank number five in the whole department." She consulted a file, then continued. "Twenty-five percent of your sales are at other counters. I like that you're not afraid to take your clients to other counters. Your product-knowledge skills are exceptional. You have fun and get the job done. I admire that."

"Thank you," Vienna said, feeling a little embarrassed at all the fuss. "Okay, you talked me into it. I will run for president!"

Melanie laughed. She closed the file, leaned back in her chair, and said, "Tammy Milton is taking a management position in the Eau Claire store. I'll need a new assistant manager in a couple of months. Will you consider training for the position?"

Vienna examined her left hand and said, "What, no ring? What kind of proposal was that?"

"I'm not getting down on my knees," Melanie said. "I'm wearing Wolford hose, Vienna. Even you aren't worth putting a run in them."

"I'll think about it," Vienna finally said.

"Fantastic! Now, go to lunch."

Vienna returned to her counter. Bianca was painting the elderly woman's nails a dark shade of red. Meg was dusting shelves, until Vienna sat down on one of the vacant stools. She turned around and said, "You look like you narrowly escaped a mortar attack. What happened?"

"She offered me a promotion," Vienna said.

"You poor thing," Meg said. "Wait. Why is that a bad thing? It's not like you lost a limb after walking through a minefield."

"Your grandfather?" Vienna asked.

"No. My uncle," Meg said.

"Do you have any aspirin? I feel a massive headache coming on," Vienna said, rubbing her temples.

"I might have some," the elderly woman said. She opened her purse with her free hand and placed several medication bottles on the counter. "What do you need? I've got verapamil, Darvocet, Diamox, Vicodin, Percocet." She continued looking through her purse. Bianca stared with her mouth hanging open. Meg and Vienna shared an amused glance. "How about some diazepam?"

"I'll get some Advil when I go to lunch," Vienna said. "Thank you, though. It's sweet of you to offer."

The woman shrugged and swept the bottles back into her purse.

She wrenched her hand from Bianca, examined it, and said, "This is hooker polish."

When the woman walked away, Bianca said, "I never do anything right." Without another word, she headed toward the women's restroom.

"That girl needs group therapy," Vienna said.

"Are you going to lunch?" Meg asked.

"I think so," Vienna said.

"I'm going to take a fifteen-minute break before you go," Meg said quickly. "Okay? Great! Bye!"

Meg dashed from their department, red-streaked hair flying behind her as she ran, before Vienna could stop her. Vienna said, "That was odd."

"You're telling me," a male voice said from behind her.

Vienna shrieked and turned around to see a large man standing there. She caught her breath and said, "You scared me! Don't do that to people."

The man ducked his head and stroked his long grizzly beard, looking like a sheepish bear, as he said, "I'm sorry."

"That's okay. Is there any way I can help you?"

"Yes. Is there a spa or something like that in this store?"

Vienna's eyes didn't move from his for a second. She used her peripheral vision to assess him, taking note of his complexion, long greasy hair, dirty jeans, and poor posture. She resisted the part of her mind that wanted to take him out back and hose him down. Instead, she said, "Not yet. They're planning on converting part of the fourth floor into a spa in the future. Probably sometime next year. The other Drayden's spas are fantastic. They have goat's milk baths, mud wraps, all sorts of treatments based on Nordic home remedies."

"Oh," the man said, looking forlorn. "Okay. Sorry to bother you."

Before he could walk away, Vienna said, "Wait. What is it you're looking for?" When he turned around again, she thrust out her hand and said, "I'm Vienna."

"I'm DeWitt," he said. "Maybe you could help me. I wanted a makeover."

"Honey, you don't need any blush or lipstick. Trust me," Vienna said. "Your friends would probably beat you up if you bought anything from my counter."

"That's just it. I don't have any friends," DeWitt said. "I want to change everything. New clothes, new hair, new me."

Meg returned to the Lillith Allure counter and asked, "Is everything okay, Vienna?"

Vienna could see the ridicule lurking behind Meg's concerned expression and realized why DeWitt wanted to become a new person. She glanced at the surrounding counters and noticed other Cosmetics associates looking her way and whispering to each other.

"No, Meg, I'm fine," she said loudly. "Now that you're back, I'm going to lunch. DeWitt, would you like to join me? Of course you would. I won't take no." She linked her arm in DeWitt's and led him toward the store's entrance. She lowered her register and said, "You don't want anything in this store anyway. It's all a bunch of overpriced crap." She took him to Bert's Bar & Grille and commandeered a table for them. "What'll you have, DeWitt? I'm buying."

"I'm really not that hungry," he said.

"Who said anything about eating?" she asked. It was three o'clock in the afternoon; most of the Drayden's staff had already been to lunch, so she wasn't worried about running into anyone she knew. She turned to their waiter and said, "I'll have a Corona." She raised her eyebrows at DeWitt, who nodded. "Make that two, please."

She engaged DeWitt in small talk and was pleasantly surprised that she enjoyed his company. She found herself talking openly with him, especially since he was reticent to talk about himself. She told him about growing up in Gary and how she never felt like she fit in. "My friends were all listening to Michael Jackson and anything R & B. I was into hair bands. Rocking out to Bon Jovi alone in my room."

"You're kidding me," DeWitt said.

"I kid you not," Vienna said. "I had all the albums. White Lion, Whitesnake, Great White, all the white bands. Come to think of it, there were no black guys in hair bands."

"Nuh-uh," DeWitt said, gesturing with his beer bottle. "Guns N' Roses. Slash was black."

"Was?" Vienna asked, and laughed. "Okay, I'll give you that one. Anyway, I could give you a good speech about how we're all different, but unique in our own little ways. But I won't. We all know that. People will make you feel like crap every now and then. That's a given. But you've obviously got some self-esteem issues going on here. I think you're a pretty cool guy. What's got you so rattled?"

"I met this man who seemed to really like me. Turns out he was using me to get back at a friend of mine. At least, I thought she was my friend. She found out what he'd done and was really mean to me. She said a bunch of horrible things; I guess some of it hit home."

"I'm not following," Vienna said. She ordered another round and took a sip from a fresh bottle. "How did this guy use you?" DeWitt rolled his eyes and stared pointedly at her. "Oh. Now I get it. God, men suck."

"If you're lucky," DeWitt joked. "No, seriously, RB wasn't so bad, even though he was kind of two-faced about it. It's Nat who was the mean one."

"Nat? Who's he?"

"She. Natasha," he explained.

Vienna nearly spit her beer all over him. "Natasha? Does she work at Drayden's?"

"She's a manager," DeWitt said with a nod. "I probably shouldn't tell you this, since you work at the same place." Then, with no encouragement from Vienna, he described Natasha's verbal abuse in vivid detail, obviously needing to get it off his chest.

Vienna shuddered with sympathy for him. Maybe he wasn't a catch, but even DeWitt was worthy of being treated with kindness and respect. He was a human being, not a cockroach. "That woman makes me want to scream," Vienna stated. "I'm sorry she treated you that way. How do you know her?"

Vienna listened with her psychologist face as DeWitt described Natasha's celebrity obsession and its manifestation. It was actually mild compared to some of the aberrant behavior Vienna had treated in her time. Apparently, the bitch was like Sears—she had a softer side, and it played with dolls. Maybe she'd invented an entire alternate universe of dolls, and her Derek doll had hurt her Natasha doll's feelings. Vienna's mind wandered into a fantasy of Derek leaving G.I. Joe on Natasha's desk with a menacing note.

"Forget her," she said and directed the subject back to DeWitt. "Let's talk about you. How'd you end up with the sewing gig in the first place?"

"I used to manage the office of a business that sold and rented heavy equipment," DeWitt said. "I scheduled employees. Jobs. Rentals. Then farms started failing and being foreclosed. We were doing a lot of repossessions. Auctions. We had to cut back staff. My life was turning into a John Mellencamp song. My granny taught me to sew when I was a little boy. Easy stuff, but also embroidery, needlepoint. I worked for myself and did whatever sewing I could get. Natasha saw one of my ads in *Hoe & Sew* and called me. She was a cash cow. I guess she was paying as much for my silence as for anything else. And now," he affected a drawl, "she ain't payin' me nothin'. I figured I need to find office work again."

"Don't let her undermine your faith in your abilities." Vienna pulled a pen from her purse and wrote down Christian's name and number on a napkin. "I'm going to hook you up with a friend of mine."

"Is he cute?"

"Yes, but he's also straight," Vienna said. "I'm thinking he could get you a lot of alterations work. Several of his clients are upscale, so you might want to think about putting forth a more professional appearance." When DeWitt reddened, Vienna added, "Just get your beard trimmed, and maybe some new pants and shirts wouldn't be a bad idea." She took the napkin back. "I'll write down the name of a couple of shops in the mall you can visit. Tell them what you're doing and that I sent you, and they'll help you. There's nothing about you that needs changing. But every now and then, a house needs a new coat of paint. Know what I'm saying?"

"I got it," DeWitt said. "Thanks, Vienna."

After he left, Vienna finished her beer and pondered her position at Drayden's. She was flattered that Melanie wanted to promote her, but she worried that accepting the position would keep her in retail. There was a side of retail that Vienna didn't like, an angle confirmed by DeWitt. She didn't like pandering to people's insecurities, making them feel inferior just because they didn't own a pair of designer jeans.

Vienna toyed with the cuff of her Dolce & Gabbana shirt and felt guilty. She appreciated the finer things in life but never felt superior because of them. Or did she? She frowned, thinking about how judgmental she could be at times.

"At least I'm nothing like Natasha," Vienna muttered. Even thinking about Natasha made Vienna bitter. People who preyed on the weak in order to feel superior nauseated her. She'd always hated the way Natasha treated the sales associates, especially Derek. As if he didn't have enough problems already. Now that she knew Natasha's wrath had spread outside of Drayden's and into the rest of the mall, affecting innocuous individuals like DeWitt, she felt compelled to do something about it.

Vienna made up her mind to stay at Drayden's long enough to bring Natasha down. Once that task was completed, she'd find another job in the mall, hopefully something that didn't exploit people's base insecurities.

"Maybe I could work in a bank," Vienna mused.

"Is this Career Day?" a voice behind her asked.

Vienna turned around and saw Cart Man sitting at the table behind her. He smiled broadly and moved to the chair DeWitt had vacated. Vienna frowned after he sat down and said, "Please, have a seat."

"Okay," he said, still smiling. "Don't worry; I wasn't eavesdropping or anything. I just got here a few minutes ago, right before your boyfriend left. I didn't know I have a rival for your affections."

"I wasn't aware that I'm such a prize," Vienna said. "Do you think I'll fit on your mantel? Or more importantly, do you think you'll win?"

"I'm fairly confident," he said.

"I can see that. However, DeWitt's just an acquaintance. He's not after my affections," Vienna explained. "You shouldn't be either."

"I can't help myself," Cart Man said, leaning forward. "I'm helpless against your charms."

Vienna riffled through her purse. She pulled a rabbit's foot off her key chain and tossed it at him, saying, "Here. Knock yourself out and leave me be." She dropped some money on the table and turned to leave.

"Vienna, wait. Would you have dinner with me on Friday night?"

"I'm sorry. I have to work."

"What about Saturday?"

"You don't give up, do you?" she asked. When Cart Man smiled again and shook his head, she said, "I'm not a prize, or any object for that matter. There's no competition. But I do have dragons of my own that need slaying. If you're still around when I've finished them off, I'll get back to you about that dinner. Okay?"

"I'm not going anywhere," Cart Man said.

"Me either, baby," Vienna said. "Ain't that the sad truth?"

"One more thing," Cart Man said as she started to leave again. "Living Colour."

"Excuse me?"

"The band. They were black, and they rocked."

Vienna shook her finger at Cart Man, about to berate him for lying to her. Obviously he'd eavesdropped much longer than he'd admitted. But she decided to be amused by his impishness. "You're right. I forgot about them. I wouldn't exactly call them a hair band."

"Why? Were they bald?" he asked.

"Bald like me," Vienna quipped. "See you later, Cart Man."

"Go slay your dragons," he called after her. "I'll be in my ivory tower, awaiting your return."

Vienna found herself smiling during the rest of her shift, and Meg finally said, "Why do you look so happy? Does it have anything to do with that man?"

"What man?" Vienna asked.

"The one who looked like death eating a cracker."

"That's so mean," Bianca said. "I'd be happy, too, if I were offered a promotion. Which will never—"

"I'm just in a good mood," Vienna said.

"You're not yourself." Meg frowned. "You haven't taken a break since you got back."

"You're right. If it's okay with you two, I'm clocking out early. I have a date."

"You could do much better," Meg said. "I surrender. Go."

Vienna waved an airy good-bye and rushed home to change. When she got to the bowling alley, Christian looked at his watch and said, "Who are you? Why are you early?"

"Don't complain. Let's bowl," Derek begged. "I'm gonna kick ass."

She and Christian exchanged a glance behind Derek's back. Christian had talked her into this bowling date so she could see Derek's erratic mood shifts, but he seemed okay to her. He was even cheerier later, when he rehashed the finer points of his game over beers.

Vienna stretched her legs out in front of herself and said, "I think the reason I never liked bowling is because of the bad shoes."

"While I share your passion for shoes," Christian said, "I think the reason you don't like to bowl is because you're really bad at it."

"I am," she agreed without a hint of dismay. "This is the last place in the mall you can expect to find me filling out a job application."

"I thought you wanted to work at every store in the mall," Derek said.

"Technically, the bowling alley is not a store."

Christian's cell phone rang, and he pulled it from his pocket with an apologetic look. She and Derek kept quiet while Christian talked and made notes on his PalmPilot.

"Let me call Riley Blake at the Congreve and see what we can work out." Christian disconnected the call and said, "Sorry. I need to take care of this."

"I'll order us another pitcher," Vienna said.

She thought about DeWitt while Christian handled his latest crisis. She considered telling Derek about Natasha and her doll fetish, then decided not to. Derek had enough to worry about with Hunter and their rocky relationship. Knowing that his manager was three sandwiches short of a picnic might be too much for him to bear.

When Christian snapped his phone shut and dropped it on the table, Derek said, "Riley's really great, isn't he? My boyfriend tells me that he's always on top of things."

"He is," Christian agreed. He winced as his phone rang again, but Vienna grabbed it. "What are you doing?"

"Although workaholism isn't *recognized* as a psychological disorder, it *is* a psychological issue," she said, "defined as when your relationship with your work is the most significant one in your life."

"I'm expecting a call from Emily-Anne. I have to make a living," Christian said defensively.

"You also have to make time for yourself."

"She's right," Derek said. His eyes went past them to the television, and he said, "What's wrong with the universe? They're showing *Hamlet* on a TV in a bowling alley bar. Although maybe Mel Gibson makes it the working man's *Hamlet.*"

Vienna laughed, and Christian asked, "What's your favorite Shakespearean play?"

"I don't know. Probably *Othello,*" Derek said.

"I never read it," Christian said. "I think I saw it on a late movie once."

"The one with Laurence Olivier?" Derek asked.

"White actor in blackface," Vienna said. "They'd never get away with that today."

"Maybe they'll remake it with Danny Glover," Christian said. "They can sell it as a set with *Hamlet.*"

"They could splice them together and call it *Lethal Weapon the Fifth,*" Vienna said.

"I like *Othello* best because of the evil Igao. What a great villain he is," Derek mused.

"Let's go rent melodramatic old movies," Christian said, "and recast them."

"Something with dragons," Vienna said, ignoring their confused stares.

"You're really going to play hooky?" Derek finally asked Christian, his tone signifying approval.

"You're like Iago," Christian said, "exerting your sinister influence over my life."

"We're not in a tragedy," Derek said.

"Honey, have you *looked* at these shoes we're wearing?" Vienna asked.

20

Rear Windows

Riley checked with the events coordinator and confirmed that three separate groups of children of hotel guests had left on their excursions to the bowling alley, planetarium, and roller rink. After marking that off his list, he wrote a stern letter to the hotel's seafood distributor, complaining about an inferior shrimp shipment the week before.

With those two tasks completed, he felt justified in stopping for a cigarette-and-coffee break, during which it occurred to him that he hadn't monitored Derek's or Hunter's e-mail for a couple of days. It hadn't seemed pressing, since the two of them apparently weren't communicating. Which wasn't surprising—he'd witnessed Derek picking up a trick in the Aurora over a month ago. He was sure it was one of many, and he appreciated having another incident to hoard in his trove of information about Derek.

He turned to his laptop, sneaking first into Hunter's account, where he found four unread e-mails from Derek. He could read those in Derek's SENT mail. He was more interested in Hunter's e-mail exchange with Garry Prophet.

> *Con,*
> *I ran away and fell in love. If I wrote down on paper everything I've been taught to want, this person wouldn't match. Isn't that great? It's made it blindingly clear that Buffy is not for me.*
> *Pro*

Pro,
Whatever you're up to, it sounds intriguing. I know you haven't asked for it, but I feel compelled to give you advice. Just tell your family once and for all that Buffy is not an option. The day is gone when we could be forced into unhappy relationships simply because our families feel a merger is suitable. This entire romance, start to finish, was put in Buffy's head by the Barlows. I never even saw evidence that she particularly liked you. Take my word for it—running away is a temporary and miserable solution.

As for my own romance, I'm starting to get the feeling that it's doomed. Sad to say, I've been avoiding contact with Derek. We seem to do nothing but fight in e-mail, and our phone calls have become formalities during which neither of us says much that isn't trivial. At least I can see that he's miserable in his job. If he were satisfied, I'd be disappointed in him. He could be doing so much more with himself. On the day he finally quits a job he hates, I'll know he's come to his senses. I would fly him here immediately if he'd let me.

I get the idea that quitting our relationship is his first priority, and to that end, he drops the names of other men into our infrequent communication. It's all very casual. "I went on break with Erik" or "Christian said . . ." or "When Davii and I . . ." Who the hell is Christian? And who spells his name Davii? I envision infidelities with the son of religious fundamentalists and maybe a male stripper. At least Derek's going for variety. Australia was a bad idea, but I'm stuck as long as the old man wants me here. I can't believe six weeks has turned into three months. I brought it on myself.

Write when you get this, if you haven't permanently gone underground as a soldier of fortune or a French chef. Bon appetit. Con

Riley closed Hunter's mail and grimaced. He had to know who all these men were and if they were really threats to Hunter's relationship. Natasha had been useless. Any time he spoke with her, she rattled on about some black woman named Vienna who talked to Derek on the phone all the time and took too many breaks. Unless Derek had found a miraculous means to change his nature and be heterosexual, Riley didn't see how that information was of any help.

He logged into Derek's account, where he found a surprising amount of e-mail.

Sweetie,
If you hate your job and you're this confused about Hunter, just come home. Maybe Hunter went away to get a fresh perspective on things. You could do that, too. Your father and I won't interfere, but we hate hearing how unhappy you are. Some time away might do you good.

Thank you for helping me set up the e-mail account. I use the computers in the library on Tuesday and Thursday. But if you need me, you can call any time. Collect. Love, Mom

Yes, move home, Riley silently begged Derek. It would be perfect if Hunter came back to find Derek gone. Although it appeared that if Derek left Drayden's, Hunter would invite him to Australia. Riley couldn't think of anything more catastrophic.

He went through several more dull e-mails from Derek's online friends, then perked up at a new address, Mercer@galaxyapt.net.

Derek—Thanks for all the help with the event planning. Your suggestions have been good ones. I've been thinking over what you told me about moving. It seems like a good solution for everyone. Have you mentioned it to Vienna yet? Let me know if I can help. Christian

C. I haven't told anyone but you. I'm still thinking things over. I don't know. Davii's absence seems to have left us all with a big void in our lives. I don't want Vienna to get the wrong idea and think I'm trying to replace him. As if anyone could. The usual time tonight? Call me. D.

Derek—Last night was great. I told you it's all in the breathing! I was dizzy afterward. Almost euphoric. How did you feel? Christian

C. I feel muscles in places I didn't know I had them. I didn't know I could hold a position for that long, LOL. Seriously, I feel good. I owe it all to you. D.

Derek—Same time tonight? I'm really enjoying this, especially talking afterward. I feel like I'm sharing things I've been keeping bottled up for so long. It's great. Christian

C. It's a date! D.

Riley smiled; he knew the man Derek was interested in. He'd often booked conference rooms for Christian Mercer. Riley had *known* he was gay, even though Christian had never flirted back with him. Obviously Christian was a closet case, like Hunter's friend Garry. Regardless, Christian was a wonderful development. Derek had a hot affair going with another man. "Hold a position for that long," indeed.

Derek could not be allowed to quit his job and join Hunter in Australia. Riley was going to have to play another hand with Natasha and make sure she kept Derek right where he was. Everything Derek was doing portended the end of his relationship with Hunter: other men, a job Hunter didn't approve of, a possible move. Hunter would never stay in Indiana without Derek as a diversion. Soon the hotel would be all Riley's, and he could start making some long overdue changes.

"Um, Riley, excuse me for bothering you, but I need to ask for a favor."

The blood drained from Riley's face, and he quickly shut his laptop before spinning around to see Derek standing on the other side of his desk. He scrutinized Derek's expression for any evidence that he had seen that it was his e-mail Riley had been reading, but Derek seemed like his usual ineffectual, mousy self.

"What can I do for you, Derek?" Riley asked politely.

"I really need to talk to Hunter, but I think he may be on another dive trip or something. He's not answering my e-mails. I was wondering if you'd heard from him? Or, if you hear from him again, if you could forward his call to me after you talk?"

Riley's thoughts moved like lightning, and he said, "As a matter of fact, I'm due to hear from Hunter tonight. I always come back to the office so he can call me here. If it's urgent—"

"It is," Derek said.

Riley pretended to think it over, keeping his face pleasant, then he said, "It sounds like it should be private, too. I know Hunter doesn't always trust our switchboard operators not to listen in on his personal calls. Deplorable, but it's impossible to find people who aren't curious about him. Why don't you come back here tonight at eight? After I talk with him, I can transfer the call to you in his office. Then you can be sure your conversation is private."

Derek brightened and said, "Thanks, Riley. I appreciate that."

"It's absolutely no trouble. I'm always happy to assist you in any way I can, Derek. I know that's what Hunter wants."

Derek didn't look too convinced, but he merely said, "I'll see you at eight, then."

"Excellent," Riley said.

After Derek walked out, Riley slumped in his chair, relieved that the little sneak hadn't seen what was on his screen. Then he rolled his eyes. Derek was so dumb. The Congreve operators would never listen in on Hunter's phone calls. Riley, on the other hand, intended to get an earful on his extension later, with nothing but twenty feet and a closed door between him and Derek. Then he'd have another little chat with Natasha.

Some days are just too good to be true, Riley thought, picking up his coffee with a smile.

21

Wake-Up Call

Derek craved coffee, but instead of going to the Brew Moon Café, as he usually did, he walked to Starbucks on the Stars level. He could always count on it to be quiet there, because it was where the professional offices were located. There were a couple of general practitioners, an ophthalmologist, an allergist, two law practices, several architects, Derek's dentist, and, tucked into one corner, an acupuncturist. There were also a few mystery corporations whose names told Derek nothing, but sounded impressive.

He considered this area of the Stars level to be one of the hidden attractions of Mall of the Universe. It was on the top floor, and hanging ferns flourished because of the skylights. The foot traffic was purposeful. People came to this part of the mall for appointments, not to shop, and there were never children screaming around the beautiful replica of Versailles' Fountain of Saturn. Even Starbucks was serene, as most of its patrons were on a break from their offices and read or sat quietly, happy for a few moments away from their busy workdays.

It was a place where Derek could think without distractions. He desperately needed to organize his thoughts before the phone call Riley had promised him with Hunter. He had only the vaguest idea of what he planned to say, and no clue whatsoever about how Hunter was going to react.

He took his coffee to an empty table. Although it was close to an elderly gentleman in a conservative business suit sitting with a boy who might have been his teenaged grandson, the two weren't talking. Derek sat down, staring out at the fountain, and tried to compose his thoughts.

"You young men," the older man suddenly spoke, "have no context that allows you to appreciate the lives you're living."

Startled, Derek glanced around; the man wasn't looking at him, but at the boy. Derek scrutinized them for a minute and realized that he wasn't a boy, after all. Like Derek, he was probably in his early twenties. He simply looked young in his jeans and flannel shirt when contrasted to his companion.

"You don't read. You know nothing of our history. The hidden nature of it. The terrible sacrifice of one's truest desires to the pressure of society. You watch your sitcoms, each with its mandatory token gay character, drug yourselves, dance in your clubs, thoughtlessly share your beautiful bodies, and think it has always been thus."

The younger man glanced at Derek, rolled his eyes, and looked back at his companion, saying, "Just give me the credit card without a lecture, please. I have a lot of shopping to do today."

The older man took a slender wallet from his inside breast pocket, removed a credit card, and silently handed it over. Then he watched as the young man rose, leaving his half-finished coffee on the table, and sauntered off without a good-bye or a word of gratitude.

Derek looked down at his cup and felt sick to his stomach. Was that how people saw Hunter and him? Hunter wasn't old, and Derek hoped he himself had never acted as rude and spoiled. But the undeniable similarity between his situation and theirs caused Derek to feel self-loathing more bitter than the taste of his coffee.

I can't do this anymore, he thought. *I love him so much, but I can't beg for his love. Why would he give it? He must feel such contempt for me.*

He picked up his coffee and walked to the fountain, sitting on the edge and staring at the pool of water. He tried to practice the breathing techniques he'd been learning in yoga class. He needed to do something to make himself feel better.

He knew if he went to Vienna or Christian, they'd offer a sympathetic ear, but that came with a price. Vienna was predisposed to dislike Hunter; anything Derek might say about him would further taint her opinion. Which wasn't fair. Hunter might be distant, but he'd never mistreated him. Derek didn't want to trash his boyfriend, nor would he make it possible for anyone else to do so.

Christian, on the other hand, seemed to better understand the world Hunter inhabited, so he probably wouldn't judge Hunter harshly. However, although Derek was finding it easier every day to confide in Christian, he still felt awkward about discussing his relationship with him. He wasn't sure what assumptions Christian might have made about his boyfriend, but he knew Christian didn't realize it was Hunter Congreve.

His cell phone vibrated, and he took it out of his pocket, smiling when he saw the 917 area code. "Hi, Davii," he said.

"What are you wearing?" Davii asked.

"Sackcloth and ashes," Derek said.

"Hot," Davii said. "I have an afternoon free, tons of cell phone minutes, and I'm sitting in Central Park at Bethesda Fountain and thinking of you."

"Weird," Derek said. "I'm sitting at the Saturn fountain and wishing I had a gay man to talk to."

"Incredible!" Davii said. "I happen to be a gay man. What's up? Is the evil Natasha tormenting you again?"

"That's a given," Derek said. "But I'm actually brooding about Hunter and trying to make a decision."

"About?"

"I'm thinking of asking Vienna if I can move in with her."

Davii dropped his playful tone when he said, "Is Hunter still in Australia?"

"Yes."

"Is this a breakup? If it is, maybe you should wait until he comes home. It doesn't seem right to break up with him when he's not there to have it out with you."

"I don't know if it's a breakup," Derek said.

Davii listened quietly as Derek told him about tricking with Mark, and about all the feelings and thoughts that had been churning inside him. He finished by describing the interchange he'd just witnessed in Starbucks. When Derek finally trailed off, Davii said, "Forget the trick. You and Hunter never discussed monogamy, so it's not an issue. Derek, I may not have known you long, but trust me, anyone who knows you at all can see that you're not some sulking boy toy. Besides, you have no idea what the story is on those two men. The old guy sounds like a pompous asshole. The young guy could be his employee, who was shopping for him. Even if your perception is accurate, they have nothing to do with you and Hunter. Agree with me, or I'm hanging up on you."

"Don't hang up," Derek begged. "I'm listening."

"If you think you're doing Vienna a favor by moving in with her, don't do it. She can stand on her own two expensively shod feet. If, however, you're doing it because you're lonely and you want some company while Hunter's away, then tell both of them that. So they know it's temporary."

"But I'm not sure it would be temporary," Derek said.

"Then it's a breakup."

"Just because I move out—"

"Don't kid yourself. You can stay with Vienna, and that's a temporary thing. But if you move out, you're breaking up with him. I'm not telling you what to do, Derek, except to be honest with yourself. And with Hunter and Vienna."

"Okay," Derek said meekly.

"If you're using the threat of moving out as some kind of ultimatum, that almost always backfires."

"I'm not," Derek said honestly. "I think Hunter has been ready for me to move out for a long time. He won't stop me. I'm just not sure I'm ready to call it quits. If I were certain that he didn't want me . . . or that things aren't going to get better . . ."

Davii sighed and said, "You sound so confused. Why don't you just tell Hunter that? That you're confused. You don't know what to do. You don't know what he wants. It's his relationship, too. He needs to help you work through this."

Derek didn't feel too optimistic, since Hunter had never been the kind of man who talked about feelings or problems. If Hunter saw a problem, he took action. He didn't worry and fret about it.

"If only I had a skill like you, and could run off with the circus," Derek said.

Davii laughed and said, "It is a circus. I don't think I've ever worked harder or had more fun. Sheila works with some bizarre people. Everyone I meet, I size them up three ways. First, by their appearance, 'cause that's my job. Then, by what kind of story you'd start writing in your head about them. And finally, by how Vienna would diagnose them. I miss you guys."

"I miss you, too," Derek said. "I promise not to whine every time you call."

"It's all going to work out," Davii promised.

Derek hoped he was right, but he had butterflies in his stomach when he went to Hunter's office a few minutes before eight that night. Riley was on the phone; he pointed to the receiver with a nod to let Derek know he was already talking to Hunter. Then he waved him toward Hunter's office. When Derek went in and sat behind Hunter's desk, Riley got up and mouthed, "It'll be just a minute," then closed the door.

Derek turned and stared toward the lights of Terre Haute, thinking about what a tactful, discreet assistant Riley was. He knew some people, including Juanita, didn't like him. But Riley had always been pleasant to Derek. Maybe, like Natasha, Riley was just hard to work for. For all Derek knew, when Natasha was away from work, she was a million laughs. That impossibility made him smile. Hunter's phone rang, and Derek swallowed and picked it up with a soft "Hello."

"Derek? Riley said you need to talk to me. I've got five businessmen waiting in the next room for a lunch meeting. Could we do this later?"

"I don't think so," Derek said, sure he'd lose his nerve if he had to wait a few more hours.

"All right," Hunter said. "Hold for a couple of minutes, and let me send them on." Derek waited, then Hunter said, "Still there?"

"Yes."

"You have my undivided attention. What's the crisis?"

His question set Derek's teeth on edge, but he said, "Why haven't you responded to my e-mails? I've been asking you for days to call me."

"I haven't read your e-mails, so I didn't know. I'm swamped here, Derek. If it's urgent, you could have called me."

"I can't get the time difference straight," Derek said. When Hunter didn't say anything, Derek figured he was about to run out of patience. He tried to remember what Davii had told him and said, "I'm really confused."

Hunter sighed and said, "It's eight P.M. there. That makes it noon the next day here. Just add sixteen hours to whatever time it is there, and—"

"I'm not talking about time zones," Derek said. "I'm talking about us. I don't understand where we are."

"Have you been drinking?" Hunter asked.

"No! I mean our relationship. I feel like things are . . ." Derek trailed off, noticing a file folder on Hunter's desk that was marked SYDNEY. Without thinking, he opened it and looked at the top page, a copy of an e-mail.

> *Hunter,*
> *I am approving your request to go to Sydney, since you insisted that you can clear your schedule for between one and three months. You are not my first choice for this assignment. I will be closely monitoring your performance there. As I outlined earlier, the situation is complicated and will require delicate handling of all personalities involved. I'm expecting at least a sixty-hour work week from you. I realize that you will want to enjoy the country, but you are there on business, not pleasure. Keep that in mind at all times. I also understand the necessity of building goodwill. If you can show me a reason for combining leisure activities with business, I'll sign off on same.*
> *Randolph Congreve*

Derek's first reaction was distaste that Mr. Congreve used his full name when signing e-mails to his son. Then, feeling like his ears were ringing, he read the first two sentences again. Hunter had *asked* to go to Sydney. He hadn't been sent there. His father hadn't even wanted him to go. It was clearly Hunter's idea.

"Have we lost our connection? Derek? Are you there?" Hunter demanded in an impatient tone.

"I'm moving out," Derek said. Before Hunter could respond, he hurried to say, "I'm moving out of the hotel. Tonight. I'll leave my credit cards and my checkbook in the apartment. You can close the bank account if you want to. I haven't used it in a while, so there are no outstanding checks. If you don't mind, I'll take all my clothes with me. I need them for work. I won't take anything else. Just my personal stuff."

"Stop," Hunter said when Derek paused to take a breath. "You are not moving out. Don't be ridiculous."

"I'm moving in with a friend," Derek said, ignoring him. "I won't have the computer account anymore, not that you read my e-mail anyway. But you have my cell phone number, and you know where I work, if you have some reason to call me."

"Derek, I can't get into this with you right now. Go back to our apartment, and I'll call you as soon as I'm free."

"Believe me, you're free," Derek said. "By the time you get back from Sydney, maybe we'll both feel like talking. Right now, I don't have anything else to say." He hung up, then stared at the phone, aghast. He'd never hung up on Hunter before. And he'd made his declaration about moving out without even talking to Vienna. Which meant that right now, he was basically homeless.

He closed the folder on Randolph Congreve's e-mail and took a deep breath. He had to keep his composure in case Riley was still outside. He didn't want anyone to see him fall apart.

When he finally walked out of Hunter's office, Riley was gone, and everything was turned off and put away. Derek made sure the office door locked behind him, then he walked to the elevator. His hand hesitated in front of the UP button, which would take him to his floor. Or rather, to Hunter's floor. He hit the DOWN button instead.

It was still early enough for him to walk through the mall to the Galaxy Building without checking in with security, so Derek left the Congreve and walked toward Vienna's. He kept his eyes straight ahead when he passed Drayden's, fearful that if he had to speak to anyone he knew, he'd start crying.

He took the elevator to the eighth floor, then rested his head against Vienna's door, reluctant to knock. If she'd be mad at him for showing up without calling, she'd have a lot more to get mad about soon after letting him in. But of all the people he could run to, somehow Vienna seemed like the one he needed most.

He knocked. After a minute, he heard a rustling on the other side of the door. She was probably looking through the peephole and weighing the wisdom of letting him in. Then the door opened, and Vienna said, "Job or boyfriend?"

"Boyfriend. How do you know when you're having a nervous breakdown?"

"Is this a professional consultation, or do you need a friend?"

He just nodded, and she pulled him into the apartment, leading him to the sofa and pushing him down. She then handed him a box of Kleenex, turned off the television, brought him a bottle of water, and disappeared toward her bedroom. When she came back, she'd changed from the silk robe she'd been wearing into a pair of jeans and a sleeveless sweater that looked so soft it made Derek want to bury his tear-stained face in it. She dropped next to him and put on a pair of socks. Finally, she sat cross-legged on the sofa, facing him.

"I can't talk yet," he said.

"My parents didn't think I should marry Kevin," she said after a pause. "They said he was wrong for me. When we got divorced, even though he was a cheating snake, my mother treated me like it was my fault. I guess for marrying him in the first place. In some ways, I was in the same boat as you. I'd made Kevin my whole world. I had professional acquaintances, but I didn't have any close friends that I could talk to. While I was hearing a lot of 'I told you so' and coping with the end of my marriage, I was facing professional censure, possible loss of my license to practice, and assault charges."

"You assaulted Kevin?"

"The other woman. I guess Davii didn't tell you everything. We'll save that story for another time. My point is, I needed to feel like somebody was on my side. I know what it's like to have your feelings and thoughts colliding around inside you like bumper cars. Your emotions can shift a dozen times in a day. The last thing you need to hear is somebody else's view of who's at fault. So all I'm going to say, as your friend and as a psychologist, is that I'm on your side, Derek." She noticed his disgruntled expression and said, "What?"

"Your breakup is a lot more exciting than mine."

She gave him a half-smile and said, "Everybody loves somebody else's misery. I should know. I loved my hundred dollars an hour."

"Damn. Is your friend rate cheaper?"

"You're covered under the Drayden's plan."

"Good. Otherwise I'd have to stay with Hunter to afford leaving him."

"You're leaving him?"

"Can I move in with you?" Derek asked.

She blinked, then said, "You're not even going to work up to that? Drop hints? Woo me?" When he shook his head, she said, "There's no room service here, Derek. No maid service. No wake-up calls."

"I don't think I need any more wake-up calls," Derek said. "I'll pay half of everything."

"When would you move in?"

"Tonight? All I have is clothes. And bathroom stuff. Some CDs and DVDs. There's not much to move if I leave my books there."

"Davii packed everything of his and put it in storage. There's nothing in his room but furniture and the residual scent of nag champa."

"I like nag champa."

"Me, too. Go get your stuff." They hugged, then Vienna walked him to the door. "I'll give you Davii's key when you get back."

"Okay."

Derek got a pass from the guard in the Galaxy lobby and walked back through the mall to the Congreve. He felt a little surreal. When he went into Hunter's apartment, he powered on his computer and wrote down all the e-mail names in his address book. He was sure Vienna would let him use her PC to open some kind of mail account and let his online contacts know his new e-mail address.

He didn't want to think, so he didn't allow himself to be still long. After packing his bathroom stuff, he went into his bedroom, looking with despair at all his clothes. He'd have to make more than one trip, which left his stomach in knots. He just wanted it over with.

When the phone rang, he froze. He wasn't ready to talk to Hunter yet, but he picked up the receiver.

"Hi, Derek, it's Liz at the front desk. Vienna is here to see you. Should I send her up?"

"Yes," Derek said, simultaneously deflated and relieved. "It's okay to give her the elevator code."

He opened the door and stared down the hall. When the elevator door opened, Vienna and Christian stepped out. Christian was pushing one of the hotel's luggage carts packed with suitcases.

"I figured you wouldn't have boxes or anything," Christian explained. "I've got garment bags, too, for your suits."

"Put on some music, and let's make this festive," Vienna said. "Nobody should have to pack alone. Got any wine?"

"You guys are great," Derek said. "Yes, I have wine. And if you want anything from Congreve's renowned room service, this is your last chance."

His spirits lifted while they packed, and he knew it wasn't the wine. His friends had taken what could have been a miserable, long ordeal and turned it into an occasion. They were better than Hallmark.

Once everything was packed, Vienna brushed her hands together and said, "Is that it? Do you have linens? Towels?"

"I didn't think of that," Derek admitted.

"Borrow some from the Congreve," Christian said. "You can return them when you get your own."

Vienna and Christian loaded the luggage cart while Derek went into Hunter's bedroom for the extra towels and sheets that Juanita kept supplied. Before leaving the room, he paused for a last look around. A picture of the two of them on the beach in P-town was on the dresser. He went over and picked it up, remembering the day it was taken. He wanted it, but he also wanted Hunter to be left with some physical evidence of their existence as a couple, so he moved it to his nightstand.

"Good-bye," he whispered.

They made a noisy group going through the empty mall, and again Derek was grateful that they'd come to help him. He'd have felt like he was walking on death row otherwise. They had a couple of giggling mishaps, and by the time they made it to Vienna's apartment, they were all giddy with exhaustion. They unloaded the luggage cart, and Christian told Derek he'd return it to the hotel. Once he'd gone, Derek and Vienna exchanged a weary look.

"If you don't mind, I'll unpack tomorrow," Derek said. "I just want to take a shower and get to sleep."

"I've got the bathroom first," Vienna said. "Seniority."

"I'll make my bed while you're in there," Derek said.

She went into the bathroom, and Derek walked to Davii's room—*his* room, he reminded himself, although he hoped that sleeping in Davii's old bed would give him good dreams. When he opened the door and turned on the light, he got a surprise. They must have done it together, because a CD player sat on the desk, freshly cut flowers adorned the dresser, and the painting of the male nude that he'd seen in Christian's apartment was hanging on the wall.

22

Children Should Be Shaken, Not Stirred

Natasha had often mused that if she were given the opportunity to remake the universe—the larger one, not the mall—to her specifications, one of her first acts would be to eliminate dreams. However much psychiatrists touted them, dreams were a nuisance that not only disturbed sleep but hung around like a stray cat yowling to be fed, only to turn on you in the end.

After she awoke from an afternoon nap, she lay on her sofa, frowning as she tried to recall the details of her dream. She'd been wearing her favorite red Ellen Tracy power suit and was surrounded by living Dollys. One Dolly was vowing that she'd get rid of invading varmints, while another insisted they should be cooked up and served with Horsey Sauce.

The dream's meaning was perfectly clear. The varmints included those weasels, Derek and Erik. And the sauce, found in packets at any Arby's, symbolized that tiresome ferret, RB.

She made herself a martini and returned to the sofa, tapping her glass with a manicured fingernail. She'd had just about enough of this whole ordeal. She was meant for bigger things, and she knew it. It was high time that everyone else understood it, too.

She'd started wadding up RB's messages at work and erasing them from her home phone without bothering to listen. He thought he was clever not giving her a callback number, merely telling her what time to expect his next call. Idiot. Even if she'd had his number, she was no longer interested in tracking him down. She'd confirmed that no police record existed that could be used against her at Drayden's. The store would never risk a lawsuit by firing her without evidence that she'd falsified her application. If petty gossip was enough to cost someone a job, even more of the country's sluggards would be on welfare.

Her options regarding Derek and Erik were a bit murkier. Erik's fate was the easier of the two. Since she knew that his father was an old classmate of Hershel's, all she had to do was shepherd his promotion out of her store, no matter how much it rankled her. He could become someone else's problem. She'd have to do a little research about what was available, but Hershel wouldn't be able to find fault with her suggestion that Erik move to a better position at another location. She'd just have to select a store in which she herself had no interest. The last thing she wanted was to run into Erik again on her career path. Unless she was driving a Humvee.

The image made her smile with grim satisfaction, and she walked into the kitchen to get an olive for her second martini. She stared into her glass as if it might provide an equally appealing vision of what to do about Derek. She hadn't dreamed he would be clever enough to evade her attempts to find out who'd handpicked his Drayden's job for him. She'd started watching every person he spoke to in the store, but the only friend he seemed to have at work was that sloth, Vienna. They were both nobodies who'd started at the same time.

Think, she commanded herself. She gripped her glass so hard that the stem snapped. She poured the rest of her drink down the sink and tossed the broken glass into the trash with frustration. If only there weren't so many stupid laws about confidentiality and privacy. Sure, they protected someone like her, who'd been guilty of nothing more than a little youthful folly. But they also thwarted her from getting access to Derek's personnel file and finding out if she had any real reason to fear his Drayden's connection.

What would Dolly do, she wondered.

She smiled again. Of course. She had to smoke the skunk out of the outhouse, which meant making Derek's time at work even more miserable. In spite of his abysmal skills, Derek had been meeting his sales goals. That was thanks not only to that glorified gofer, Christian Mercer, but to the other shoe sellers, who were apparently protecting Derek from Natasha's ire by directing customers his way.

She would put a stop to that by assigning Derek more tasks off the sales floor. If he thought he was unhappy now, he'd have greater reason to whine when his paychecks began to shrink. Money talked. If Derek did likewise, sooner or later his benefactor would confront Natasha, and her enemy would finally have a face and a name. Once she knew, she could plan her next step for eliminating Derek without risking her own career.

In fact, it wouldn't hurt to be a little proactive in that regard. The upcoming Planter's Day Sale would provide the perfect opportunity to shift her focus from Erik, Derek, and every other unpleasant part of her job and renew her acquaintance with the Lvandssons. Rumor had it that all three siblings would be present. Sven had the flaccid personality of an overcooked noodle, and Henrietta was essentially a boorish, overpaid stockroom clerk. But Drayden had always been pleasant to her.

She'd have to make sure everything was just right at the sale. She'd have a mental list of her accomplishments ready to share with Drayden, as well as visible signs that Women's Shoes was one of the best-managed departments in the store.

She allowed herself the luxury of daydreaming about what she wanted next at Drayden's: Hershel Wicks's job. She was dazzled by the brilliant prospects available to her as the store's manager. She could get rid of the slugs, slackers, and sluts who kept Drayden's from realizing its full potential. Once she'd fixed things, she would rapidly progress up the ladder that she'd been climbing for years and escape this hellhole.

She looked around her dreary apartment and came back to reality with a dull thud. How had she ever ended up in this backwoods, at the mercy of sexist pigs and rodents like RB? It was the opposite path Dolly had taken when she escaped the Appalachians for Nashville and then Hollywood.

In her bedroom, Natasha retrieved her hidden key, then she let herself into the Doll House, as she liked to call it. After locking herself in, she sat down and picked up one of the Dollys. She absentmindedly began to run a tiny comb through the doll's hair and thought about growing up in Beverly Hills.

She'd been ten years old the day she came home from school to find that in eight hours, her bedroom had been transformed into an environment as sterile and uncluttered as the rest of the Deere house. "Toys are for children," she'd been told. "Dolls are for little girls. You don't want people to think you're a baby, do you?"

No one had thought to consider that she actually was a child. She was advised to begin focusing on her schoolwork. Her parents had high expectations that didn't allow the time or space for playing or daydreaming.

She became more reclusive at home and at school. She knew well what was demanded of her in either setting, and she learned to stifle her desire to run and play, to giggle and have friends over, to jump rope and twirl in endless circles that would make the skirts she wore flare outward in broad umbrellas of fabric.

Those things didn't fit in with the image of who Natasha was supposed to be. She was to be seen and not heard, or heard only after being spoken to. She should be perfectly manicured and dressed in case Daddy had a client over. She was to keep her room spotless, her grades high, and her manners in check. She was supposed to be the Perfect Daughter. And she always did what she was supposed to.

She turned the doll over in her hands, barely seeing it as she continued to brush its hair, her lips pursed together.

When she was twelve years old, she'd awakened in the middle of the night with a stomachache. She endured it for as long as she could before going downstairs. Her parents were watching *The Tonight Show Starring Johnny Carson,* and Natasha paused in the doorway, listening to the woman who sat on the guest couch talking to Johnny. She was entranced by the way her clothes sparkled, and by the pile of blond hair on her head. The woman laughingly recounted tales of growing up in a poor family of twelve children. But Johnny told the audience that determination and hard work had been her means of escape and made her one of the most successful performers in the world.

Something simple and honest about the woman had clutched Natasha's heart. In spite of all the makeup and the wig, the long fake fingernails, and what had to be surgically enhanced breasts, she seemed like the most real person Natasha had ever seen. When Johnny introduced her song and called her Dolly Parton, Natasha's stomachache went away. She felt like she'd been given a new doll, one that was her own special secret.

That night had steeled her resolve. If Dolly could flee the mountains of Tennessee, then Natasha could also escape. She had demanded to be sent away to school, and her parents, sensing something new and frightening about her, had gladly acquiesced. It was a concession that would be repeated many times. They were always willing to spend money to keep her from becoming a problem, including the bribe her father had paid to get her out of that little shoplifting indiscretion.

Ultimately, she'd severed all her ties with them, always moving farther away from Beverly Hills, with only one constant in her life: her secret Dolly collection. She didn't need a family or friends. She didn't need the esteem of her employees or the respect of her bosses. Any rare moment of weakness, when she felt sad or lonely, would vanish in an instant, just like her childhood stomachache, in the reassuring company of her dolls.

DeWitt and RB had violated that sacred, solitary world, but just like Dolly, she would not be kept down by anyone. All she needed was a chance to impress Drayden Lvandsson at the sale, and she could set in motion her eventual escape from Mall of the Universe.

Then one day, when she had all the professional security she craved, she could be more like Dolly. She could charm people with a bright smile and nurture deserving employees with patience and understanding, so that they, too, would become successes.

She combed the doll's long blond tresses with increasingly rapid strokes until she looked down to see a wad of hair on her skirt next to the bald doll head.

23

Close Encounters of the Spurred Kind

Vienna pulled back the long braids of her wig and felt annoyed all over again by the edict from management to dress in overalls for the night. Drayden's had two huge sale events every year: the Planter's Day Sale in the spring and the Harvest Day Sale in autumn. Employees were strongly encouraged to dress as if they were about to plow the north forty. It all smacked of conformism to Vienna. She loved wearing denim, but the overalls looked peculiar with her Lillith Allure smock, which she was still required to wear.

According to Drayden's lore, the Lvandsson family threw a party in the original Drayden's store the night before their first Planter's Day Sale. Everybody in town attended to polka till dawn, then returned a few hours later to snatch up half-price Cattle Cozies, manure spreaders, and farm wear.

Sven Lvandsson saw the marketing genius of keeping the store open the night before the big sale, but he had long since discontinued the polka party aspect. Now the event was referred to as Planter's Day Preview Night. Drayden's best customers, especially those with the best credit ratings, were invited to grab discounted items the night before the big sale began.

The Planter's Day Sale was when Drayden's made the lion's share of its profits, so it was considered a big deal. The actual sale lasted two weeks. Shifts were extended to twelve-hour days, since business would nearly triple during that time frame. Drayden's employees had already run themselves ragged for over a week, marking down merchandise, reorganizing stockrooms, and preparing for the general mayhem that lay ahead.

Vienna had been scheduled for the evening shift of Preview Night, which meant she had to work six hours, help close the department at the end of the day, clean and restock her entire counter, then change at the last minute to work for the rest of the night. At least the people on the morning shift got four hours off before returning to work the sale. Nobody could tell the employees exactly how long Planter's Day Preview Night would last. By the time customers began trickling into the store, Vienna was already exhausted.

Her counter became swamped within minutes, and she delegated Bianca to stay on the cash register while she and Meg assisted as many customers as they could. Luckily, the first hour flew by, and when the crowd around their counter thinned, Vienna said, "I need a break. I'll see if I can manage to bring back bottles of water."

"Oh, man," Meg said, adjusting the straps of her overalls. "This better not be one of your infamous half-hour breaks, Vienna. I'm all for slacking, as you know, but not tonight. Okay?"

"Okay. I promise I'll be right back," Vienna insisted. "I still can't believe you actually wore overalls."

"Like we had a choice. I'm sure if we didn't follow the dress code, we'd be sold and shipped off to work in some Drayden's factory in Idaho. I may have conformed, but don't worry. I'm still me," Meg said, lifting a foot to show off her combat boot. "You never know when the enemy will strike. If one of these bitches gets out of line, I'll dropkick her to the other end of the mall." An elegantly dressed woman had walked up to the counter and apparently overheard Meg's comment, since she looked taken aback. Meg smiled broadly, waved Vienna away, and said, "Hi, may I help you?"

Bianca suddenly gasped and ducked beneath the counter. When Vienna turned around, she found herself face-to-face with the store manager, Hershel Wicks. He was flanked on one side by a hatchet-faced woman in a red denim suit with a walkie-talkie clipped to the pocket of her blazer, and on the other side by a grinning man in a royal blue Versace suit. Hershel's friends looked like backup singers for Elton John being escorted to the stage by a Jewish farmer.

"Good evening, Vienna," Hershel said pleasantly. "I'd like to introduce to you Henrietta and Drayden Lvandsson."

"It's lovely to meet—" Vienna was drowned out when Henrietta's walkie-talkie suddenly screeched with feedback.

"The pleasure's all—" Drayden stopped and frowned at Henrietta when her walkie-talkie squawked again. "Turn the damn thing off, Henri!"

Henrietta grabbed the walkie-talkie and bellowed, "What? Over."

"Shipment number twelve out of Bologna to Detroit was accidentally diverted to Dayton," a voice reported through a crackle of static. "Do we reship to Detroit? Over."

"Yes! And call me on my cell phone! Over!" Henrietta said.

"Security breach in sector seven," a different voice said. "Customers copulating in copy room on four. Over."

"I'm on it. Over," Henrietta said. She slapped Hershel on the back and said, "These sale events get crazier every year. I'll catch up to you guys later."

As she strode away, Drayden said, "You'll have to excuse my sister's impropriety. All those years working with pit crews has sullied her femininity. What little there was to begin with." Drayden laughed at his own joke, and Hershel joined in nervously. Vienna's polite smile clashed with her scrutinizing stare as she studied Drayden. He remained in close proximity to Hershel, even putting his arm around the store manager's shoulders as he continued speaking. "Hershel told me about your heroic efforts with the Lillith Allure people. I had to meet the woman who practically brought a bull to its knees."

"With all due respect, sir, I had nothing to do with stopping the bull," Vienna said. "What have you been telling him, Hershel?"

Drayden tightened his grip on Hershel's shoulder and shook him playfully as he said, "Have you been pulling my leg, old man? You could at least be a gentleman and pull the other one, too, while you're at it."

Hershel reddened and said, "Vienna was instrumental in making Sheila Meyers feel at home during her visit to Drayden's."

"Yes. I received a call from Lillith Parker and Frank Allen," Drayden said. "Despite the incident, they reported that Sheila had nothing but wonderful words for our Miss Vienna."

Vienna felt like a child who'd eaten all of her vegetables; both men gazed at her with dopey smiles. She looked around uneasily, as if searching for an escape route. Instead, she saw Derek standing on the edge of the carpet in Women's Shoes, greeting people as they entered his department. He looked cute in his overalls and floppy straw hat.

"Actually, I can't take all the credit for Sheila's happy times in Indiana," she said, stepping between Hershel and Drayden. She linked arms with Drayden and led him toward Derek, deciding to gloss over the fact that she'd called in sick the day of Sheila's appearance. "It's true; I did everything I could to welcome Sheila and make her in-store appearance run smoothly. But anyone could've done that. It was my friend Derek who went above and beyond the call of duty outside the store."

"How so?" Drayden asked.

"I'll let Derek tell you," Vienna said. She introduced Derek to Drayden and said, "I was telling Mr. Lvandsson about your stellar encounter with Sheila Meyers."

"My what?" Derek asked.

"He's so modest," Vienna stated. "You know, Derek. The way you comforted Sheila after that horrible incident with the bull, then called your friend Davii onto the scene when her hairdresser was incapacitated." She turned to Drayden and added, "It was a brilliant idea. She took Davii with her for the rest of her tour."

"Quick thinking, Derek," Drayden praised, wrapping his arm around Derek's shoulders and knocking the straw hat from his head. "Obviously Hershel was brilliant to hire you."

Vienna noticed that Natasha, who'd been conversing with a customer, was now slowly moving closer to them with a menacing expression. She, too, was wearing the requisite overalls, but hers were pressed, bore a DKNY logo, and were dressed up with a fitted blazer and dangerously pointed high heels.

"I completely agree," Vienna said. "In fact, Derek was in a few of my training classes. I hate to admit this, but at the time I wasn't sure that Drayden's was the right place for me. Derek convinced me to stick it out and not give up. He knew the job was made for me. He's so good at reading people."

"Vienna's manager recently recommended her for the management program," Hershel added.

"See? Derek knew I was management material," Vienna said. Natasha was now standing almost directly behind Derek. Vienna knew she had to throw all her eggs in one basket and do it quickly, before they boiled under Natasha's wrath. "Anyway, it was Derek who realized that the situation with the bull might mar Drayden's relationship with Lillith Allure. He did everything he could to smooth things over with Sheila. He even took her out that evening for a tour of the mall. She left with a good impression of Drayden's, instead of memories of a raging, snorting beast."

"Derek, we have customers who require your attention. Is this your hat on the floor?" Natasha interjected, handing him his hat as if it were his head on a platter. "We're here to make money, not stand around and—oh, Hershel! I didn't see you. I thought Derek and Vienna were loitering on company time. As usual. I didn't realize they were talking with you and—" She looked at Drayden, as if noticing him for the first time. "Mr. Lvandsson! It's so good to see you again."

"Drayden, I'm sure you remember Natasha Deere, manager of Women's Shoes," Hershel said politely.

"Of course," Drayden replied. Vienna noted with satisfaction that Drayden made no move to touch Natasha. His arm remained fraternally on Derek's shoulders while he said, "I was learning how lucky we are to have Derek on our team."

Vienna wondered to which team he was referring.

"I'm afraid I might have to disagree with that assessment," Natasha said curtly. Vienna scowled, especially when Natasha's expression changed from dour to frosty delight as she continued. "While Derek may not be my best associate, he isn't without his charm. In fact, I was going to recommend a transfer. Perhaps Derek would be better suited to Customer Service. He loves to talk on the phone, as Vienna can attest, since they're constantly chatting with each other." Before Vienna could protest, Natasha motioned to Derek and Drayden and added, "As you can see, Derek really shines when interacting with people."

"I'm not sure what you're implying, Natasha," Drayden said, pulling Derek in closer, "but I do agree that Derek seems to have excellent people skills. Perhaps those abilities *are* being squandered here, since there seem to be so few actual human beings in this department."

Vienna resisted the urge to gasp and cover her mouth, remembering that sudden noises and movements had caused Belle the bull to charge. Drayden locked eyes with Natasha, as if daring her to strike. Vienna noticed that Natasha's jaw was set and her hands were clenched into fists at her sides, as if straining not to stupidly lash out at the company's namesake. Derek was pale, and Hershel looked equally uncomfortable.

Drayden broke the tension by saying, "I think Hershel and I are being horrible hosts. It's Planter's Day Preview Night, and we're so wrapped up in one another that we're neglecting our guests." He released Derek but took his hand, saying, "I look forward to seeing you again, Derek. You're quite charming, and I'm sure you'll go far with our company. In fact, I'll see to it."

"It was an honor to meet you, sir," Derek said and quickly walked away.

"Ms. Deere," Drayden said, "I'm quite dismayed by your lack of tact this evening. There's an employee relations seminar in Chicago that I'm sure will benefit you. I'll book you and forward the details. I trust that won't be a problem?"

Natasha said icily, "Not at all."

"Perfect," Drayden said. Once Natasha skulked away, he turned to Vienna and said, "As for you, Miss Vienna, if we turn our backs on you for a second, somebody's liable to steal you away from us. You're obviously overqualified to stand behind a makeup counter."

"I can't imagine who, or what, could tempt me to leave your store, Mr. Lvandsson," Vienna said.

"What a fantastic liar you are, Vienna!" Drayden exclaimed. "You can't fool me. I couldn't wait to get away from this business when I was younger. There's nothing more boring than retail. I thought I'd die if I tried to live out my father's dreams. But I've learned that other aspects of the business can be fascinating. The fashion, the people who buy it, the people who sell it. Once I figured that out and conquered my fear of failure, nothing could hold me back."

"Atychiphobia," Vienna said absentmindedly.

"Excuse me?" Drayden asked. When Vienna shook her head, he said, "I'll be in town for a while. I'll make it a point to see you again."

As he kissed both her cheeks, Vienna said, "I can't wait."

"Once you've vanquished your demons, we'll figure out a way to get you out from behind that counter," Drayden said.

"Who said anything about demons?" Vienna asked.

"Perhaps I should've used the singular?" Drayden coyly asked. "Hershel, old man, let's see if we can find Henrietta. I'll get her to tell you the story about when she won a race against our neighbor in my father's horse and wagon."

After Drayden and Hershel walked away, Vienna peered into Women's Shoes. She couldn't spot Derek among the customers and hoped Natasha wasn't browbeating him. She returned to the Cosmetics area, wending through the crowd until she reached her counter.

"Where the hell have you been?" Meg demanded. "I thought you said you'd be right back. I was starting to think you'd been captured and tortured."

"Something like that," Vienna said.

"You forgot our bottles of water," Meg complained.

"It's okay," Bianca insisted. "I'm sure if Drayden Lvandsson wanted to meet me, I would have forgotten, too. Not that he'd ever want to meet me."

"I'm sorry. I'll go get them," Vienna said.

"No!" Meg and Bianca exclaimed in unison.

"Don't be silly; I'll be right back," Vienna vowed and hurried away from the sales floor.

24

I'll Take What's Behind Door Number One

Derek climbed the stairs to the second level of the stockroom. His head was pounding, his stomach felt inverted, and he wanted to throw up. He remembered those exact sensations from his rides on the Indy Cyclone when he was a kid. Every year when the garish little carnival returned to their shopping center in Evansville, Derek vowed he wouldn't ride the Cyclone. Reuben and his other friends would taunt him mercilessly until he gave in. He still had occasional nightmares about it.

As he stared unseeingly at rows of shoeboxes, it occurred to him that the Indy Cyclone was an apt comparison for his job. The punch of the time clock initiated the same dread he'd felt when the bolt slid into place on the ride. He could view daily life teeming around him, but he was trapped in a cage. Then the cage began moving in an endless loop, tossing and turning, sometimes suspending him upside down, then unexpectedly wrenching him upright before the next circuit.

The Cyclone was also like Natasha, whose behavior left him nauseatingly addled. Within the duration of one shift, she might show him disarming sweetness, turn on him with vicious criticism, or ignore him altogether, treating him to icy indifference. Her behavior never seemed related to either his personality or his job performance. He didn't need Vienna's advanced degrees to know that his boss could use extensive psychotherapy.

He slumped down, pulling his knees against his chest, grateful that Natasha had banished him from the sales floor, although she probably would appear any minute and begin screeching at him about his indolence. He puzzled over her earlier behavior. It seemed to him that as his manager, she should have been delighted to hear Drayden Lvandsson commending him. Instead, it had fine-tuned her hostility. She was determined to humiliate him in front of every customer he helped.

Derek didn't get it. If he'd been a stellar employee, he might have suspected that she felt threatened by him. If he was ever rude or unhelpful to a customer, she'd have been justified in protecting the store's interests. If his behavior indicated a tendency toward laziness, treachery, or thievery—but he was average in every sense of the word. He wasn't the kind of person who aroused great passion in others, whether anger, lust, hatred, or love. But if he wasn't the cause of it, if it was just Natasha's own demented personality, why was he the only one of her employees who had to endure her Sybil-like conduct? She either tolerated people or showed contempt for them. But he'd never seen her treat anyone else with the wide array of behaviors she directed toward him.

He no longer cared when she did it in front of his co-workers. They understood how she was. As embarrassing as it was around Christian or Vienna, at least he knew they were on his side. He didn't flatter himself that any of his customers gave him more than a cursory thought. But the way she'd belittled him in front of Drayden Lvandsson was totally unprovoked and uncalled for.

He tried to make himself invisible as the doors beneath him opened with a soft whoosh. He heard Natasha hiss, "How *dare* you push me—"

"Listen, you officious, self-important viper," a male voice cut her off, and Derek went rigid. "I've been watching you all night. You either back off of Derek Anderson or you'll no longer be employed by the Drayden's organization. Or any similar company. In any capacity."

"You wouldn't—"

"Don't tempt me," he said.

Before Natasha could respond, Derek heard her name paged on their speaker system, and the doors whooshed again. He tossed his straw hat aside, clattered down the stairs, and headed for a different set of doors, reluctant to leave the stockroom and come face-to-face with Natasha. He didn't want her to stop him from catching up with his defender and thanking him.

He slipped through the stockroom door that was closest to the mall entrance and frowned when he realized that his view was blocked by the stupid bales of hay they'd stacked up. He stuck his head through an opening and saw his quarry walking toward the exit into the mall. He crouched down and darted in the same direction, hoping that if Natasha happened to glance his way, she wouldn't spot him stalking the man who'd just threatened her job.

Within seconds, they were moving side by side, invisible to each other because of the hay piled between them. As he reached the last stack, he was able to grab the man's arm before he could leave the store.

He saw a flash of shocked blue eyes turn his way, then he was being pushed backwards. When he extended his free hand behind him to brace himself against the wall, he felt a doorknob and instinctively turned it. The force of the other man's movement propelled them both through the door into total darkness.

"Where the hell are we?"

Derek thought for a second, then said, "Storage closet. Behind the display window you can see from the mall."

Then he stopped talking because his mouth was full of another tongue. The kiss was so deeply fulfilling that it left his entire body throbbing with desire. Their mouths stayed locked together as overalls and suit coat were pulled off, shoes went flying, and snaps, buttons, zippers, and belts were negotiated. Then Derek laid back with a moan as the tongue finally abandoned his to travel down his body. After an eternity of being teased and tantalized, he heard the tearing noise of a condom wrapper. What began slowly and gently quickly intensified until both men's ragged breathing ended in a tempest of moans and gasps as they collapsed together in sweaty, sticky pleasure.

As much as he enjoyed watching his lover's face when they had sex, fucking unexpectedly and spontaneously in total darkness with dozens of people only a few feet away was the hottest thing Derek had ever done with Hunter. He couldn't catch his breath to say any of the things that were tumbling through his mind, including thanking him for his threats to Natasha. Or asking when he'd gotten back from Sydney. Or telling him how much he'd missed him over the last four months. Or apologizing for moving out and begging to come home.

None of it mattered. Hunter had taken delicious possession of him again, and Derek's senses were singing in an ecstasy of surrender. All he needed or wanted was to hear Hunter express his love. Then he'd do anything he was asked to do. But he understood Hunter well enough to know those words wouldn't come easily. If he said it first . . .

"Hunter, I have to tell you—"

"You don't have to tell me anything," Hunter insisted. "Don't talk. Not yet."

Derek relaxed in Hunter's arms, allowing himself to enjoy the physicality of the moment. Hunter was right. As long as their bodies were so eloquent, they didn't need words. Hunter began softly kissing his neck, moving up to his ears, then back down to his throat. Derek's hands traveled over Hunter with purpose, until he heard the sharp intake of his breath.

"I need to see you," Derek moaned. "I need to see your eyes. I'm nothing but need; I need you so much."

Hunter pulled away and said, "Get dressed. Go tell that bitch that you quit. Or don't tell her. Leave with me now."

"Why, Hunter? Why should I quit?" Derek asked, silently imploring, *Tell me you need me. Tell me you miss me. Tell me you love me.*

"You don't have to stand for that kind of treatment. You don't need this job."

"Why don't I need this job?"

"You don't need the money."

"Because you'll take care of me," Derek said.

"Of course."

"I'm not quitting my job," Derek said. "And I'm not moving back to the Congreve."

"Was it so bad that anything, even this, is better? Do you like being unappreciated and mistreated?"

"Not anymore," Derek said. "Do you have your cigarette lighter? I have to find my clothes. I'm still on the clock." He heard Hunter rummaging around, then the click of the lighter. He avoided looking in that direction as the flame illuminated the darkness.

"You're really not coming with me."

Derek didn't answer, getting himself back together while Hunter held the lighter aloft. The last thing he did was reach down and pick up the condom and the torn wrapper, dropping them into a Drayden's bag so he could throw them away in the men's restroom. Although how he was going to get there without being seen by his boss was a mystery.

"See that door over there?" Derek asked. "If you crack it, you'll get light in here from the display window. So you can see to get dressed. I have to go."

"Fine," Hunter said.

Derek dared a look at him, but just then the lighter flickered out, so he groped his way to the exit door and opened it, saying, "Call me sometime when you can talk without giving me orders."

After the door closed behind him, he leaned against it for a few seconds. He subdued an overwhelming urge to cry and looked down at the Drayden's bag, realizing that he could easily slip from the store and go to the mall restroom without Natasha catching him.

He hurried in that direction, grateful that no one seemed to glance his way as they loitered around Gert the fiberglass cow. When he went into the little hallway that led to the men's room, the door of the women's restroom opened and Vienna emerged.

Derek squirmed as her gaze raked him from head to toe, then his face flushed when she said, "You might want to clean that . . . genetic material . . . out of your eyebrow before you go back to work."

He stared at her in an agony of embarrassment. "It was Hunter. I was with Hunter."

"I know," she said. "I tried to let you know that he was in the store checking you out. But Natasha was watching you like a hawk. She picked up the phone every time I called."

"So you're the stupid customer who kept calling with infuriating questions," Derek said. "I thought her brain was going to explode."

"We should be so lucky," Vienna said. "Anyway, I guess he caught up with you." Derek nodded mutely, unsure whether to laugh or cry. "And it didn't go entirely well. Your night has really sucked, hasn't it?"

"Yes," Derek concurred.

"Why don't you leave? I'll clock you out."

"We could both lose our jobs for that."

"So what? I'd just move on to number twenty, or whatever it is. And I may be useless in affairs of the heart, but I'm great at vocational guidance. I could find you a better job in this mall faster than Natasha could say, 'You're fired.' Go home and do something nice for yourself."

"All right," Derek said reluctantly.

Vienna reached into her smock pocket, shoved a sample of skin cleanser into his hand, and turned him toward the men's room, saying, "*After* you wash your face."

Derek viewed himself in the restroom mirror with relief that no one but Vienna had seen him looking so disheveled. His shirt was buttoned wrong. An overall strap was twisted and only half hooked. His hair stuck out in all directions and still had straw in it from that stupid hat. He definitely looked like he'd just gotten off the Indy Cyclone.

After he made himself presentable, he trudged through the mall toward the Galaxy Building. Only Drayden's was still open, for Preview Night, and his footsteps were abnormally loud in the large, empty space. He could hear the tinny sound of a radio playing, so he figured he'd be accosted by a security guard any minute. Then he spotted the source of the music.

One of the Cart People, as Vienna called them, was sitting at a kiosk, humming along to the radio. Derek didn't avoid the Cart People like everyone else did. He liked to think of them as the modern equivalent of gypsies, and he was usually interested in their pitches. Tonight, however, he wasn't really in the mood, so he was glad it was after hours.

As if in keeping with Derek's gypsy concept, the man's kiosk was designed to look like the traveling wagon of an old-time peddler. Derek saw the name "Nature's Marvels" painted on the side. He watched as the man polished a crystal from among the collection of stones and rocks on the shelves of the cart. He also saw bottles of essential oils and flower essences, which amused him. The peddler really was the New Age version of a snake-oil salesman.

The man glanced up, smiled at Derek, and said, "Did you lose your raft?" When Derek didn't answer, the man nodded toward several paper containers of chili dogs and said, "These were left over when Sirius Dogs closed tonight. They were free. You're welcome to have one."

Derek smiled. Eating a stale hot dog would top off his feeling that he'd spent a night at the carnival. He sat on the extra bar stool, took a bite, and examined the man's wares.

"See anything that interests you?"

"You can't sell after hours," Derek reproached him.

"I didn't ask you to buy anything. I asked if anything interested you."

"Sorry," Derek said, feeling chastened. "I'm Derek Anderson."

After a pause, the man said, "Nice to meet you, Derek. I'm Ed Rochester."

Derek lifted an eyebrow and said, "Ed Rochester? I was an English major. I assume you picked the name because Edward Rochester disguised himself as a gypsy in *Jane Eyre*?"

"Oops," the peddler said.

"Really," Derek said. "Give me some credit. But it's okay with me if you want to be incognito, Ed. We all have our secrets." He picked up a greenish blue stone and said, "What's this one?"

Ed looked at it and said, "Chrysocolla. It's a healer."

"What does it heal?"

"It helps regenerate the pancreas, regulate insulin, and balance blood sugar."

"I don't have any of those problems," Derek said and started to replace the stone.

"It also eases heartache, purifies and harmonizes the home, and increases the capacity to love. You can keep it. It's small and will fit easily into your pocket."

"Thanks," Derek said, taking another bite of his hot dog as he studied the stone. "So, Ed, do you tell fortunes?"

"Not all gypsies do," Ed said.

"But since Mr. Rochester's gypsy did—"

"Everything you need is in your own backyard," Ed smoothly interrupted.

"I'll be sure to tell my roommate that. Vienna practically killed people to get away from the smokestacks and slag piles of Gary."

"Gary very well may be in her future," Ed intoned. "It's the circle of life."

Derek slid off the stool and said, "Thanks for the chili dog and the rock."

"Don't mention it," Ed said. "See you around, Derek."

Derek finished his walk to the Galaxy Building and took the elevator to the apartment, feeling forlorn. Neither Vienna's nor Ed's kindness could erase his post-Hunter letdown. He'd been so touched to hear his lover threaten Natasha, then thrilled to be in his arms again, only to end up more miserable than ever. Any man would know that a simple "I love you" could have brought him back home. But an honest man, which Hunter was, wouldn't have said it unless it were true.

He realized that his overalls smelled like Marc Jacobs cologne, so he changed into sweatpants and a T-shirt and curled up on the sofa, intending to wait up for Vienna. It was pathetic how his intention to be a good friend seemed to always turn into running to her for comfort. He could tell Davii anything, and could rely on Christian for good-humored companionship, but Vienna was his rock. He jumped up and went to his bedroom, finding the stone from Gypsy Ed in the bib pocket of his overalls. Then he went back to the sofa and napped.

When he awoke, he was still clutching the rock in his palm. He opened his fingers to let his hand cool off, then he heard voices from Vienna's bedroom. He sat up, wondering if he should leave the apartment to give her more privacy. As he stood, the rock slipped from his grasp and hit the coffee table. The voices stopped, and he heard Vienna call, "Derek? Are you awake? Come here, baby."

He wandered down the hall and found her sitting on the bed next to Christian. Both of them were fully dressed, although Vienna had undone the straps of her overalls. Derek blushed and said, "I didn't mean to interrupt."

Vienna shook her head and said, "We were just rehashing your bad night."

"Natasha," Christian clarified.

"And Hunter," Vienna added, as if friendship required full disclosure.

"Hunter?" Christian asked.

"Right," Vienna said.

"Hunter Congreve?" Christian turned to stare at Derek. "Your boyfriend is Hunter Congreve?"

"Ex-boyfriend," Derek said.

"How could you not know that?" Vienna asked. "What do men talk about? Whose apartment did you think we moved him out of in the dead of night?"

"I don't know," Christian said. "I knew his boyfriend worked at the Congreve—"

"Ex-boyfriend," Derek said again. He went to the bed when

Vienna patted it and slid between the two of them, lying on his back and pulling one of her pillows over his head.

After a pause, Vienna said, "It makes my blood boil the way Natasha treats people and gets away with it."

"It sounds like Drayden Lvandsson's on to her, though," Christian said.

"It's not enough," Vienna stated. "Sure, she'll be inconvenienced by going to Chicago, sitting through monotonous seminars, and participating in role-playing games about how to treat people nicely. But that's as far as it's going to go. You know she'll come back and pick up right where she left off, treating everyone like shit. No, I want retribution. For Derek's sake."

"It sucks that he has to deal with that bitch on top of his situation with Hunter," Christian said.

"I'm still here," Derek moaned from behind his pillow.

"Christian, has a man named DeWitt called you?" Vienna asked.

"Actually, yes. I've been meaning to ask you about that. What's his story?"

"I'm so glad you asked," Vienna said. "DeWitt was doing some sewing for Natasha, and they had a falling out. She was vicious to him. If you could've seen how beaten down the poor guy was, your heart would've broken."

"Trust me, I think I understand his misery," Derek said, having removed the pillow so he could listen to Vienna's story.

"Why don't you just quit, Derek? There must be something else you could do instead of selling shoes," Christian said.

"Not tonight," Derek said. "I know you have my best interests at heart, but I've already had this discussion once tonight. Maybe tomorrow, okay?"

"Fine," Christian said. "So DeWitt was Natasha's tailor? Did he mess up a hem or something?"

"He wasn't *her* tailor," Vienna stated with a strange grin. "He was her dolls' tailor."

Derek maintained a stupefied silence, and Christian finally said, "Okay, I'll bite. He made clothes for her doll?"

"Not doll. Dolls. Apparently she has a lot of them," Vienna said.

"She collects dolls?" Christian asked. "That's weird, but how does this information help you get retribution against her?"

"They're all Dolly Parton dolls," Vienna stated. "It's not a collection. It's an obsession. They could be instruments in avoidance behavior. Or they play a part in an obsessive-compulsive personality disorder. Maybe a combination of the two. I'm not sure yet. But when DeWitt told a mutual acquaintance—" she broke off with a frown. "Hoagie? Something like that. It's not like me to forget a name. Anyway, when she found out that DeWitt told someone about her collection, she decimated him. Obviously she feels she has something to hide."

"Maybe I *should* quit," Derek said.

"Based on this information, I have a plan," Vienna said. "I could use a little help, though."

Derek turned to Christian and said, "Or maybe I'll get fired."

"It could be more fun that way," Christian agreed. "I have the feeling that Vienna's going through with her plan whether or not we help her."

Vienna shrugged and said, "Laura Bartlebaum had a breakthrough after I stabbed her."

"You what?" Christian asked.

Derek enjoyed watching Christian's face as he heard the tale of the unfaithful husband and the careless patient. He found it reassuring that Vienna could so calmly discuss what had once been her darkest secret. He couldn't wait to tell Davii about her progress.

"In the end," Vienna finished, "Laura dropped Kevin like a bad habit and decided to remain faithful to her husband. She even agreed not to press charges against me and wrote to the Board of Psychiatry on my behalf. Sometimes patients just need a little push to get better. We're going to push Natasha gently toward sanity."

She looked expectantly at Christian, who finally said, "I'm in. And not because I'm afraid of you now."

Vienna laughed, then they both turned to Derek, who stared back at them, wondering what Vienna was planning. After a pause, he said, "We're not going to break the law, are we?"

"Laws are like hearts," Vienna said sagely. "Some of them work better after a little breaking."

25

It's Everywhere You Want to Be

Riley broke the lead of his pencil when Hunter called his name for the tenth time in two hours. He was beginning to wonder if he couldn't devise some way to get his boss sent back to Sydney. He'd been a beast since his surprising return to Indiana. Although his mood was satisfying evidence that relations between Hunter and his boy toy continued to deteriorate, Riley's months as acting head of the Hotel Congreve had left him with little patience for Hunter's resumption of power.

Still, Riley had other consolations. For one, although it still annoyed him that Natasha Deere had dodged his phone calls, he no longer needed her. Derek was doing a marvelous job of ending his love affair, as Riley had seen in a terse note that Hunter sent to Garry Prophet to apprise him of the state of the disunion.

> *Pro,*
> *Situation with Derek completely fucked. His refusal to quit his job is either a childishly willful gesture, or he lacks the self-esteem to want more and better. Either is a huge disappointment. Coming home accomplished nothing, and I think he definitely has another boyfriend. I've seen them together. Is there anything more pathetic than a scorned lover who turns to stalking? Yours in stealth mode.*
> *Con*

The e-mail left Riley with a velvety feeling of contentment. Apparently, Hunter had glimpsed Derek with his limber sex pal, Christian. Which would explain his vile mood. But should Riley detect any thawing in relations between the crown prince and the pea brain, he still had a few aces up his sleeve, and they didn't require Natasha's cooperation.

In fact, since Hunter was being such a pest, Riley decided to give himself a special treat and throw a card on the table. He went into Hunter's office with his usual obsequious expression and said, "Sorry, did you call me? I was trying to confirm some charges on Derek's Visa account."

Hunter looked up with a frown and said, "Derek is still using his Visa?"

"I haven't received the current statement," Riley said. "I'm just verifying unusual charges on the last one I have."

Hunter seemed to be lost in thought, then he said, "Are any of the Lvandssons still guests of the hotel?"

"Miss Lvandsson left after Drayden's Planter's Day Preview Night," Riley said. "Mr. and Mrs. Sven Lvandsson are still here. I believe Mrs. Sven has just been appointed to the board of a Terre Haute art group—Vigo County Stages, Wabash Symphony—I'm not sure."

"Find out exactly which organization and send her one of the hotel's fruit-and-chocolate baskets," Hunter said. "With a note of congratulations. Drayden Lvandsson? Is he still a guest?"

"Yes," Riley said, wondering why it mattered. He'd have to do some reconnaissance. Maybe Drayden was Hunter's new romantic interest.

Hunter frowned again, then said, "Derek's Visa bill. Let me look at it."

"I'll get it," Riley said. He went back to his desk, pulled the entire file of Visa statements, and took it to Hunter, who waved him out of his office.

Riley smiled as he turned away. The file should keep Hunter busy for a while. For months, Derek's charges had followed a pattern. Books at Patti's Pages, an occasional meal so inexpensive that it was obviously for one, a charge or two a month at Aveda, and a clothing purchase every couple of weeks. Then there were the online purchases of porn DVDs. For all Riley knew, Derek and Hunter had enjoyed those together. In any case, month after month, the charges were innocuous and consistent.

Until the last two bills, when there had suddenly been a dramatic increase in purchases of new clothes, hair products, and haircuts, along with large bar tabs and steep meal charges indicating that Derek had not been drinking and dining alone. Then there were the gift cards. Those were Riley's favorite charges. They made it look as if Derek had expected Hunter to pay for his lavish generosity to his new friends and fuck buddies. Visa provided a satisfying means of assisting the slow, painful suicide of a relationship. It was a mercy killing.

Riley was given a few hours of peace while Hunter shut himself in his office. Not only didn't he emerge for lunch, but he didn't ask Riley to order from the hotel restaurant. Riley took advantage of his boss's preoccupation to enjoy a leisurely meal at Bert's Bar & Grille. When he returned, Hunter came out of his office and dropped the Visa folder on his desk. He looked tired.

"Just pay the damn thing," he said. "I want to see the next one when it comes."

"Certainly," Riley said. When Hunter didn't leave, he asked, "Was there something else?"

Hunter appeared to hesitate, then he finally asked, "Did you see much of Derek while I was away? Did he spend a lot of time in the hotel? Have friends over? Before he moved, I mean."

Riley pretended to be flustered and dropped his eyes as if embarrassed, saying, "I'm sure it would be better if you asked Derek. His answers would be more accurate than mine. It's often easy to misunderstand what one sees. When one doesn't know all the details."

Hunter scowled and said, "And what did one see, Riley?"

"Derek seemed to make a few friends here and there. Of hotel guests. Maybe he considered himself a bit of a goodwill ambassador in your absence."

"Hotel guests?" Hunter repeated, as if he hadn't heard Riley correctly. "Are you implying that he tricked with men in this hotel?"

"I didn't say that," Riley quickly responded in a tone that sounded horrified but with an underlying trace of regret that Hunter had figured it out. "I never saw him take anyone to *your* suite."

"I see," Hunter said. "And this went on until he moved out?"

Riley dropped his eyes again and said, "I honestly didn't keep tabs on Derek's nocturnal activities. It was nice to see him making new friends that he could go to dinner with or catch a movie with or . . . whatever they did. Like his friend Davii. And Christian. Well, that's what had me concerned about the Visa bill."

"I don't follow," Hunter said.

"Christian's last name is Mercer."

"Okay," Hunter said with a blank look.

"Apparently, he's the son of Patricia Mercer. She's quite the celebrated Midwestern artist."

"Your point, Riley?"

"Maybe you noticed a rather steep charge to the Rania Gallery in New York? That was for a signed Mercer print. It was such an unusual high-dollar item that I confirmed the purchase. But I suppose you've seen it hanging in your suite."

"There's no new art in my apartment," Hunter said. He went back to his office without another word.

Riley smiled. In time, Derek would undoubtedly wonder why his check for the last Visa bill had never been deposited in Hunter's account. It had been accommodating of him to slide it under the door to Riley's office without actually confirming that Riley had received it. If Derek ever got around to asking about it, Riley could say he'd never seen it and suggest that the cleaning crew had thought it was trash and disposed of it.

The damage was done. As far as Hunter knew, Derek had stuck him with a lot of charges involving other men. Even if Derek swore he'd tried to pay the bill himself, the only proof of that had been shredded by Riley long ago.

Riley sharpened a new pencil and began drawing an approximate version of the Manhattan skyline on his desk pad while he made business calls.

26

Love at First Stroke

Christian worked his fingers into the pastel, defining the sparkle in the eyes of Perky, Emily-Anne's West Highland terrier. He sat back from the easel, satisfied with the actual rendering but discomfited by what he thought was a lifeless portrait. Frustrated, he plucked a bright red pastel from the container to his left and began filling and enlarging the dog's lips.

He tossed the chalk back into the box and thought, *Like mother, like dog.*

He wondered if collagen injections might mar Perky's chances at the next AKC show. Then again, Emily-Anne appeared to suffer no ill effects from her surgical enhancements. Christian had tactfully tried to guide his client to the realization that her efforts to defy aging were turning her into a caricature. Much like Perky. With a sigh, he pulled the archival paper from the easel and crumpled it, tossing it over his shoulder.

A glance at the clock alerted him that he needed to dust himself off before beginning his cloak-and-dagger foray into Mall of the Universe. While he exfoliated in the shower with an apricot scrub, he thought about Derek's horror at his array of grooming products. He decided to boldly skip the after-cleansing moisturizing gel, but once he'd dried off, he couldn't force himself to disregard the rest of his routine. When he was finally satisfied with his hair, he dressed in dark indigo jeans and a camouflage shirt with a printed eagle on the chest. He wouldn't blend in with the pinks and oranges that were currently popular in Couture and Women's Shoes, but his choice of greens and yellows seemed appropriate for his duties.

Just before leaving the apartment, he picked up his PalmPilot and his phone. His conscience did battle with itself. He wanted to devote his full attention to Derek's situation, but he couldn't be inaccessible to his clients. He left the phone turned on as he began a brisk walk to Drayden's. Just as he reached the store, "Morning Train" pealed from his belt, and he switched his headset on with exasperation.

"Christian, thank goodness. It's Courtney. Mama's fighting with me in Drayden's Wedding Salon. She's insisting on an empire waist. What is this, 1976? You've got to come talk sense into her."

Christian grimaced. He loved Courtney. She was adorable, and he appreciated that she trusted him more than her wedding planner and her strict mother. Maybe he could delay her.

"Courtney, I'm helping another client right now. Why don't you and your mother grab an appetizer in Drayden's café on the fourth floor? I'll meet you there later, and we can—"

"Christian, please," Courtney begged, sounding tearful. "I'm standing here in this white undergarment that looks like my grandma's nightgown, and I've been through more dress changes than Stevie Nicks. I had to lock myself in the fitting room with the phone just to call you."

"I'll be right there," Christian promised. "But I've only got minutes. I'm really pressed for time."

"Thank you," Courtney said with a sob.

He switched the phone to vibrate and took the UP escalator, looking down at Women's Shoes. There was no sign of Derek, but he saw Natasha circling the department, which appeared busy. With any luck, Derek had already begun their mission involving Natasha's secret lair of Dolly madness.

He found Courtney blowing her nose in the middle of a group of chattering women, none of whom were listening to each other or saying anything helpful that he could discern. She gave a relieved yelp when she saw him and rushed over to throw her arms around him. He felt a pang of regret that he'd encouraged her relationship with her fiancé, Barry. She looked delectable in the white cotton sheath.

"Gaynell," he said sternly to the most forbidding member of the group of women, "your daughter is a size five. She has exactly the kind of body the current styles were designed for." When Gaynell's expression remained unmoved, Christian played his trump card. "I remember when Barry told me he fell in love with Courtney's tiny waist. He said that everyone would know she was getting married for love and not because she had to."

Gaynell, a staunch pillar of her church, blanched and said, "No one would dare—"

"That's exactly what they'll say if they see a high waist," Christian warned.

"I love you," Courtney murmured as Gaynell began directing the saleswomen to bring a different style of dress. "She said the sleeker dresses plunge too low in the back."

"Remind her that the veil will cover your back," Christian said. "I really have to go, hon. If she picks a veil you don't like, just remember how fragile they are. An accident on the morning of your wedding, and you can rip the whole thing off and use just the headpiece."

"I'm naming my first child Christian," Courtney vowed.

"Your mother will approve," Christian said with a grin, then hurried toward the DOWN escalator.

Christian rarely made use of the game functions on his PalmPilot, but today was a good opportunity to finally learn Desdemona. He selected it as he wandered around Natasha's department, pretending to take note of new arrivals for his clients as he manipulated the game on the screen. Enjoying the mild excitement of his mall espionage, he was prepared to intercept Natasha if she seemed likely to return to her office.

Natasha, armed with a clipboard, bar code scanner, and commands for the stockroom staff, hovered over cartons of shoeboxes. She tucked the clipboard under her arm and scanned the boxes, then tore the top sheet of paper from the clipboard and officiously handed it to Erik. When she turned to stride away, Christian slid around a column to follow her but was overrun by masses of green, yellow, pink, and purple gingham.

He clutched a table as the quiet of mid-afternoon Drayden's was suddenly broken by the whoops, hollers, and yeehaws of nearly fifty women dressed for a hoedown. As a woman with brown hair swept into a beehive flew by him, he caught a glimpse of white paper pinned to the back of her dress. Apparently, she was contestant 23 in the Midwest Square Dancing Competition. Behind the group of women, an equal number of men dressed in cowboy boots and bolo ties swaggered onto the floor.

With the sudden influx of customers, Christian figured that Natasha wouldn't be returning to her office any time soon. He wandered to Cosmetics, where he could still keep an eye on her. He'd return to Women's Shoes if the ruckus subsided, signaling that Natasha might escape the herd of flared skirts and puffy sleeves.

After rounding a display of face creams claiming to benefit laugh and worry lines even better than Botox, he watched for a second as Natasha assisted a woman with unusually full blond hair. Her resemblance to Dolly Parton explained the look on Natasha's face. She seemed genuinely amicable and willing to aid the customer in finding the right fit for her feet, which were clad in chunky fuchsia clogs.

As Christian moved deeper into Cosmetics, he felt his phone vibrate at his side. He lifted it in front of his eyes, but a flash of red caught his peripheral vision. When he turned to obtain a full view, he felt his heart lurch. Behind the Lillith Allure counter, Bianca stood directly beneath a halogen spot lamp intended to highlight the latest products. Instead, it cast a glow on the long tresses of her head. Her pale skin seemed to radiate from within.

Christian stared as if seeing her for the first time. He'd never really talked to her after a brief introduction by Vienna several weeks before. His mind had been on something else at the time, and beyond noting to himself that she was attractive, he hadn't given her much thought. Today, her appearance made him mentally grope for some image.

One of Botticelli's three Graces, he thought.

He stashed his phone back in its holder without looking at the caller ID and dashed toward the counter. As she saw his intense expression, Bianca looked startled and backed up, causing a few bottles on the display shelves to teeter.

"You have to leave," he said.

"Huh?" Bianca asked with a stricken look. "Did I do something wrong?"

"You have to leave now. I need you."

"For one of your clients?" she asked, glancing around as if to see who might be with him.

"For me," he said. "I've got a . . . uh . . . situation. I need your help. You need to leave the store."

"I still have two hours on the clock," she protested.

"Please, Bianca, for everyone's sake, go," Meg said, appearing suddenly from around the other side of the counter. She looked with great interest at Christian's choice of T-shirt.

Christian reached in his pocket and took out a business card, saying, "This is my apartment. I'll meet you there. Please don't make me wait two hours."

"I can't just walk out of here," Bianca said with a gasp.

"Thirty minutes," Christian begged.

"I told you those cream-filled donuts were weapons of mass destruction," Meg said. "Now you've gotten food poisoning. You'll have to clock out early." She looked at Christian and swore, "She'll be there. Thirty minutes."

Christian nodded and practically flew back up the escalator to the third floor. Fortunately, Courtney and Gaynell were busy in a fitting room, and he grabbed the arm of one of the sales associates.

"That thing Courtney was wearing a while ago."

"Mr. Mercer, even if you don't like them all, our gowns are not 'things'—"

"No, the camisole, or whatever you call it. I need to buy one. Now. Where can I get it?"

"We don't sell them. We just provide them for our brides between fittings."

"I have to have one," Christian said, starting to feel frantic.

The woman looked at him and said, "Oh, all right. Heaven knows, you've brought enough business—" she broke off with a wicked smile. "We'll just add it to the cost of Courtney's dress. The least that dreadful mother can do—"

"Anything; I don't care," Christian exhorted. "Hurry."

Half an hour later, he arrived at his apartment just ahead of Bianca. When he opened the door, she still looked confused and uncertain, and he ushered her inside. "Mr. Mercer—"

"Christian," he said.

"I don't understand—"

"I need you to sit for me," he said.

Her eyes darted around, and she said, "You have a child?"

He thrust the bag at her and said, "Can you change into this?"

Bianca pulled the garment from the bag and gave him an incredulous stare. "I don't know what kind of woman you think I am, but—"

"Oh, God, no," Christian said with remorse. "I want to paint you. Wearing this."

"Paint me?"

"I'm an artist," he said. He paused, hearing his own words, then he smiled and repeated, "I'm an artist. Seeing you a while ago . . . I knew I had to paint you. Haven't you heard that all artists are slightly mad? Indulge me. Please."

She looked into his eyes, as if assessing whether he was trustworthy, and after a minute said, "Where can I change?"

"Anywhere," he said. "I'll be in the first room on the right when you're ready."

Christian went into his studio and stared at the sketch pads, pencils, and pastels with a frown. Then he crossed the room to the closet and dug through the chaos on the floor, tossing items back out over his shoulder, until he found what he was looking for. He removed a large wooden box from the darkest recess of the closet, carried it to his easel, and blew dust from the top just as Bianca walked in. The cloud billowed in front of her, causing her to sneeze.

"Bless you."

"Thank you," she said.

He cleared training materials from an antique tapestry love seat that he'd salvaged from one of his mother's moves. He'd often wondered why he kept it, but now he was grateful, especially after Bianca settled herself there and waited patiently while he dragged in different lamps until he got the lighting he wanted. He tossed his phone and headset to his desk and left the room to change into an old white T-shirt and a pair of faded, ripped jeans. When he returned, Bianca was yawning.

"Are you hungry? Thirsty? Do you need anything?"

"I'm just sleepy," she said. "What do I have to do?"

"Whatever you want," he said. "Be comfortable. If you want to lie down, I'll get you a pillow."

He darted to his bedroom and came back with a pillow. He settled it under her head, then fanned her lush red hair around her, dying to get a paintbrush in his hands. When his cell phone began to vibrate against his desk, he ignored it.

Bianca yawned again and closed her eyes while Christian cleared his easel and set a large canvas on it. He arranged his paints as he'd done many years before, falling back into step as if the last time he'd painted was a week ago instead of years. Then finally, wonderfully, he was painting, looking from Bianca to his canvas. He was dimly aware that the phone continued to vibrate occasionally, but he didn't care. Nothing was as important as drowsy Bianca and the vision of her that began to appear in his imagination, where it would be transported through his muscle, bone, and nerves to the canvas.

"May I use your bathroom?"

Bianca's question brought Christian out of his fog. He hadn't even realized she was awake. He nodded, turned his attention back to his canvas, then looked at the clock. When Bianca came back, he said, "I had no idea we'd been like this for nearly two hours. If you need to leave, I'll understand."

"I'm fine," Bianca said and stretched. "I had a good nap." She settled on the love seat again. "Is it okay if I talk?"

"Of course."

"I have to admit, I don't have a very high opinion of artists."

"Really? Why not?" Christian asked, using his palette knife to blend pigments.

"Even though I'm not that great at it, I really love my job at Drayden's. I like the store and my manager, and the benefits are fantastic."

"Uh-huh," Christian said, wondering how she'd gone from artists to Drayden's and whether she was about to ask him for career advice.

"And redheads usually get along with other redheads," Bianca mused.

"I've generally found that to be true."

Bianca frowned and said, "Your hair is more brown than red."

"It's auburn," Christian said.

Bianca stared at his hair for a few seconds, then said, "Sydney was definitely a redhead, like me."

Christian decided that either he needed a break, or he was spoiled by Derek's ability to tell a story, because Bianca left him mystified. He put down the palette and knife, cleaned off a chair so he could sit down, and said, "Go on."

"I'd only been working at Drayden's about a month when they did this exhibit. Of paintings."

"On that wall outside the café? On the fourth floor?"

"Yes," Bianca said. "Rumor had it that the artist was related to some important person in the Drayden's organization, and everyone was excited about it. Supposedly she was famous. The artist, I mean."

"Sydney the redhead," Christian guessed.

"Yes. Anyway, I looked at the paintings and, while I know nothing about art, I wasn't impressed. It was just a lot of color with stuff sticking out of it."

"Stuff?"

"Uh-huh. Like broken glass, pieces of mirrors, cosmetics brushes gunked with paint. Pretty much everything I work with every day, stuck on a canvas with a bunch of paint."

"I see," Christian said, glad that he didn't. "So you felt like maybe this Sydney person was attacking a career that you love?"

"Well, honestly, no. I didn't get that. I just thought it was crap."

"Okay," Christian said, starting to enjoy Bianca's way of telling a story.

"Then the artist—maybe she *is* famous. Sydney Kepler?"

"Never heard of her," Christian said.

"She did an in-store appearance. Someone from the paper came to interview her, all these big shots were there, and she gave a little talk. Whatever; I didn't go. But I saw her later, walking with the reporter and a group of people. She was a beautiful woman, and in spite of the fact that I wasn't crazy about her paintings, her hair caught my eye, and I started to feel nicer toward her."

"As a fellow redhead," Christian said.

"Yes. When she walked by my counter, I gave her a big smile and said hello, and she stopped with her entourage. She sort of swept her arms out, like she was on a game show presenting a prize of Lillith Allure products, and said, 'This is exactly what my art protests. The cosmetics industry plays on women's fears of inadequacy and aging.' All those people were hanging on every word, and as Meg said later, they looked at me like I was personally responsible for the glass ceiling, domestic violence, and the failure of the Equal Rights Amendment."

"That's awful," Christian said.

"No, what's awful is that I blurted out, 'Your paintings play on my fears of bad dreams and acid reflux.' The reporter laughed so hard that I thought he was going to wet his pants, sort of like you're doing now."

"Sorry," Christian said, composing himself.

"Less than a half hour later, my manager was asked to escort me upstairs. Melanie's really cool, and all the way there, she kept saying she wished I hadn't done it, because she liked me and didn't want to lose me. That maybe if I apologized to Sydney and the store manager, I'd just get a reprimand, and she'd do everything she could to help me keep my job."

"No wonder you like your manager," Christian said.

"We went into this little conference room, and Hershel, the store manager, came in. His face was all grim, and he shut the door, looked at me, then started laughing, too. Apparently, Sydney's father owns the *building* that's used by Drayden's in Eau Claire, Wisconsin. The Lvandsson family was doing him a favor by showing her work; she wasn't nearly as important as she thought. Plus, she gave Hershel all kinds of headaches about her exhibit. I didn't get in trouble at all. Hershel wanted to see me to make sure I wasn't upset. That's why I love Drayden's."

"And why you don't love redheaded artists," Christian said. "Although I think it's important for you to know that I in no way hold you responsible for the failure of the Equal Rights Amendment."

"Thank you," Bianca said. "In return, I'll give you the benefit of the doubt and won't blame you for Sydney. I didn't mean to distract you."

"I needed a break. I'm also hungry. Are you?"

Bianca nodded and followed him to the kitchen. She made sandwiches while he made tea. Their conversation ranged from Emily-Anne's dogs to Bianca's family. She was the youngest of three girls. Not only were both her parents doctors, but both her sisters were in medical school.

"I'm the dumb one," Bianca said.

"You're not dumb," Christian protested.

"Trust me, in my family, I'm the dumb one. But they all love me and spoil me, so it's okay. Plus I give my sisters all my free samples. Med school isn't cheap."

Christian's customary need to validate people asserted itself, and he said, "You shouldn't put yourself down because of your job. All that matters is loving what you do and doing your best. There's nothing worse than having a compulsion to do one thing and being forced by circumstances or a lack of confidence to do something else."

"Uh-huh," she said, looking like he'd given her something to think about.

When they finished eating, she expressed her willingness to continue sitting for him. He had no trouble getting right back into his work, and Bianca dozed again.

The ringing of his phone jarred the room's tranquility, and Bianca's eyes fluttered open. Christian ignored it, just as he had his cell phone, and suddenly his mother's voice pierced the silence from his answering machine.

"Listen, young man, I don't know what you're up to, but I've left five messages on your cell phone. I want you to return my call at once. I'm at the Rania Gallery overseeing my new installation. Betsy Pelham stopped in after a trip that took her through Terre Haute. Apparently—"

The machine cut off, and Bianca's eyes met his, then moved to his paintbrush, which was poised midair. Christian turned toward the phone, then looked back at the canvas and started painting again.

This time, the machine picked up after two rings, and his mother continued, "Betsy unrolled a sketch she bought at some charity auction in Indiana. It's signed 'Mercer,' and she wanted to know if it was mine. Is this your handiwork? Are you starting to pick up your art hobby after all these years? You can't just sign your work 'Mercer,' dear. I'm Mercer. And if you intend to—"

Again the machine cut her off, and Christian continued to paint, although Bianca sat up with a contemplative expression. The third time the phone rang, Christian's death grip on the brush was a clear sign of his internal fury. Bianca narrowed her eyes.

"If you intend to try your hand at art again, then I insist you join me in New York and find someone to study with, Chrissie." Christian was startled when Bianca jumped to her feet and crossed the room to the desk, unplugging the phone as his mother was saying, "Your technique has always been—"

"That's better," Bianca said when his mother's voice was cut off. She glanced around with a frown until she spotted the stereo, and after pawing through his CDs, selected one and put it in. The room resounded with the first notes of Chopin, and Bianca lowered the volume a notch, then appeared to be satisfied. She turned to stare at him. "You look hot. I'm sorry to interrupt you again, but I'm getting us both some water. Is there anything else you need from the kitchen?"

"No, thanks," Christian said.

Bianca started to leave, then turned back and reached for his cell phone, examining it until she figured out how to turn it off. "Keep painting," she ordered and left the room.

Christian looked at the canvas and, after a few seconds, reached for a different brush and went back to work.

27

He's a Magic Man, Mama

Vienna practically collapsed into the chair, thankful to finally be away from work and sitting in Die Mondeklipse Weingarten. Immediately after being seated, she ordered a glass of wine without the slightest bit of guilt. She knew she should have stayed at Drayden's through her lunch break to make sure her plan was carried through to fruition, but she had faith in her boys. Besides, she'd come up with the plan. Wasn't that enough?

Her wine arrived, and she took a grateful sip before ordering a pastrami on rye. She was famished. She'd been working nonstop for six hours because of the ongoing Planter's Day Sale and still had to return for another several hours of work. Vienna hated working during sales and cursed herself for not quitting beforehand, as she usually did. But the Planter's Day Sale had crept up on her. She blamed Natasha. If she hadn't been so focused on taking care of Derek and saving him from Natasha's evil clutches, she would have found another job by now.

Vienna allowed herself to admit that being offered a promotion played a small part in her decision not to leave Drayden's sooner. She still hadn't accepted or declined the offer. It was far too busy in the store for anyone to follow through and force an answer from her. Not until the sale was over, which gave her another week or so to make up her mind. Or to find another job.

Vienna sipped her wine and looked at her watch. Christian should be at Drayden's keeping an eye on Women's Shoes so Derek could carry out his part of the plan without interruption. She'd bribed one of the boys in Shipping to hold off that day's shoe delivery until the middle of the day. She rolled her eyes, remembering how difficult it was to persuade him to leave the boxes in the middle of the sales floor, since it would put him at great risk of incurring Natasha's wrath. It had cost her forty dollars, but it would provide the diversion Derek needed to do his deed. With Christian there to make sure everything went off without a hitch, she was fine to actually sit down for a few minutes and rest her aching butt. She closed her eyes and began to massage one of her feet.

"I'd be glad to do that for you while you enjoy your wine."

"Cart Man," she said without opening her eyes. She leaned back in her chair, extended her leg, and felt two strong hands move her foot into his lap. She sighed as he began to rub her instep. "You don't know how good that feels."

"I hear that slaying dragons is rather hard on the feet," Cart Man said.

"Did I say dragons? I meant deer. One big-mouthed Deere in particular," Vienna said.

She opened her eyes and found Cart Man smiling appreciatively at her. She smiled back but shook her head in amazement at the same time. Even though they'd had a few conversations here and there, he was still a stranger, and she couldn't believe she was letting him rub her feet. She chalked it up to the wine, which she assumed was beginning to go to her head.

"I didn't know it was deer season," Cart Man said.

"It's open season on Our Miss Deere," Vienna said.

"So the deer has a name," Cart Man said. "Give me your other foot, please. Thank you."

"Please don't tell me you know her. I'd hate to have to poison you or something if you tried to interfere."

"It wouldn't work. I know my poisons. Don't forget my mother's birds. Don't worry. I have no idea who you're talking about," Cart Man assured her. "I have no intention of interfering in whatever you're doing. However, if I can be of any assistance, please let me know. I love a good prank. Besides, if my helping you would expedite things and free you to go out with me—"

"I'm a big girl," Vienna interrupted. "I can handle things on my own, thank you."

"That was never in question," Cart Man said, still smiling. When her sandwich was put down, he offered, "Should I give you the full treatment and feed you?"

"After you touched my feet? I think not," Vienna said and took a hearty bite of pastrami on rye.

As she chewed, Cart Man said, "Now that your mouth's otherwise engaged, let me tell you how much I've been looking forward to going out with you. How beautiful I think you are. How much I love that tiny mole near your eye and often think about it before I fall asleep at night. How just being able to humbly rub your feet for you gives me more pleasure than you'd ever imagine."

Vienna was suddenly glad she'd ordered pastrami, since it required a lot of chewing and gave her time to formulate a tactful response to Cart Man's words. She wondered how long she could get away with chewing. Maybe if she chewed long enough, he'd just go away. But she had only a half hour, ten minutes of which had already gone by, and she couldn't be late returning for work or Meg would probably kick her ass.

Cart Man was grinning again. Vienna studied his teeth, which were perfectly straight and gleaming white, and she wondered if he'd worn braces. Even sitting down with her foot in his lap, he looked tall. His skin was flawless, save for a small scar near his eyebrow. She imagined that he'd been a rough-and-tumble sort of youth who probably got into all sorts of trouble. She wondered what path had led him to the mall, how he'd ended up behind a cart, and if he was ambitious enough to want more from his life.

She was somewhat ashamed to realize that she was embarrassed at the idea of going out with Cart Man. There was a caste system in Mall of the Universe, a fact she couldn't deny. Everybody knew it. The people who worked in the hotel and the anchor stores were at the top of the pyramid. Next came the smaller boutique employees, then the attractions staff, and after them, the food court workers. Somewhere at the bottom were the Cart People and the mall's service staff. The different groups never associated with one another. Vienna wouldn't even consider having lunch with a food court employee, or "foodie," as they were commonly known. She would never see a movie with one of the parking attendants. She was always polite to everyone in the mall. Friendly, even. Which invited them to be nice to her in return, offering gossip and information as needed. But she never associated with them after hours.

Still chewing, she regarded Cart Man with trepidation, resisting the urge to look around and make sure nobody she knew was watching them. She was reminded of DeWitt and how he'd made her feel about herself. How petty her job really was, and how unnecessary it sometimes seemed to spend every dime on designer this, that, and the other thing.

But in spite of his station, Cart Man was extremely appealing. She liked the way the skin around his eyes crinkled when he smiled. She figured it meant that he laughed a lot. Vienna decided she could use a little more laughter in her life. That was why she liked Davii so much. And Derek.

As she finally swallowed, Cart Man said, "I've taken up enough of your time for one day." He gave her foot a firm squeeze, gently placed it on the floor, and rose to leave.

"Wait!" Vienna exclaimed, dropping her sandwich on its plate. She saw crumbs falling to the floor from her blouse as she jumped up and felt a little foolish, but she didn't care. "I don't know how strict your work schedule is, but I have another break later. Probably in four hours. It's just a half hour, but we could do something."

"I was hoping for dinner and a movie," Cart Man admitted.

"I can't promise anything like that for a while. We're in the middle of a hellish time at work, and I'm working longer hours. In fact, I need to get back now." She riffled through her purse and dropped some money on the table, then picked up her sandwich and said, "I hate to eat and run, but I'm a busy career gal and all that. So what do you say? Meet me in four hours on the Earth level outside Drayden's?"

Cart Man bowed slightly and said, "I'd be honored to spend any amount of time with you."

Vienna felt flushed as she walked back to Drayden's. She felt like she had a secret, which made her happy. She loved anything clandestine and sneaky. Which reminded her of her other furtive duties. She pitched the remaining half of her sandwich into a garbage can before running into Drayden's. After punching back in at the time clock, she meandered slowly through the stockroom, hoping to encounter Derek and assess the status of Operation Deere Slayer. But she saw only Tremaine, one of the stockroom associates, who was loading stacks of shoeboxes onto a shelf.

"You got a shipment this late in the day?" Vienna asked.

He stopped his work, wiping sweat from his brow. "Yeah. Can

you believe it? The stupid Shipping dude left the carton on the sales floor, too. He must have been new or something. Anybody with half a brain knows you don't do that. Of course, the bitch took it out on me." Vienna didn't have to ask who he meant. "Somehow it was my fault. She started yelling at me, but I cut her off, saying, 'Don't worry, Miz Natasha! I put dem boxes on duh shelves fo' you real good! You don't need to whup me!' That shut her up. Haven't seen her for about an hour, in fact."

Vienna smiled, then asked, "Have you seen Derek?"

"Nah. Not for a while. He must be on break or something."

Vienna thanked him and walked away, assuming that everything was going according to plan, since Christian and Derek were both gone. She returned to her counter to find Meg at her most hostile, growling something about the world being filled with bitches and how Bianca had gone home because of a stomachache. Vienna had little time to wonder if the two were related, because their counter was swamped with women wanting the Gifts with Purchase that came with buying different Lillith Allure combinations.

Vienna hated sales because they attracted the worst possible customers: tightwads who wanted everything for nothing, who didn't care about Drayden's stellar customer service, and most of whom were downright rude. Enticed into the store by deep discounts, they couldn't understand why nothing in her department was marked down, and she heard herself repeatedly explaining that cosmetics and fragrances never went on sale; discontinued items sold at the normal price until they were gone; they'd run out of free samples by the third day of the sale; and the Gift with Purchase came only when a customer spent a certain dollar amount.

Four hours later, a beleaguered Vienna was relieved by the Cosmetics manager so she could take another break. She'd been yelled at, had generally been hassled by everyone, and had even had one customer throw a compact at her head when Vienna told her that it wasn't on sale.

Cart Man was waiting for her outside the Drayden's entrance. When he saw her weary gait, he stepped forward and wrapped his arms around her. She rested her head on his shoulder and didn't want to move. Ever.

"Those women are all insane," she said. "It's makeup, for God's sake. I've never been that aggressive over a tube of lipstick in my life. Or anything."

"I find that hard to believe," Cart Man said. "You strike me as the kind of woman who would stop at nothing to get what she wanted."

"Well, yeah," Vienna agreed, carefully extricating herself from his arms. "But I'd never spit at anyone. Someone actually spit at Meg. Can you believe it? I need a drink. Let's get the hell away from this joint."

Moments later, they were sitting in the courtyard outside the planetarium, each sipping an ice cream float paid for by Cart Man. He'd insisted on buying them and called them therapy. Vienna had to admit that she felt soothed by the taste of the vanilla ice cream mingling with the sharp carbonation of the soda. It reminded her of riding her bike in the summertime as a little girl, collecting discarded bottles from the side of the road so she could redeem them at the drugstore in exchange for an ice cream soda or a candy bar. Suddenly she wanted a Mars bar, too.

She realized Cart Man was staring at her, which made her blush. "I was just having a sense-memory moment," she explained. "What are you thinking about?"

"I'm wondering what you'd rather be doing," Cart Man said.

"I'm right where I want to be," Vienna said.

"I don't mean now," Cart Man explained. He seemed to rethink what he'd just said, and amended, "Maybe I do. I mean with your life. I don't want to offend you, but I think you're a whole lot smarter than the average cosmetics salesperson."

Vienna laughed and said, "I'm not offended. But I can't speak for my co-workers. Some of them are quite dedicated to the world of cosmetics. It's not a bad job. It can be fun sometimes. But to answer your question, no, it's not what I want to do with my life. I guess I'm in a holding pattern. Trying to figure it all out. But I know I won't be doing it forever. How about you?"

"Same here. I know I'm low man on the totem pole in this mall. But I don't mind. This is a fun place," he said, looking around them. "I don't know how many times I've circled this mall, and I always see something new. New people, new stores, you name it. There's magic all around us." He looked at Vienna again and said, "I know I've tried this before, but would you please have dinner with me tonight?"

Vienna realized that he was right. There must be magic in Mall of the Universe. It had made Derek appear out of thin air. It had found Davii a fabulous new life. It made funny things happen when she was bored. But how much of that was her own doing? Or fate? Regardless, she couldn't deny the magic that was happening between her and Cart Man. She resisted the voice screeching inside her head—her mother's voice—that said, *A white boy? You know what that got you last time. Divorced, that's what!*

"I'd love to," Vienna said and happily sipped her ice cream float.

A few hours later, she was looking at Cart Man's face in the warm glow of candlelight and decided she'd never seen anyone more handsome. His eyes danced, matching the candle's flame as it sputtered and flickered like an angel dancing on the head of a pin. She stared into his eyes as she sipped red wine from a paper cup and attempted to twirl spaghetti onto a plastic fork. They both laughed when Cart Man's forkful of pasta stubbornly unwound midway to his mouth and seemed to leap from his fork, plummeting to the floor like a suicide victim.

"This seemed more romantic in the planning stages," Cart Man said apologetically.

Vienna shifted on her stool, leaning across the surface of the cart to pat his arm, and said, "It's fine. Really. This is nice. I love the mall after hours. It's so quiet in here."

Cart Man opened one of the drawers in his cart and said, "Let's see if you're telling me the truth. Ah. Here we are." He held up a ring with a large oval stone and beckoned for Vienna's finger. He slid the ring on and said, "Mood rings never lie."

"I'm going to ignore the implication that I'm untruthful. Instead, I'll silently wonder about your trust issues," Vienna said, holding up her hand and watching as the stone turned a murky blue. "I haven't seen one of these things in years. I used to wonder how they work."

"They're magic," Cart Man said and laughed when Vienna rolled her eyes.

"What does blue mean?"

"Is it dark blue, or just regular?" he asked.

"I don't know," Vienna said.

"Let's see," he said and took her hand. They leaned over the cart, heads almost touching as they examined the ring. "Blue means you're calm."

"I'm definitely calm," Vienna agreed, although she also felt a little nervous. She didn't know if it was her rapid heartbeat or the silly ring, but she felt half her age. She tried to remember her first date, but it seemed like a hundred years ago. What was the boy's name? Frank something? They'd gone to see a movie, and she remembered being annoyed that he hadn't tried to kiss her. She looked at her hand, framed by Cart Man's, and liked the way they looked together. His hands were warm and comforting. She wanted him to kiss her. She succumbed to her true feelings and said, "Maybe I'm not as calm as I thought."

Cart Man frowned playfully, pretending to study the ring more intently, and said, "Yes. I see what you mean. This is definitely dark blue. Romantic."

"That sounds about right," Vienna said.

"Passionate," Cart Man said, staring at her.

"Yes," Vienna confirmed, nodding when he leaned forward.

"Happy," he whispered, his face inches from hers.

"Definitely," she said. When he kissed her, she was ecstatic. Her entire being was focused on the moment, carefree and satisfied.

"I hope this is okay," he said, his hand on her cheek, thumb lightly brushing her lips. She nodded, and he asked, "Would you like to see my place? I'm not pushing. I'm not suggesting that we—"

"It's okay," Vienna interrupted. "I know what you mean. Why don't we go to my place? It's nearby. I'm pretty sure my roommate is out for the evening, and I really need to get home and feed my kitty."

28

The Dinosaur from Our Imagination

What the hell am I doing? Derek wondered, skittering through the mall like a cat in a roomful of rocking chairs. *I'll never get out of this alive.*

He flinched as he reached into his pocket for his cell phone and his fingers brushed Natasha's keys. He kept expecting to feel the clamp of her hand on his neck. Every few seconds, he glanced nervously over his shoulder, even though he knew how guilty that made him look. He'd be lucky if he didn't end up surrounded by security guards, although it was hard to consider them a serious threat when they were always crashing their golf carts through glass doors and windows.

In spite of his anxiety, the thought of mall security made Derek smile. The first time he'd ever heard Hunter call them the "Barneys" he'd tentatively asked what they had to do with purple dinosaurs. Hunter had looked perplexed at Derek's question, and Derek had been embarrassed about missing Hunter's reference to Barney Fife, bumbling deputy from Mayberry. Hunter had brushed it off, making Derek explain the purple dinosaur cult. In time, the two different Barneys had merged in their private jokes, which included creating their own lyrics to the "I Love You" song whenever they heard new evidence of mall security's ineptitude. And occasionally at other times . . .

After they settled into their room at the guesthouse, Hunter left to take a walk. Derek lay on the bed with a novel, trying not to wonder what Hunter was up to, if he was cruising or maybe tricking. He knew he should be out enjoying his first trip to Key West, but he thought maybe Hunter wanted some time away from him. He didn't realize he'd fallen asleep until Hunter slid onto the bed next to him and woke him. The book fell from Derek's chest to the floor between the bed and the wall. When he reached for it, his hands touched cold metal. Confused, he brought up a pair of handcuffs left behind by a former occupant of the room.

He and Hunter stared at each other for a few seconds, then used the cuffs as the catalyst for hours of electrifying sex. Sometime during the night, Hunter made him hysterical by unexpectedly singing in his ear, "I frisk you. You fuck me. We are mall security."

Stop, he ordered himself, remembering that he'd been about to call Christian to tell him that he'd successfully stolen Natasha's keys from her desk. Instead, he stared at the unusually large crowd of people between him and Hal's Hardware Heaven. He'd known it was a bad idea to get the keys duplicated at the mall. He'd asked Christian if he could borrow his car to do it elsewhere. Christian had said that would take too long. It was vital that Natasha never have a chance to miss the keys.

Derek's concern was Hunter, who was always dashing in to Hal's to buy little wrenches, screwdrivers, and other assorted items that he used to maintain his bikes. Derek had been deliberately avoiding any of the places where he might run into his ex. But Christian was right. Time was the most important consideration. Which forced Derek to negotiate his way through a hundred potential witnesses to get to the hardware store.

He didn't understand why so many people were lingering on the Sun level until he finally saw the group of magicians entertaining the crowd in the common area. Rings of children watched, spellbound, as bunnies and doves disappeared and reappeared, balls were juggled, and brightly colored scarves were pulled from unexpected places amid puffs of smoke. As Derek scanned the crowd, his eye was caught by Gypsy Ed, the man he'd met on Preview Night.

Ed's focused expression was full of affection and pleasure, and Derek realized that he was actually quite handsome. But he wasn't looking at the magicians. Derek followed the trajectory of his gaze until he spotted the person in the crowd that Ed was watching so intently. It wasn't a thrilled child, as Derek had expected. It was Hunter. Derek felt a little put out that his lover was being cruised by another man. Then, as he stared at Hunter, he understood why Ed was smiling, and his heart melted.

Hunter was watching the magicians with rapt fascination. When a dove fluttered from a box, his eyes widened. When a coin was taken from behind a little boy's ear, Hunter smiled along with everyone else. The simple, standard tricks that most people had seen from the time they were toddlers, but of course, Hunter had never really been a child. Probably the only magic he'd seen as a boy was the Congreve accountants making money appear out of thin air.

Like Gypsy Ed, Derek was mesmerized by the appearance of a Hunter who rarely surfaced. The little boy who'd never seen a magic show. Whose parents had never taken him to a circus or a carnival. The Hunter that Derek instinctively understood and wanted to protect from the judgment of others. Derek's gaze went from Hunter to Ed, then back to Hunter. It hurt that another man could not only see Hunter the way he did, but might not fail to win his heart, as Derek had. Someone else might magically release the child in Hunter who needed a sympathetic companion.

Derek's jealousy struggled against his love, and he turned away, his heart aching as he thought, *If not me, then someone. I want him to be happy.*

He slowly skirted the crowd and went into Hal's, taking the keys off Natasha Deere's chain and handing them over to be duplicated. He looked down, trying to figure out how to teach his heart to say good-bye and mean it. He was pushing the brass *D* in a circle over the wooden counter when he smelled Marc Jacobs and smoke, and he looked up into Hunter's eyes.

"You're so sad," Hunter said. "Is there anything I can do for you, Derek?"

Derek swallowed and shook his head. That was the root of their problem. In Hunter's world, they were locked into roles. Hunter was the one who took care of things. Derek was the one who was taken care of. Hunter would never have kicked him out, because he wasn't cruel. But as long as they were together, Derek would always be treated like a child. Hunter would always be the adult.

Hunter reached over and gently touched Derek's hair, saying, "I like this haircut. It suits you."

When Derek didn't answer, Hunter dropped his eyes, following the path of the *D* that Derek still pushed around the counter.

Derek felt his face get hot. He was practically begging the world to notice that he'd stolen Natasha's keys. Vienna might suggest that he wanted to get caught.

"Making keys to your new place for your new boyfriend?" Hunter asked, staring hard at Derek's red face.

Taken off guard, Derek merely grunted, "Huh?"

"Drayden?" Hunter asked. When Derek's mouth fell open, Hunter said, "I saw him with you at the store that night." Derek didn't have to ask which night Hunter meant, blushing again at the memory of his encounter with Hunter in the storage room at Drayden's. Before he could reply, Hunter went on. "He's obviously crazy about you. I guess it's a good match."

After his first wave of shock subsided, Derek realized there was no reason for Hunter not to think he'd simply traded one sugar daddy for another. It didn't speak highly of Hunter's opinion of him, but he guessed he deserved it.

"How do you know the *D* isn't for Derek?" he asked wearily.

"A big brass *D* on a key chain, Derek? That's so not you. Do you think I don't know you at all?" When Derek only stared at him, Hunter shrugged and left the store.

Derek paid for the duplicate keys and a small ring to put them on, then walked back to Drayden's in a trance. He couldn't think of any moment during Preview Night that would have given Hunter the impression that he had something going with Drayden Lvandsson. He'd only met the man that night. As gratifying as it was to think that Hunter was jealous, if that had been what prompted their sex, it was no healthier than any of the other negative emotions they shared. It was time to move on.

When he went inside Drayden's, he checked out Cosmetics. Vienna was swamped with customers. He saw no sign of Christian, who was supposed to be keeping an eye on Natasha. Derek went through the stockroom doors and approached Natasha's desk with a fatalistic attitude, unsurprised but also undismayed to see her standing there with Erik. He was ready to hand over her keys, get fired, and leave the mall for the comfort of his parents and Evansville. Or maybe he'd go stay with Davii in New York. There wasn't a reason in the world why he should be enduring the fucked-up population of a vindictive manager, an ex-boyfriend, a roommate who shunned the profession that had cost her so much time and money, and a friend who was too cowardly to use his artistic talent. The universe sucked, and Derek wanted out.

"I know they were right here on my desk," Natasha said furiously. "Someone must have taken them."

Derek reached into his pocket, his eyes meeting Erik's, and Erik said, "Oh, good. Derek, help me move this desk. I'm sure Natasha's keys are wedged between it and the wall."

"I need—"

"Hurry up!" Natasha snapped, cutting off Derek's attempted confession. "God, why must I always be subjected to imbeciles and laggards?"

Erik's gaze didn't waver, and Derek felt sympathy for him. If Vienna successfully crushed Natasha, it would benefit a lot more people than just Derek. Derek could leave Drayden's without a trace of regret, but Erik loved his job. He was good at it. It wasn't fair that Natasha had so much power to make it miserable for him.

As they moved the desk, Derek pulled the keys from his pocket and let them fall to the floor.

"See?" Erik said, smiling faintly at Derek while Natasha dropped to her knees and reached under the desk to retrieve the keys.

"Please try," Natasha said as she stood up, "not to let anything else go wrong today." She grabbed her purse and stalked away without a word of thanks or farewell.

"Erik—"

"I don't want to know," Erik said, waving him away. "Just tell me it won't hurt the store."

"It won't hurt the store."

Vienna wasn't home when he got in that evening. Nor did Christian answer his phone. Apparently they'd roped him into their scheme, persuading him to steal and copy the keys, then abandoned him. Not that he could be mad, since they were doing it for him in the first place. Well, for him and to conquer the forces of evil.

He grinned, realizing that his mood had lifted. He no longer felt like running away. He really didn't even mind having some time to himself. It had been a while since he hadn't had to work or wanted to watch TV, go out with Vienna, or join Christian for yoga. He decided to make the most of it.

After he showered, he bought a new novel at Patti's Pages and took it to dinner with him at Stargrazers. Then he walked slowly through the mall, window-shopping, people-watching, and enjoying his own company. It wasn't until he stepped into the lobby of the Congreve that he realized what he'd done. Force of habit had led him home. Except it wasn't home anymore.

As he turned to retrace his steps, he heard Sheree's musical reminder that home without Hunter was no home for him. Sheree had to be a witch; what else explained the way she seemed always to sing his thoughts, even when she couldn't possibly know he was there?

He went inside the Aurora to listen to her *Showboat* set. The bar stools were full, so he had to take a table, where he ordered a drink and sat back, admiring his favorite chanteuse. A few songs later, his glass was empty and she was about to take a break, so he pushed back his chair to leave.

"Derek, right?" he heard a man say. Looking up, he saw Drayden Lvandsson standing next to his table.

"Yes, sir," he said, his spine straightening as he prepared to stand up.

Drayden placed his hand on Derek's shoulder to restrain him and said, "Mind if I sit down? Could I buy you a drink?"

"Sure," Derek said with a nervous swallow. He watched as Drayden smiled and nodded toward their waiter, then said, "I didn't know you were still in town, Mr. Lvandsson."

"Please call me Drayden. Really. Even at work."

"Yes, sir," Derek said, and Drayden smiled. "I mean—"

"We're just a couple of men listening to a beautiful woman sing wonderful old songs," Drayden said. He glanced toward the bar, where Sheree was getting her water. "Isn't she marvelous?"

"I've always thought so," Derek said.

"So, Derek, any new accounts of heroism to share? Rescued any more supermodels? My father was quite entertained by the story of a shoe seller by day, bull whisperer by night."

Derek blushed and said, "Mr. Lvandsson—"

"Drayden."

"—I have to tell you the truth. I'm probably the lousiest shoe seller Drayden's has ever had. I'm always screwing something up. The only thing I've got going for me is good manners. Gert the cow could do a better job than I do."

Drayden's eyes crinkled with amusement, and he said, "But you obviously think fast on your feet."

"Vienna, the woman who told you that story? She and our friend Davii are actually the ones who saved the day. I was cowering behind a table most of the time, trying to come up with clever bon mots about the bull. Vienna wanted to make me look good to you."

"Then obviously you have something other than good manners going for you. You have a good friend," Drayden said. "Even if your sales are soft, lots of people have to grow into a job, Derek."

"In my case, I'd pretty much need the retail equivalent of Viagra," Derek said, and Drayden let out a gratifying bellow of laughter.

Derek glanced toward the stage as Sheree began singing "My Buddy," wondering if she was trying to tell him something, since that was her nickname for him. If so, it seemed insensitive; the song was about someone who missed all the gay days he'd spent with his buddy. Sheree didn't seem to be singing to him, though. Derek shifted to see who she was watching and spotted Hunter staring at him from the door to the Congreve lobby. Or rather, he was staring at Drayden. Then Hunter looked at Derek for a moment before turning and leaving the bar.

29

Indiana Talbot and the Temple of Doom

Vienna waited outside the main entrance of Drayden's, scanning the courtyard for Derek and Christian. She impatiently glanced at her watch and frowned; they were ten minutes late. She turned and gazed at her reflection in one of Drayden's display windows, patting the curls of her latest wig into place. She examined her cuticles, then checked her watch again. Even though the interior of the mall remained open because of the clubs, bars, and some of the restaurants, Vienna worried that loitering in the courtyard might attract the attention of mall security.

Finally she spotted Christian walking toward her in the distance. He was dressed head to toe in black and was wearing gloves. Vienna rolled her eyes and thought, *So much for being subtle.*

"Sorry I'm late," he said. "A client called right before I left. She's asking her boss for a raise tomorrow and needed encouragement. Where's Derek?"

"I have no idea," Vienna stated. "What the hell are you wearing? I told you to dress inconspicuously."

Christian looked down at his outfit and said, "I thought I did."

"You look like a cat burglar. Get that thing off your head," she said, snatching off his black stocking hat. She opened her large Kate Spade tote bag and stuffed it inside.

"Hey!" Christian exclaimed, his hands flying up to his head. "My hair!"

"Are we ready?" Derek suddenly said, causing both Vienna and

Christian to yelp in surprise. He grinned at their reactions, pointed to his Diesel sneakers, and said, "I'm wearing my sneakiest shoes."

"That's great," Vienna said sarcastically. She gestured to Christian and said, "At least you're not dressed like Ethan Hunt here."

"Ethan Hunt?" Derek asked blankly.

"Mission: Impossible," Vienna said with a sigh. "I'm starting to understand the title."

"We're breaking into Natasha's apartment. What did you expect me to wear, a clown suit?" Christian asked, sounding miffed as he continued to smooth his hair. "I'll bet nobody ever messed up Ethan Hunt's hair."

"We don't have to do this tonight," Derek said. "Natasha's not due back for two more nights. We could do it tomorrow."

"Let's get it over with," Vienna said, leading the way to Natasha's condominium. "If you're afraid, the best course of action is to confront your fears head on, instead of putting it off."

"I'm not afraid," Derek said.

"I was talking to myself," Vienna said.

As they approached the Final Frontier Passage, Christian asked, "We're going to just walk right in?"

"Do you have a better idea?" Vienna asked. "What did you think we were gonna do, scale the side of the building?"

"He's certainly dressed for it," Derek said.

"If you two don't stop making fun of my clothes, I'm out of here," Christian huffily replied.

"Think about it. If we sneak in, we look guilty and draw attention to ourselves. We have keys to Natasha's apartment, so all we have to do is look like we belong there and security won't give us a second thought, right?"

"In theory," Christian said.

"Makes sense to me," Derek agreed.

"Let's go," Vienna urged. "If we get stopped, we're there to water a friend's plants while she's out of town."

They strode purposefully through the Final Frontier Passage and directly into Natasha's building. Vienna looked at the butter-soft leather furniture, lush foliage, and expensive art on the lobby walls and felt envious. It was nicer than her building. Why did the evil harridans of the world always get all the breaks? She smiled at the concierge as they passed the front desk and cheerfully said, "Hi!"

"Good evening," he replied, nodding his head once and returning her smile.

When they stopped in front of the elevators, Christian whispered, "What floor?"

"Thirteen," Derek said.

"Why doesn't that surprise me?" Christian said.

"I never realized how nice it is in the Rings of Uranus," Vienna said with hushed awe as she continued to look at the lobby.

"Why, thank you," Derek said demurely.

It took Vienna a minute to get the joke. Christian snorted once, then bit his thumb to keep from drawing the concierge's attention. Vienna grinned and said, "I never get invited to the Rings of Uranus."

"The last time I tried to get into the Rings of Uranus, I got lost," Derek said.

"They should really put up a sign," Christian said. "This way to the Rings of Uranus."

"I wish I lived in the Rings of Uranus," Vienna said.

"I can't believe how easy it was to get into the Rings of Uranus," Christian added.

"Once you get inside the Rings of Uranus," Derek said, "you never want to leave."

Vienna watched the elevator's display count down to one. The doors opened; once they rushed inside and the doors closed, they burst out laughing, hanging on to each other for support.

"Vienna, I never thought breaking in to the Rings of Uranus would be so much fun!" Derek said.

"Stop," Vienna gasped. "I can't breathe."

"No more Rings of Uranus jokes," Christian decreed.

"Right. This is serious. We can't slip up," Vienna said once she'd regained breath control. She patted the curls of her wig back into place while Derek tucked his shirt back in. Christian studied his hair in the reflective surface of the elevator doors, muttering something about Paul Mitchell hairspray. Vienna couldn't help herself and asked, "Do you think the payments are high in the Rings of Uranus?"

They became serious again when the doors of the elevator opened on the thirteenth floor, consumed with the task of locating Natasha's apartment. When they found the right door, Vienna said, "Okay, Derek. You've got the keys."

Derek put the key in the lock and they all drew in their breath before he turned it, not knowing what to expect. The click of the tumblers falling into place sounded like a cannon in the quiet stillness of the hallway. When nothing bad happened, they all sighed audibly. Derek looked to Vienna, who nodded, so he turned the doorknob.

Once they'd crept quietly inside, Derek closed the door softly behind them, while Vienna peered into the darkness.

"Where's the light switch?" Christian asked.

"I don't know," Vienna hissed. "I'm kind of waiting for a three-headed dog to appear."

"She called Erik today from Chicago, so she's definitely out of town," Derek whispered. There was a crash and he said, "Damn it! Stupid table."

"I'm turning on the lights," Christian said, and Vienna could hear him running his hands along the walls to find a switch.

She took three steps forward, then stopped, saying, "What was that?"

The scrape of Christian's hand stopped, and he asked, "What was what?"

"I heard something. It sounded like someone walking," she said, frozen in place.

"It was your heels on the parquet, silly," Derek said as the room was flooded with light.

They blinked for a second as their eyes adjusted. Once she could focus, Vienna saw why the sound of her heels had echoed in the apartment. The main rooms were vast, and the furnishings were expensive, yet sparse. The floors were devoid of carpet, and the majority of the walls were bare. There were no bookshelves, no pictures, and no knickknacks. Natasha's apartment had all the love and warmth of an operating arena in a hospital.

"So much for my watering the plants excuse," Vienna muttered.

"Talk about minimalism," Christian said, looking around the room.

"I don't see any dolls," Derek said, sounding panicked. "Where would you put a doll in this place? Where are the dolls?"

"Don't make me slap you," Christian warned.

"That only works on television," Vienna stated. "Slapping a hysterical person rarely quiets them. On the contrary, it usually provokes them and results in an equally violent—"

"Excuse me! Hello!" Derek exclaimed. "I hate to interrupt, but I don't think either of you is grasping the gravity of this situation. We've broken into my manager's apartment. We're committing a felony."

"Oh, Derek, don't be such a pussy," Vienna said. She wandered farther into the apartment and began nosing around. "If we were going to be busted by security, it would've happened by now. Let's spread out. If you move anything, be sure to put it back exactly where you found it."

Derek, looking worried, wandered down a hallway. Christian started opening drawers in the kitchen. Vienna continued observing everything. The lack of pictures in the apartment was telling. Since there were no photos of friends or family anywhere, Vienna could ascertain that Natasha had no fond memories. She frowned at her realization that she and Natasha had something in common.

She noticed a television remote on the coffee table and gingerly picked it up with two fingers. There was a faint outline of dust where the remote had been, which caused Vienna to frown again in thought.

"What is it?" Christian asked, returning from the kitchen.

"Did you find anything suspicious?" she asked, coming out of her reverie.

"The refrigerator holds the bare minimum for survival. The baking dishes have no brown stains on them. I'd say our girl orders in a lot. Other than that, there's nothing," Christian said. "No refrigerator magnets. Nothing incriminating in the trash. The only things in the dishwasher are coffee cups and martini glasses."

"There aren't any fingerprints on this remote control," Vienna said. She carefully set it on the coffee table, making sure it was within the dust outline. "If there's any life happening on a daily basis in this apartment, it isn't going on in here."

Derek appeared in the hallway and said, "I think whatever it is we're looking for is down here." Before he could lead them to the end of the hall, Christian stopped short and said, "Natasha's bedroom?" When he darted inside, Vienna followed, with Derek on her heels.

She hastily looked around the nondescript room. The bed was made with military precision, had no frilly pillows, and the comforter was a solid black. The top of the dresser was barren. The bedside tables had steel lamps with dark shades. Like the living area, it had no artwork on the walls, save for one lone mirror above a barren desk.

"This place scares me," Christian said. "It's like an apartment in one of those decorating or architecture magazines. They look nice, but it's just for show. You'd think she'd have at least one picture of herself, a stuffed animal, an old yearbook. Something that shows she lives here."

Vienna opened the closet and recognized the clothes she'd seen Natasha wearing at work. Everything was meticulously hung and arranged by color. It was all perfectly merchandised and could have been displayed on a rack at Drayden's. Natasha's shoes were all in boxes stacked neatly on the floor.

"I checked, and the shoes are arranged by color and heel height," Derek said. "Just like we do at work."

"But where are the dolls?" Christian asked. "Do you think DeWitt lied about that?"

"I think what we're looking for is in the next room," Derek said, motioning for them to follow him. He led them to a padlocked door at the end of the hallway. "None of the keys I duplicated fit this lock. I didn't find another key in the bedroom. Did either of you find a key?"

Christian shook his head while Vienna eyed the padlock and said, "This has to be it, boys. We've got to get in this room."

"I'll be right back," Christian said and ran back down the hallway.

"Maybe there's a screwdriver somewhere," Vienna said. She left Derek and went into Natasha's bathroom. She was momentarily distracted by the toiletries and cosmetics on the counter, which were carefully arranged by product and rivaled any display Vienna had ever seen. She found what she was looking for under the sink and said, "Jackpot!"

Just then, she heard several loud crashes coming from the hallway, followed by Christian exclaiming, "Jackpot!"

Screwdrivers in hand, she stepped into the hallway and found Christian wielding a fire extinguisher. The lock on the door was broken and hanging limply from the door frame. Christian waved the fire extinguisher and said triumphantly, "I remembered seeing it under the sink in the kitchen."

"You fool!" Vienna shrieked. "Now she's going to know there was a break-in! We used a key before, so technically we didn't break in.

Now something's broken! I can't believe you'd do something so stupid."

"Ew," Derek said. "You sound just like Natasha."

Vienna clasped her hand over her mouth and looked horrified.

"It's this apartment," Christian said. "It's evil, I tell you."

"Don't be absurd," Vienna finally said. "Apartments and inanimate objects can't be evil. Evil is in the mind of the beholder. I'm sorry I snapped at you. Let's just see what's inside."

Like before, Derek cautiously pushed open the door and hit the light switch, and they gazed inside before entering.

"Holy flying crap," Vienna said.

An entire wall of the room was lined with display shelves filled with Dolly Parton dolls. There were framed Dolly Parton pictures and posters on the walls. A throw rug with Dolly's image covered the floor. A curio cabinet held a collection of Dolly plates, pins, and patches. Possibly every book or magazine published about the country singer was crammed into a bookshelf next to a life-sized cardboard cutout of Dolly. A sign affixed to the wall opposite the door read "Dolly Parton Drive." There was even a Dolly Parton pinball machine in the corner.

They were speechless as they walked into the room. Christian examined a media cabinet with a television, VCR, DVD player, stereo, and every possible Dolly Parton movie, album, and compact disc stacked inside. Vienna opened a closet door and found an array of glittering dresses, jeans, and shirts. There was a shoe rack filled with high-heeled shoes in every color, as well as a collection of cowboy boots.

"DeWitt wasn't kidding," she finally said. She turned around and saw Derek staring with horror at twenty wigs on a table, each perched on a Styrofoam head. "Are you okay, Derek?"

"I don't know why, but all of this scares me," he said. "I feel like I'm in a horror movie and something terrible is about to happen. I think I'm going to quit my job tomorrow. I don't want to be around Natasha another second. Look at all this. She's obviously deranged."

"I wouldn't go that far," Vienna said. "She's obsessed with Dolly Parton. This is where the life of her apartment begins."

"Or where life ends," Derek said. "Let's get out of here."

"Not so fast," Vienna said. "We're fine. Judging by the clothes in that closet, Natasha might sometimes dress like Dolly. But she doesn't seem to live her life as Dolly. At least, not twenty-four/seven. I don't think she has any Dolly personalities or anything like that. But there was a lock on the door, so she wants to protect Dolly. Keep her safe from society. I seriously underestimated the magnitude of her obsession, though. I thought we'd just find a few dolls."

"What do we do now?" Christian asked.

"I'm not sure. I want to have a look around," Vienna said.

She examined the dolls on the display shelves and took down one doll that had a bald patch on the side of its head. Derek stood in the middle of the floor wringing his hands, obviously not daring to touch anything. Christian sighed and sat down in a chair with a Dolly afghan slung over its back.

Just then, a loud voice screamed, "Why'd ya come in here looking like that?"

Vienna shrieked and involuntarily launched the doll across the room, where it knocked over the wig stands as if they were bowling pins. Derek jumped backward and jarred the curio cabinet, causing the doors to swing open and several plates to crash to the floor. Christian leaped from the chair, looking wildly around the room, as if searching for whoever was screaming at them.

"It's the stereo!" Vienna yelled, trying to be heard above the din.

Christian opened the media cabinet and shut off the stereo. He looked at the chair and held up a remote. "I must've sat on it."

"I almost peed my pants," Derek said. He looked at the broken plates on the floor and at the overturned wigs, and said, "We're never going to be able to fix this stuff."

"He's right," Christian said. "Let's grab the dolls and get out of here."

"I don't think that's such a good idea anymore," Vienna advised.

"I thought that was the plan," Christian said.

"If these dolls are what's holding her together, I don't think we should take them away. Maybe I can talk her into getting therapy," Vienna insisted. "That would be better for her."

"Come on, Vienna. You know Natasha. Do you really think you can talk her into anything?" Christian asked. "The woman is living in a fantasy world. I thought we were going to push her back toward sanity?"

"Who can say she was ever sane to begin with?" Vienna argued. She thought about it for a moment and sighed, finally giving in. She opened up her Kate Spade tote and doled out pillowcases to

Christian and Derek. "Fine. We'll remove the stimulus and deal with the emotional repercussions as they're revealed."

"Even if we didn't take the dolls, this mess is probably enough to send her over the edge," Derek said. "We may as well finish what we started."

"Don't forget, the door to this room was locked," Christian reminded them as he and Derek began filling their pillowcases. "If she didn't want people to get in and was keeping this place under lock and key, I seriously doubt she'll go to the police when she finds her dolls missing."

"The last thing we need is the police getting involved in this," Derek said. He looked at his pillowcase full of dolls and noticed the Congreve logo. "Hey, these are my pillowcases."

"You didn't think I'd use mine, did you?" Vienna asked. "They're Egyptian cotton."

Derek frowned, then pointed to a large doll on the wig table. It was a two-foot replica of Dolly in blue jeans, a red top with white polka dots, and a cowboy hat. The partially bald doll that Vienna had thrown lay at its feet like a victim slain by her gigantically malicious Dolly doppelgänger. He said, "What about that one?"

Vienna shrugged and said, "Might as well. Why stop now?"

Derek picked it up and was about to put it in his other empty pillowcase when a piercing alarm was activated. He dropped the doll and the pillowcase, bellowing, "You've got to be kidding me!"

"Do you think it's just in here?" Christian yelled. "Or do you think it's connected to building security?"

"Holy crap! Who cares? Let's get out of here!" Vienna screamed.

"The dolls!" Christian hollered.

They each grabbed a pillowcase full of dolls and ran from the apartment. Vienna had the presence of mind to make sure the front door was locked behind them to keep up appearances that nothing was wrong on the other side. She sprinted down the hall to find Derek frantically pressing the elevator buttons while Christian danced in place behind him.

"Are you kidding me? The last thing we want is to be trapped in an elevator. The stairs! Where are the stairs?" she insisted.

They found the stairwell and began racing down as fast as they could. A few flights down, Derek stopped short and said, "Wait. There were four pillowcases. We have three. We left a pillowcase in the Dolly room."

Vienna, panting, said, "It's too late for that now. We've got to get out of here."

Derek thrust his pillowcase full of dolls into Christian's free hand and said, "If she finds it, she might connect it to me. Go on without me. I'll only hold you back. Save yourselves."

"What is this, *Gunsmoke*?" Vienna asked incredulously. As Derek darted through a door to the hallway of the eighth floor, Vienna pushed Christian onward. "You heard him; keep moving!"

Christian continued their flight from danger, calling back, "I had no idea it would be so perilous to steal from the Rings of Uranus."

30

The Scene of the Crime

When he was five years old, Derek stole a pack of M&M's from a small grocery store in his neighborhood. He didn't realize he was stealing, because the grocer always let him take a piece of candy, then charged his mother for it afterward. Mrs. Anderson had warned the man that Derek wasn't making the connection, so when he showed up at home one afternoon happily crunching his M&M's, she grabbed his arm and returned him to the store to apologize. Confused, Derek broke away from her on their walk back home and climbed a tree. She left him there. His father's arrival a while later alerted him that he'd done something really serious. Confusion turned to shame. When his father asked him to climb down, he declined, insisting that he was just going to live in the tree for a while.

As the elevator doors opened on the thirteenth floor of Rings of Uranus, Derek relived that childhood moment of shame when he found himself face-to-face with a Barney. The security guard took one look at his guilty face and said, "Which apartment do you live in?"

"I don't live here," Derek said.

"Which resident are you visiting?"

"Um . . ."

"I think you'd better come with me," the guard said, stepping into the elevator and hitting the lobby button.

While the elevator made its descent, Derek weighed his options.

A full confession was out of the question. He was hardly going to embrace a criminal record for breaking and entering, nor was he going to implicate his friends, who were the ones holding the stolen goods. At the moment, he looked guilty of nothing more than trespassing. Unless they searched him and figured out he had keys to Natasha's apartment, especially if the alarm in the Dolly room was linked to a security system and their crime was exposed.

Making a run for it when the elevator doors opened was a gamble. The security guard didn't have a weapon, but he did have a radio. Even if Derek eluded an entire battalion of Barneys, his home and employer were both at the mall. Running didn't seem like a good alternative.

Which left him with no choice but to try to bullshit his way out of it, and his mind raced through possible scenarios as the guard directed him through the lobby of Rings of Uranus to a door marked SECURITY. He noted with relief that there was a different concierge on duty. At least Vienna and Christian were safe.

Another Barney was in the office, and the two men grunted at each other. Derek's captor said, "No sign of forced entry. No one answered the door. There's no noise now. Probably an alarm clock."

"According to the computer, it wasn't the smoke detector. Did you go inside?"

"*Her* apartment? Are you joking? Besides, I found him," the guard said, pointing at Derek.

"In the vicinity?"

"No, on the elevator. Arriving. Not leaving."

"Why am I here?" Derek asked. "I didn't do anything."

"All you gotta do is tell me which resident you're visiting. I'll check it, and you can go."

"I wasn't visiting anyone," Derek said.

"Why are you in the building? It's a private complex." When Derek didn't answer, the guard muttered, "Teenagers. No respect."

Derek bit off his protest that he wasn't a teenager, wondering if the misconception might work to his advantage.

"Give me your parents' phone number," the second guard said, his hand hovering over the phone. "We'll let them straighten this out."

Derek tried to imagine his parents' reaction should he actually let the security guard call them. It was tempting. *You're holding him for* what*? Riding an elevator? What kind of Mickey Mouse outfit are you?*

"Can't you give me a break?" he asked. "I haven't done anything wrong."

"The number," the security guard repeated, unmoved. His phone rang, and he picked it up, barking "Uranus Security" into the receiver.

Derek started giggling, which might have reinforced the idea that he was a teenager but provoked withering glances from both the guards. While the desk guard talked on the phone, his guard said, "Look, kid, do us all a favor. We ain't gettin' paid to babysit you. Give me your parents' name and number."

Derek sighed, knowing there was no way Vienna could pass as his mother. Even if she could fake being old enough, she couldn't fake being white. He thought of Juanita, but he couldn't fake being Spanish. There was no one else.

"Come on, buddy. We ain't got all night."

Buddy . . .

"Call the Congreve," he said. "Ask for Sheree Sheridan."

"Sheree's your mother?" the guard asked with a shocked look. When Derek maintained a sullen silence, the guard went to another desk and dialed the number, asking to be connected to Sheree. Then he said, "Miss—er—Mrs. Sheridan, this is Uranus Security. We have your son here." He winced at whatever her reaction was and said, "All's I know is, we asked for a parent, and the kid gave us your name." After another pause, he held out the receiver to Derek.

"Hi, Ma, it's Buddy."

"Oh," Sheree said. "I guess you can't tell me what this is about."

"No, ma'am."

"Does this mean I need to come get you?" she asked.

"I think so."

"Tell them I'm on the way."

"Yes, ma'am," he said and handed the receiver back to the guard. "She's on her way."

The other guard had finished his call, and the three of them stared at one another without talking for what seemed like forever. Finally there was a rap on the door, and they let Sheree in.

"Buddy," she said sadly, looking for all the world like a disappointed mother. She turned to the guard and said, "What did you catch him doing?"

"He wasn't doing anything," the guard said. "But he wouldn't tell us why he's here or if he's visiting someone. He's gotta be hiding something. And anyway, he's breaking teen curfew."

Sheree looked at Derek again, allowing her lovely blue eyes to fill with tears, and said, "You were here to see *her,* weren't you? After her father told you to stay away. Oh, Buddy. You're going to cost me my job." She sniffed and turned back to the guard. "It's just like *Romeo and Juliet.*"

"Look, Sheree, I didn't even know you had a kid," the guard said, handing her a tissue. "I don't wanna cause you no trouble. Just take Buddy home, and we'll act like this never happened."

"Thank you," Sheree said, giving him a melting look.

"And you, kid, stay out of Uranus. You should be ashamed, upsetting your mother like this."

"I'm sorry," Derek said, pretending to hang his head so they couldn't see that he was on the verge of laughing again. *Stay out of Uranus.*

"I can drive you back to the hotel in the cart—"

"No!" Sheree and Derek objected simultaneously and avoided each other's eyes. She thanked the guards profusely, then they were allowed to leave. Sheree glanced at him as they walked across the lobby and said, "You'd better come home with me. In case they've got surveillance cameras. A Congreve car can drive you around to the Galaxy Building later."

"As long as Hunter doesn't find out," Derek said.

"He's not likely to," Sheree said. They crossed the mall in silence, then Derek went with Sheree to her suite. When she opened the door, her Italian greyhound pattered up to greet them. Derek rubbed his ears, then Sheree said, "Go lie down, Ajax. Make yourself comfortable, Buddy. Would you like something to drink? I was having wine."

"Wine would be nice," Derek said. "Thanks." While she was gone, he glanced around with appreciation. Except for the soft leather sofa and tapestry armchairs, everything in the room looked like an antique. Subtle lighting illuminated what was obviously expensive art, and other than a few pictures in silver frames on the baby grand piano, all the surfaces were uncluttered. Her suite was elegant and comfortable. Everything that Natasha's apartment hadn't been.

When she returned, she handed him his glass and sat across from him, sipping her wine. Ajax, curled on a pillow at her feet, let out a contented sigh.

"This is really nice," Derek said. "I'd never know we were in a hotel."

"Thank you," Sheree said. "I do like nice things."

"I guess I should explain about tonight."

"You don't have to," she said. "What you do is your business. I know you'd never do anything wrong."

"Actually," Derek said miserably, "you'd better hear this. Because I did something really bad. When it's discovered, you might get stuck answering questions."

"I see," Sheree said.

She listened with a grave face as he told her about Natasha and the dolls. The only time she reacted was when he mentioned Dolly Parton's name. Her gaze became intense, and she seemed to be contemplating something, but she remained quiet until he was done. He waited for her to chastise him for involving her in their blundering attempt at vigilante justice. The silence was oppressive as she continued to look stern, then she crumbled, throwing her head back and laughing until tears streamed down her face.

"Oh, Buddy, how I wish I could have seen the three of you when the stereo started blaring. I have to meet Vienna someday." She began laughing again, wiping her eyes. Finally she composed herself and said, "I seriously doubt that you have to worry about Natasha reporting the theft. It sounds like she's determined to keep her little collection a secret."

"But the Congreve pillowcase—"

"You don't live here anymore," Sheree said with a shrug. "Anyone who's ever been a guest of the hotel could have a pillowcase. What are you going to do with the dolls now?"

"I have no idea," Derek said. "If Vienna has a plan, she hasn't shared it. I don't know whom to fear more. Her or Natasha."

"How much worse could things get at Drayden's, even if Natasha does suspect you?"

"She could fire me, thereby validating Hunter's poor opinion of me."

Sheree stared at him for a moment, then stood and walked to

the piano, saying, "Come here. I want you to see something." Derek followed her and looked at photographs as she picked them up one at a time and handed them to him. "This is Randolph and me on his yacht. Have you ever met him?"

"No," Derek said, studying the weathered face of Hunter's father. He was striking, with gray hair and piercing blue eyes. Other than the eyes, there was no similarity between him and Hunter. Derek turned his attention to a much younger version of Sheree, whose long blond hair was blowing away from her face. "You're so beautiful, Sheree."

Sheree smiled and said, "Thank you. I used to be quite the thing."

"You're still quite the thing," Derek insisted. She took the photograph from him and replaced it, then handed him another one, taken on the lawn of a house that reminded Derek of pictures of the Kennedys in Hyannisport. A group of people of various ages dressed in shorts and polo shirts were squinting at the sun as they faced the camera. The girls were pretty and long-legged, and the boys had the same ruddy good looks as Randolph Congreve.

"Who's who?" Derek asked.

Sheree tapped the glass and said, "That's Randy—Randolph Jr.—who's now at the Washington Congreve. Then Elizabeth, who's married to a symphony conductor. Dinah and her husband manage the Manhattan Congreve. Peyton is at the London Congreve. These are cousins; they're all at Congreve hotels, too. The two boys standing back-to-back, refusing to look at the camera, are Hunter and his friend Garry, who were inseparable from prep school through college."

Derek wished Hunter was facing the camera; he looked like a young teen. He tried to remember if he'd ever heard him mention Garry, whose face was indistinguishable because of Peyton's shadow.

"They're a handsome brood," Derek said, "but they're not exactly . . ."

"Jumping for joy?" Sheree finished his sentence after he trailed off. "Heaven only knows what they'd been up to. Randolph's idea of developing character pitted them all against each other at various sports. Here; this is one of my favorites."

Derek smiled as she handed him a picture of Hunter standing next to a bike in front of a stone building. He looked happy. "How old was he?"

"Seventeen," she said. "He was at school. He sent me this picture himself. Hunter is the only one of the children who . . . I guess I always felt close to him because I met Randolph about the time Hunter was born. In some ways, we grew up together. I was delighted when his father sent him here. I think the world of him."

"He thinks highly of you, too. He'd be horrified to find out what I've been up to tonight," Derek said ruefully.

"He might surprise you. He and Garry were such a handful as boys. There was a time or two when I got them out of a jam."

"Really?" Derek asked. "For doing what?"

Sheree smiled and said, "Do you know why Hunter called me when he was in trouble?"

"Because he was afraid of his father?"

"The same reason you did. He knew I'd never tell."

"But the statute of limitations has to have run out on Hunter's misdeeds," Derek wheedled.

"There's no expiration date on trust," Sheree said firmly.

Derek sighed and went back to his chair, picking up his wine. When Sheree settled across from him again, he said, "Is there anything you *can* tell me about Hunter?"

"Such as?"

"I was with him for three years, and I never heard of Garry. Are they still friends?"

Sheree frowned and said, "They'd have to be. Nothing could ever break up those two. Garry is a Prophet."

"Like a holy man?" Derek asked, bewildered.

Sheree laughed. "Have you ever heard of Seventeen Provinces Gin?"

"Sure."

"That's the Prophet family. They started making gin in the Netherlands in the seventeen hundreds and brought it to the New World not long after the Congreves arrived from England. After he got his MBA, Garry was sent to Europe to work in one of their distilleries. That's also about the time I came to Indiana. So I'm a little out of the loop, but I'm sure that Hunter and Garry will always be friends."

"Oh," Derek said. It was just one more thing Hunter hadn't shared with him. "Is Garry gay, too?"

"No," Sheree said.

"Were Hunter's parents upset when they found out he was?"

Derek regretted the question as soon as it was out of his mouth. It was glaringly inappropriate on so many levels. "I'm sorry. I shouldn't have asked that."

Sheree seemed amused and said, "You're always such a gentleman. I can't speak for Charlotte, but Randolph is a pragmatist. He won't waste his time trying to change what can't be changed. It helps that Randy and Peyton have supplied him with an ample number of Congreves to carry on the name and the business. It also helps that Hunter has always been fearless. Even as a child. If he wanted something, he went after it. If he wanted to do something, he did it. When he knew he was gay, it became a fact of life for everyone. When he decided not to work for Congreve after he got his MBA, he didn't. In some ways, he's like his father."

"He almost never talks about his family with me," Derek admitted.

Sheree sighed and said, "They aren't a warm family. They'll close ranks quickly against any kind of outside threat. But by and large, they stay out of one another's private lives. The Congreves are a well-run corporation whose highest ranking members happen to be related."

"How did you end up here?" Derek asked.

"You mean, why was I banished? Or, why to Indiana?"

"You must think I'm so rude."

"No. I understand your curiosity. I was young when I met Randolph, and it's true that we had a love affair for many years. He made me very comfortable financially. Without going into detail, it was time for me to leave. I grew up in this area; I chose to come back. I don't have to live in the hotel. I certainly don't have to work here. I'm here because I want to be. Randolph and I are still quite good friends. And I enjoy being close to Hunter." Derek jumped when someone knocked on the door, and Ajax rose from his pillow. Sheree looked at her watch and said, "That's one of the bellhops here to take Ajax for his last walk of the night."

"I should be going," Derek said. "Sheree, thank you so much—"

"It was no trouble, and I got an entertaining story and good company in return," she said. "I'll call the desk and arrange for someone to drive you to the Galaxy." As they walked to the door, she put her hand on his arm. "One more thing, Buddy. Don't confuse your situation with mine. They aren't the same."

Derek was pondering her words as he crossed the Congreve

lobby. He finally realized someone was calling his name, and he looked toward the desk.

"Hi, Derek," Liz called. "Come here." When he got to the desk, she reached over and clasped his hand, saying, "We miss you."

"Thanks," he said. "I miss everybody here, too."

"Come back and visit us," Liz said. "Or if you ever want to go to Pluto with us, or hang out, just call."

"I will," he promised.

She looked past him and said, "Your car's ready."

He nodded and walked outside, where Benjamin opened the limo door with a flourish and said, "It's good to see you, Derek."

"Can I just sit in front with you?" Derek asked.

"Sure you can." They settled into the car, and Benjamin pulled out, saying, "You should visit more often. Juanita sure does miss you. *Everybody* at the hotel misses you."

Derek smiled faintly, wishing he could know whether that was true.

31

Diamond in the Rough

One of the advantages of Riley's position at the Hotel Congreve was the inside information he had about Mall of the Universe. Thus he knew that the security cameras on the top floor of the largest parking garage were connected to nothing. Nor was that level commonly patrolled by mall security, unless a guard sought the area for the same reasons other mall employees did. It was a good place to park one's car to avoid dings and scrapes, because shoppers used it only during the busy holiday seasons. Since it had no roof, the only smokers it attracted were mall employees who liked to occasionally light up a midshift joint to take the edge off their workdays. But its major appeal was in providing a place for quick and anonymous sexual encounters.

It was the last that drew Riley after a particularly long, irksome day of taking orders from Hunter. He was only halfway through his first cigarette when a Jeep Cherokee with darkly tinted windows circled the perimeter before coming to Riley's corner to idle a few feet away. The driver lowered his window and made eye contact with Riley, who tossed his cigarette and slid into the passenger seat. Conversation was eschewed in favor of getting right to business. Within a half hour, Riley was back inside the mall, wearing a smirk and the faint scent of another man's cologne.

One appetite taken care of, Riley decided that dinner could wait for a drink or two, so he returned to the Congreve. He settled at the bar in the Aurora and made small talk with Steve the bartender while he looked idly around the lounge. He spotted Sheree Sheridan at a corner table talking to Drayden Lvandsson. He frowned, wondering again if Drayden was someone he should worry about. Drayden lived in Minnesota, and Riley had a sudden horrifying fear that Hunter might drag him from Mall of the Universe to Mall of America. Then he reminded himself that there was no Hotel Congreve in the Twin Cities area.

When he realized that Sheree was looking at him, he idly turned away. He was surprised a few minutes later when he heard her greeting the Aurora's patrons from the stage. She wasn't scheduled to go on for at least an hour. He turned around and saw her accompanist hastily taking the stage. Sheree spoke to him, then turned back toward the room and started singing.

It took Riley a moment to recognize her lament as a Dolly Parton song. He was sure it was merely coincidence that Sheree seemed to be singing in his direction as she wondered whether a lover left behind would be waiting at the end of the road. Still, it unnerved him enough to make him leave the lounge. He wanted no reminders of the way he'd wasted energy on anyone as ineffectual as Natasha Deere.

He looked at his watch. Hunter must have surely left the office, and Riley decided it was a good time to look at his boss's e-mail for any clues about Drayden Lvandsson. The executive floor was quiet when Riley stepped off the elevator, but when he let himself into his office, light was spilling from Hunter's doorway. Just as Riley started to back out, he heard Juanita Luna's voice and froze. It was Riley's job to schedule Hunter's meetings with hotel employees. This one had not been on the calendar, which alarmed him.

"Mr. Hunter," Juanita was saying, "I know you didn't ask me here to talk about Australia. You must have something on your mind."

"You're right," Hunter said. "I've been looking at the hotel's financial reports with an eye to turning a greater profit."

Riley smiled, thinking of the recommendations he'd given Hunter. Maybe the blockhead actually intended to take his advice. It was possible that Riley's wildest dream was about to come true and Juanita would no longer be an annoying part of the staff. His pulse accelerated at Hunter's next comment.

"I've been advised to cut staff. A five-percent reduction of some of our most highly paid employees would save us not only their wages, but the cost of their benefit packages."

Riley was gratified to hear his own words coming out of Hunter's mouth, making it abundantly clear which of them should be running the hotel. He cursed the luck that had allowed Hunter to be born a Congreve.

"That's shortsighted," Juanita said. "Congreve hotels are known for the service we provide our guests. If we cut staff, service will go down. Why would our guests pay premium prices for bad service? They might as well stay in a motel. And there are other reasons why it's a bad idea."

"What do you think those are?" Hunter asked.

"Our people need their jobs. They have families to support. Many of them are poorly educated. There aren't a lot of jobs out there. And what about our college students? Where are they going to work? Will they need more financial aid? Will they have to drop out of school?"

"My father would be completely unmoved by the human element of the equation," Hunter said.

"I'm not talking to your father. I know my audience."

Hunter laughed and said, "Good point. But pretend you are talking to my father. He'd like the part about guest services. What else would you tell him?"

"Cutting costs is a negative solution. Instead, you should make more money."

"How?" Hunter asked.

Riley clenched his fists as Juanita rambled on about creative bookings, working with economic development organizations and the universities, and seeking more nonlocal business and tourist dollars. In Riley's opinion, she needed to spend more time counting sheets and towels, and less time spewing her half-baked ideas at Hunter.

She echoed his thoughts when she said, "Mr. Hunter, you have an MBA from Yale, and I'm a hotel housekeeper. I'm telling you things that are like nursery school for you. What's this really about?"

Hunter laughed and said, "You're one of the smartest people I know. I enjoy hearing your thoughts, and you're right. Unlike my father, I always consider the human side of my business. That's one of the things that makes me enjoy what I do."

"You're a good person."

"Thank you. So are you. Which is why I hate to lose you as my housekeeper."

Yes! Riley thought. *Fabulous! Hunter is finally wising up.*

"You're getting rid of me?" Juanita asked.

"I'm afraid I have to. I can't stand to see potential wasted. I want you in our management training program."

Riley's mood plummeted. Was Hunter insane? The woman was a maid.

Hunter talked for a while about the management program while Riley seethed, trying to figure out his boss's plan. Did Hunter intend to replace him with Juanita? Or was Hunter finally sending him out of this godforsaken hole to a hotel more deserving of his talents?

"Mr. Hunter—"

"Stop being so Third World."

She laughed and said, "I call you that because I respect you, not because you're my boss. Of course I'm interested in your offer. But I can't make a decision without talking to Consuela."

"Trust me, I understand and respect that," Hunter said.

After a brief silence, Juanita said, "I don't think Derek meant to upset you by getting a job. He thought he was being responsible."

Can this get any worse? Riley wondered.

"By wasting his potential?" Hunter asked.

"He isn't."

"Are you joking? He could be doing so much more."

"There's nothing wrong with selling shoes."

"Putting aside the fact that his parents didn't send him to college to sell shoes, he hates it."

"Then he'll learn that he's not a shoe salesman. Or anything else that makes him unhappy just to get a paycheck. That's a good lesson."

"It's a lesson that took him away from me."

"He didn't go far. Derek is trying to be his own man. You should respect him."

"I've always respected him."

"Not if your respect depends on Derek doing what you think is right. You've been in his shoes, haven't you?"

"I'm not his father. I never asked him for obedience. I never threatened to withdraw my approval or affection if he made his own decisions."

"You left him."

"I didn't leave him. I went away on business."

"So the timing was a coincidence?"

After a long pause, Hunter said, "No. Sometimes the way I speak to Derek is inappropriate, especially if I'm in work mode. It sounds like I'm giving him orders. I didn't want him to take the job, and I knew I had to step back. I thought some space would do us both good."

"It wasn't good for him. He moved out. Was the space good for you? What did you get out of it?"

"I was miserable," Hunter confessed. "We haven't been apart for more than a week at a time in years. I love being with Derek and seeing the world through his eyes. He's my Scheherazade."

"I don't know what that means," Juanita said.

"Scheherazade enchanted her husband with stories to keep him from killing her. I'll get you the book. Derek is my storyteller. He takes everything he sees and hears, and turns it into stories. Whenever we're out in public or we travel, I'm the audience for his imagination. Australia would have been so much better if he'd been there."

"Did what's-her-name live or die in the end?"

"Scheherazade? The sultan fell in love with her, so he allowed her to live. Good news for Derek. Bad news for me. He's telling his stories to someone else now, and Indiana has lost its charm. I have to start thinking of my own story and what I'll do next. I've kept you long enough. Say hello to Consuela—"

Riley hastily backed out of the office and exhaled. Hunter was ready to move on, and if he was grooming Juanita to take over, he obviously had even bigger plans for Riley.

He walked briskly to Stardate Tavern, to savor an expensive meal and celebrate his good fortune. There would be no more Lollipop Guild. No more Juanita Luna. No more Sheree Sheridan. No more Derek, whose relationship with Hunter was deader than . . .

Riley stopped midthought when he saw a vaguely familiar face across the restaurant. When he couldn't place it after a few minutes, he decided it was because he was seeing the man out of context. He was probably a mall employee, and Riley began listing stores to satisfy his nagging sense that he was somehow significant. It wasn't until the man took a long pull off his bottle of Budweiser that it clicked.

DeWitt. The loser who'd told him about Natasha before giving him a great blow job. It was astounding to see him looking like he belonged in an upscale restaurant like Stardate. DeWitt's hair and beard were clean and neatly trimmed, and his jeans were dressed up with an attractive sport coat. He was far more doable than when Riley had met him in Galileo's Glass, and Riley's gaze shifted to his companion, a handsome older man who was laughing at whatever DeWitt was saying.

Riley's regret over missed opportunities turned into a smile of self-congratulation. Obviously their fleeting encounter had been good for DeWitt, inspiring him to strive for a better class of man. If Hunter wanted to know about spotting a diamond in the rough and polishing it, he'd be well-advised to take lessons from his assistant.

32

One Shoe Over the Cuckoo's Nest

Natasha barely registered the chipped polish on her fingernails when she pulled back her long dark hair and wound it into a tight bun. One lock of hair simply wouldn't stay put and kept sliding down her forehead, falling over her right eye. She coated it with hairspray in hopes of gluing it to her scalp. Then she put on her makeup and dressed in a cream-colored suit with an emerald green blouse. She brought her lukewarm coffee to her mouth too quickly and spilled the liquid down the front of her blouse and suit. After releasing a string of profanity and changing clothes, she swished some mouthwash around and spit, missing the sink and staining the wall.

Mondays had always been her favorite day, but this particular Monday was proving to be a challenge. Instead of seeing herself as the driving force of her own destiny, she felt like a helpless passenger while her destiny skidded out of control.

As she passed through the employee entrance into Drayden's, Natasha didn't notice the curled edge of the rug inside the door. She tried to maintain her balance after she tripped, but her heel broke, causing her to twist her ankle and fall down. The pain in her ankle was so excruciating that it took her breath away. Natasha lay on the floor, her mouth frozen in an *O* that made her look like a fish out of water. A single tear rolled down her cheek, leaving a trail of mascara. When she was able to compose herself, she got up and limped onward.

She hobbled past the security desk, grimacing when the graveyard shift guard said, “Good morning, Ms. Deere.”

“Right,” she replied with a curt nod, keeping her pace as steady as possible.

“Had a good day yesterday, did we?”

“Unghuh,” Natasha grunted in return.

“Is everything okay, Ms. Deere?”

She didn’t answer. Hot, salty tears started to stream down her cheeks, leaving black streaks that Natasha wiped and smudged with the back of her hands, not wanting to stain a second outfit.

She turned the corner and went into the women’s restroom. When the door closed behind her, she leaned against it and slid to the floor, where she put her head in her hands and sobbed.

How could this have happened? What sort of twisted individual had taken advantage of her in this way? She felt violated. Yet in some strange fashion, she blamed herself. As if she hadn’t taken enough precaution. She should have seen it coming.

Impossible. Who could have known such a sicko lurked out there?

Her home—her sanctuary from the hellish abyss known as Indiana—had been broken into. Worse, the Doll House had been molested, the dolls all removed from the safety of their home. Taken. Kidnapped, in fact. That was it; they’d been kidnapped. Who would do such a terrible thing? And what were they doing to Dolly now? Hundreds of Dollys?

She let out another sob. She wasn’t aware of how long she’d been sitting on the floor until someone pushed on the restroom door and bumped the back of her head. She stood up, her ankle throbbing, and moved to a sink. Jonquil came into the restroom and did a double take upon seeing Natasha so disheveled.

“Oh!” Jonquil exclaimed. “Natasha! Are you okay?”

“Fine,” Natasha answered, taking makeup out of her bag and repairing her face. Jonquil left without another word, and Natasha followed shortly after, dropping everything on her desk. She took off her good shoe and placed it next to the broken pump she’d already slipped off. She limped from the stockroom to the sales floor in her stockings, holding a shoebox.

“Would you ring this up for me, please, Erik?”

He gave her a cautious look and said, “Sure. Do you want me to put it on your Drayden’s charge?”

"Yes, please." Natasha reached across the counter for a piece of scratch paper and a pen. She scribbled on the paper. "Here's my account number. Just enter it manually." She replaced the pen and took the shoes out of the box, carefully slipping them onto one foot at a time.

She saw an improperly placed stiletto on a display and thought, *I'll fix it later.* Then she tottered around the perimeter of the floor, barely noticing that Jonquil and Missy were frantically trying to straighten up from the night before.

"Since the shrinkage manager will most likely be making a visit later," Erik said, "I should probably let you know that we had a shoplifter last night. I was helping a customer try on a pair of Andrea Pfister shoes. She asked me for a larger size, so I went to the stockroom. She was gone when I came back. So were the shoes. Nobody saw her leave. She left her old shoes in the box. I'm sorry, Natasha. I should've been paying better attention."

"It's okay," Natasha answered dully.

Erik stared at her. "It is? It's a four-hundred-dollar loss. Are you sure?"

"It could happen to anybody," Natasha said.

She continued her awkward walking tour of the department. Erik followed her as if on an invisible leash. When Natasha approached the table where Missy was cleaning and rearranging displays, Missy clumsily knocked several shoes to the floor. Natasha stepped over the shoes without uttering a single word. Then she stopped in her tracks. She turned and looked from Erik to Missy.

"Which one of you closed last night?" she asked in a hollow tone.

"I did," Erik said. Missy looked scared.

"Everything is fine," Natasha said with no expression whatsoever.

She returned to the stockroom and checked the previous evening's sales figures on her computer. *Good enough,* she thought. *Who really cares how many stupid shoes you all sell, anyway?*

She got up from her desk, feeling physically drained, although her day had barely started. She sighed and returned to the sales floor, meandering listlessly to the register area. She was indifferent to the sight of Drayden Lvandsson standing at the counter.

"Good morning!" Drayden boomed.

"Good morning," Natasha answered tonelessly and absently tidied the counter area. The lock of hair she'd lacquered into place fell down again. It was firm and scraped against her skin. She didn't care.

"Well?" Drayden asked as Erik approached them.

Natasha finished opening a new pack of sales slips, then looked blankly at Drayden, saying, "Well, what?"

"How was Chicago? The seminar? What did you learn?"

Natasha's eyes again welled up with tears, and her hands shook. She heard an unintelligible and high-pitched whining noise, and was startled to realize that it was coming from her own mouth. Her hands were shaking, and she dropped the sales slips to the floor. As she staggered from the department like a woman possessed, the last thing she heard was Drayden Lvandsson saying to Erik, "Funny. My brother, Sven, had the same reaction after *he* attended that seminar."

33

Chitty Chitty Big Bang

Vienna couldn't understand what had possessed her to buy a dress with a zipper that she couldn't reach. She had her arms twisted behind her, straining to get the zipper past the middle of her back. She finally shouted an obscenity, took off the dress, and hurled it across her bedroom, not caring where it landed. Frustrated, she removed a simple black pantsuit from her closet and put it on over a lace camisole. Just as she was slipping on a pair of Anne Klein pointed-toe pumps, her phone rang.

"Hello."

"You sound rushed. Is this a bad time?"

"Davii!" Vienna exclaimed. "How did you know I'm in a rush?"

"My experience in the Zodiac Traveling Circus," Davii replied. "I'm used to listening to harried models on their cell phones now."

"Plural? I thought you belonged to Sheila."

"Yeah, and if I'm lucky, she puts on my muzzle and takes me for a walk," Davii said. "I belong—I'm *employed* by Lillith Allure. Sheila's my number-one project. And get this—I have a team."

"Wasn't that always a fantasy of yours?" Vienna asked as she applied mascara.

Davii laughed and said, "Not that kind of team. There's another hairdresser on the Zodiac shoots who does the other models while I get Sheila ready. I oversee her work and the makeup artist's. But it's temporary until the other guy comes back."

"The other guy," Vienna mimicked. "Even I remember that poor man's name. Rex." She hastily blotted her lipstick and added, "I'm proud of you, Davii. And to think, a management position is something you used to eschew."

"Bless you," Davii said. When he got nothing but her silence, he said, "I had to grow up sooner or later. What's up? Where are you off to in such a hurry? Hot date?"

Vienna paused, assessing her look in the mirror. She smiled and said, "If you can believe it, yes. I, Vienna Talbot, have a hot date."

"I knew you had it in you. You're a hot lady. You deserve a hot date," Davii said. "Who's the lucky man? Wait. Let me guess. An ad exec who looks amazing in Armani, but even better out of it?"

"No," Vienna said.

"You don't have to sound so incredulous. They do exist. I've seen a lot of them around here."

"You're in New York, baby," Vienna said, pillaging her closet for the right purse. "This is Terre Haute. Try again."

"Um, a hot farmer?"

Vienna laughed. "No. He's just a really great person. A gentleman among men. We've gone out a few times, and he's very sweet. That's all I can tell you for now. Do you want to talk to Derek?"

"Of course," Davii said. "How's he doing?"

Vienna paused to drop her wallet and a lipstick into a Stuart Weitzman clutch and said, "About the same. Remember Natasha?"

"The überbitch? Of course."

"We . . . did something—"

"Oh, no."

"—and now she's not herself. She's repressing, but I can tell she's about to snap. Her focus isn't on her job at all. Which has taken a lot of pressure off Derek at work. But he's still not happy."

"I'm sure that's because of Hunter," Davii said.

"Kind of," Vienna said. "It's more about Derek and his needs. He's responsible for his own—"

"I get the picture, Dr. Talbot."

"Anyway, he's sullen and needs to get out of the apartment. I'm going to the Big Bang tonight—"

"You are?" Davii interrupted. "You hate that thing. I tried to get you to go every year, but you never would."

"It's a whole new Vienna, baby," she said. "The point is, I want Derek to go, but he won't. Try to talk him into it. It would be good for him to be out with his friends, instead of home sulking about Hunter."

"I'll do what I can," Davii promised.

Phone in hand, Vienna knocked on the door to Derek's bedroom. He opened the door and said, "Hey."

"I'm on my way out. Sure you won't come along?" she asked.

Derek shook his head and said, "Nah. I'd rather stay in."

"I'm sure there'll be lots of Congreve guests at this thing," Vienna said. "I'll bet Hunter will be there, too. Why don't you get dressed up and show him what he's missing?"

"Trust me. He knows," Derek said. "You go and have fun."

"Suit yourself," Vienna said and kissed him on the cheek. "Your navy Hugo Boss suit would be great."

"Nice try," Derek said.

She handed him the phone and said, "Talk to Davii. See you later."

A half hour later, she was waiting outside the planetarium for Cart Man. The courtyard of Mall of the Universe was decorated with pink streamers, twinkling lights, and lots of flowers. The center was cleared for dancing, although everybody was standing in small groups or sitting at tables. Cater waiters carried trays of appetizers through the crowd, and Sheree Sheridan was singing on a bandstand, accompanied by a pianist, bass player, and drummer.

Vienna spotted Emily-Anne Barrister greeting guests while hanging on the arm of a distinguished gentleman that Vienna assumed was her husband. She saw Christian, Bianca, Meg, Drayden—everybody but Cart Man. She assumed she was on time but couldn't be sure, since she hadn't worn her watch.

"Vienna, you look fabulous," Christian said as he approached her.

"Thank you," Vienna said. "Do you know what time it is?"

"A little after seven."

"I'm right on time," she mused. She'd mentally prepared to be escorted to the Big Bang and felt a little awkward standing in one spot on her own. She considered going to the bar to get a drink but didn't want to move in case Cart Man showed up and couldn't find her. Unless he'd stood her up. She reminded herself that he was only a few minutes late. She was obsessing over nothing, and Christian was staring at her with curiosity, so she said, "You've done a great job getting this thing together. I love all the pink lilies."

"Thank you," Christian said. "And thanks for the suggestions you made about the mall restaurants. Did you come alone?"

Suddenly Vienna wanted to slap Cart Man. If only he were there to be slapped. *But then I wouldn't need to slap him,* she thought.

"I meant to say, is Derek coming?" Christian clarified.

"Oh. I don't think so," Vienna replied. "He's probably worried about running into Hunter."

"I haven't seen Hunter," Christian said. A loud crash pierced the din, followed by people shrieking. Christian groaned and said, "But Emily-Anne's here! Excuse me."

Vienna scanned the crowd again. More people had arrived, and some had begun dancing. She began wandering around, wondering what was keeping Cart Man, until she nearly ran into Bianca. "Bianca! Hi."

"I'm sorry. I wasn't watching where I was going," Bianca said.

"Actually, I wasn't either," Vienna said.

"No, really, it's my fault. I'm so clumsy," Bianca insisted.

"If you say so. You look pretty," Vienna said, instantly regretting offering the compliment. Not because it wasn't true. Bianca looked radiant. Her dress was stark white, simple, with clean lines. Her hair was twisted up and piled on top of her head, with one wisp floating over her face, sometimes hooking around her ear as she moved. Vienna had always imagined that Bianca would fade into the woodwork in white, leaving a mass of red hair hovering on its own. Instead, she seemed lit from within, like a star. Vienna studied her curiously and asked, "Are you pregnant?"

"No!" Bianca squealed. Several heads turned in their direction. Bianca put one hand on her stomach and cupped the other around her mouth as she whispered, "Why? Do I look fat in this dress? Be honest."

Vienna put her hands on Bianca's cheeks and said, "Look at me and listen. You are beautiful. Do you believe me?"

"I'm in love with Christian Mercer," Bianca said in lieu of an answer.

"You are?" Vienna asked with surprise.

"I've been spending time with him. Sitting for him."

"He's got a kid? I had no idea," Vienna said, wondering how Christian could hide such a thing.

"No. For a portrait. I was so nervous, being stared at for hours. But after a while, I loved it. It was like he needed me so much. It felt good. He's wonderful, kind, everything I dreamed he'd be. I know it sounds silly."

"It sounds wonderful," Vienna said. "Good for you."

"He doesn't know. I mean, there's no reason to tell him because—can you let go of my face?"

"Oh. Sorry."

Before Vienna could find out why Christian had to be kept in the dark, he walked up and said, "Vienna? Do you mind if I steal Bianca? I'd like to introduce her to the Barristers, now that Emily-Anne is finished terrorizing the waiters."

"Yeah, sure," Vienna said. "I'll talk to you guys later."

As she watched them drift away, she felt a pang of jealousy. They were gorgeous together. She walked to an out-of-the-way table and sat down, still looking for Cart Man, angry because he was late. She'd wanted to introduce him to her friends. She wanted them to see the same wonderful things about him that she'd experienced. Now she was starting to regret putting so much faith in him, trusting him. Maybe he was already getting bored with her, like Kevin had.

"Is this seat taken?" Vienna looked up to see Drayden Lvandsson standing next to the table, martini in hand. She shook her head, and he sat down. "This is a great party. They do this every year?"

Vienna nodded, then decided she should probably answer properly. She heard her mother's nagging voice in her head, reminding her that Drayden was her superior and deserved respect. "When the planetarium opened, they threw an annual Spring Solstice celebration. Even with partial funding from the mall, it became expensive, so Emily-Anne Barrister partnered with them to turn it into her Big Bang Benefit for Breast Cancer. This year, they're raising money for a mobile mammogram unit. Drayden's is one of the sponsors. But you probably knew that part."

"I'm sure it will be a success," Drayden said, looking around. "I'll have to make a hefty personal donation. Who was the event planner? The original Drayden's is going through a renovation. We've installed a herring pond on the main floor. I want to throw a party when everything's finished."

"Christian Mercer," Vienna said. "Hershel Wicks can put you in touch with him."

"Fantastic," Drayden said. "Mind if I talk shop?"

"Be my guest," Vienna replied.

"I hear you haven't accepted Melanie's proposal." When Vienna gave him a blank look, he clarified, "For you to enter the management training program."

"I have thought about it. I just got busy with the sale," Vienna replied, thinking it was probably the safest answer she could give.

"Why do I feel like I'm being stalled? Do you have another offer?"

Vienna hesitated, thinking that the only offer she'd received had been from Cart Man, who obviously wasn't going to be serving it up with a side dish of hope that evening. She wished she did have a legitimate reason for declining the promotion. She didn't want to make Melanie look bad.

"It's an important decision, Mr. Lvandsson," she stated. "As I told Melanie and Hershel, I need to give it careful consideration. I don't want to let anyone down, including myself."

Drayden clapped his hands, saying, "Well said, Miss Talbot. Let's put our party hats back on." He looked around. "I suppose I should meet Mrs. Barrister. Which one is she?" Vienna pointed her out, and Drayden said, "We'll talk again later."

After he left, Vienna put her head in her hands and said, "I have to get out of this place."

"If it's the last thing you ever do?"

"Derek!" She looked up and saw that he was wearing the navy Hugo Boss suit she'd suggested.

He sipped at his cosmopolitan before he rested it on the tabletop, then sat down, crossed his legs, and asked, "What have I missed? Anything exciting happen?"

"Of course not. In fact, you're just in time for my dramatic exit," Vienna said.

"Got a pumpkin to catch?" Derek asked. "Please don't go. Not after Davii worked so hard to get me to come here."

"Oh, sure. I tell you to come and you decline. It's because I don't have a penis, isn't it?"

"It's the accessory of the season," Derek said. "Speaking of dicks, have you seen Hunter?"

"Stop that. You know that's not how you really feel." When Derek made no comment, she added, "Although he is a man. My opinion of men is rapidly deteriorating. Present company excluded, of course."

"Let me guess. The guy you've been seeing in secret stood you up?"

"Damn Davii!" she said vehemently. "That boy has a mouth bigger than the Grand Canyon."

"He also told me that I should come here to support you," Derek said. Vienna eyed him warily, wondering what other information Davii had divulged. "That's pretty much all he said. That it's a big deal that you came to this thing, and I should be here for you in his place."

Vienna bit her lip, holding back the words that threatened to tumble from her mouth like an avalanche. Derek's eyes were full of concern. He reminded her briefly of Davii, and she realized she could trust Derek with anything. They were, after all, partners in crime.

"My mother died of breast cancer shortly after my divorce was finalized," Vienna said. Before Derek could respond, she continued. "I had no idea she was sick. None. Mama and I were a lot alike. If anything was wrong, we'd deal with it on our own. We put our faith in ourselves and the Lord, everybody else be damned. That's just what she did with her cancer. She didn't even tell my father until it was too late."

"I'm sorry," Derek said when she paused for breath.

"I never got to say good-bye to her. Our last conversation was an argument. She was angry that I'd gotten myself into a bad marriage, accusing me of not looking out for number one. She said that I'd allowed Satan to lead me down his path and all sorts of other nonsense. Did you know that Satan's path leads to Bloomington?"

"Sounds reasonable to me," Derek said.

"I didn't want to hear any of that," Vienna said, remembering how angry and defensive she'd been. "I didn't want to be Vienna the Preacher's Girl any longer. I couldn't even be in Bloomington without being under their thumbs. I didn't tell anyone where I was going. Just up and moved here quietly. When Mama died, Kevin's lawyer tracked me down, and Daddy called with the bad news. I was such a mess."

"That's understandable," Derek said quietly.

Vienna nodded and dabbed at her eyes with a napkin. "Daddy and I had a long talk after the funeral. He took me to a park near the cemetery and explained a few things to me. Mama was hard on me because she wanted so much for me. She was proud of everything I accomplished—getting my degrees on my own, being in a practice and helping people. He said she bragged about me to everyone. What bothered her was my shame. How I ran from Gary and did everything I could to hide where I came from. That I latched on to the first boy who came along and got into a loveless marriage. And she was right. That's exactly what I did. I was just too stupid to see it. Too ashamed to admit it." Neither of them said anything for a minute. She took a deep cleansing breath and exhaled slowly. She felt free. "Anyway, that's why I'm here. Here in this mall. Here in Terre Haute. Here at this party. To' up from the flo' up, and stood up."

"What kind of idiot would leave you here alone?" Derek asked.

Before Vienna could answer, Sheree announced that she was taking a short break. She stepped offstage and into Drayden's arms, receiving a kiss on her cheek.

"That's interesting," Derek said obliquely.

Vienna grabbed Derek's arm and pointed, saying, "Derek, look."

Natasha Deere had just paid her entrance fee and was scanning the crowd. A woman on the greeting committee tried to pin a pink ribbon on her dress, but Natasha swatted at her hands and stalked away.

"She doesn't look so distraught anymore," Derek observed.

"What are you talking about? Her hair's a mess," Vienna countered. "And look—she's wearing two different shoes."

"But her determined stare and evil glow are back," Derek said.

Vienna scrutinized Natasha. Her jaw was set as she walked around the courtyard, seeming to look for something or someone. A man holding a slice of cake accidentally stepped into her path. He said something and laughed, but stopped when Natasha knocked the plate out of his hands, sending the cake flying. She pushed him out of her way and moved on.

"Uh-oh," Vienna said.

"Remember that dramatic exit you were about to make?" Derek asked.

"Yeah," Vienna replied.

"Can I come with you?"

"Uh-huh," Vienna said. "Only let's change it to a covert exit."

"I'm right behind you," Derek said.

They slowly got out of their chairs and crouched down, ready to crawl away unnoticed, when Vienna bumped into a pair of legs. She looked up and said, "Cart Man. You came."

"Did someone lose a contact?" Cart Man asked.

"Hey, Ed," Derek said.

"Ed? Is that your name?" Vienna asked. "Where have you been?"

"You're dating Ed? That's great," Derek said. He glanced back and warned, "She's getting closer. Can we work this out somewhere else?"

Vienna, indifferent to anything but Cart Man, said, "No. I want to know where he's been. I've been waiting here forever, and he hasn't even apologized. I don't know who you think you are, but—"

"There you are!" Natasha said, pointing at Derek and advancing toward him.

"Save yourself," Derek said to Vienna.

"Derek!" Emily-Anne cried, emerging from a nearby crowd of people. "Everybody's been complimenting me on my shoes all night! Thank you so much." She stepped forward and flung out her arms to hug Derek. Unfortunately, her left hand connected with Natasha's nose, sending her reeling into a waiter who was carrying a tray of champagne flutes. "Oh, no! That's the second time tonight I've done that."

Natasha held her bleeding nose and shrieked, "You bitch! I've never liked you. I hate you, Emily-Anne Barrister!" Emily-Anne's mouth dropped open, and Natasha pushed her aside and looked at Derek. "You! Where are my dolls?"

"Cortlandt!" Emily-Anne shouted. "Call security!"

"I don't know what you're talking about," Derek stammered.

"Natasha," Vienna said as calmly as she could, "why don't we talk about this rationally?"

"Don't give me that crap," Natasha said, her eyes fixed on Derek. "I've got it all figured out."

"Natasha? Are you okay?" Drayden Lvandsson interceded while Sheree looked on. "Is there something wrong here?"

"He took my dolls," Natasha said, pointing a bony finger at Derek. "I was at home, watching *Straight Talk,* and it reminded me of *you.*" Her finger jabbed the air in front of Vienna, and Vienna felt Cart Man's hands fall protectively on her shoulders. "Dolly is a newly separated woman who gets a job as a radio show psychiatrist. Which instantly made me think of Miss Talbot."

"Me?" Vienna asked.

"I know all about you," Natasha proclaimed. A piece of spittle flew from her mouth as she spoke, and she absentmindedly wiped her mouth with the back of her hand, smearing her lipstick. "RB's not the only one who can find out people's secrets."

"RB," Sheree and Vienna said at the same time.

Vienna wasn't sure what the name meant to Sheree, but she had a feeling it was one of those details she shouldn't have overlooked when Natasha whirled around to stare at Sheree and said, "You know him, don't you?"

"It's on the Sun level," Sheree said. "I love their roast beef sand—"

"Not Arby's," Natasha hissed. "RB. You're all connected. Jonquil told me that Derek lives with you," Natasha said, pointing at Vienna again, "but he used to live at the Congreve." She reached into her purse and pulled out a pillowcase, waving it in their faces.

"Oh, crap," Derek said.

"You left this when you took my dolls," Natasha accused. "Who has them? You or him?"

"Who?" Derek asked.

"RB!" Natasha said, sounding exasperated.

Vienna saw Drayden slip his cell phone to Sheree, who began frantically dialing as she stepped away. When he turned back, Vienna caught his eye and said, "And you wanted me to get into the management program." She pointed to Natasha. "If this is what happens, I want no part of it."

"*Her*? You're going to make her a manager?" Natasha asked. "Are you insane?"

"No, but you obviously are," Vienna said.

"She has no sense of responsibility! She takes breaks all day!" Natasha shouted.

"I don't believe this," Derek said.

"Shut up, dollnapper!" Natasha said.

"That's it!" Derek exploded. "I'm so tired of dealing with you. You're the meanest bitch I've ever met in my life."

"Don't you have a way to screen out people with behavioral disorders when you're hiring?" Vienna asked Drayden. "Anyone can see she's bipolar!"

"I didn't hire her," Drayden protested.

"I'm not bipolar!" Natasha shrieked.

"You're a nutjob!" Derek yelled. "Everybody thinks so. Nobody likes working for you."

"I'm the most responsible person in that store," Natasha said.

"What's going on here?" Christian asked, stepping between Derek and Natasha. "Are you okay, Derek?"

"No!" Derek answered.

"Get out of my way, errand boy!" Natasha ordered, trying to push past Christian to get to Derek.

Vienna again pointed at Natasha and continued her tirade to Drayden. "If this is your idea of the trophy manager, count me out. Forget the whole thing."

"I never wanted to sell shoes anyway!" Derek said. "I hate shoes!"

"I quit!" Vienna and Derek bellowed together.

"That's her!" Emily-Anne was pointing at Natasha. Two mall security guards stepped forward to grab Natasha's arms. Emily-Anne turned to Drayden and said, "I'm *never* shopping in your store again."

"Stop!" Natasha wailed as the guards dragged her away. "I just want my dolls back! They've got my dolls!"

"I knew I shouldn't have come here," Vienna said.

"Are you okay?" Cart Man asked.

"I'm out of here," Derek muttered, pushing past Christian.

"Derek, wait!" Drayden exclaimed.

"Forget it. There's no way in hell I'm going back to that store. Natasha or no Natasha. I've had it," Derek said.

"I had no idea, Derek," Drayden said. "Please let me make it up to you. I feel terrible. We can work this out."

Derek was silent for a long time, staring straight ahead. Vienna turned and followed his gaze, seeing Hunter standing among the onlookers who'd gathered. Sheree stood behind him, still holding Drayden's cell phone. Neither Hunter nor Derek made a move toward each other. Hunter's expression was unreadable, but Derek's look was pure longing. Finally, Derek's expression changed, and he said, "I'm leaving."

"Derek, stop!" Drayden said, hurrying after him.

The two of them nearly ran over a woman, who called out, "Garry!"

"Oh, God," Cart Man moaned.

"Pro?" Hunter said, suddenly staring at Cart Man.

"Con," Cart Man said in a pleading tone as he took a half step toward Hunter.

"Wait a minute," Vienna said. "Poe? Your last name's Poe? Ed Poe, as in Edgar Allan Poe?'

"What are you doing here?" Hunter asked Cart Man.

"Garry!" The woman finally made it to their group. Her huge hoop earrings were swinging wildly, as were the sequined fringes on her top. Her ash blond hair was teased and sprayed into impossible heights, and her boots were made for two-stepping. Vienna couldn't understand why the woman was pointing at Cart Man as she said, "Why in Sam Hill did you run out on me? We weren't done talkin'."

"Buffy, I can explain," Cart Man said.

"Buffy?" Vienna said incredulously. "You made me wait because of a woman named Buffy?"

"Who's this, Garry?" Buffy asked, looking at Vienna. "Is she servin' drinks? I'd love a Tequila Sunrise."

"Hey!" Vienna exclaimed indignantly.

"Are you going to be okay, Pro?" Hunter said to Cart Man as Sheree tugged at his arm. "I need to—"

"Yeah," Cart Man said. "I'll catch up with you later. I know where to find you."

"Which is it?" Vienna demanded. "Ed Poe or Garry Poe?"

"Pro," Sheree corrected before she followed Hunter. "Short for Prophet."

Vienna clenched her hands and gritted her teeth with annoyance, finally saying, "Somebody better start explaining really fast."

"I'll explain everything," Cart Man promised. He kissed Vienna, then added, "Later. I swear."

"Why the hell are you kissin' *her*?" Buffy demanded as Cart Man dragged her away.

Vienna intercepted a look between Christian and Emily-Anne. Emily-Anne grabbed her husband's arm, and they began herding the crowd away as Emily-Anne said, "Come. We've still got tons of food. And games. With prizes! Everyone inside the planetarium."

"Are you okay?" Christian asked Vienna.

"Do you want something to drink?" Bianca asked, stepping forward to put an arm around Vienna's shoulders. "I don't have any idea what just happened. But if it were me, I'd need a stiff drink."

"I'm okay," Vienna said, dazed. "I just don't know who I'm dating. Cart Man. Ed. Garry. For over two years I was single, and suddenly I'm dating three people. Only they're all the same guy, apparently."

"Bummer," Bianca said.

"Yeah," Vienna agreed. "It's crazy." She remembered Natasha. "Christian, give me your keys."

"What?"

"I've got to get those dolls," Vienna explained. "You saw Natasha. She's breaking down, not breaking through, like I'd hoped. At any rate, she's with mall security, and we don't want them on the case. Maybe if I return her dolls, she'll forget about everything. This is my fault, and I've got to fix it before we all end up in jail. Now give me those keys!"

Christian held out the keys and said, "They're in my bedroom closet."

"Thanks!" Vienna said, snatching the keys and leaving Christian and Bianca standing in the empty courtyard.

34

A Temperamental Journey

Two cups of Earl Grey tea hadn't quite cleared Christian's foggy head or bleary eyes. For too many days, he'd been trying to keep up with his clients' needs while spending his nights painting. Bianca had an advantage over him, because she usually napped while he painted. He could have shown some mercy and sent her home; he didn't need her constantly in front of him when he worked. But asleep, her presence was comforting, and when she awoke, she was entertaining. Especially when she talked about art.

He'd enjoyed her story about the cosmetics-hating artist at Drayden's, so he was intrigued when she stared at his mother's wheat-field painting and asked, "Is that yours?"

"No."

Before he could tell her it was his mother's, Bianca said, "Good. I don't like it."

"You don't? Why not?"

"It's stupid. Is it the country or the city? It's like the artist couldn't decide what he wanted to paint. Who puts a skyscraper in the middle of a wheat field? And that parking lot. Who's going to use it? There's no road going there." She listened as he talked about surrealism and the conflict in the painting between nature and progress that was perhaps indicative of the artist's inner struggle. When he paused for breath, she said, "I still think it's stupid. But what do I know about art? I can't even draw good eyebrows on my customers."

After that, he always contrived to leave an art book or two in his studio, delighted when she flipped through the pages and provided a running critique of some of the most sacred cows in art history. She hadn't yet seen the canvas she was inspiring, a moment he looked forward to with terrified exhilaration.

He pulled his thoughts back to the present when DeWitt entered the Brew Moon Café. He was hardly the wounded man that Christian had first met. He looked well put together, with a finely trimmed beard, slightly spiky hair parted on the right side, and a freshly pressed white button-down shirt tucked into fashionably faded jeans. Vienna had done a great job of helping DeWitt emerge from behind all his hair and soiled denim, but Christian liked to think that he'd also played a part in assisting DeWitt to overcome his low self-esteem.

DeWitt nodded to let Christian know that he'd seen him, then got his coffee before approaching him. Christian stood and waited until DeWitt put his cup on the table next to an organizer before shaking his hand. He could have sworn his bones crunched. Maybe DeWitt still needed a lesson in formal greetings.

"You look great," Christian said.

"Thank you. You and Vienna have really helped me make some good changes."

"I'm glad to hear it."

They both sat down, and as DeWitt took his first sip of coffee, he looked at Christian's hands and frowned. "Have you been working on your car or something?"

"What?" Christian asked.

"Is that grease under your nails?"

"Oh," Christian said, looking at his hands with surprise. "No. Paint. I woke up realizing something I did wrong on my painting last night, and I had to take care of it. I didn't have time for more than a quick shower before meeting you."

"Oh, good," DeWitt said. "I was having a *Freaky Friday* moment."

Christian's mind had wandered back to his painting, and he said, "Huh? Is it Friday already?"

"The movie," DeWitt explained patiently. "I thought maybe we'd switched lives. Are you okay? You seem a little out of it."

"Just tired," Christian said. "Sorry. Why did you want to see me?"

DeWitt took a deep breath and said, "I need to talk to you about Leslie Harper. I met with her, like you suggested, and I'm altering all her suits. She's worried herself into a fifteen-pound weight loss, and nothing fits."

"Uh-huh," Christian said.

"I didn't mean to step on your toes," DeWitt continued sheepishly, "but Leslie asked me to help facilitate her move to Indianapolis. She's had trouble getting in touch with you."

"That's fine," Christian said. "I'm glad you could help her."

"Well, she wants to pay me, and I don't feel like I should—"

"Of course you should," Christian said firmly. "Don't ever provide your services for free, DeWitt. In fact, the more you charge, the more you're valued."

"But she's your client, and it seems like you should get the money. I wouldn't even know her except for you."

"What do you use your barn for?" Christian asked. DeWitt stared at him with a perplexed look, and Christian said, "The barn. On your property. You obviously don't farm, so what do you use it for?"

"I keep my tools and my bikes in there," DeWitt said. "I've got this really sweet vintage Harley that I'm restoring—"

"Is there a lot of empty space in the barn? Is it relatively airtight? Or could it be weatherproofed?"

"I guess," DeWitt said, still looking mystified.

"I'd like to rent it. I mean, you could still use it, but I need some big interior space. I want to work on larger canvases and—"

"Are you sure you're okay?" DeWitt asked. "You're not yourself."

"I'm sorry. My mind is all over the place. Yes, it's fine for Leslie Harper to pay you. Have you gotten alterations work from any of my other clients?"

"Yeah," DeWitt said, reaching for his organizer.

"You have to get rid of that thing," Christian said, dismayed, as he looked at the Post-It Notes sticking out of the sides of the organizer. He held up his PalmPilot. "You need one of these. I can't tell you how much easier it has made my life. Plus, when you came to the table? You had to struggle with your coffee and your organizer, put everything down, then shake my hand. You want your client to know that he or she is the most important thing to you. You never want to look awkward or to keep anyone waiting to shake your hand." He nudged his PalmPilot across the table and said, "I've got all the information on this one stored on my computer, so borrow it. Start getting used to it. We'll buy you one later and input your clients' information."

"I don't really have clients—"

"You're going to," Christian said. "Why don't we barter? You let me use space in your barn, and I'll slowly transition my clients over to you."

"Are you kidding?"

Christian considered it. A part of him felt regret, but people always missed something about jobs they left, even jobs they hated, and he'd loved his. He would miss the craziness of his clients and the challenge of meeting their demands. Mostly, though, he felt relieved. At least he wasn't abandoning them. He was leaving them in capable hands. Not to mention extremely strong hands.

He realized that DeWitt was making eye contact with a man who'd just come in and said, "There is something you'll need to handle carefully. The gay thing."

"I grew up in rural Indiana," DeWitt said. "I think I've got the gay thing under control."

Christian blushed and said, "I have a confession to make. There are times that being gay works to your advantage. Some clients are more likely to trust your guidance in certain areas if you're gay. Also, men tend to be more comfortable when you're spending a lot of time with their wives and girlfriends if they think you're gay."

"Christian Mercer," DeWitt scolded, "are you telling me that you pretend to be gay for money?"

"You make it sound like I'm hustling," Christian said with a huff. "I never have sex with my clients. Female or male. Do you have any teaching experience?"

"No," DeWitt said.

"We can work on that, too. Seminars. That's where the money is. For the same investment of time, lots more people are paying you."

"Why are you doing all this for me?" DeWitt asked.

"I'm not," Christian said. "After all these years of teaching people to follow their dreams, to set goals and work toward them, to believe in themselves, I'm finally ready to take my own advice. I won't be able to give it up all at once, but with your help—" He broke off with a sigh when "Morning Train" blared at them. He couldn't believe he'd forgotten his headset. As he pulled the phone from his pocket, DeWitt reached across the table and snatched it away from him.

"Christian Mercer's office. This is DeWitt; how may I help you?" Christian's mouth fell open, but DeWitt just grinned at him. "I'm sorry, Mrs. Barrister, but Christian is unavailable right now. Is there any way I can assist you? Dr. Brown said what? That's *terrible.* I'm sure Jitters *is* a wonderful dog. Since I haven't seen him myself, I can't say if he's overweight, but it never hurts to get a second opinion. There are several excellent veterinarians in the area."

"Fax," Christian hissed.

"I can fax you a list later."

"Within the hour," Christian said.

"Within the hour," DeWitt repeated.

As DeWitt continued to listen to Emily-Anne's troubles with her canine offspring, Christian stood and whispered, "I'll fax the list from my apartment. I can get my phone and PalmPilot from you later."

DeWitt nodded, and Christian left the café with a lighter load and spirit. He stopped at Nebula Art Supply, transfixed by the wide array of oil colors. He'd laid down all of the base coats for his painting of Bianca and had made progress with painting her form and the background, but he needed the right colors to capture the translucency of her skin, the small indentation just below her bottom lip, and the natural golden highlights in her red hair.

As he gathered the necessary paints, some new brushes, and a few impulse items, he heard a man say, "Where have you been hiding?"

Christian turned to see one of his clients standing behind him; he looked perturbed. He scanned his mental data banks until he got the name. Brett Larson was an attorney who'd hired Christian to organize his office after blaming his business difficulties on the clutter that surrounded him. Christian hoped he hadn't missed an appointment with Brett or mislaid any of his extensive files of divorce actions and prenuptial agreements. "I've been swamped the last few weeks," he said apologetically.

Brett stared at the art supplies and said, "If I were a different type of attorney, I'd probably sue you for breach of contract." When he saw Christian's look of concern, he smiled. "I'm kidding. Since your 'Order in the Court' seminar, I've made great progress in keeping myself organized, instead of relying on everyone else to do it for me. What's been keeping you so busy?"

Christian cast a guilty look at his art supplies and said, "I found a muse."

"Lucky you," Brett said, reaching into his inside pocket and removing a business card, "but if it doesn't work out, here's my card."

"I have your number already, Brett. I won't be needing it, though."

"You never know."

Brett left, and Christian paid for his supplies. While he ran other errands, he dropped Brett's card into a trash can. He wouldn't need it. He couldn't deny that he was forming a bond with Bianca, but he intended to move slowly. He didn't want to repeat the mistakes he'd made years ago with Aline, and he also sensed some hesitation on Bianca's part. She didn't seem uncomfortable with him. In fact, at times she seemed almost too comfortable, as if she didn't regard him as a potential romance. He'd gotten accustomed to her meandering conversations and liked the way he could never anticipate what she might say next. But it had dawned on him that she never made flirtatious or suggestive comments that could lead to anything more intimate than friendship. He didn't know if she was shy, inexperienced, or just uninterested. He'd decided it was best to be patient until he figured it out.

When he picked up his dry cleaning, Kate handed it over, took his debit card, and said, "Somebody finally caught you, huh?"

"I'm sorry?" Christian asked, unsure what she meant.

"Me, too," Kate said. When she returned his debit card, she noticed his baffled look. "I know the signs. In all the time we've done your cleaning, you never brought your comforter in. The next phase is when your dry cleaning includes items that aren't yours." When Christian blushed, she laughed. "Satisfy my curiosity. Which side of an unfamiliar shirt will the buttons be on?"

"Stay tuned," Christian said, grinning as he left.

The sight of Bianca looking radiantly beautiful as she sat outside his apartment door reminded him that it wasn't going to be easy to restrain himself. "I'm sorry; did I keep you waiting long?"

"No," she said. "I'm early. I know it's a terrible habit, because it always makes the other person feel like he's in the wrong, but I can't seem to break it."

"I can solve this dilemma," Christian said, leading her inside. He reached into his pocket and took out a shiny new key. "Now you can come and go as you please."

Bianca took the key and said, "And I can always water your plants or something."

Christian stopped himself from glancing around his plant-free apartment. While Bianca went into the kitchen to make tea, a habit they'd fallen into, he made a list of local veterinarians and faxed it to Emily-Anne. Then he put the clean comforter on the bed and looked around the room with satisfaction. Nothing was out of place. He went to his studio and began unloading his new art supplies.

When Bianca joined him, she said, "Have you heard from Derek yet?"

"No," Christian said with renewed concern for his friend, who'd been missing in action since the night of the Big Bang. "Has Vienna?"

"Nope," Bianca said. "She says she's not worried; he just needs a vacation from all the drama of his life at the mall."

"Have you gotten the other story out of her yet?"

"About the man with multiple identities?" Bianca asked. When he nodded, she said, "No. You know how Vienna is. She never talks about herself." She started unbuttoning her blouse. Although she seemed comfortable with having him there, Christian left the room and changed into his paint-stained jeans and T-shirt. His clothes were beginning to look a little like their own work of art.

His new fine brushes allowed him to capture the nuances of Bianca's skin. His concentration was so intense as he worked that it took a while for him to realize that Bianca was speaking.

"What?" he asked.

"Your doorbell," she said. "Didn't you hear it?"

"My doorbell rang?"

"Four times."

"Shit," Christian said, dropping his paintbrush and leaving the room. "Nooooo," he moaned as he looked through the peephole. His mother's face was stretched out as if she were made of Silly Putty. She didn't look happy. Christian braced himself before he opened the door.

Patricia stormed in, then turned on her high heels as she entered the living room. The two of them assessed each other. Her formerly brown hair, now mahogany, was swept into a loose knot. Her fierce pink lips were puckered, and her brow was furrowed, a look Christian hadn't seen since he was seven and had tried to "help" his mother by adding paint to a canvas that was slated for her first major exhibit in Manhattan.

"You look great," Christian said, hoping to head off a tantrum.

"You look terrible. Your eyes are hollow. Your hair is a mess. Have you shaved recently?" Her eyes swept his clothes. "You're *painting*?"

"No. This is Indiana's hot new look."

"Don't give me any of your sass," Patricia ordered. She reached into her small handbag, took out a cigarette, and lit it in one fluid motion.

"Please don't smoke in my apartment."

"Fine," Patricia said as she walked into the kitchen and extinguished the cigarette in the sink. She returned to the living room. "Although it's not going to be your apartment for long if you neglect your clients' calls the way you've been ignoring mine."

"I needed to be in the moment. You should understand that better than anyone. How many times did you just disappear because you were inspired?"

"Oh, for heaven's sake. Don't act like I neglected you. I'm certainly not neglecting you now. I want you to come to New York. You need proper tutelage."

"I've had proper instruction."

"From Mrs. Grim at Highland Day School?"

"Grimes. Mrs. Grimes." Christian stared intently at his mother. "You think I've learned nothing from you?"

Patricia's face went slack. She flopped into the armchair behind her and rested her chin on her fist. Her expression became thoughtful as she looked past him, and Christian turned around to see Bianca, still dressed in her sheer cotton shift.

"I'm Bianca. You must be the mother."

"Patricia Mercer," his mother said a little acidly. "Lovely to meet you." She looked at Christian. "Is this your reason for not coming to New York?"

"I'm happy here. I can go to New York whenever I want."

"I'm not going to support you. Even a successful artist—"

"I wouldn't take your money if you offered it," Christian said. "I still have clients. I have savings. I'll manage."

"It's a tough road," Patricia warned, sounding almost motherly.

"I'm prepared for it."

"That doesn't mean he doesn't need you," Bianca said. Christian and Patricia turned to look at her with similarly indignant expressions. Her voice had a confident tone that Christian wasn't used to hearing. "You must have lots of insight that would help Christian.

About unscrupulous dealers. Galleries he can trust. Pitfalls to avoid. People who can help him."

Patricia's gray eyes were a little cold, so Christian was shocked when she said, "Actually, he knows more about all that than I do. I've always depended on Christian to help my manager deal with those details."

"I'm not surprised," Bianca said. Christian began to suspect she had an agenda when she continued. "Christian's always ready to help anyone. You must be so proud of him."

"Well, of course," Patricia said.

"You should be proud of yourself, too, since you're the one who raised him to be that way."

"True," Patricia said, looking pleased. She shifted her gaze to Christian. "I'm staying at the Congreve. Why don't we meet for drinks later and talk all this over? May I look at your—"

"No," Christian said. "Not until it's finished. But I will meet you later."

"You come, too, Bianca," Patricia said. "You seem like a sensible young woman."

"I'd love to," Bianca said sweetly.

After he'd walked his mother out, Christian turned to Bianca and said, "What a smooth operator you are. Sometimes I feel like I'm dealing with a feral cat instead of a mother, but you'll have her eating out of your hand in no time."

"How *are* you going to support yourself?" Bianca asked. "Judging by the shelves in your bathroom, you're very high maintenance."

"You could always support me," Christian joked.

"I guess I'll have to sell a lot of lip liner, huh?"

"Tons."

"I've always wanted to be the benefactress to a gay artist."

"Gay? I think we can clear up that little misunderstanding right now," Christian said, finally comprehending what had been holding Bianca back.

Her eyes widened when he walked across the room and leaned in for a kiss. She returned it with fervor, and her arms crept around his neck. He wasn't sure who was dragging whom toward the bedroom as she said, "I think this might be the best clarification I've ever had."

35

The Wichita Lying Man

Riley took a drag off his cigarette and nearly spit it across the alley. Generic. Like his whole flavor-free life. How was it possible that a man of his genius had been reduced to buying cheap cigarettes? There was no justice in the world. Not as long as scheming bitches like Juanita Luna and Sheree Sheridan were out to get hardworking, talented people like him.

He thought of all the years he'd been a slave to the Congreve dynasty while Sheree feathered her nest by screwing that domineering, ungrateful old man. Riley had obviously made the wrong choice. He should have been sleeping with Hunter instead of working his ass off to make him look good. Apparently that was how one guaranteed security with a Congreve.

He smiled bitterly. It hadn't worked for Derek, though, thanks to Riley's efforts. Maybe Riley had been banished from the kingdom, but Derek was no longer whoring with the crown prince. There was some satisfaction in that.

He'd always suspected that Sheree was the old man's spy and had taken pains not to run afoul of her. Christ, he'd even given her skinny dog a present every Christmas. She had no sense of gratitude or even basic human decency. It still stunned him to remember the day she'd helped bring the universe crashing down around him.

That had been such a productive morning. Hunter hadn't come in, leaving Riley a message that he'd be away in meetings until midafternoon. Since Riley had no information about meetings on his calendar, and there was nothing on Hunter's desk to indicate where he'd be, he'd powered on his laptop to check Hunter's e-mail, almost having a stroke at what he found.

> *Derek,*
> *I don't know why you quit your job and left the mall. I've called your cell phone, and all I get is some out-of-area message. Your parents either don't know where you are or they aren't telling me. In the unlikely event that you access our private network to check your e-mail, I'm asking you to call me. Please.*
>
> *Don't be afraid that I'm going to lecture you or say I told you so. I only want to know that you're okay.*
> *Love,*
> *Hunter*

Riley had hastily logged out of Hunter's account and into Derek's, nearly crazy with relief when he saw that Hunter's e-mail was unread. He deleted it without opening it, ensuring that Derek would never see it. Then he changed Derek's password. Even if the little idiot figured out how to access the network, which Riley found improbable, he wouldn't be able to get into his account. He was gone. It was over. Riley had won.

The phones had been abnormally quiet that morning, giving him the opportunity to catch up on all of his work. Then he treated himself to a long lunch, indulging himself by getting a manicure and stopping by Mercury Man to put a new suit on layaway.

When he went back to work, he glanced toward Hunter's office, but the desk was still empty. He called Craig at Drayden's and confirmed that Derek had, in fact, quit his job without notice, but that was the extent of Craig's information.

After making a few more business calls, Riley opened his file drawer to remove the laptop and reconnect it. Except the laptop wasn't there. The hair on the back of his neck stood up, and he began looking in other drawers without success. He knew he hadn't taken it with him when he went to lunch. If someone on the staff had stolen his computer, there was going to be hell to pay. He'd fire every one of them, from Juanita down to the lowliest laundress or bellhop, until somebody returned it.

"Looking for this?" Hunter asked, and Riley whipped around to see his boss leaning against the door frame of his office, Riley's laptop in his hand.

He felt the blood drain from his face, but he kept his voice casual when he said, "I'm so glad you have it. That's my personal property."

"Come in here, please," Hunter said.

Riley followed him in, stopping short when he saw Natasha Deere in Hunter's guest chair. She gave him a cold look and said, "Yes. That's him. RB. He's the one who wanted me to spy on Derek."

"What are you talking about?" Riley asked indignantly. "I've never seen this woman before in my—"

"Oh, but you have," Sheree said smoothly as she emerged from the corner of Hunter's office. "You made a request, as I recall. You asked if I'd do a Dolly Parton set when you came into the Aurora one night. I did. This is the woman you sat with while I was singing."

"Thank you, Sheree," Hunter said. "Ms. Deere, we'll talk later. I need to see Riley alone now." When the women were gone, Hunter looked at him and said, "Why?"

"I have no clue who or what they're talking about," Riley said. "I've completely devoted my time and energy to you, Hunter."

"With some help from our computer people, I know exactly how much time and energy you've devoted to me," Hunter said. "What I don't know is why. You're the only one who can tell me that." Riley didn't answer, and Hunter said, "My father wants to press charges against you. Our lawyers assure us we have grounds. You tampered with my e-mail. You accessed my private financial records. You used my funds, without my knowledge or permission, to alter the work order for my computer network. Drayden Lvandsson is weighing his options, too. You blackmailed Natasha into harassing a Drayden's employee. I could probably stop my father and Drayden. Just explain why you singled out someone who never mistreated you in any way."

"You had everything I should have had," Riley spat, thrilled to finally direct his venom at Hunter. "I worked for years while you squandered your time and opportunities in Europe. But when you decided on a whim to get into the business, they made me your assistant. I could have run this hotel in my sleep, but I had to take orders from you and put up with crap from bleeding hearts like

Juanita, while you and Derek partied your way from one resort to the next. You used my expertise and my hard work to run this hotel, taking all the credit, not to mention the bonuses, and you don't think you mistreated me?"

"Actually," Hunter said, "I was talking about Derek. He's the person you injured. But I've heard enough. I'm afraid I can't return your 'personal property' to you, Riley. We'll keep it as evidence. Your severance check will include the cost of replacing it. You can pick that up from Juanita at the front desk when she confirms that you've vacated your apartment and turned in your keys. Be careful about using the Congreve for a reference. Good luck."

That had been the final humiliation: to give Juanita his keys and take his last check from her. "You'd better hope that boy's okay, or you're going down," was all she'd said. His only satisfaction had been in telling her that the one going down was Derek, on his new boyfriend, Christian Mercer, knowing that she'd relay that information to Hunter.

The second cigarette wasn't quite as bad as the first, but Riley smoked it quickly, unwilling to spend his time in a stinking alley brooding about Hunter Congreve and that loser, Derek Anderson. What a fucked-up world, when men like those two thrived while *he* was punished for being too dedicated to his career.

He went back inside the motel lobby, suppressing a shudder at the stale smell. He was sure there was mold under the indoor-outdoor carpet. At least it was newer than the shag carpet in the motel's forty rooms.

He slipped behind the counter and sat down at his battered metal desk, staring through the lobby window at the neon sign blinking next to the highway: LARUE INN OF WICHITA. SWIMMING POOL. CABLE IN EVERY ROOM. VACANCY.

36

The Spy Who Bagged Me

Vienna rued having ever embarked on her mission to take Natasha's dolls. She'd honestly thought it could only help to remove the objects of Natasha's fixation. But Vienna's evaluation had been made under duress, with panic and a blaring alarm hindering her thought process. She hadn't counted on Dolly being an omnipresent figure in Natasha's world. Vienna could remove the dolls, but they were just things, mere objects. Dolly was everywhere. She was in movies, on television, on compact discs, on posters, and obviously in Natasha's heart and soul.

Nobody would ever believe that Natasha had a heart, let alone a soul, but Vienna had come to know that it was absolutely true. Natasha's pain was real, and Vienna knew she was the catalyst that had caused Natasha to break. She wanted to help her in any way she could. She owed it to herself, as a psychologist. She owed it to her mother, who always had faith that Vienna was a good girl. She owed it to Derek, because she'd practically coerced him into letting her help him. But most of all, she owed it to Natasha, for violating her home and heart.

After she left the Big Bang and retrieved the dolls from Christian's apartment, she went straight to Natasha's condo and banged on the door for hours, but Natasha never answered. Vienna finally gave up and went home. Natasha's phone number was unlisted; Vienna's only option was to go to Drayden's and convince someone there to break the rules and give it to her.

Erik was her unlikely hero. The people in Human Resources refused to give out an employee's personal information, so Vienna decided to appeal to Erik. Even if he didn't know the number, she figured he'd know where to look in Natasha's desk.

"Her desk's been cleaned out," Erik informed her, which made Vienna gasp. "They told me that Natasha resigned this morning. Her personal stuff was delivered to her residence, I guess. I don't know."

"Did you get promoted?" Vienna asked, running her hand over her head and wondering what she'd do next. When Erik nodded happily, she said, "Congratulations, Erik. You really deserve it."

"Thanks," Erik said. "I wish it had happened under better circumstances, though. I know she was awful, but in some ways, I admired Natasha. She was very dedicated to her job."

Vienna felt as though she'd been punched in the stomach. She winced and said, "If you have any idea how I can get in touch with her, please tell me. I beg of you. I can't tell you why, but you've got to."

Erik paused, then began writing on a scrap of paper. "She told me to call her only in case of an emergency, but what the hell. Here's her number."

"Thanks!" Vienna exclaimed and rushed home.

She'd called Natasha all that night, but there was no answer. Not even an answering machine. The situation seemed hopeless. And with Derek missing in action, Vienna felt like an asteroid had hit Earth, wiping out civilization and leaving her all alone.

But that wasn't the case, as she learned a few mornings later, when a persistent knocking woke her. She rose from the sofa and groggily walked to the door, startled to find Natasha on the other side.

"I'm leaving Indiana," Natasha stated. She was less disheveled than she'd been the last time Vienna had seen her, but her eyes were red and she looked as though she hadn't slept in days. "This is your last chance to return what's mine."

"Of course," Vienna said. "Come in." Natasha took a few tentative steps into Vienna's apartment but made it clear she wasn't about to sit down. Vienna asked, "How did you know I'd have your dolls?"

"I didn't. You just told me," Natasha said.

Vienna nodded and couldn't help but smile, feeling slightly out of practice with facilitating discussion. She pointed to the pillowcases leaning against the sofa and said, "There they are."

Natasha's eyes widened, her expression resembling that of a little girl who'd been presented with a pony: thrilled, but not quite sure she should believe it was really for her.

When she didn't move, Vienna said, "I want you to know that I'm very sorry for all the trouble I caused."

Natasha was still staring at the pillowcases. Vienna followed Natasha's gaze and saw a pair of Dolly legs sticking out from the top of one of them, an arm reaching out of another, as if frantically waving to be rescued.

"I never meant to hurt you, Natasha," Vienna said, trying again to provoke a response. "You didn't deserve to be violated like that. You may treat people badly. People I care about. But that doesn't give me the right to retaliate. I'm sorry."

Natasha finally looked at Vienna and asked, "You? You did it all?"

"Yes," Vienna said. "I broke in to your apartment, broke the lock on your . . . shrine, and took your dolls. It was all me."

"What about RB?" Natasha said. She sounded confused and completely muddled, as if trying to fight the effects of a narcotic. "I thought it was RB."

"I don't know who that is," Vienna said. As much as it annoyed her that there was something or someone at Mall of the Universe that she'd overlooked, she didn't want Natasha to continue to fixate on RB. That might provoke her into going after the hapless DeWitt again, which he didn't deserve. "Would you like some orange juice, Natasha? Coffee?"

Natasha waved away the offer and walked slowly to the sofa, sinking down and extracting a doll from one of the pillowcases. She smoothed the doll's messy hair and touched its patchwork coat. She looked up at Vienna and said, "This one's my favorite."

"Oh, yeah?" Vienna said. She sat down on a nearby chair and asked, "Why's that?"

"Everyone laughs at her and taunts her. They make fun of her patchwork coat, because it's made from old clothes and isn't storebought. It's the things they say behind her back that hurt the worst, though."

"It's a very pretty coat," Vienna said. She almost wished she'd taken the time to examine DeWitt's handiwork while she had the dolls. Then again, the quicker their sinister influence could be removed from her apartment and her life, the better off she'd be.

"Her mother made it," Natasha said.

"Does her mother love her?" Vienna asked tentatively.

She watched as Natasha struggled to answer, obviously toeing a thin line between fantasy and reality. Her voice wavering, she finally said, "I don't know."

"That's okay," Vienna said. "Questions without answers are fine. But it's important to explore the possibilities. It keeps us going. It's also important to accept other people's help."

Natasha stared at her dully and asked, "You just feel guilty, don't you?"

"No. I want to help you. I want you to get help. If not from me, then from someone," Vienna pleaded. "You can't deny that you've got problems, Natasha. I don't want you to hurt anyone else. Or yourself."

"Fine," Natasha said. She stood up and walked resolutely to the door. Vienna wasn't used to someone else announcing that time was up, but she knew the moment had passed and could only hope she'd gotten through. Natasha stopped before she opened the door and said, "I may have misjudged you. I don't think you're irresponsible."

"Thank you," Vienna said. "You're not taking your dolls with you?"

"I won't be needing them anymore." Natasha held up the doll in her hand. "I'll keep this one, though, as a reminder."

"Don't hold on to the past, Natasha," Vienna implored. "Deal with it, but put it behind you at some point. You've never struck me as someone who's happy. Find something or some place that truly brings you joy."

Natasha seemed to think it over before she said, "I will if you will, Miss Talbot."

That was the end of Natasha. Or, as Vienna preferred to think, it was a beginning for Natasha.

Alone again, Vienna listened to the messages on her machine. She'd been preoccupied trying to sort through the madness of the past few days and set things right again, virtually ignoring the outside world. Unfortunately, in spite of all the juggling she'd done, there was still one ball up in the air. The majority of the messages were from Cart Man.

"Garry," Vienna said aloud, reminding herself of his real name.

She wasn't ready to deal with him yet, so she did what her mother had always done. She cleaned. From her empty bedroom to Derek's, and all points in between. Unfortunately, it wasn't a large apartment, nor was it dirty, so it didn't take much time. With a sigh, she plundered her kitchen cabinets and baked, although with no one there to eat her cooking, it would go to waste. She could almost feel her mother's disapproval, and she took a long bath to wash that sin away. Then she cleaned the bathroom again.

Finally, disgusted with all her avoidance behavior, she poured a glass of wine and sat down at the table, sipping as she took stock of her feelings. She couldn't deny that she felt somewhat betrayed by Garry. He'd pretended to be something he wasn't. Hadn't he? Vienna had never pressed for details about his life. She'd simply enjoyed his company. He was sweet and comforting. She loved spending time with him.

"Oh, man," she moaned, suddenly pinching the bridge of her nose. She'd slept with someone without knowing his name. She'd never done anything like that before. When had she become so reckless? *Davii would approve,* she mused. Her eyes fluttered toward the ceiling, and she said, "Oh, Mama. I don't know who I am anymore."

Had Cart Man really been so different from the rest of them? Hadn't Davii pretended to be happy for her sake, when what he really wanted was a life outside Indiana? Or Derek. He'd defiantly clung to a job he hated and wasn't suited for just to make a point to Hunter. Christian had masked his frustrated artistic needs by staying busy and making over everyone else. And she, Vienna Talbot, had been running in place for two years, trying to convince herself that she was getting away from a past that was, in fact, an important part of who she'd become.

Her doorbell sounded, and she glared at the door, refusing to move. After the third ring, there was an insistent knocking, so she relented and opened the door. She wasn't surprised to see him there. He'd always known exactly when to show up.

"Come in, Cart Man," she said, returning to her wine. She took a long drink and pointed to the kitchen. "If you'd like a glass, they're in the cabinet above the sink. I hate to seem rude, but since you've been here before, not to mention inside me, you're no longer a guest."

Vienna saw the corners of his mouth twitch before he went into the kitchen for a glass, saying, "I'd never have shown up uninvited, but it's been hard to keep my eye on all four levels of the mall hoping for a glimpse of you. I've been worried. Did you get my messages?"

Vienna suddenly sat up straight in her chair and smacked her forehead. "I'm sorry! Did I call you Cart Man a minute ago? I meant to say Ed. Or is it Garry today?" He filled his glass, topped off hers, then sat down beside her. Vienna put her hand on his arm and said, "Sybil? Are you in there? Are you comfortable in the big chair?"

"Are you finished?" Garry asked.

"No. I think I have one more," Vienna said. "Was this a big game for you? Bag the black woman, then brag to your friends? String along poor Vienna and play her for a fool, while you've got another piece of chicken on the side?"

"Piece of chicken?" Garry asked.

"That honey blond piece of white meat you were with at the Big Bang Benefit," Vienna clarified. "You know who I mean. Meaty thighs, but probably very dry?"

"Right. Buffy," Garry said.

"What are you smiling about, Cart Man?" Vienna asked.

"Nothing," Garry said quickly, putting on a poker face. "Absolutely nothing."

"I thought not. I'm not gonna be played like that. Who is she?" Vienna sipped her wine again, and when she looked at Garry, poker face intact and lips pressed firmly together, she added, "You may speak now."

"Her name is Buffy Barlow—"

"Oh, Lord," Vienna muttered.

"—a pimento heiress—"

"Of course she is."

"—whom my parents hoped I'd marry for the good of our family business," he explained. "I came here to get away from all of them. I wanted to step back and have some time on my own to figure out what I wanted to do."

Vienna stared into his eyes, which didn't move from hers. Even though his story sounded as implausible as something Derek would invent, she knew he was telling the truth. She understood his need to get away, to take stock and figure out how to move forward with his life. She'd been doing the same thing for two years. She said, "Go on."

"That's it," he said. "The night I spent 'inside you,' you told me about your past with Kevin. Maybe I should have told you then. However, not only was it five in the morning, but it would have made Buffy seem as significant to my life as Kevin was to yours. Which would have been inaccurate. I feel nothing for her. She's a nice girl, but that's the best I can say about her."

"Woman," Vienna corrected.

"Woman," Garry parroted.

"What about your family?" Vienna asked. "Where does this put you with them?"

Garry thought for a moment before saying, "I'm really not sure. I hope they'll support me in any decision I make. Unfortunately, I can't be certain. This was very important to them. Her family is in olives. Mine's in gin. To them, it makes logical business sense to merge the families. But I don't love her."

"Prophet," Vienna said, recalling Sheree's words at the Big Bang Benefit. "Seventeen Provinces Gin?" When Garry nodded, she said, "Davii will be calling you Daddy in no time."

"Who? What?" Garry asked.

"Nothing," Vienna dismissed. "Your family is one of the largest manufacturers of gin in the world."

"Third largest, I believe. But I've been out of the loop for a while. It could be fourth by now."

"Right," Vienna said slowly, trying to take it all in. "You really had me fooled. I thought you were . . ."

"Just a cart person," Garry said, finishing her sentence.

"You're so much more than that," Vienna said, her reserve softening. "I knew that even before everything went haywire. Before Buffy showed up. But when she did, I thought, 'Oh great, Vienna. Another guy's cheating on you, and this time it's happening before you've gotten out of the starting gate.'"

"I wasn't cheating on you with Buffy," Garry said firmly. "My parents tracked me down through my credit cards and told Buffy where to find me. She cornered me on the night of the Big Bang Benefit, when I was on my way to meet you, and demanded to know why I'd been avoiding her. I was trying to let her down gently. That's why I was late."

"Oh," Vienna said softly.

"She wouldn't take no for an answer, so I finally just walked out on her," Garry said. "I couldn't bear the idea of you thinking I'd stood you up."

"I did think that."

"I know," Garry said. He took her hands in his and said, "I'm sorry."

"Okay, so Boobie—"

"Buffy."

"Right. Buffy. She means nothing to you. She's out of the picture, and you'll probably be disinherited," Vienna clarified.

Garry moved closer to her, kissed her hand, and said, "Will you still love me if I'm penniless?"

"I thought you were penniless when I met you. And you can stop smiling, because that was *not* an admission of love. I've still got questions."

"I might be out of the gin business, but I'm a very enterprising man."

"I have no doubt. How did you end up at Mall of the Universe?"

"Ah," Garry said. "We have my oldest and best friend to thank for that. He lives and works here, so I thought I'd pay him a visit while I was in hiding. Since he manages the Congreve, I figured why not hide in style?"

"Hunter Congreve."

"Right. But he left for Australia. I considered visiting friends in Montreal, then decided to come here anyway. Hunter was supposed to be gone for only a few weeks, and I intended to wait for him. I knew he and Derek were having problems, and I thought I'd keep tabs on Derek while Hunter was away."

Vienna drew back slightly and said, "You were spying on Derek?"

"No," Garry insisted. "I just wanted to be around in case either of them needed me."

"It's okay," Vienna said, patting his hand. "I approve of observation. So you went undercover. What did you learn?"

"That you're a stunning woman. I don't know how good a friend I was to Hunter, since the only thing on my mind was you."

"You really lay it on thick, Cart Man," Vienna observed.

He leaned in and kissed her. When his hand moved up her arm, Vienna remembered how he held her and the way his hand cradled her neck when they made love. His tongue flicked at her earlobe, and he whispered, "My name is Garry."

"Okay," Vienna relented, "Garry."

He lightly put his hands on her face, looked into her eyes, and said, "But don't ever stop calling me Cart Man. I kind of like it."

Vienna laughed. She felt infinitely better. She kissed him quickly, then went into the kitchen. She returned with another bottle of wine and offered Garry the corkscrew. "If you would, sir."

He jumped from his chair and took the corkscrew from her, but held onto her hand, moving to stand behind her. Nuzzling her neck, he carefully removed the cork while she held the bottle and laughed.

"That tickles!" She took the bottle from him and poured, saying, "I can't believe Hunter Congreve is your best friend."

"Why?" Garry asked.

"Because you're nothing alike," Vienna stated. "You're sweet and funny. Kind. He's cold. Insensitive. And a big old stuffed shirt."

"How well do you know him?"

"I've only met him a couple of times," Vienna admitted. "None of which were very memorable. I know he's your friend, but I wish he'd treat Derek better. The guy's a cad."

"You know I adore you," Garry said and kissed her. "I think you're very intelligent, and I'd never disrespect you."

As he folded her into his arms, Vienna said, "But?"

"But you've got Hunter all wrong."

37

Fables of the Reconstruction

Hunter Congreve believed that his place in the world had been determined not by birth, as most people thought, but by one of his earliest memories. At four years old, he'd been mesmerized by a story Nanny Lynn told the Congreve children, as much because of her lilting Irish brogue as the tale of the baby cuckoo. Cuckoos left their eggs in the nests of other birds, and this particular mother cuckoo chose a nest inside the hollow of a tree. The baby cuckoo was hatched and brought up with the young of his foster parents. By the time he was strong enough to fly away, the cuckoo had grown too large to fit through the tree's opening. For a while, his parents brought him food, but when they were no longer in need of their nest and were distressed by his cries, they finally abandoned him. After a few more mishaps, the tree was severed by a stroke of lightning, and the young cuckoo flew away unharmed.

"Hunter is the cuckoo!" Elizabeth shouted, making the rest of them laugh.

"He's always screaming his idiot head off," Randy agreed.

"Hunter's not like the rest of us," Dinah said.

"Hunter is not a Congreve," Peyton pronounced with finality.

Nanny Lynn had been giving them all a scolding when his mother made one of her rare visits to the nursery. In an attempt to keep Peyton from telling her why Hunter was mad, Randy tried to kick him under the nursery table, but it was Nanny Lynn who gave a yelp of pain when Randy's foot made contact with her shin.

"Hunter," Mrs. Congreve had said wearily, "don't abuse the servants. They're too hard to replace."

Hunter was left with a number of impressions from the incident. He was annoyed with his mother for not realizing that his leg wasn't long enough to have reached Nanny Lynn, so he developed a strong dislike of injustice. He liked Nanny Lynn better than his family, so he never learned to be condescending toward people his grandmother called "inferiors." And though he might have been genetically a Congreve, thanks to this early rejection by his siblings, he wasn't locked into behaving like one. It was a liberation he never regretted.

His first blow toward being his own person came when he was fifteen and fell hopelessly in love at Phillips Academy. Garry would never be able to return his feelings, but Hunter gained two things from the experience: his best friend and an understanding of his own nature. Garry handled the situation with grace, and they became each other's champions, confidants, and partners in the usual schoolboy pranks. Garry knew their close friendship caused people to suspect his sexuality, but he never made Hunter feel like that was any kind of burden. It wasn't as Prophet and Congreve, children of privilege, that they considered themselves beyond the censure of others. It was as Pro and Con, two sides of a single, unbreakable connection called friendship.

The first adult to whom Hunter confided his newfound knowledge about himself was Sheree Sheridan. He'd always felt a bond with her, almost as if she'd been the cuckoo who left him in the Congreve nest. Sheree heard him out, then put her arms around him and said, "Hunter, this will be your saving grace." It was years before he understood that being among his family without being a full-fledged part of them was like having the best of two worlds.

He'd boldly proclaimed his sexuality to his father while he was on summer break, and after a few minutes of stony silence, in an eerie repetition of his mother's reprimand, his father said, "Just don't fuck the staff, Hunter. It's hard to find good help." Which had been bewildering, since they were in their Marblehead house at the time and the only servants were their fifty-five-year-old housekeeper and their sixty-year-old gardener.

For the most part, Hunter did what was expected of him. He stayed out of serious trouble and studied hard. When he had to choose a sport at school, he decided on cycling because he didn't particularly enjoy games with balls and he hated being trapped inside a gym. He considered running, but he liked the speed of racing and the challenge of competing against his own body, a machine, other cyclists, and nature. He continued cycling through his college and post-graduate years.

His next declaration of independence came when he completed his MBA and refused to go to work for Congreve. When Garry was sent to Europe to work for his family's business, Hunter went with him and began competitive racing in earnest. He was in France when he fell in love for the second time, although his lover was also an American. Barrett was a model, and Hunter was so stupidly dazzled by his beauty that it took him a long time to notice his less attractive qualities. These included a tendency to use Hunter's name and connections to advance his career, an eagerness to treat Hunter's money as his own, and an ability—somewhat amazing in a boy from Newark—to affect an attitude of world-weariness that ultimately doomed the relationship. Hunter had no patience with snobbery.

Hunter's cycling career was also doomed when his bike skidded on a wet road and he was thrown down a steep embankment, mangling one of his knees. His father saw to it that he had outstanding surgeons, but Hunter understood that there was only so much they could do. He accepted the inevitable without bitterness, but his father had no intention of letting his earlier rebellion go completely overlooked, and he sent him to Indiana when Hunter agreed to work for the Congreve hotel chain.

Hunter had mentally prepared himself to start at the bottom and work his way up at either the Boston or Manhattan Congreve, so his father's decision surprised him. To an outsider, being made manager of his own hotel appeared to be a reward. But Hunter recognized it as his father's punishment. Terre Haute was not the kind of city where the upscale Congreve hotels were usually located. The hotel existed only because of the supermall, and it was expected to lose money. Providing it an untested, untrained manager nearly guaranteed that it would be a tax write-off.

Randolph Congreve had not known that his youngest son took other lessons from the story of the cuckoo. Yelling one's head off was rarely productive, and sometimes what seemed like catastrophe was actually, in the words of the Congreve forefathers, a chance at life, liberty, and the pursuit of happiness. Hunter had no illusions about himself. He'd been born with all the comforts that came with being a Congreve, and he had no intention of tossing them aside out of stubborn pride.

Still, he missed his friends and the places where he felt at home. He especially missed Garry, who was sent by the Prophets from one European distillery to another to learn every facet of the family business. Although Hunter resented his father's domination, he tried to follow Garry's example and find the positive aspects of accepting his familial responsibilities.

Gradually, his sense of humor asserted itself. He loved his staff, who provided him with an endless set of challenges and diversions. He enjoyed his hotel guests, many of whom saw a journey to Mall of the Universe and their stay in a Congreve hotel as a fantastic adventure. He liked the hardworking, decent spirit of the people of Indiana. As a gay man who'd grown up among the leisure class, he'd anticipated ostracism and rejection, but he was treated as a valuable part of the business community. And there were plenty of fair-minded citizens who made him feel welcome as a person, as well.

The biggest advantage of being in Indiana was the presence of Sheree. They were each other's connection to a life from which they'd both been banished, but it was more than that. Hunter knew that for whatever reason, Sheree genuinely loved him in the same way Garry did. During times when he was overwhelmed by the responsibilities that had been placed on him, or he just needed the sight of a friendly face, Sheree was the one he turned to.

When Hunter was finally settling into his new life, not exactly happy, but not entirely unhappy, he'd fallen in love for the third and final time. From the first moment he saw Derek, he knew he wanted him. Like the cuckoo's tree, he'd been struck by lightning, and nothing would ever be the same.

In time, Hunter had come to know that Derek had an infinite number of appealing qualities—sweetness, trust, humor, incorruptibility, and tolerance—but he'd never really understood the initial attraction. Derek was cute, but Hunter had known great beauties. He was cocky, but Hunter had grown up surrounded by brash people. He was an eager, uninhibited lover, but Hunter had enjoyed an abundance of good sex. As mystifying as it was, however, from their first days together, he'd believed that Derek was meant to be with him. He'd found Derek bewitching. He loved the way Derek's conversations filled the empty spaces in his apartment and in his heart. He loved holding him until they fell asleep. He loved waking up with him, and finding him there each time he came back. When Derek had left to go home for the summer, Hunter was lonelier than he'd ever been.

He endured the separation for two weeks before he was provoked into a rare display of Congreve ferocity, going to Evansville to talk honestly with the Andersons. He intended to have a relationship with their son, and nothing was going to stand in his way. Overwhelmed as they were by having their suspicions about Derek confirmed, they were not meek. It wasn't until they understood that Hunter had no intention of letting Derek neglect his studies or be nothing more than Hunter's diversion that they agreed to let their son make the decision for himself.

Hunter had never thought any of them regretted it; he certainly hadn't. For three years, Derek had been the source of a happiness Hunter hadn't known existed. Hunter worked hard, surprising his father and everyone else except Sheree by making the hotel profitable. But Hunter knew he could never have stuck it out without Derek, who'd given him a home in a little place that was supposed to have been exile.

Best of all, Derek was his storyteller. By day, Derek could adapt any person or situation into an observation or tale that enthralled Hunter. Derek's talent with words was mysterious and magical, and Hunter encouraged it in every way he could. He made sure Derek had a computer, so he could write, and online access to information, to simplify any research he needed to do. When they traveled, he always visited bookstores with Derek, and he encouraged him to buy and read as many books as he wanted.

Hunter wanted to provide Derek with an awareness of the larger world. For Hunter, going to circuit parties was a chance to relax and blow off steam in places where gay men converged in a celebration of their existence. But he also meant for their trips to give Derek a look at the world outside Indiana. Hunter believed that the more Derek saw, the more honest and brave he would be with what he wrote. Derek had grown up feeling safe inside the love of a family, and he'd recreated a safe place for himself at college, then at the mall. Hunter liked it that Derek felt secure, but he never wanted Derek to feel that he'd missed out on anything.

At night, Derek lulled Hunter to sleep with a continuing story of two princes. The two princes were Derek's metaphor for the things they shared. Their physical passion. The hurt that an unsympathetic world could sometimes cause two gay men. The place where they lived, or the ones they visited. The men they found handsome, or the women who touched their lives. Sometimes the stories were funny, other times romantic, but for Hunter, they became a way to measure the depth of the love that grew from their initial attraction. He believed that they belonged to each other heart, body, and soul.

Their relationship was not without its difficulties. From time to time, he sensed Derek's frustration with him. Hunter didn't have Derek's easy ability to express his thoughts and feelings. When Hunter was angry with his father or annoyed by work, his moodiness baffled Derek. Sometimes they bickered over petty things, but to Hunter, that was all part of the package. He never doubted that the strength of what they shared could withstand their individual flaws.

He also never worried about the disparity between them. Although he was older and had more responsibility and money than Derek, Hunter believed that love leveled everything out. In fact, he sometimes thought that his love was smothering. He kept reminding himself that Derek was seven years younger and in his first relationship. He tried to give him space to explore and experiment, sure that if he put too many conditions or limitations on Derek, he'd be stuck like the cuckoo in the tree, watching Derek fly to freedom.

It unsettled him when Derek graduated and seemed disinclined to do anything with his time or his talent. He didn't feel taken advantage of, as he had with Barrett. But his sense that Derek was unhappy was confirmed when his lover began lying on the sofa watching movies until Hunter fell asleep. Sometimes he urged Hunter to go to bed without him while he stayed at his computer, not writing, as Hunter hoped, but talking to people that Hunter knew nothing about. The bedtime stories of the princes tapered off, then stopped.

Derek's decision to work at Drayden's played on Hunter's single fear—losing Derek. His first thought, which came at him out of nowhere, was that Derek took the job to be close to some man he was interested in. That was so threatening that Hunter quickly searched for other possibilities. Since he didn't believe for a minute that Derek had any real interest in a retail career, he decided his motive had to be money. Not only money that didn't come from Hunter, but money from a job that was in no way connected to Hunter, who would happily have introduced Derek to contacts who could have used his gift with words.

His instinct was to tell Derek that he couldn't take the Drayden's job, and he bit off the words before they left his mouth. Derek was no more likely to appreciate an attempt to control him than Hunter had been, and Hunter didn't intend to make his father's mistakes. When Derek left his office after telling him about the job, Hunter fought his urge to find him and use whatever emotional or financial power he had to change his mind. He kept telling himself that it was only a job, not a good-bye, but that wasn't how it felt.

Sydney had seemed like a solution. Physical distance would prevent Hunter from interfering with Derek's choices. In retrospect, it was the worst decision he'd ever made. Their communication had been frustrating, then it had become something that Hunter hadn't expected. Hostile. Hurtful. His attempts to convey Australia's beauty had misfired. He simply didn't have Derek's gift with words.

But Derek had found words. Words for men. Erik. Davii. Christian. Who they were to him, what they did with him, was left vague, and Hunter knew that was deliberate, because it wasn't in Derek's nature to be secretive. It was, however, in Hunter's nature to retreat behind a wall of silence as his only defense.

When Derek told him that he was moving out, Hunter had done exactly what he'd promised not to, giving his lover orders as if Derek was one of his employees or subservient in some way. Then he'd infuriated his father by threatening to quit if he wasn't allowed to come home as soon as possible.

He'd been too late to stop Derek from moving out, so his only hope was to see him and bring him home so they could talk things through. On Planter's Day Preview Night, watching Derek's manager belittle him, and seeing Drayden Lvandsson hang all over him, made Hunter crazy. He knew he should leave before he made things worse. When Derek came after him, the lonely months of anger and frustration dissolved under the thrill of being able to make love to him again. It hadn't been enough to bring Derek home.

The weeks after that had been the worst of Hunter's life. To have Derek so close, but unavailable. To see him with Drayden and wonder about the nature of their relationship, which defied everything he understood about Derek. To listen to Riley's innuendos about what Derek had been doing with his time, which hurt Hunter's pride even though it didn't diminish his love. Hunter knew Derek loved him. He could see in Derek's eyes that something was wrong. But Hunter couldn't find a way to reach past the months apart or the people between them.

It had all come to a head at the Big Bang when Sheree's frantic phone call had summoned Hunter. He watched Derek's drama play out and tried to determine what was going on. He didn't want to repeat his mistake of giving Derek orders, so he kept his mouth shut and hoped that Derek would turn to him. Instead, Derek walked out, with Drayden Lvandsson on his heels. Nonetheless, Hunter had a feeling, later confirmed by Sheree, that nothing was going on between Drayden and Derek.

He'd looked for Derek most of the night, banging on his apartment door, calling his cell phone, walking the mall. He'd gone back to the hotel and alerted the staff that if anyone saw Derek, he wanted to be told immediately. Near dawn, he'd gone back to the Galaxy Building. When the elevator doors opened on Derek's floor, Garry was standing there.

"Don't bother," Garry said. "No one will come to the door. I honestly don't think they're there."

"Who the hell is 'they'?" Hunter asked. "What are you doing here?"

Garry stepped into the elevator, and the doors closed. The two men stared at each other for a few seconds, then Garry hugged him. Hunter gratefully held on until they got to the lobby, then they walked silently together back to his apartment at the Congreve, where they caught each other up.

"I can't believe you fell in love with Derek's roommate," Hunter finally said.

"When I fell in love with her, she wasn't his roommate," Garry said. "I'd seen them together. I knew they were friends. But Vienna never told me anything about him."

"If she had, would you have told me?"

"And risked Vienna's wrath?" Garry asked. He grinned. "Of course I would have told you. I might have come here to get away from my family and Buffy, but if I'd seen a way to help you and Derek, I would have."

"You couldn't have screwed it up any worse than I did," Hunter said and told him about Preview Night.

Garry shook his head and said, "Instead of telling him what to do, you should have told him how you feel. I blame myself."

"For what?"

"I spoiled you, Hunter. You never have to express your thoughts or feelings to me because I know you so well. You assume that Derek knows you the same way."

"He does," Hunter said.

"Indulge me. Did you ever tell Derek that the reason he shouldn't be selling shoes is because you think he's a gifted writer? Or that your world would be a sadder, duller place without him in it?"

"I don't have to tell him that. He knows it."

"Maybe," Garry said doubtfully. "In any case, it's clear there are things you don't know about Derek."

Hunter had to admit the truth of that. In the days that followed, Vienna continued to avoid Garry, and no one seemed to know where Derek was. Hunter turned to the people that he trusted for answers. Juanita hadn't heard from him, nor had Sheree. But Sheree, with Natasha Deere, had been able to help him discover the ways that Riley had undermined his relationship. Hunter's sense of betrayal at Riley's hands was nothing compared to his rage over any pain Riley might have caused Derek. His analysis of Riley's sly innuendos and outright interference made him wonder what lies or suspicions his assistant might have planted in his lover's head. Hunter knew he was still missing pieces of the puzzle in understanding Derek's feelings and actions.

Juanita reluctantly told Hunter about Riley's final accusation, but she refused to believe that Derek and Christian Mercer were lovers. Hunter wasn't as sure, and though he sensed that Derek wasn't in the mall, he finally decided he had to see for himself. He found Christian's address and went to the Galaxy Building.

The visit was enlightening, but not in the way he'd expected. Hunter had obviously interrupted a romantic evening, but Christian's companion wasn't Derek. The tousled redhead named Bianca watched Hunter with a thoughtful expression as Christian assured him that he had no idea where Derek was. Hunter had seen enough to believe him, but when he turned to leave, Bianca said, "Christian, tell him. About the dolls."

Christian was obviously uncomfortable explaining that he, Derek, and Vienna had broken into Natasha's apartment and stolen her property. As shocked as Hunter was—it seemed very out of character for Derek—on his walk back to the hotel, he'd started laughing so hard that he had to sit down. He kept envisioning Derek fending off the Uranus security guards; it was like he'd gotten trapped in one of his own outrageous stories.

It was the first time Hunter had laughed in so long, and it felt like a gift from Derek. At least the mystery of the key chain was cleared up. The brass *D* had been for "Deere," not "Drayden." And not . . .

Davii. Hunter finally knew where Derek was. His parents weren't covering for him in Evansville. Derek was in New York with Davii. All the relief he'd felt upon realizing that Derek had never been involved with Drayden Lvandsson and wasn't with Christian Mercer evaporated. He'd lost him to another man after all. No one—Garry, Vienna, Sheree, or Juanita—could explain it away. Derek was really gone.

Hunter walked back to his apartment in a daze. For hours, he relived his life, beginning with the childhood story of the cuckoo and ending with Derek's flight to freedom. But he didn't simply mentally replay his memories. He sat down at Derek's computer and typed them all out, knowing that he could never tell them the way his storyteller would, but that they had to be told. He held nothing back, struggling to find words for his love, his fear, his need, and his hope.

The sun was coming up when he finished. He printed everything out and, not pausing for a chance to talk himself out of it, sealed it in an envelope, wrote Derek's name on the outside, and took it to Vienna's apartment, sliding it under the door. Even if she wouldn't talk to Garry and give him and Hunter the chance to explain themselves, Hunter had a feeling that Vienna would make sure Derek got the envelope.

He waited, knowing that only Derek would be able to find the right ending for his story. Several days passed, until one morning, after he finished getting ready for work, he walked into his living room. He saw the envelope lying where it had been pushed under his door. With a leaden feeling in his stomach, he crossed the room, bent, and picked it up.

38

The Short-Terminator

"Finally," Vienna said when the sound of the doorbell cut through the silence in her living room. Like a Pavlovian response, relief washed over her, and she felt as if a weight had been lifted from her shoulders. She opened the door and greeted the woman on the other side, ushering her into the apartment and pointing toward the pillowcases full of dolls. "There they are."

"I know a lot of little girls who'll be thrilled to have them," the woman said. She peered inside a pillowcase, saying, "And so many! What darling little clothes. I can't thank you enough for donating them to our charity. Let me write out a receipt."

"You don't have to do that," Vienna insisted impatiently. "Please just take them away."

The woman shrugged and said, "If you say so. Thank you again."

"Just one second, please," Vienna said. She went into her bedroom and returned a moment later, handing the woman a plastic bag. "Can you use these? They're my wigs. You probably know women who need them far more than I do."

"How wonderful!" the woman exclaimed. "I'll pass these on to Emily-Anne Barrister. She works with Locks of Love, and I'm sure they'll have use for them. Thank you so much for your generosity."

Once the dolls and wigs were gone, Vienna felt liberated. It had been two weeks since the Big Bang Benefit, and her house, except for Derek's absence, was in order. She had to complete only one more task to return harmony to her universe. As she had so often since moving to the mall, she left her apartment to fill out an application.

An hour later, she was chewing on the end of her pen until she realized what she was doing and stopped. Oral fixations were so unbecoming. She flipped through the rest of the application, looking at the probing questions, realizing how daunting it all seemed. She'd never trusted applications to completely represent her as a complex and multifaceted individual. She pored over every answer, hoping she'd covered all the bases, leaving nothing open for interpretation.

"A fifteen-page statement following guidelines from sections one and two. Done," Vienna said to herself, putting the essay into a manila envelope. "Release form. Done. Statements from Kevin and Laura. Thanks, kids," she said, adding the photocopies to the envelope. "Proof of malpractice insurance. Yes. Bless your little heart, Chubb. Couldn't have done it without you."

She added the application to the envelope and addressed it to the Committee on Professional Practice and Ethics. Reapplying for her license to practice psychology was the most daunting task she'd faced in a long time, and she felt nervous just sealing the envelope. Her suspension had expired the previous month, and it was time to get her life back on track, to make her mother proud again.

Vienna sipped her tea, then added another packet of sugar, idly stirring as she surveyed the mall. Everybody looked happy, energetic, or full of purpose as they walked down the corridors. It was a busy day, and the mall was filled with families, couples, and friends, all walking, laughing, and talking without a care in the world.

Construction had begun that morning on Mall of the Universe's latest attraction. A roller coaster, The Universal Express, was being built on the mall's roof. Slated to open within a year, it would feature dizzying drops, twists, and speeds up to seventy miles per hour. Vienna couldn't wait, since she'd always loved a good thrill. Although perhaps nothing would ever compare to the ride with Derek and Company that began the day she walked into employee orientation at Drayden's.

She missed Derek. She missed the way he'd filled Davii's space in the apartment with his sweetness and his wacky stories. Then again, his stories were no more outlandish than the real-life craziness he'd brought with him. Breaking and entering and doll theft were not the norm for a preacher's kid or a doctor of psychology.

She missed prank-calling with him at work, although she knew they were better off moving on from Women's Shoes and Cosmetics. She would never regret the job, though, since it had brought Derek, Christian, Bianca, Meg, Emily-Anne, DeWitt, Drayden, and even Natasha into her life. She'd learned something from all of them.

Vienna finished her tea, collected her things, and walked through the mall. Moments later, she walked out of Mail Boxes Etc. feeling light and happy, one step closer to professional joy. She imagined a time in the not-so-distant future when she'd have her license again. She would open an office on the Stars level and start her own practice, facilitating group therapy sessions, helping families, and offering discounted sessions to mall employees. If she'd learned anything over the past two years, it was that the mall was rife with people in need of therapy.

She walked through the crowds on the Earth level until a man approached her and asked, "Would you like a sample of our almond hand cream? It's infused with essential oils!"

Instead of running away from the Cart Person, Vienna said, "Take me to your leader."

"He's over there," the Cart Person said, pointing toward the courtyard.

"Thank you," Vienna said. She walked to the courtyard, and before sitting down at Cart Man's table, she opened her purse and removed a tissue. She handed it to him and said, "I've been meaning to return this to you for quite some time. Thanks for loaning it to me."

"Cleaned and pressed, too," Garry said, taking it from her. "How thoughtful."

Vienna sat down, and Garry moved his chair closer, drawing her forward and pressing his lips to hers. The only voice Vienna heard in her head was her own, cheering loudly. She kissed him again and said, "I'd love to do this all day, but I have to get back to work."

"No. You have to stay with me and be Queen of the Cart People," Garry said, pulling her onto his lap and holding her tight.

"That is enticing," Vienna said. "But I always wanted to be an overlord."

"It's always a power struggle with you."

"Do you see me struggling?" Vienna asked. "Did you talk to your parents yet?"

"Yes. They're not amused that their son is now in the cart industry," Garry said with a sigh. "However, my mother called me back later and said she'd work on my father. Regardless, I'm not going anywhere."

"Music to my ears," Vienna said. She kissed Garry's hand, then wriggled free of his grasp. She collected her things and said, "I'll see you later. I'm making you dinner tonight."

"Okay," he said, grinning.

"And every night," she said, calling over her shoulder as she walked away, "forever!"

She walked to Drayden's, smiling the entire way and wondering what she should cook for Garry. She frowned suddenly, remembering that she'd agreed to meet Meg and her girlfriend that night for drinks. She shrugged, knowing that Meg would understand. She'd make some joke about Vienna's heart being captured by the enemy and agree to reschedule.

Vienna took the escalator to the top floor of Drayden's and walked past the Customer Service counter, waving brightly when the representatives greeted her. She entered the Human Resources offices, stopped at an assistant's desk, and asked, "Did I get any calls, Charmaine?"

"No. But here's a new copy of the employee conduct manual," Charmaine said. "There's a conflict between two employees in Fine Jewelry that you need to resolve when you have a moment."

"Commission again?" Vienna asked.

"What else?" Charmaine answered.

"I love a good conflict," Vienna said. "Bring it on."

"You're the only one around here who does," Charmaine said, shaking her head. "It's a good thing Mr. Lvandsson talked you into taking this job."

"It's only a short-term arrangement," Vienna said emphatically. "Don't get used to my being here."

"Whatever you say," Charmaine said. "Oh. There's a man in your office."

"New hire?"

"I don't think so."

"Okay. Tell the Fine Jewelry manager that I'll be downstairs shortly," Vienna said and walked into her office. When she saw Davii sitting with his feet on her desk, she laughed and said, "Comfy?"

"You're so lucky," he said as he got up and hugged her. "I don't have an office."

"What are you doing here?" she asked.

"I heard there was trouble in paradise. I've got some free time, so I thought I'd come see my number-one girl," he replied.

"And she's so happy you did," Vienna said. "But this is a trouble-free zone now." She threw her arms around him again and said, "I've missed you!"

"I've missed you, too," he said. "Oh, my aching butt. We flew into Indianapolis this morning, then took the shuttle from hell. This has been the longest day ever!"

Vienna pulled back and said, "Child, I've got stories."

"Me, too," Davii said. "Let's have lunch."

"Okay!" Vienna agreed. They walked out of her office arm in arm, and Vienna said, "Charmaine, call Fine Jewelry and tell them I'll see them later this afternoon, okay? I'll be right back!"

39

Across the Universe

Derek sat on the other side of Cortlandt Barrister's desk and tried not to squirm. Watching a blue pencil dance its way down pages of words he'd written fell on the discomfort scale somewhere between final exams and prostate exams. Even if he didn't expect to fail, the experience made him anxious. It didn't help that Mr. Barrister never stopped frowning while he read. Davii had laughed when he read it. But Davii loved him, and as gratifying as that was, Derek knew he wasn't his toughest critic.

Even if things didn't turn out the way Derek hoped, he was glad he'd taken the risk. He'd spent the entire night after the Big Bang on the roof of the Congreve, brooding over his next move. Before the sun came up, he slipped into his apartment in the Galaxy Building without waking Vienna and threw some basics into an oversized backpack. He wrote her a note telling her that he was okay; he just needed to get away for a while.

His first call had been to Emily-Anne Barrister, who'd helped him connect with her husband. Then he'd rented a car, driven to Indianapolis, and caught the first flight he could get to New York, where he'd practically collapsed into Davii's arms at LaGuardia. He'd slept through almost two full days before he felt ready to explore Manhattan with Davii as his guide.

His cell phone vibrated. As discreetly as he could, he pulled it from his pocket and glanced down. After a moment, the display alerted him that he had a text message. He looked at Mr. Barrister, who was still frowning while he read. Derek carefully pushed buttons until the message appeared: "Daddy and I are thinking about you. Good luck! Mom."

He grinned, wondering which century she'd been researching on the Web at the library when she remembered that she was living in the electronic age and could wish her son well. Hopefully when he called her later to thank her, he'd have good news. Although Mr. Barrister's expression wasn't very promising when he dropped the pages to his desk and let the blue pencil fall on top of them.

"I can always tell when a writer's background is in English instead of journalism," Mr. Barrister commented. "When you turn in your column each week, I want you to pick up my previous week's edits. In time, I'm sure you'll grasp that brevity is a virtue in the newspaper business."

Derek stared at him for a few seconds before saying, "You mean you're going to publish it?"

"Yes, Derek." Mr. Barrister jammed a soggy, unlit cigar in his mouth. "When you came to me with your proposition, I told you what I wanted. An Oz-like microcosm. You've delivered."

"You don't think the gay character might be a little too much?"

"Which one's gay?" Mr. Barrister asked. When Derek just gazed at him, he emitted either a grunt or a laugh; Derek couldn't tell. "My point being, it's subtle, Derek. You might know he's gay; maybe some readers will, too. Some won't. Maybe they'll figure it out when someone writes an outraged letter to the editor. So what? I told you I wanted a diverse set of characters who were funny, flawed, and sympathetic. That's what you gave me. I told you to plug the mall stores. You did. Half the people who take the paper are using it to line their litter boxes. If some old Holy Roller gets his knickers in a twist and complains, those people might read the paper before they let the cat crap on it. It's all good. I've never used my papers to anesthetize the public; I'm not starting now. Make it funny, don't get me sued for libel, and we'll be working together until merchants stop advertising or I drop dead, whichever comes first."

"Don't start smoking again," Derek begged.

After he left the Barrister building, Derek took a shuttle to the mall, eager to see Vienna. He'd missed her and wondered which mall store she'd decided to work in next. He also wanted to see Christian and thank him for never pointing out the obvious: that

Derek should be writing stories, not selling shoes. And he was curious to find out what Davii was up to on his visit back to the mall.

It was a letdown to find no one in his apartment. He decided to unpack before he started trying to track them down. An envelope was lying on his bed, and he picked it up, his heart pounding as he recognized Hunter's handwriting. For a while, he was afraid to open it. He didn't want to know what had happened during the two weeks he'd been in New York, or what new heartbreak he might be facing. Finally, he took out the pages and started reading Hunter's story of his life and of the way *his* heart had been broken. He didn't understand it all, especially the parts about Riley and Garry, but he finally had the answer to the single question that had tormented him for so long.

After he stopped crying, he sat down at Vienna's computer and wrote an account of his feelings before and after Hunter left, and of some of his experiences while Hunter was away. He finished by describing Cortlandt Barrister's agreement to serialize his fictitious stories about the people in the mall in the *Terre Haute Times.*

He printed the letter, put it in Hunter's envelope, and walked to the Congreve, feeling a little anxious, because after he slid the envelope under the door, all he could do was wait for Hunter either to come home and read it, or to read it and open the door.

Hunter, he thought, *please open the door.*

When Hunter opened the door, Derek was sitting on the floor, leaning against the wall. Hunter held up the pages Derek had left, then extended his free hand. Derek took it, letting Hunter pull him into the apartment.

After Hunter closed the door, he looked at Derek and said, "What was the question?"

"Do you love me?" Derek asked.

"How could you not know the answer to that?" Hunter asked.

"You've never said it."

"Of course I have."

"No, you haven't," Derek argued. "Trust me. I'd remember."

Hunter appeared to think it over, then he said, "Does a man tell air that he loves breathing it?"

"Maybe a man should, if he wants to keep breathing."

Hunter smiled and said, "Derek, I love you." Derek wasn't sure what expression flickered across his face that made Hunter suddenly embrace him. His mouth against Derek's ear, Hunter whispered, "I love you *more* than the air I breathe. I'm glad I told you everything, even though I'm too late."

"Why do you think you're too late?" Derek asked, his voice as low as Hunter's.

Still holding him, Hunter ran his hand over Derek's hair and said, "Somebody was there for you when I wasn't. Somebody loved you when you thought I didn't. Somebody didn't let you down."

Derek smiled and said, "Part of that's true. Somebody was there. Vienna and Christian. Somebody does love me. Sheree and Juanita. Somebody didn't let me down. Davii. Davii would have failed me as a friend if he hadn't told me to try everything before I gave up on you and me. If he hadn't urged me to give you a chance to work things out. If he hadn't been there for me in New York when I needed him. If he hadn't told me it was time to come home, even coming back with me, because he's a true friend who knows that more than anything in the world, I love Hunter Congreve, who also never, *never* let me down, which is why I'm home."

The most enlightening part of making love with his new knowledge of Hunter's feelings was that nothing was different. Their bodies had the same intuitive sense of when to please and when to be pleased. When to hold back. When to let go. Hunter's eyes had the intensity they always had during sex. And when it was over, they both still felt the need to keep holding on, to keep touching, to keep looking at each other.

"How could I have not understood that this is how you say 'I love you'?" Derek wondered aloud.

"How could I have failed to realize that a man who's in love with words would need to hear them?" Hunter asked. He lit a cigarette, then settled back so Derek could nestle against him.

"Once there were two princes," Derek said. He couldn't see his lover's face, but he could tell by the way Hunter's arm tightened around him that he'd needed this as much, if not more, than sex. Derek smiled and went on. "One's wealth was tangible. The other's wealth was not. One was born to everything. The other worked for it. The funny thing is, neither of them knew which was which. But it didn't matter, because together, they had it all."

"Thank you," Hunter whispered. They were quiet until he finished his cigarette, then Hunter repositioned himself so that he was the one being held.

"I love what you wrote to me," Derek said. "Sheree once told me that you're fearless. I understand the courage it took to open yourself up even though you thought I was gone. I don't want you to worry about that ever again. I'll never fly far without you."

"I'll never try to stop you from flying." Hunter said. "I've been so happy with you and our life together. I didn't realize how lonely you were when I traveled or worked long hours. I'm glad you've found friends. I want you to hold on to those friendships. I'd like to know them, too."

"I'd love that," Derek said, grinning at the thought of his lover fending off Vienna's clinical appraisals. Relishing Meg's wicked sense of humor. Coping with the flirtatious rapport that Derek and Christian shared. Watching Emily-Anne wreak havoc in his hotel. Grappling with Davii's complexities. It would do Hunter good to have his life populated with Derek's friends.

"Have you written your first column yet?" Hunter asked.

"I gave it to Mr. Barrister today," Derek said.

"What did he say?"

"Pulitzer," Derek said, and Hunter laughed. "He said I use too many words."

"What does he know?" Hunter asked.

"I wanted to ask you about Garry and—" Derek broke off, noticing a new addition to Hunter's artwork on the wall. He sat up, his voice gently reproachful when he said, "Hunter."

Hunter followed the direction of his gaze and said just as softly, "That's a very expensive piece. I bid on it for a worthy cause."

"You got robbed," Derek said.

"It's a pretty good likeness of Miss Indiana to have been done by a three-year-old," Hunter disagreed.

Derek looked at Hunter, then reached over to lightly cuff his chin. "You do love me."

"I do," Hunter said.

work. She paid no heed to the birds or the music of the leaves. She was indifferent to the brilliant sunlight. What she noticed about the walk was how people moved aside on the narrow path when they saw her determined stride. She liked that part.

Nodding curtly at the guard, she walked through the employee entrance. She found a locker for her handbag, checked to make sure she was properly creased, tucked in, and tidy, then went to her workstation.

The other employees greeted her with warm smiles when she took her place on the platform. Her return smile was faint. Just because she'd adopted her policy of not destroying people didn't mean she intended to befriend them. That issue had been brought up in her recent thirty-day review.

"Natasha," the management rep said, "you've gotten glowing input from your co-workers about how capable you are. Thorough, punctual, professional. Also, comments about how amazing you are with our small guests. They say you have a way of keeping everything orderly and organized. But no one feels that they know you. We want to know that you enjoy your job!"

"I love it," she'd answered tonelessly.

The odd thing was, she did love it. Because she knew it was temporary. If there was anything she understood, it was how to move up a ladder. This time, she intended to get to the top. Eventually, she'd be running the entire organization. Although she might never meet its founder—she shuddered momentarily at the thought of Drayden Lvandsson—she'd make damn sure that the business was a credit to the person whose name was on it.

The Tennessee Tornado clattered to a stop, and its occupants exited the opposite side as Natasha motioned the line to move forward. A small boy and girl clambered eagerly toward her, and Natasha barked, "No running."

Chastened, they slowed down, then stared up at her with huge eyes as she held up a hand to stop them. She whipped a tape measure from her pocket and held it against them, then nodded. Car by car, she checked to make sure everyone was seated and properly secured. Another pair of children were pinching each other and giggling, and Natasha stopped at their car and gave them a look that could have inspired a new Peter Benchley novel. They immediately settled down.

"That's better," Natasha said. "We don't act like little animals at Dollywood, do we?"

"No, ma'am," they said in unison.

She nodded approvingly, then stepped back to let her gaze sweep the occupants of the cars one last time.

"Enjoy the ride," she said, and the faces of those who watched her showed that they were almost afraid not to.